DARK CA

Ray Bradbury (22 August 1920 – 5 June 2012) published some 500 short stories, novels, plays, and poems since his first story appeared in *Weird Tales* when he was twenty years old. Among his many famous works are *Fahrenheit 451*, *The Illustrated Man*, and *The Martian Chronicles*.

By Ray Bradbury

Ahmed and the Oblivion Machines
The Anthem Sprinters
Bradbury Speaks
The Cat's Pajamas
Dandelion Wine
Dark Carnival
The Day it Rained Forever
Death is a Lonely Business
Driving Blind
Fahrenheit 451
Farewell Summer
From the Dust Returned
The Golden Apples of the Sun
A Graveyard for Lunatics
Green Shadows, White Whale
The Halloween Tree
I Sing the Body Electric!
The Illustrated Man
Killer, Come Back to Me
Let's All Kill Constance
Long After Midnight
The Machineries of Joy
The Martian Chronicles
A Medicine for Melancholy
Moby Dick (screenplay)
Now and Forever
The October Country
One More for the Road
Quicker Than the Eye
R is for Rocket
Ray Bradbury Stories Volume 1
Ray Bradbury Stories Volume 2
S is for Space
The Small Assassin
Something Wicked this Way Comes
A Sound of Thunder
The Toynbee Convector
When Elephants Last in the Dooryard Bloomed
Where Robot Mice and Robot Men Run Round in Robot Town
The Wonderful Ice Cream Suit
We'll Always Have Paris
Yestermorrow
Zen in the Art of Writing

RAY BRADBURY

Dark Carnival

Harper*Voyager*
An imprint of
HarperCollins*Publishers* Ltd
1 London Bridge Street
London SE1 9GF
www.harpercollins.co.uk

HarperCollins*Publishers*
Macken House
39/40 Mayor Street Upper
Dublin 1
D01 C9W8
Ireland

First published in the United States by Arkham House in 1947
This edition published in the United Kingdom by HarperCollins*Publishers* 2024
3

A catalogue record for this book is available from the British Library

ISBN: 978-0-00-855431-6

Set in Meridien by Palimpsest Book Production Limited, Falkirk, Stirlingshire

Printed and bound in the UK using 100% Renewable Electricity by CPI Group (UK) Ltd

This book contains FSC™ certified paper and other controlled sources to ensure responsible forest management.

For more information visit: www.harpercollins.co.uk/green

Contents

To

Grant M. Beach

THE HOMECOMING

"Here they come," said Cecy, lying there flat in her bed.

"Where are they?" cried Timothy from the doorway.

"Some of them are over Europe, some over Asia, some of them over the Islands, some over South America!" said Cecy, her eyes closed, the lashes long, brown, and quivering, her mouth opening to let the words whisper out swiftly.

Timothy came forward upon the bare plankings of the upstairs room. "*Who* are they?"

"Uncle Einar and Uncle Fry, and there's Cousin William, and I see Frulda and Helgar and Aunt Morgianna, and Cousin Vivian, and I see Uncle Johann! They're all coming fast."

"Are they up in the sky?" cried Timothy, his little grey eyes flashing. Standing by the bed, he looked no more than his fourteen years. The wind blew outside, the house was dark and lit only by starlight.

"They're coming through the air and traveling along the ground, in many forms," said Cecy, in her sleeping. She did not move on the bed; she thought inward upon herself and told what she saw. "I see a wolf-like thing coming over a dark river—at the shallows—just above a waterfall, the starlight shining up his pelt. I see a brown oak leaf blowing far up in the sky. I see a small bat flying. I see many other things, running under the forest trees and slipping through the highest branches; and they're *all* coming this way!"

"Will they be here by tomorrow night?" Timothy clutched the bedclothes. The spider on his lapel swung like a black pendulum, excitedly dancing. He leaned over his sister. "Will they all be here in time for the Homecoming?"

"Yes, yes, Timothy, yes," sighed Cecy. She stiffened. "Ask no more of me. Go away now. Let me travel in the places I like best."

"Thanks, Cecy," he said. Out in the hall, he ran to his room. He hurriedly made his bed. He had just awakened a few minutes ago, at sunset, and as the first stars had risen, he had gone to let his excitement about the party run with Cecy. Now she slept so quietly there was not a sound.

The spider hung on a silvery lasso about his slender neck as he washed his face. "Just think, Spid, tomorrow night is All Hallows' Eve!"

He lifted his face and looked into the mirror. His was the only mirror allowed in the house. It was his mother's concession to his "illness." Oh, if only he were not so afflicted! He opened his mouth, surveyed the poor, inadequate teeth nature had given him. No more than so many bean kernels, round, soft and pale in his jaws. The canines were nothing at all! Some of the high spirit died in him.

It was now totally dark and he lit a candle to see by. He felt exhausted. This past week the whole family had lived in the fashion of the old country. Sleeping by day, rousing at sunset to move about. There were blue hollows under his eyes. "Spid, I'm no good," he said quietly, to the little creature. "Can't even get used to sleeping days like the others."

He took up the candle. Oh, to have *strong* teeth, with incisors like spikes. Or strong hands, even; or a strong mind. To have the power to send one's mind out, free, as Cecy did, while lying on her soft bed, sleeping. But, no; he was the imperfect one, the sick one. He was even—he shivered and drew the candle flame closer—afraid of the dark. His brothers snorted at him. Bion and Leonard and Sam. They laughed because he slept in a *bed*. With Cecy it was different; her bed was part of her comfort for the composure necessary to send her mind abroad to hunt. But Timothy, did *he* sleep in the wonderful polished boxes like the others? He did *not!* Mother allowed him his own bed, his own room, his own *mirror!* No wonder the family skirted him like a holy man's crucifix.

If only the wings would sprout from his shoulder blades. He bared his back, stared at it. He sighed again. No chance. Never.

Downstairs were exciting and mysterious sounds. The slithering sound of black crepe going up in all the halls and on the ceilings and doors. The smell of burning black tapers crept up the banistered stairwell.

Mother's voice, high and firm. Father's voice, echoing from the damp cellar. Bion walking from outside the old country house, lugging vast two gallon jugs of liquid that gurgled as he moved.

"I've just got to go to the party, Spid," said Timothy. The spider whirled at the end of its silk, and Timothy felt alone. He would polish cases, fetch toadstools and spiders, hang crepe, but when the party started he'd be ignored. The less seen or said of the imperfect son the better.

All through the house below, Laura ran. "The Homecoming!" she shouted gaily. "The Homecoming!" her footsteps everywhere at once.

Timothy passed Cecy's room again, and she slept soundly. Once in a great while she went below stairs. Mostly she stayed in bed. Lovely Cecy. He felt like asking her, "Where are you now, Cecy? And *in* who? And what's happening? Are you beyond the hills? and what goes on there?" But he walked on to Ellen's room instead.

Ellen sat at her desk, sorting out all kinds of blonde, red and dark hair and little clips of fingernail gathered from her manicurist job at the Mellin Town beauty parlor five miles over. A sturdy mahogany case lay in one corner with her name on it.

"Go away," she said, not even looking up at him. "I can't work with you gawking."

"All Hallows' Eve, Ellen!" he said, trying to be friendly. "Just think!"

"Huh!" She put fingernail clippings in small white sacks and labeled them. "What's it mean to you? It'll scare the hell out of you. Go back to bed."

His cheeks burned. "I'm needed to polish and work and help serve."

"If you don't go, you'll find a dozen raw oysters in your bed tomorrow," said Ellen, matter-of-factly. "Goodbye, Timothy."

In his anger, rushing downstairs, he bumped into Laura.

"Watch where you're going!" she shrieked from clenched teeth, out of which stuck tiny flat-headed nails. She hammered them into doors and upon them hung—what a joke!—imitation wolfsbane! "Won't this give Uncle Einar a fright!" she shouted to everybody.

She swept away. He ran to the open cellar door, smelled the channal of moist earthy air rising from below. "Father?"

"It's about time," Father shouted up the steps. "Hurry down, or they'll be here before we're ready!"

Timothy hesitated only long enough to hear the million other house sounds. Brothers came and went like trains in a station, talking and arguing. If you stood in one spot long enough the entire household passed with their pale hands full of things. Leonard with his little black medical case, Samuel with his large, dusty, ebon-bound book under his arm, bearing more black crepe, and Bion excursioning to the wagon outside and bringing in many more gallons of liquid.

Father stopped polishing to give Timothy a rag and a scowl. He thumped the huge mahogany box. "Come on, shine this up, so we can start on another. Sleep your life away."

While waxing the surface, Timothy looked inside.

"Uncle Einar's a big man, isn't he, papa?"

"Umm."

"How big?"

"The size of the box'll tell you."

"Seven feet tall?"

"You talk a lot."

Timothy made the box shine. "And he weighs two hundred and five."

Father blew. "Two hundred and *fifteen*."

"And space for wings!"

Father elbowed him. "You're doing that wrong. *This* way. Watch!"

About nine o'clock Timothy ran out into the October weather. For two hours in the now-warm, now-cold wind he walked the meadows collecting toadstools and spiders.

He passed a farm house. If only you knew what's

happening at *our* house! he said to the glowing windows. He climbed a hill and looked at the town, miles away, settling into sleep, the church clock high and round white in the distance. The town didn't know, either.

He brought home many jars of toadstools and spiders. In the cellar chapel a brief ceremony was celebrated, with father incanting the dark lines, mother's beautiful white ivory hands moving in the reverse blessings, and all the children gathered except Cecy, who lay upstairs in bed. But Cecy was present. You saw her peering from now Bion's eyes, now Samuel's, now mother's, and you felt a movement and now she was in you, fleetingly, and gone.

Timothy prayed to the Dark One with a tightened stomach.

"Please, please, help me grow up, help me be like my brothers and sisters. Don't let me be different. If only I could put the hair in the plastic images as Ellen does, or make people fall in love with me, as Laura does with people, or read strange old books as Sam does, or work in a fine job like Leonard and Bion do. Or even raise a family some day, like mother and father've done . . ."

At midnight the first relatives arrived!

Grandmother and Grandfather, all the way from the old country; cheery and talkative. There was much greeting!

After that, people arrived every hour. There were flutters at side windows, raps on the front door, knocks at the back. Noises from the cellar and rustlings from the attic, and the chimney whistled with autumn wind. Mother filled the large crystal punch bowl with a fluid. Father hurried from room to room lighting more tapers. Laura and Ellen hammered up more imitation wolfsbane. And Timothy stood in the center of the excitement, no expression on his face, his hands trembling a little at his sides, gazing now here, now there, quickly, quickly! See everything! Banging of doors, laughter, darkness, the sound of wine fluidly poured, sound of wind, the rush of feet, the welcoming bursts of talk at the doors, the transparent rattlings of windows, the shadows passing, re-passing, whirling, vanishing.

The party was begun!

Five, ten, fifteen, thirty people! And sixty more to come!

"Well, and *this* must be Timothy!"

"What?"

A chilly hand took his hand. A long beardy face leaned down over Timothy's brow. "A good lad, a good lad," said the man.

"Timothy," said mother. "This is your Uncle Jason."

"Hello, Uncle Jason."

"My, my, you don't sound very happy, nephew Timothy."

"I'm all right."

"Thanks for telling me, my boy. Perk up." The man buffed Timothy's chin with his cold fist, gently.

"And over *here*—" Mother drifted Uncle Jason away. Uncle Jason glanced over his caped shoulder, winked at Timothy, glassily.

Timothy stood alone.

From off a thousand miles in the candled dark, he heard a high fluting voice; that was Ellen. "And my brothers, they *are* clever. Can you guess their occupations, Aunt Morgianna?"

"I have no *idea*."

"They operate a mortuary in town."

"What!" A gasp.

"Yes!" Shrill laughter. "Isn't that *priceless!*"

"Wonderful!"

They all roared.

Timothy stood very still.

The laughter quieted. "They bring home sustenance for us all, you know."

Laura cried, "Oh, yes! Are you familiar with how a mortician works, Auntie darling?"

Aunt Morgianna was uncertain of the details.

"Well," began Laura, scientifically. "They push little silver needles attached to red rubber tubing into the bodies, draw out the blood. They inject preservative. Most morticians flush the blood down the drain. But not Leonard and Bion, ah no! They carry it home in gallon casques for mama and papa and all of us. Of course—Timothy . . . ."

Timothy jerked his mouth, softly.

"No, no," cried mother in a swift whisper to Laura.

"Timothy," drawled Laura, reluctant to leave the word alone.

An uneasy silence. Uncle Jason's voice demanded. "Well? Come on. What *about* Timothy?"

"Oh, Laura, your tongue," sighed mother.

Laura went on with it. Timothy shut his eyes. "Timothy doesn't—well—he doesn't *like* blood. He's—delicate."

"He'll learn," explained mother. "Given a little time," she said very firmly. "He's my son, and he'll learn. He's only fourteen."

"But I was *raised* on the stuff," said Uncle Jason, his voice passing from one room to another. The wind played the trees outside like harps. A little rain spattered on the window. "Raised on the stuff . . ." passing away into faintness.

Timothy bit his lips and opened his eyes.

"Well, it was all *my* fault." Mother was showing them into the kitchen now. "I tried forcing him. You can't force children, you only make them sick and then they never get a taste for things. Look at Bion, now, he was thirteen before he'd drink b----"

The last word was lost in a rise of wind.

"I understand," murmured Uncle Jason. "Timothy'll come around."

"I'm *sure* he will," said mother, defiantly.

Candles flamed as shadows crossed and recrossed the dozen musty rooms. Timothy was cold. He smelled the hot tallow in his nostrils and instinctively he grabbed at a candle and walked with it around and about the house, pretending to straighten the crepe.

"Timothy." Someone whispered behind a patterned wall, hissing and sizzling and sighing the words. "Tim-o-thy iss—a—fraid—of—thee—dark." Leonard's voice. Hateful Leonard! "So—mother sometimes—let's him take—a candle. You see them up and down the stairs together—the candle and Timothy's two grey eyes just behind the flame—close to it for warmth and color—shining."

"I *like* the candle, that's all," said Timothy, in a reproachful whisper.

"He'll be all right. Children are children," said an aunt's voice way over in the dining room blacknesses.

More noise, more laughter, more thunder! Cascades of wild laughter! Bangings and clickings and shouts and whisperings of clothing and capes! Moist fog swept through the front door like powder from exploded cannons! Out of the fog, settling his wings, stalked a tall man.

"Uncle Einar!"

Timothy propelled himself on his thin legs, straight through the fog, under the green webbing shadows. He threw himself into Uncle Einar's arms. Einar lifted him!

"You've wings, Timothy!" Light as thistles, he tossed the boy. "Wings, Timothy, fly!" Faces wheeled under. Darkness rotated. The house blew away. Timothy felt breeze-like. He flopped his arms. Einar's fingers caught and threw him again to the ceiling. The ceiling fell like a charred wall. "Fly! Fly!" shouted Einar, loud and deep. "Fly with wings! Wings!"

He felt exquisite agonies in his shoulder blades, as if roots grew, burst to explode and blossom into fresh long, moist membranes! He babbled wild stuff; again Einar hurled him high!

Autumn wind broke in a tide on the house, rain crashed down, shaking the beams, causing chandeliers to tilt their enraged candles. And the one hundred relatives stared out from each black enchanted niche and room, circling inward, all forms and sizes, to where Einar balanced the child like a puppet in the roaring spaces. "Beat your wings! Take off!"

"Enough!" cried Einar, at last.

Timothy, deposited gently to the floor timbers, exaltedly, exhaustedly fell against Uncle Einar, sobbing happily "Uncle, uncle, uncle!"

"Good flying, eh, Timothy?" Einar patted Timothy's head. "Good, good."

It was almost dawn. Most had arrived and were ready to bed down for the daylight, sleep motionlessly with no sound until the following sunset, when they'd jump out of their mahogany boxes for the revel.

Uncle Einar, followed by round dozens of others, moved toward the cellar. Mother directed them downward to the crowded row on row of highly polished boxes. Einar, his wings like sea green tarpaulins tented behind him, moved with a curious whistling and sussurus through the passageway; where his wings touched they made a sound of drum heads gently beaten.

Upstairs, Timothy lay wearily, thinking, trying to *like* the darkness. There was so much you could do in darkness that people couldn't criticise you for, because they never saw you. He *did* like the night, but it was a qualified liking; some times there was so much night he cried out in rebellion.

In the cellar, mahogany lids sealed downward, drawn in upon gesturing pale hands. In corners, certain relatives circled three times to lie down, heads on paws, eyelids shut.

The sun rose. There was a sleeping with no snores in it.

Sunset. The revel exploded like a bat nest struck full, shrieking out, fluttering, spreading! Box lids banged wide! Steps rushed up from cellar damp! More late guests, kicking on front and back portals, were admitted, and apologized.

It rained, and sodden visitors flung their capes, their water-pelleted hats, their sprinkled veils over Timothy who bore them to a closet, where they hung like mummified bats to dry. The rooms were crowd-packed. The laughter of one cousin shot from the hall, angled off the parlor wall, ricocheted, banked and returned to Timothy's ears from a fourth room, accurate and cynical. It was followed by a volley of laughs!

A mouse ran across the floor.

"I know *you*, Niece Leibersrouter!" exclaimed father.

The mouse spiraled three women's feet and vanished in a corner. Moments later a beautiful woman rose up out of nothing, stood in the corner, smiling her white smile at them all.

Something huddled against the flooded pane of the kitchen window. It sighed and wept and tapped continually, pressed against the glass, but Timothy could make nothing of it, he saw nothing there. In imagination he was outside, staring in. The rain was on him, the wind at him, and the taper-dotted darkness inside was inviting. Waltzes were being waltzed; tall thin figures pirouetted and glided to outlandish music. Stars of light flickered off lifted bottles; small earth clods crumbled from the handled casques, and a spider fell and went silently legging over the floor.

Timothy shivered. He was inside the house again. Mother called him to run here, run there, help, serve, out to the kitchen, fetch this, fetch that, bring plates, heap the food, be careful, don't stumble, here now, and here—on and on—the party happened around him but not *to* him. Dozens of towering black shapes pressed by him, elbowed him, ignored him.

Finally, he turned and slipped away up the stairs.

He stood by Cecy's bed. There was not a tremor in her long narrow white face; it was completely calm. Her bosom did not rise or descend. Yet if you touched her you felt warmth.

"Cecy," he called, softly.

There was no response until the third call, when her lips parted a little. "Yes." She sounded very tired and happy and dreaming, and remote.

"This is Timothy," he whispered.

"I know," she said, after a long wait.

"Where are you tonight, Cecy?"

After he had repeated the question twice, she said,

"Far west of here. In California. In the Imperial Valley, beside the Salten Sea, near the Mud Pots and the steam and the quiet. I'm a farmer's wife, and I'm sitting on a wooden porch. The sun's going slowly down."

"What's it like, Cecy?"

"You can hear the mud pots talking," she said, slowly, as if talking in church. "The mud pots lift little grey heads of steam, pushing up the mud like bald men rising in the thick syrup, head first, out in the broiling channals, and the grey heads rip like rubber fabric and collapse with a noise like wet lips moving. And little plumes of steam escape from the ripped tissue. And there is a smell of sulphur and deep burning and old time. The dinosaur has been abroiling here ten million years."

"Is he done yet, Cecy?"

Cecy's calm sleeper's lips turned up. "Yes, he's done. Quite done." The languid words fell slowly from her shaping mouth. Nothing else of her moved. She was quite still save for the tremor of lips when they answered. "You know what a surrey top is like, Timothy? Well, that's how the night comes here in this shallow between the mountains. The sun pulls the dark cover down after it. I'm inside this woman's head, looking out through the little holes in her skull. I don't even know her name, while I'm listening to the silence. The sea doesn't move on the shore, it just lies there, so quiet it makes you afraid. I'm smelling the salt of it, quietly. And over me a number of bombers and pursuit planes float across the first stars. They resemble pterodactyls on huge wings. Further over in the sumpland, the iron spine of a steam shovel shows—a brontosaurus frozen in metal pantomime, gazing at those aluminum reptiles flying high. And I am watching these prehistoric things, and smelling the smells of prehistoric cookings. It is so quiet, so quiet . . . ."

"How long will you stay in her, Cecy?"

"Until I've listened and looked and felt enough. Until I've changed her life some way. Living in her isn't like living anywhere in the world. Her valley with her little wooden house is a dawn world. Black mountains lift on the west, north and south, all enclosing this huge, solemn valley. Two concrete roads rim the sea, emptied by the war. Once in half an hour I see a car run by, shining its headlights. But the dark closes behind it. I sit on the porch all day, and watch the shadows run out from the trees, join and become one big night at sunset. I wait for my husband to come back from town. The sea is on the shore, salted and making no noise. Once in a while a fish leaps up, starlight catching its scales, falls back. The valley, the sea, the few cars, the porch, my rocking chair, myself, the silence."

"What *now*, Cecy?"

"I'm getting up now," she said.

"Yes?"

"I'm walking off the porch, toward the mud pots. Another flight of planes goes overhead, flinging off noise in every direction that propellors whirl in. They take the silence apart and the sound gets into my bones."

"And now?"

"Now, I'm walking along the board planks to where the tourists before the war used to stand watching the grey bubbles rise. My feet make hollow knocks on the planks, slowly."

"Now?"

"Now the sulphur fumes are all around me. The bubbles come up in breaking clusters, smoothing again. A bird flies over, crying sadly. Suddenly I'm in that bird! I fly away! And as I fly, inside my new small glass-bead eyes, I see something, a woman, below me, on a board walk, take one two three steps forward into the mud pots! I hear a sound as if a boulder has been dropped into molten depths! I keep on flying, ignoring this sound. I circle. As I come back I see a white hand, like a spider, wriggling, disappearing into a pool of grey lava. The lava seals over.

"Now, I'm flying home, swift, *swift!*"

Something rattled hard against the window.

Cecy flicked her eyes wide, full, bright, happy, exhilarated.

"Now, I *am* home!" she said.

Cecy lay upon her pillow, letting her eyes wander for a time. Finally, she saw Timothy.

"Is the Homecoming on?" she asked.

"Everybody's here."

"Then why are you upstairs?" She took his hand. "Well?" She smiled slyly. "Ask me. Go on. Ask me what you came up to ask."

"I didn't come to ask anything," he said. "Well, almost nothing. Well, oh, Cecy!" It came from him in one long rapid flow. "I want to do something at the party, to make them look at me, something to make me good as them, something to make me belong and there's nothing I can do and I feel funny and, well, and I thought you might—"

"I might," she said, closing her eyes, smiling inwardly. "Stand up straight, and stand very still." He obeyed. "Now, shut your eyes and blank out your thoughts."

He stood very straight and thought of nothing, or at least thought of thinking nothing, which was almost as good.

She sighed.

"Shall we go downstairs now, Timothy?"

Like a hand into a glove, Cecy was within him.

"Look, everybody!"

Timothy lifted the crystal of warm red wine, wine that veins had distilled, muscled hearts had pushed and pumped through thinking minds.

He held the glass so that the whole house turned to watch. Aunts, uncles, cousins, brothers, sisters!

He drank it straight down.

He jerked a hand at sister Laura. He held her gaze, whispering to her in a subtle voice that kept her silent, frozen. He felt tall as the trees as he walked to her. The party, a regular vortex, now slowed. It waited on all sides of him, watching. From all the doors the faces peered. They were not laughing. Mother's face was astonished.

Father looked bewildered, but pleased and getting prouder every instant.

Timothy took Laura's hands behind her, she didn't fight him, her eyes were glazed. He spoke and reached up, gently moving her head back, exposing her long white neck.

Gently, over the neck vein, he nipped her.

Candle flames swayed drunkenly. Wind climbed around the roof above. Relatives stared and shifted in the dark and stared again.

He released Laura, turned, popped toadstools in his mouth, swallowed, then, seized, he beat his arms against his flanks and dashed about. "Look, Uncle Einar! I'll fly, at last!" Beat! went his hands. Up, down, pumped his feet! Faces flashed by him!

At the top of the stairs before knowing it, flapping, Timothy heard his mother cry, "Stop, Timothy!" far below. "Hey!" shouted Timothy, and leaped off the top of the well, thrashing!

Half way down, the wings he thought he owned dissolved. He screamed.

Uncle Einar caught him.

Timothy flailed whitely in the receiving arms. A voice burst from his lips, unbidden:

"This is Cecy! This is Cecy!" it announced, shrilly. "Cecy! Come see me, all of you! Upstairs, first room on the left!" Followed by a long trill of laughter. Timothy tried to cut if off with his tongue, his lips.

Everybody laughed. Einar set him down. Running

through the crowded blackness as the relatives flowed upstairs toward Cecy's room to congratulate her, Timothy kicked the front door open. Mother called out behind him, anxiously.

Flap! went his dinner, straight down upon the cold earth.

"Cecy, I hate you, I hate you!"

Inside the barn, in deep shadow, Timothy sobbed bitterly and threshed in a stack of odorous hay. Then he lay still. From his blouse-pocket, from the protection of the match-box he used for his retreat, the spider crawled forth. Spid walked along Timothy's arm. Spid explored up his neck to his ear and climbed in the ear to tickle it.

Timothy shook his head. "Don't, Spid. Don't."

The feathery touch of a tentative feeler probing his ear drum set Timothy shivering. "Don't Spid!" He sobbed somewhat less.

The spider traveled down his cheek, took a station under the boy's nose, looked up into the nostrils as if to seek the brain, and then clambered softly up over the rim of the nose to sit, to squat there peering at Timothy with green gem eyes until Timothy filled with ridiculous laughter.

"Go away, Spid!"

In answer, the spider floated down to his lips and with sixteen delicate movements tacked silver strands back and forth, zig-zag, over Timothy's mouth.

"Mmmmmm," cried Timothy.

Timothy sat up, rustling the hay. The land was very bright with moon now that the rain had retired. In the big house he could hear the faint ribaldry as MIRROR MIRROR was played. In that game a huge mirror was set against one wall. Celebrants shouted, dimly muffled, as they tried to identify those of themselves whose reflections did not, had not ever, and *never would* appear in a mirror!

"What'll we do, Spid?" The mouth-web broke.

Falling to the floor, Spid scuttled swiftly toward the house, until Timothy caught him and returned him to his blouse pocket. "Okay, Spid. Back in it is. We'll have fun, no matter what."

Outside, a green tarpaulin fell from the sycamore as Timothy passed and pinned him down with yards of silken goods. "Uncle Einar!"

"Timothy." The wings spread and twitched and came in with a sound like kettle-drums. Timothy felt himself plucked up like a thimble and set on Einar's shoulder. "Don't feel badly, nephew Timothy. Each to his own, each in his own way. How much better things are for you. How rich. The world's dead for us. We've seen so much of it, believe me. It's all one color; grey. Life's best to those who live the least of it. It's worth more per ounce, nephew, remember that."

From midnight on, Uncle Einar bore him about the house, from room to room, weaving, singing. Late arrivals by the horde set hilarities off afresh. Great-great-great-great and a thousand more greats grandmother was there, wrapped in Egyptian cerements, roll on roll of linen bandage coiled about her fragile dark brown bird bones. She said not a word, but lay stiff as a burnt ironing board against one wall, her eye hollows cupping a distant, wise, silent glimmering. At the four a.m. breakfast, one-thousand-odd-greats grandmama stiffly seated the head of the longest table and red toasts were pantomimed to her.

Grandfather Tom wandered about through the throng at all hours, tickling young nieces, holding them, gumming their necks, a look of unbearable desperation flushing his features as time passed. Poor grandpapa, in *his* profession, and no teeth!

The numerous young cousins caroused at the crystal punch bowl. Their shiny olive-pit eyes, their conical, devilish faces and curly bronze hair hovered over the drinking table, their hard-soft, half-girl, half-boy bodies wrestling against each other as they got unpleasantly sullenly drunk.

Laura and Ellen, over and above the wine-sated tumult, produced a parlor drama with Uncle Fry. They represented innocent maidens strolling, when the Vampire (Uncle Fry) stepped from behind a tree (Cousin Anna). The Vampire smiled upon the Innocents.

Where were they going?

Oh, just down to the river path.

Could he escort them along the way?

He might if he were pleasant.

He walked with them, grinning secretly, from time to time licking his lips.

He was just preparing to attack one of them (at the river) when the Innocents, whirling eagerly, knocked him flat and drained him vacuum-dry of his blood. They sat down on his carcass as on a bench, and laughed and laughed.

So did everybody at the Homecoming.

The wind got higher, the stars burned with fiery intensity, the noises redoubled, the dances quickened, the drinking became more positive. To Timothy there were thousands of things to hear and watch. The many darknesses roiled, bubbled, the many faces mixed, vanished, reappeared, passed on. Mother moved every where, gracious and tall and beautiful, bowing and gliding, and father made sure that all the chalices were kept full.

The children played COFFINS. Coffins, set in a row, surrounded by marching children, Timothy with them. A flute kept them marching. One by one coffins were removed. The scramble for their polished interiors eliminated two, four, six, eight contestants, until only one coffin remained. Timothy circled it cautiously, pitted against his fey-cousin, Roby. The flute notes stopped. Like gopher to hole, Timothy made it, popped into the coffin, while everyone applauded.

Once more the wine cups were full.

"How is Lotte?"

"Lotte? Did you not hear? Oh, it is too good to tell!"

"Who's Lotte, mama?"

"Hush. Uncle Einar's sister. She of the wings. Go on, Paul."

"Lotte flew over Berlin not long ago and was shot for a British plane."

"Shot for a plane!"

Cheeks blew out, lungs bulged and sank, hands slapped thighs. The laughter was like a cave of winds.

"And what of Carl?"

"The little one who lives under bridges? Ah, poor Carl. Where is there a place for Carl in all Europe? Each bridge has been devastated. Carl is either dead or homeless. There are more refugees in Europe tonight than meet mortal eyes."

"True, true. *All* the bridges, eh? Poor Carl."

"Listen!"

The party held its breath. Far away the town clock struck its chimes, saying six o'clock. The party was ending. As if at a cue, in time to the rhythm of the clock striking, their one hundred voices began to sing songs that were four hundred years old, songs Timothy could not know. They twined their arms around each other, circling slowly, and sang, and somewhere in the cold distance of morning the town clock finished out its chimes and quieted.

Timothy sang.

He knew no words, no tune, yet he sang and the words and tune came correctly, round and high and good.

At the verse end, he gazed at the stairs and the closed door at the top of the stairs.

"Thanks, Cecy," he whispered.

He listened.

Then he said, "That's all right, Cecy. You're forgiven. I know you."

Then he just relaxed and let his mouth move as it wished, and words came out in their own time, rhythmically, purely, melodiously.

Goodbyes were said, there was a great rustling. Mother and father and the brothers and sisters lined up in grave happiness at the door to shake each hand firmly and kiss each departing cheek in turn. The sky, beyond the open door, colored and shone in the east. A cold wind entered.

Again Timothy was forced to listen to a voice talking and when it finished he nodded and said, "Yes, Cecy. I would like to do that. Thanks."

And Cecy helped him into one body after another. Instantly, he felt himself inside Uncle Fry's body at the door, bowing and pressing lips to mother's pale fingers, looking out from the wrinkled leather face at her. Then he sidestepped out into the wind, the draft seized him, took him in a flurry of leaves away up over the house and awakening hills. The town flashed under.

With a snap, Timothy was in another body, at the door, saying farewell. It was Cousin William's body.

Within Cousin William, swift as a smoke puff, he loped down the dirt road, red eyes burning, fur pelt rimed with morning, padded feet rising, falling with silent sureness, panting easily, again over the hill and into a hollow, and then dissolving away . . . .

Only to well up in the tall cold hollows of Uncle Einar

and look out from his tolerant, amused eyes. And he was picking up the tiny pale body of Timothy. Picking up himself, through Einar! "Be a good boy, Timothy. I'll see you again, from time to time."

Swifter than the bourne leaves, with a webbed thunder of wings, faster than the lupine thing of the country road, going so swiftly the earth's features blurred and the last stars rotated to one side, like a pebble in Uncle Einar's mouth, Timothy flew, accompanied him on half his startling journey.

He came back to his own body.

The shouting and the laughing bit by bit faded and went away. Dawn grew more apparent. Everybody was embracing and crying and thinking how the world was becoming less a place for them. There had been a time when they had met every year, but now decades passed with no reconciliation. "Don't forget, we meet in Salem in 1970!" someone cried.

Salem. Timothy's numbed mind turned the word over. Salem—1970. And there would be Uncle Fry and Grandma and Grandfather and a thousand-times-great Grandmother in her withered cere-clothes. And mother and father and Ellen and Laura and Cecy and Leonard and Bion and Sam and all the rest. But would *he* be there? Would he be alive that long? Could he be certain of living until then?

With one last withering wind blast, away they all shot, so many scarves, so many fluttery mammals, so many sered leaves, so many wolves loping, so many whinings and clustering noises, so many midnights and ideas and insanities.

Mother shut the door. Laura picked up a broom.

"No," said mother. "We'll clean up tonight. We need sleep, first."

Father walked down into the cellar, followed by Laura and Bion and Sam. Ellen walked upstairs, as did Leonard.

Timothy walked across the crepe-littered hall. His head was down, and in passing the party mirror he saw himself, the pale mortality of his face. He was cold and trembling.

"Timothy," said mother.

He stopped at the stairwell. She came to him, laid a hand on his face. "Son," she said. "We love you. Remember that. We all love you. No matter how different you are, no matter if you leave us one day," she said. She kissed his cheek. "And if and when you die your bones will lie undisturbed, we'll see to that, you'll lie at ease forever, and I'll come see you every Hallows' Eve and tuck you in the more secure."

The house echoed to polished wooden doors creaking and slamming hollowly shut.

The house was silent. Far away, the wind went over a hill with its last cargo of small dark bats, echoing, chittering.

He walked up the steps, one by one, crying to himself all the way.

SKELETON

It was past time for him to see the doctor again. Mr. Harris turned palely in at the stair-well, and on his way up the flight he saw Dr. Burleigh's name gilded over a pointing arrow. Would Dr. Burleigh sigh when he walked in? After all, this would make the tenth trip so far this year. But Burleigh shouldn't complain; after all, he was paid for the examinations!

The nurse looked Mr. Harris over and smiled, a bit amusedly, as she tiptoed to the glazed glass door, opened it, and put her head in. Harris thought he heard her say, "Guess who's here, Doctor?" And didn't the doctor's acid voice reply, faintly, "Oh, my God, *again*?" Harris swallowed uneasily.

When Harris walked in, Dr. Burleigh snorted thinly. "Aches in your bones again! Ah!!" He scowled at Harris and adjusted his glasses. "My dear Harris, you've been curried with the finest tooth combs and bacteria-brushes known to science. You're only nervous. Let's see your fingers. Too many cigarettes. Let me smell your breath. Too much protein. Let's see your eyes. Not enough sleep. My response? Go to bed, stop the protein, no smoking. Ten dollars, please."

Harris stood there, sulking.

The doctor glanced up from his papers. "*You* still here? You're a hypochondriac! That's *eleven* dollars, now."

"But why should my bones ache?" asked Harris.

Dr. Burleigh addressed him like a child. "You ever had a sore muscle, and kept at it, irritating it, fussing with it, rubbing it? It gets worse, the more you bother it. Then you leave it alone and the pain vanishes. You realize you caused most of the soreness, yourself. Well, son, that's what's with you. Leave yourself alone. Take a dose of salts. Get out of here and take that trip to Phoenix you've stewed about for months. Do you good to travel!"

Five minutes later, Mr. Harris riffled through a classified phone directory at the corner druggist's. A fine lot of sympathy one got from blind fools like Burleigh! He passed his finger down a list of BONE SPECIALISTS, found one named M. Munigant. Munigant lacked an M.D., or any other academical lettering behind his name, but his office was conveniently near. Three blocks down, one block over . . . .

M. Munigant, like his office, was small and dark. Like

his office, he smelled of iodoform, iodine, and other odd things. He was a good listener, though, and listened with eager, shiny moves of his eyes, and when he talked to Harris, he had an accent and seemed to whistle every word, undoubtedly due to imperfect dentures. Harris told all.

M. Munigant nodded. He had seen cases like this before. The bones of the body. Man was not aware of his bones. Ah, yes, the bones. The skeleton. Most difficult. Something concerning an imbalance, an unsympathetic coordination between soul, flesh and bone. Very complicated, softly whistled M. Munigant. Harris listened, fascinated. Now, *here* was a doctor who understood his illness! Psychological, said M. Munigant. He moved swiftly, delicately to a dingy wall and rattled down half a dozen x-rays and paintings of the human skeleton. He pointed at these. Mr. Harris must become aware of his problem, yes. He pointed at this and that bone, and these and those, and some others.

The pictures were quite awful. They had something of the grotesquerie and off-bounds horror of a Dali painting. Harris shivered.

M. Munigant talked on. Did Mr. Harris desire treatment for his bones?

"That all depends," said Harris.

M. Munigant could not help Harris unless Harris was in the proper mood. Psychologically, one had to *need* help, or the doctor was of no use. But (shrugging) Mr. Munigant would "try."

Harris lay on a table with his mouth open. The lights were switched off, the shades drawn. M. Munigant approached his patient.

Something touched Harris' tongue.

He felt his jawbones forced out. They cracked and made noises. One of those pictures on the dim wall seemed to leap. A violent shivering went through Harris and, involuntarily, his mouth snapped shut.

M. Munigant cried out. He had almost had his nose bitten off! It was no use. Now was not the time. M. Munigant raised the shades. He looked dreadfully disappointed. When Mr. Harris felt he could cooperate psychologically, when Mr. Harris really *needed* help and trusted M. Munigant to help him, then maybe something could be done. M. Munigant held out his little hand. In the meantime, the fee was only two dollars. Mr. Harris must begin to think. Here was a sketch for Mr. Harris to take home and study. It would acquaint him with his body. He must be aware of himself. He must be careful. Skeletons were strange, unwieldy things. M. Munigant's eyes glittered. Good day to Mr. Harris. Oh, and would he have a breadstick? He proffered a jar of long hard salty breadsticks to Harris, taking one himself to chew on, and saying that chewing breadsticks kept him in—ah—practice. See you soon, Mr. Harris. Mr. Harris went home.

The next day was Sunday. Mr. Harris started the morning by feeling all sorts of new aches and pains in his body. He spent some time glancing at the funny papers and then looking with new interest at the little painting, anatomically perfect, of a skeleton M. Munigant had given him.

His wife, Clarisse, startled him at dinner when she cracked her exquisitely thin knuckles, one by one, until he clapped his hands to his ears and cried, "Don't do that!"

The remainder of the day he quarantined himself in his room. Clarisse was seated at bridge in the living room with three other ladies, laughing and conversing. Harris himself spent his time fingering and weighing the limbs of his body with growing curiosity. After an hour of this he suddenly stood up and called:

"Clarisse!"

She had a way of dancing into any room, her body doing all sorts of soft, agreeable things to keep her feet from ever quite touching the nap of a rug. She excused herself from her friends and came to see him now, brightly. She found him reseated in a far corner and she saw that he was staring at that anatomical sketch. "Are you still brooding, darling?" she asked. "Please don't." She sat upon his knees.

Her beauty could not distract him now in his absorption. He juggled her lightness, he touched her knee-cap, suspiciously. It seemed to move under her pale, glowing skin. "Is it supposed to do that?" he asked, sucking in his breath.

"Is what supposed to do what?" she laughed. "You mean my knee-cap?"

"Is it supposed to run around on top your knee that way?"

She experimented. "So it *does,*" she marveled. "Well, now, so it does. Icky." She pondered. "No. On the other hand—it doesn't. It's only an optical illusion. I think. The skin moves over the bone; not vice-versa. See?" she demonstrated.

"I'm glad yours slithers, too," he sighed. "I was beginning to worry."

"About what?"

He patted his ribs. "My ribs don't go all the way down, they stop *here*. And I found some confounded ones that dangle in mid-air!"

Beneath the curve of her small breasts, Clarisse clasped her hands.

"Of course, silly, everybody's ribs stop at a given point. And those funny little short ones are floating ribs."

"I just hope they don't float around too much," he said, making an uneasy joke. Now, he desired that his wife leave him, he had some important discovering to do with his own body and he didn't want her laughing at him.

"I'll feel all right," he said. "Thanks for coming in, dear."

"Any time," she said, kissing him, rubbing her small pink nose warm against his.

"I'll be damned!" He touched his nose with his fingers, then hers. "Did you ever realize that the nose bone only comes down so far and a lot of gristly tissue takes up from there on?"

She wrinkled hers. "So what?" And, dancing, she exited.

He felt the sweat rise from the pools and hollows of his face, forming a salten tide to flow down his cheeks. Next on the agenda was his spinal cord and column. He examined it in the same manner as he operated the numerous push-buttons in his office, pushing them to summon the messenger boys. But, in these pushings of his spinal column, fears and terrors answered, rushed from a million doors in Mr. Harris' mind to confront and shake him. His spine felt awfully—bony. Like a fish, freshly eaten and skeletonized, on a china platter. He fingered the little rounded knobbins. "My God."

His teeth began to chatter. "God All-Mighty," he thought, "why haven't I realized it all these years? All these years I've gone around with a—SKELETON—inside me!" He saw his fingers blur before him, like motion films triply speeded in their quaking apprehension. "How is it that we take ourselves so much for granted? How is it we never question our bodies and our being?"

A skeleton. One of those jointed, snowy, hard things, one of those foul, dry, brittle, gouge-eyed, skull-faced, shake-fingered, rattling things that sway from neck-chains in abandoned webbed closets, one of those things found on the desert all long and scattered like dice!

He stood upright, because he could not bear to remain seated. Inside me now, he grasped his stomach, his head, inside my head is a—skull. One of those curved cara-paces which holds my brain like an electrical jelly, one of those cracked shells with the holes in front like two holes shot through it by a double-barreled shot-gun! With its grottoes and caverns of bone, its rivetments and placements for my flesh, my smelling, my seeing, my hearing, my thinking! A skull, encompassing my brain, allowing it exit through its brittle windows to see the outside world!

He wanted to dash into the bridge party, upset it, a fox in a chickenyard, the cards fluttering all around like chicken feathers burst upward in clouds! He stopped himself only with a violent, trembling effort. Now, now, man, control yourself. This is a revelation, take it for what it's worth, understand it, savor it. BUT A *SKELETON!* screamed his subconscious. I won't stand for it. It's vulgar, it's terrible, it's frightening. Skeletons are horrors; they clink and tinkle and rattle in old castles, hung from oaken beams, making long, indolently rustling pendulums on the wind . . . .

"Darling, will you come in and meet the ladies?" called his wife's sweet, clear voice.

Mr. Harris stood up. His SKELETON was holding him up. This thing inside him, this invader, this horror, was supporting his arms, legs and head. It was like feeling someone just behind you who shouldn't be there. With every step he took he realized how dependent he was upon this other Thing.

"Darling, I'll be with you in a moment," he called weakly. To himself he said, "Come on, now, brace up. You've got to go back to work tomorrow. And Friday you've got to make that trip to Phoenix. It's a long drive. Hundreds of miles. Got to be in shape for that trip or you won't get Mr. Creldon to put his money into your ceramics business. Chin up, now."

Five minutes later he stood among the ladies being introduced to Mrs. Withers, Mrs. Abblematt, and Miss Kirthy, all of whom had skeletons inside them but took it very calmly, because nature had carefully clothed the bare nudity of clavicle, tibia and femur with breasts, thighs, calves, with coiffure and eyebrow satanic, with bee-stung lips and—LORD! shouted Mr. Harris inwardly—when they talk or eat, part of their skeleton shows—their *teeth!* I never thought of that.

"Excuse me," he said, and ran from the room only in time to drop his lunch among the petunias over the garden balustrade.

That night, seated on the bed as his wife undressed, he pared his toenails and fingernails scrupulously. These parts, too, were where his skeleton was shoving, indignantly growing out. He must have muttered something concerning this theory, because next thing he knew his wife, in negligee, slithered on the bed in animal cuddlesomeness, yawning, "Oh, my darling, fingernails are *not* bone, they're only hardened skin growths."

He threw the scissors away with relief. "Glad to hear that. Feel better." He looked at the ripe curves of her body, marveling. "I hope all people are made the same way."

"If you aren't the darndest hypochondriac I ever saw," she said. She snuggled to him. "Come on. What's wrong? Tell mama."

"Something inside me," he said. "Something—I ate."

The next morning and all afternoon at his downtown office, Mr. Harris found that the sizes, shapes and constructions of various bones in his body displeased him. At ten a.m. he asked to feel Mr. Smith's elbow one moment. Mr. Smith obliged, but scowled suspiciously. And after lunch Mr. Harris asked to touch Miss Laurel's shoulderblade and she immediately pushed herself back against him, purring like a kitten, shutting her eyes in the mistaken belief that he wished to examine a few other anatomical delicacies. "Miss Laurel!" he snapped. "Stop that!"

Alone, he pondered his neuroses. The war just over, the pressure of his work, the uncertainty of the future, probably had much to do with his mental outlook. He wanted to leave the office, get into his own business, for himself. He had more than a little talent at artistic things, had dabbled in ceramics and sculpture. As soon as possible he'd get over into Arizona and borrow that money from Mr. Creldon. It would build him his kiln and set up his own shop. It was a worry. What a case he was. But it was a good thing he had contacted M. Munigant, who had seemed to be eager to understand and help him. He would fight it out with himself, not go back to either Munigant or Dr. Burleigh unless he was forced to. The alien feeling would pass. He sat staring into nothing.

The alien feeling did not pass. It grew.

On Tuesday and Wednesday it bothered him terrifically that his outer dermis, epidermis, hair and other appendages were of a high disorder, while the integumented skeleton of himself was a slick clean structure of efficient organization. Sometimes, in certain lights while his lips were drawn morosely downward, weighted with melancholy, he imagined he saw his skull grinning at him behind the flesh. *It had its nerve, it did!*

"Let go of me!" he cried. "Let go of me! You've caught me, you've captured me! My lungs, you've got them in a vise! Release them!"

He experienced violent gasps as if his ribs were pressing in, choking the breath from him.

"My brain; stop *squeezing* it!"

And terrible hot headaches caught his brain like a bivalve in the compressed clamp of skull-bones.

"My vitals! All my organs, let them be, for God's sake! Stay away from my heart!" His heart seemed to cringe from the fanning nearness of his ribs. Ribs like pale spiders crouched and fiddling with their prey.

Drenched with sweat, he lay upon the bed one night while Clarisse was out attending a Red Cross meet. He tried to gather his wits again, and always the conflict of his disorderly exterior and this cool calciumed thing inside him with all its exact symmetry.

His complexion: wasn't it oily and lined with worry?

Observe the flawless, snow-white perfection of the skull.

His nose: wasn't it too large?

Then observe the small tiny bones of the skull's nose before that monstrous nasal cartilage begins forming Harris' lopsided proboscis.

His body: wasn't it a bit plump?

Well, then, consider the skeleton; so slender, so svelte, so economical of line and contour. Like exquisitely carved oriental ivory it is, perfected and thin as a reed.

His eyes: weren't they protuberant and ordinary and numb looking?

Be so kind as to note the eye-sockets of the skeleton's skull; so deep and rounded, sombre, quiet, dark pools, all knowing, eternal. Gaze deeply into skull sockets and you never touch the bottom of their dark understanding with any plumb line. All irony, all sadism, all life, all everything is there in the cupped darkness.

Compare. Compare. Compare.

He raged for hours, glib and explosive. And the skeleton, ever the frail and solemn philosopher, quietly hung inside of Harris, saying not a word, quietly suspended like a delicate insect within a chrysalis, waiting and waiting.

Then it came to Harris.

"Wait a minute. Hold on a minute," he exclaimed. "You're helpless, too. I've got you, too. I can make you do anything I want you to! And you can't prevent it! I say put up your carpels, metacarpels, and phalanges and—sswtt up they go, as I wave to someone!" He giggled.

"I order the fibula and femur to locomote and *Hunn* two three four, *Hunn* two three four—we walk around the block. There."

Harris grinned.

"It's a fifty-fifty fight. Even steven. And we'll fight it out, we two, we shall. After all, I'm the part that *thinks!*" That was good, it was a triumph, he'd remember that. "Yes, by God, yes. I'm the part that thinks. If I didn't have you, even then I could still think!"

Instantly, he felt a pain strike his head. His cranium, crowding in slowly, began giving him some of his own treatment back.

At the end of the week he had postponed the Phoenix trip because of his health. Weighing himself on a penny scales he saw the slow glide of the red arrow as it pointed to: 164.

He groaned. "Why, I've weighed 175 for ten years. I can't have lost ten pounds." He examined his cheeks in the fly-dotted mirror. Cold primitive fear rushed over him in odd little shivers. "Hold on! I know what you're about, *you*."

He shook his finger at his bony face, particularly addressing his remarks to his superior maxillary, his inferior maxillary, to his cranium and to his cervical vertebrae.

"You rum thing, you. Think you can starve me off, make me lose weight, eh? A victory for you, is that it?

Peel the flesh off, leave nothing but skin on bone. Trying to ditch me, so you can be supreme, ah? No, no!"

He fled into a cafeteria.

Ordering turkey, dressing, creamed potatoes, four vegetables, three desserts, he soon found he could not eat it, he was sick to his stomach. He forced himself. His teeth began to ache. "Bad teeth, is it?" he wanted to know, angrily. "I'll eat in spite of every tooth clanging and banging and rattling so they fall in my gravy."

His head ached, his breathing came hard from a constricted chest, his teeth pulsed with pain, but he had one small victory. He was about to drink milk when he stopped and poured it into a vase of nasturtiums. "No calcium for you, my boy, no more calcium for you. Never again shall I eat foods with calcium or other bone-fortifying minerals. I'll eat for one of us, not both, my lad."

"One hundred and fifty pounds," he said, the following week to his wife. "Do you see how I've changed?"

"For the better," said Clarisse. "You were always a little plump for your height, darling." She stroked his chin. "I like your face, it's so much nicer, the lines of it are so firm and strong now."

"They're not *my* lines, they're his, damn him! You mean to say you like him better than you like me?" he demanded indignantly.

"Him? Who's *'him'*?"

In the parlor mirror, beyond Clarisse, his skull smiled back at him behind his fleshy grimace of hatred and despair.

Fuming, he popped malt tablets into his mouth. This was one way of gaining weight when you couldn't keep other foods down. Clarisse noticed the malt pellets. "But, darling, really, you don't have to regain the weight for me," she said.

"Oh, shut up!" he felt like saying.

She came to him and sat down and made him lie so his head was in her lap. "Darling," she said. "I've watched you lately. You're so—badly off. You don't say anything, but you look—hunted. You toss in bed at night. Maybe you should go to a psychiatrist. But I think I can tell you everything he would say. I've put it all together, from hints you've let escape you. I can tell you that you and your skeleton are one and the same, one nation, indivisible, with liberty and justice for all. United you stand, divided you fall. If you two fellows can't get along like an old married couple in the future, go back and see Dr. Burleigh. But, *first,* relax. You're in a vicious circle, the more you worry, the more your bones stick out, the more your bones stick out, the more you worry. After all, now, who picked this fight—you or that anonymous entity you claim is lurking around behind your alimentary canal?"

He closed his eyes. "*I* did. I guess I did. Oh, my darling, I love you so."

"You rest now," she said softly. "Rest and forget."

Mr. Harris felt buoyed up for half a day, then he began to sag again. It was all very well to say every thing was imagination, but this particular skeleton, by God, was fighting back.

Harris set out for M. Munigant's office late in the day. Walking for half an hour until he found the address, he caught sight of the name Mr. Munigant initialled in ancient, flaking gold on a glass plate outside the building. Then, his bones seemed to explode from their moorings, blasted and erupted with pain. He could hardly see in his wet, pain-filled eyes. So violent were the pains that he staggered away. When he opened his eyes again he had rounded a corner. M. Munigant's office was out of sight.

The pains ceased.

M. Munigant was the man to help him. He *must* be! If the sight of his gilt-lettered name could cause so titanic a reaction in the deepness of Harris' body, why, of course M. Munigant *must* be just the man.

But, not today. Each time he tried to return to that office, the terrible pains laid him low. Perspiring, he had to give up, and stagger into a cocktail bar for respite.

Moving across the dim room of the cocktail lounge, he wondered briefly if a lot of blame couldn't be put on M. Munigant's shoulders; after all, it was Munigant who'd first drawn such specific attention to his skeleton, and brought home the entire psychological impact of it! Could M. Munigant be using him for some nefarious purpose? But what purpose? Silly to even suspect him. Just a little doctor. Trying to be helpful. Munigant and his jar of bread-sticks. Ridiculous. M. Munigant was okay, okay.

*

There was a sight within the cocktail lounge to give him hope. A large fat man, round as a butterball, stood drinking consecutive beers at the bar. Now *there* was a successful man. Harris repressed a desire to go up, clap the fat man's shoulder, and inquire as to how he'd gone about impounding his bones. Yes, the fat man's skeleton was luxuriously closeted. There were pillows of fat here, resilient bulges of it there, with several round chandeliers of fat under his chin. The poor skeleton was lost, it could never fight clear of *that* blubber; it may have tried once—but now, overwhelmed, not a bony echo of the fat man's supporter remained.

Not without envy, Harris approached the fat man as one might cut across the bow of an ocean liner. Harris ordered a drink, drank it, and then dared to address the fat man:

"Glands?"

"You talking to me?" asked the fat man.

"Or is there a special diet?" wondered Harris. "I beg your pardon, but, as you see, I'm down. Can't seem to put on any weight. I'd like a stomach like that one of yours. Did you grow it because you were afraid of something?"

"You," announced the fat man, "are drunk. But—I like drunkards." He ordered more drinks. "Listen close. I'll tell you—"

"Layer by layer," said the fat man, "twenty years, man and boy, I built this." He held his vast stomach like a globe of the world, teaching his audience its gastronomical geography. "It was no overnight circus. The tent was not raised before dawn on the wonders installed within. I have cultivated my inner organs as if they were thoroughbred dogs, cats and other animals. My stomach is a fat pink Persian tom slumbering, rousing at intervals to purr, mew, growl, and cry for chocolate titbits. I feed it well, it will most sit up for me. And, my dear fellow, my intestines are the rarest pure-bred Indian anacondas you ever viewed in the sleekest, coiled, fine and ruddy health. Keep 'em in prime, I do, all my pets. For fear of something? Perhaps."

This called for another drink for everybody.

"Gain weight?" The fat man savored the words on his tongue. "Here's what you do; get yourself a quarreling bird of a wife, a baker's dozen of relatives who can flush a covey of troubles out from behind the veriest molehill. Add to these a sprinkling of business associates whose prime motivation is snatching your last lonely quid, and you are well on your way to getting fat. How so? In no time you'll begin subconsciously building fat betwixt yourself and them. A buffer epidermal state, a cellular wall. You'll soon find that eating is the only fun on earth. But one needs to be bothered by outside sources. Too many people in this world haven't enough to worry about, then they begin picking on *themselves,* and they lose weight. Meet all of the vile, terrible people you can possibly meet, and pretty soon you'll be adding the good old fat!"

And with that advice, the fat man launched himself out into the dark tide of night, swaying mightily and wheezing.

"That's exactly what Dr. Burleigh told me, slightly changed," said Harris thoughtfully. "Perhaps that trip to Phoenix, now, at this time—"

The trip from Los Angeles to Phoenix was a sweltering one, crossing, as it did, the Mojave desert on a broiling yellow day. Traffic was thin and inconstant, and for long stretches there would not be a car on the road for miles ahead or behind. Harris twitched his fingers on the steering wheel. Whether or not Creldon, in Phoenix, lent him the money he needed to start his business, it was still a good thing to get away, to put distance behind.

The car moved in the hot sluice of desert wind. The one Mr. H. sat inside the other Mr. H. Perhaps both perspired. Perhaps both were miserable.

On a curve, the inside Mr. H. suddenly constricted the outer flesh, causing him to jerk forward on the hot steering wheel.

The car plunged off the road into deepest sand. It turned half over.

Night came on, a wind rose, the road was lonely and silent with little traffic. Those few cars that passed went swiftly on their way, their view obstructed. Mr. Harris lay unconscious until very late he heard a wind rising out of the desert, felt the sting of little sand needles on his cheeks, and opened his eyes.

Morning found him gritty-eyed and wandering in thoughtless, senseless circles, having, in his delirium, gotten away from the road. At noon he sprawled in the poor shade of a bush. The sun struck into him with a keen sword edge, cutting through to his—bones. A vulture circled.

Harris' parched lips cracked open, weakly. "So that's it?" he whimpered, red-eyed, bristle-cheeked. "One way or another you'll wreck me, walk me, starve me, thirst me, kill me." He swallowed dry burrs of dust. "Sun cook off my flesh so you can peek forth. Vultures lunch and breakfast from me, and then there you'll lie, grinning. Grinning with victory. Like a bleached xylophone strewn and played by vultures with an ear for odd music. You'd like that. Freedom."

He walked on through a landscape that shivered and bubbled in the direct pour of sunlight; stumbling, falling flat, lying to feed himself little mouths of flame. The air was blue alcohol flame, and vultures roasted and steamed and glittered as they flew in glides and circles. Phoenix. The road. Car. Water. Safety.

"Hey!"

Somebody called from way off in the blue alcohol flame.

Mr. Harris propped himself up.

"Hey!"

The call was repeated. A crunching of footsteps, quick.

With a cry of unbelievable relief, Harris rose, only to collapse again into the arms of some one in a uniform with a badge . . . .

*

The car tediously hauled, repaired, Phoenix reached, Harris found himself in such an unholy state of mind that the business transaction was more a numb pantomime than anything else. Even when he got the loan and held the money in his hand it meant nothing. This Thing within him like a hard white sword in a scabbard tainted his business, his eating, colored his love for Clarisse, made it unsafe to trust an automobile; all in all this Thing had to be put in its place before he could have love for business or anything. That desert incident had brushed too closely. Too near the bone, one might say with an ironic twist of one's mouth. Harris heard himself thanking Mr. Creldon, dimly, for the money. Then he turned his car and motored back across the long miles, this time cutting across to San Diego, so that he would miss that desert stretch between El Centro and Beaumont. He drove north along the coast. He didn't trust that desert. But—careful! Salt waves boomed, hissing on the beach outside Laguna. Sand, fish, and crustacea would cleanse his bones as swiftly as vultures. Slow down on the curves over the surf.

If anything happened, he wanted cremation. The two of them'd burn together that way. None of this graveyard burial stuff where little crawling things eat and leave nothing but unmantled bone! No, they'd burn. Damn Him! He was sick. Where could he turn? Clarisse? Burleigh? Munigant? Bone specialist. Munigant. Well?

"Darling!" trilled Clarisse, kissing him, so he winced at the solidness of her teeth and jaw behind the passionate exchange.

"Darling," he said, slowly, wiping his lips with his wrist, trembling.

"You look thinner; oh, darling, the business deal—?"

"It went through. Yeah, it went through. I guess. Yeah, it did," he said.

She enthused. She kissed him again. Lord, he couldn't even enjoy kisses any more because of this obsession. They ate a slow, falsely cheerful dinner, with Clarisse laughing and encouraging him. He studied the phone, several times he picked it up indecisively, then laid it down. His wife walked in, putting on her coat and hat. "Well, sorry, but I have to leave now," she laughed, and pinched him lightly on the cheek. "Come on now, cheer up! I'll be back from Red Cross in three hours. You lie around and snooze. I simply *have* to go."

When Clarisse was gone, Harris dialed the phone, nervously.

"M. Munigant?"

The explosions and the sickness in his body after he set the phone down were unbelievable. His bones were racked with every kind of pain, cold and hot, he had ever thought of or experienced in wildest nightmare. He swallowed all the aspirin he could find in an effort to stave off the assault; but when the doorbell finally rang an hour later, he could not move, he lay weak and exhausted, panting, tears streaming down his cheeks, like a man on a torture rack. Would M. Munigant go away if the door was not answered?

"Come in!" he tried to gasp it out. "Come in, for God's sake!"

M. Munigant came in. Thank God the door had been unlocked.

Oh, but Mr. Harris looked terrible. M. Munigant stood in the center of the living room, small and dark. Harris nodded at him. The pains rushed through him, hitting him with large iron hammers and hooks. M. Munigant's eyes glittered as he saw Harris' protuberant bones. Ah, he saw that Mr. Harris was now psychologically prepared for aid. Was it not so? Harris nodded again, feebly, sobbing. M. Munigant still whistled when he talked; something about his tongue and the whistling. No matter. Through his shimmering eyes Harris seemed to see M. Munigant shrink, get smaller. Imagination, of course. Harris sobbed out his story of the Phoenix trip. M. Munigant sympathized. This skeleton was a—a traitor! They would *fix* him for once and for all! "Mr. Munigant," sighed Harris, faintly. "I—I never noticed before. You have such an odd, odd tongue. Round. Tube-like. Hollow? Guess it's my eyes. Don't mind me. Delirious. I'm ready. What do I do?"

M. Munigant whistled softly, appreciatively, coming closer. If Mr. Harris would relax in his chair, and open his mouth? The lights were switched off. M. Munigant peered into Harris' dropped jaw. Wider, please? It had been so hard, that first visit, to help Harris, with both body and bone in rebellion. Now, he had cooperation from the flesh of the man anyway, even if the skeleton was acting up somewhat. In the darkness, M. Munigant's voice got small, small, tiny, tiny. The whistling became high and shrill. Now. Relax, Mr. Harris. NOW!

Harris felt his jaw pressed violently in all directions, his tongue depressed as with a spoon, his throat clogged. He gasped for breath. Whistle. He couldn't breathe! He was corked. Something squirmed, cork-screwed his cheeks out, bursting his jaws. Like a hot water douche, something squirted into his sinuses, his ears clanged! "Ahhh!" shrieked Harris, gagging. His head, its carapaces riven, shattered, hung loose. Agony shot into his lungs, around.

Harris could breathe again, momentarily. His watery eyes sprang wide. He shouted. His ribs, like sticks picked up and bundled, were loosened in him. Pain! He fell to the floor, rocking, rolling, wheezing out his hot breath.

Lights flickered in his senseless eyeballs, he felt his limbs swiftly cast loose and free, expertly. Through streaming eyes he saw the parlor.

The room was empty.

"M. Munigant? Where are you? In God's name, where are you, M. Munigant? Come help me!"

M. Munigant was gone.

"Help!"

Then he heard it.

Deep down in the subterranean fissures of his bodily well, he heard the minute, unbelievable noises; little smackings and twistings and little dry chippings and grindings and nuzzling sounds—like a tiny hungry mouse down in the red blooded dimness, gnawing ever so earnestly and expertly at what may have been, but was not, a submerged timber . . . !

Clarisse, walking along the sidewalk, held her head high and marched straight toward her house on Saint James Place. She was thinking of the Red Cross and a thousand other things as she turned the corner and almost ran into this little dark man who smelled of iodine.

Clarisse would have ignored him if it were not for the fact that as she passed he took something long, white and oddly familiar from his coat and proceeded to chew on it, as on a peppermint stick. Its end devoured, his extraordinary tongue darted within the white confection, sucking out the filling, making contented noises. He was still crunching his goodie as she proceeded up the sidewalk to her house, turned the doorknob and walked in.

"Darling?" she called, smiling around. "Darling, where are you?"

She shut the door, walked down the hall and into the living room.

"Darling . . . ."

She stared at the floor for twenty seconds, trying to understand.

She screamed.

Outside in the sycamore darkness, the little man pierced a long white stick with intermittent holes; then, softly, sighing, lips puckered, played a little sad tune upon the improvised instrument to accompany the shrill and awful singing of Clarisse's voice as she stood in the living room.

Many times as a little girl Clarisse had run on the beach sands, stepped on a jelly-fish and screamed. It was not so bad, finding an intact, gelatin-skinned jelly-fish in one's living room. One could step back from it.

It was when the jelly-fish *called you by name* . . . .

THE JAR

It was one of those things they keep in a jar in the tent of a sideshow on the outskirts of a little, drowsy town. One of those pale things drifting in alcohol plasma, forever dreaming and circling, with its peeled dead eyes staring out at you and never seeing you. It went with the noiselessness of late night, and only the crickets chirping, the frogs sobbing off in the moist swampland. One of those things in a big jar that makes your stomach jump like it does when you see an amputated arm in a laboratory vat.

Charlie stared back at it for a long time.

A long time, his big raw hands, hairy on the roofs of them, clenching the rope that kept back curious people. He had paid his dime and now he stared.

It was getting late. The merry-go-round drowsed down to a lazy mechanical tinkle. Tentpeggers back of a canvas smoked and cursed over a poker game. Lights switched out, putting a summer gloom over the carnival. People streamed homeward in cliques and queues. Somewhere, a radio flared up, then cut, leaving Louisiana sky wide and silent with stars peppering it.

There was nothing in the world for Charlie but that pale thing sealed in its universe of serum. Charlie's loose mouth hung open in a pink weal, teeth showing, eyes puzzled, admiring, wondering.

Someone walked in the shadows behind him, small beside Charlie's giant tallness. "Oh," said the shadow, coming into the light-bulb glare. "You still here, bud?"

"Yeah," said Charlie, irritated his thoughts were touched.

The carny-boss appreciated Charlie's curiosity. He nodded at his old acquaintance in the jar. "Everybody likes it; in a peculiar kinda way, I mean."

Charlie rubbed his long jaw-bone. "You—uh—ever consider selling it?"

The carny-boss' eyes dilated, then closed. He snorted. "Naw. It brings customers. They like seeing stuff like that. Sure."

Charlie made a disappointed, "Oh."

"Well," considered the carny-boss, "if a guy had money, maybe—"

"How much money?"

"If a guy had—" the carny-boss estimated, squinting eyes, counting on fingers, watching Charlie as he tacked it out one finger after another. "If a guy had three, four, say, maybe seven or eight—"

Charlie nodded with each motion, expectantly. Seeing this, the carny-boss raised his total, "—maybe ten dollars, or maybe fifteen—"

Charlie scowled, worried. The carny-boss retreated. "Say a guy has *twelve* dollars—" Charlie grinned. "Why he could buy that thing in that jar," concluded the carny-boss.

"Funny thing," said Charlie, "I got just twelve bucks in my denims. And I been reckoning how looked up to I'd be back down at Wilder's Hollow if I brung home something like this to set on my shelf over the table. The guys would sure look up to me then, I bet."

"*Well,* now, listen here—" said the carny-boss.

The sale was completed with the jar put on the back seat of Charlie's wagon. The horse skittered his hoofs when he saw the jar, and whinnied.

The carny-boss glanced up with an expression of, almost, relief. "I was tired of seeing the damn thing around, anyway. Don't thank me. Lately I been thinking things about it, funny things—but, don't mind me, I'm a big-mouthed so-and-so. S'long, farmer!"

Charlie drove off. The naked blue light bulbs withdrew like dying stars, the open dark country night of Louisiana swept in around wagon and horse. The brass merry-go-round clanking faded. There was just Charlie, the horse, timing his gray hoofs, and the crickets.

And the jar behind the high seat.

It sloshed back and forth, back and forth. Sloshed wet. And the cold gray thing drowsily slumped against the glass, looking out, looking out, but seeing nothing, nothing, nothing.

Charlie leaned back to pet the lid. Smelling of strange liquor his hand returned, changed and cold and trembling, excited. He was bright scarlet happy about this. *Yes, sir!*

Slosh, slosh, slosh . . . .

In the Hollow numerous grass-green and blood-red lanterns tossed dusty light over men huddled, chanting, spitting, sitting on General Store property.

They knew the creak-bumble of Charlie's vehicle and did not shift their raw, drab-haired skulls as he rocked to a halt. Their cigars were nicotine glow-worms, their voices were frog mutterings in summer nights.

Charlie leaned down at an eager angle. "Hi, Clem! Hi, Milt!"

"Lo, Charlie. Lo, Charlie," they murmured. The political conflict continued. Charlie cut it down the seam:

"I got somethin' here. I got somethin' you might wanna see!"

Tom Carmody's eyes glinted, green in the lamp-light, from the General Store porch. It seemed to Charlie that Tom Carmody was forever installed under porches in shadow, or under trees in shadow, or if in a room then in the farthest niche, shining his eyes out at you from his dark. You never knew what his face was doing, and his eyes were always funning you. And every time they looked at you they laughed a different way:

"You ain't got nothin' we wants ta see, you dumb sheebaw!"

Charlie made a fist with a blunt knuckle fringe. "Somethin' in a jar," he went on. "Looks kine a like a brain, kine a like a pickled wolf, kine a like—well, come look yourself!"

Somebody snicked their cigar into a fall of pink ash and ambled over to look. Charlie grandly elevated the jar lid, and in the uncertain lantern light the man's face changed. "Hey, now, what in hell *is* this—?"

It was the first thaw of the night. Others shifted lazily upright, leaned forward; gravity pulled them into walking. They made no effort, except to keep one shoe afore the other to keep from collapsing upon their unusual faces. They circled the jar and contents. And Charlie, first time in his life, seized upon some strategy and clapped the lid down with a glass clatter:

"You want to see more, drop aroun' my house! It'll be there," he declared, generously.

Tom Carmody spat from out his porch eyrie, "Ha!"

"Lemme see that again!" cried Gramps Medknowe. "Is it a brain?"

Charlie flapped the reins and the horse stumbled into action.

"Come on aroun'! You're welcome!"

"What'll your wife say?"

"She'll kick the tar off'n our heels!"

But Charlie and wagon were gone over the hill. They stood around, all of them, chewing tongues, squinting after. Tom Carmody swore softly from the porch . . . .

As Charlie climbed the steps of his shack, carrying the jar to its throne in the living room, he thought that from now on the place would be a palace. The incumbent king swam without moving in his private pool, raised, elevated upon his shelf over the skinny table.

This jar was the one thing that dispelled the gray sameness that hung over the place on the swamp-rim.

"What've you got there?"

Thedy's thin soprano turned him from his admiration. She stood in the bedroom door glaring out, her thin body clothed in faded blue gingham, her hair drawn to a drab knot behind red ears. Her eyes were faded like the gingham. "Well," she repeated. "What is it?"

"What's it look like to you, Thedy?"

She took a thin step forward, making a slow indolent pendulum of hips. Her eyes were intent upon the jar, her lips drawing back to show feline milk teeth.

The dead pale thing hung in its serum.

Thedy snapped a dull-blue glance at Charlie, then back to the jar, once more at Charlie, once more to the jar, then she whirled quickly to clutch the wall.

"It—it looks. It—looks just like—*you*—Charlie!" she shouted hoarsely.

The bedroom door slammed behind her.

The reverberation did not disturb the jar's contents. But Charlie stood there, longing after her, neck muscles long, taut, heart pounding frantically, and then after his heart slowed a bit, he talked to the thing in the jar:

"I work the bottom land to the buttbone ever' year, and she takes the money and rushes off down home visitin' her folks nine weeks at a stretch. I can't keep holt of her. She and the men from the store they make fun of me. I can't help it if I don't know the ways to hold or touch or work her. Damn, but I *try!*"

Philosophically, the contents of the jar gave no advice.

"Charlie?"

Someone stood in the frontyard door.

Charlie turned, startled, then broke out a grin.

It was some of the men from the General Store.

"Uh—Charlie—we—that is—we thought—well—we came up to have a look at that—stuff—you got in that there jar—"

July passed warm and it was August.

For the first time in years, Charlie was happy as tall corn growing after a drought. It was gratifying of an evening to hear boots shushing through the tall grass, the sound of men spitting into the ditch prior to setting foot on the porch, the sound of heavy bodies creaking across it, and the groan of the house as yet another shoulder leaned against its frame door and another voice said, as a hairy wrist wiped clean the questioning mouth:

"Kin I come in?"

With elaborate casualness, Charlie'd invite the arrivals in. There'd be chairs, soap-boxes for all, or at least carpets to squat on. And by the time crickets were itching their legs into a summertime humming and frogs were throat-swollen like ladies with goiters shouting in the great night, the room would be full to bursting with people from all the bottom lands.

At first nobody would say nothing. The first half hour of such an evening, while people came in and got settled, was spent in carefully rolling cigarettes. Putting tobacco neatly into the rut of brown paper, loading it, tamping it, as they loaded and tamped and rolled their thoughts and fears and amazement for the evening. It gave them time to think. You could see their brains working behind their eyes as they fingered the cigarettes into smoking order.

It was kind of a rude church gathering. They sat, squatted, leaned on plaster walls, and one by one, with reverent awe, they stared at the jar upon its shelf.

They wouldn't stare sudden like. That would've been irreverent. No, they kind of did it slow, casual, as if they were glancing around the room—letting eyes fumble over just *any* old object that happened into their consciousness.

And—just by accident, of course—the focus of their wandering eyes would occur always at the same place. After awhile all eyes in the room would be fastened to it, like pins stuck in some incredible pin-cushion. And the only sound would be someone sucking a corn-cob. Or the children's barefooted scurry on the porch planks outside. Maybe some woman's voice would come, "You kids git away, now! Git!" And with a giggle like soft, quick water, the bare feet would rush off to scare the bull-frogs.

Charlie would be up front, naturally, on his rocking chair, a plaid pillow under his lean rump, rocking slow, enjoying the fame and looked-up-toedness that came with keeping the jar.

Thedy, she'd be seen way back of the room with the women folks in a bunch like grey grapes, abiding their menfolk.

Thedy looked like she was ripe for jealous screaming. But she said nothing, just watched men tromp into her living room and sit at the feet of Charlie staring at this here Holy Grail-like thing, and her lips were set as seven day concrete and she spoke not a civil word to nobody.

After a period of proper silence, someone, maybe old Gramps Medknowe from Crick Road, would clear the phlegm from his old throat's cavern, lean forward, blinking, wet his lips, maybe, and there'd be a curious tremble in his calloused fingers.

This would cue everyone to get ready for the talking to come. Ears were primed. People settled as much as sows in warm mud after the rain.

Gramps looked a long while, measured his lips with a lizard tongue, then settled back and said, like always, in a high thin old man's tenor:

"Wonder what *it* is? Wonder if it's a he or a she or just a plain old *it?* Sometimes I wake up nights, twist on my corn-matting, think about that jar settin' here in the long dark. Think about *it* hangin' in liquid, peaceful and pale like an animal oyster. Some times I wake Maw and we both think of it . . . ."

While talking, Gramps moved his fingers in a quavering pantomime. Every body watched his thick thumb weave, and the other heavy-nailed fingers undulate.

". . . we both lay there, thinkin'. And we shivers. May be a hot night, trees sweatin', mosquitoes too hot to fly, but we shivers jest the same, and turn over, tryin' to sleep . . . ."

Gramps lapsed back into silence, as if his speech was enough from him, let some other voice talk the wonder, awe and strangeness.

Juke Marmer, from Willow Sump, wiped sweat off his palms on the round of his knees and softly said:

"I remember when I was a runnel-nosed kid. We had a cat who was all the time makin' kittens. Lordamighty, she'd a litter ever time she turned around and skipped a fence—" Juke spoke in a kind of holy softness, benevolent. "Well, we usually gave the kittens away, but when this one particular litter busted out, everybody within walkin' distance had one-two our cats by gift, already.

"—So Ma busied on the back porch with a big two gallon glass jar, fillin' it to the top with water. It slopped in the sunlight. Ma said, 'Juke, you drown them kittens!' I 'member I stood there, the kittens mewed, runnin' 'round, blind, small, helpless and snuggly. Just beginnin' to get their eyes open. I looked at Ma, I said, 'Not *me*,

Ma! *You* do it!' But Ma turned pale and said it had to be done and I was the only one handy. And she went off to stir gravy and fix chicken. I—I picked up one—kitten. I held it. It was warm. It made a mewin' sound. I felt like runnin' away, not ever comin' back."

Juke nodded his head now, eyes bright, young, seeing into the past, making it stark, chiseling it out with hammer and knife of words, smoothing it with his tongue:

"I dropped the kitten in the water.

"The kitten closed his eyes, opened his mouth, tryin' for air. I 'member how the little white fangs showed, the pink tongue came out, and bubbles with it, in a line to the top of the water!

"I know to this day the way that kitten floated after it was all over, driftin' aroun', aroun', slow and not worryin', lookin' out at me, not condemnin' me for what I done. But not likin' me, neither. Ahhhh . . . ."

Hearts beat fast. Eyes shifted quickly from Juke to the shelved jar, back to him, up again; a spectators' game, like one sees at a tennis tournament, interest changing from moment to moment, apprehensively.

A pause.

Jahdoo, the black man from Heron Swamp, tossed his ivory eyeballs like a dusky juggler in his head. His dark knuckles knotted and flexed—grasshoppers alive.

"You know what thet is? You know, you *know?* I tells you. That am the center of Life, sure 'nuff! Lord believe me, it am so!"

Swaying in a tree-like rhythm, Jahdoo was blown by some swamp wind nobody could see, hear or feel, save himself. His eyeballs went around again, as if loosened from all mooring. His voice needled a dark thread pattern picking up each person by the lobes of their ears and sewing them into one unbreathing design:

"From that, lyin' back in the Middibamboo Sump, all sort o' thing crawl. It put out hand, it put out feet, it put out tongue an' horn an' it grow. Little bitty amoeba, perhap. Then a frog with a bulge-throat fit ta bust! Yah!" He cracked knuckles. "It slobber on up to its gummy joints and it—it AM A MAN! That am the center of creation! That am Middibamboo Mama, from which we all come ten thousand year ago. Believe it!"

"Ten thousand year ago!" reiterated Granny Carnation.

"It am old! Looky it! It donn worra no more. It know betta. It hang like pork chop in fryin' fat. It got eye to see with, but it donn blink 'em, they donn look fretted, does they? No, man! It know betta. It know thet we done come *from* it, and we is goin' back *to* it!"

"What color eyes has it got?"

"Grey."

"Naw, *green!*"

"What color hair? Brown?"

"Black!"

"Red!"

"No, *grey!*"

Then, Charlie would give his drawling opinion. Some nights he'd say the same thing, some nights not. It didn't matter. When you said the same thing night after night in the deep summer, it always sounded different. The crickets changed it. The frogs changed it. The thing in the jar changed it. Charlie said:

"What if an old man went back into the swamp, or maybe a young kid, and wandered aroun' for years and years lost in the drippin' trails and gullies, the wet ravines in the nights, skin a turnin' pale, and makin' cold and shrivelin' up. Bein' away from the sun he'd keep witherin' away up and up and finally sink into a muck-hole and lay in a kind of—solution—like the maggot 'skeeters sleepin' in liquid. Why, why—for all we know, this might be someone we know. Someone we passed words with once on a time. For all we know . . . ."

A hissing from among the women folk back in the shadow. One woman standing, eyes shining black, fumbling for words. Her name was Mrs. Tridden. She said:

"Lots of little kids run stark naked into the swamp ever year. They runs around and they never comes back. I almost got lost maself. I—I lost my little boy, Foley, that way. You—you DON'T SUPPOSE!!"

Breaths were taken in, snatched through nostrils, constricted, tightened. Mouths turned down at corners, bent by grim facial muscles. Heads turned on celery stalk necks, and eyes read her horror and hope. It was in Mrs. Tridden's body, wire-taut, holding onto the wall back of her with straight fingers stiff.

"My baby," she whispered. She breathed it out. "My

baby. My Foley. Foley! Foley, is that you? Foley! Foley, tell me, baby, is that YOU!"

Every body held their breath, turning to see the jar.

The thing in the jar said nothing. It just stared blind-white out upon the multitude. And deep in raw-boned bodies a secret fear juice ran like spring thaw, and the resolute ice of calm life and belief and easy humbleness was cracked down the middle by that juice and melted away in a gigantic torrent! Someone screamed.

"It moved!"

"No, no, it didn' move. Just your eyes playin' tricks!"

"Hones' ta God," cried Juke. "I saw it shift slow like a dead kitten!"

"Hush up, now! It's been dead a long, long time. Maybe since before you was born!"

"He made a sign!" screamed Mrs. Tridden, the mother woman. "That's my baby, my Foley! My baby you got there! Three year old he was! My baby lost and white in the swamp!"

The sobbing broke out of her.

"Now, now, there now, Mrs. Tridden. There now. Set yourself down and stop shakin'. Ain't no more your child'n mine. There, there."

One of the women folk held her and faded out the sobbing into jerked breathing and a fluttering of her lips in butterfly quickness as the breath stroked over them, afraid.

When all was quiet again, Granny Carnation, with a

withered pink flower in her shoulder length grey hair, sucked the pipe in her trap mouth and talked around it, shaking her head to make the hair dance in the light:

"All this talking and shoving words. Like as not we'll never find out, never know what it is. Like as not if we could find out we wouldn't *want* to know. It's like them magic tricks them magicians do at the show. Once you find the feke, it ain't no more fun 'n the innards of a jackbob. We come collecting around here every ten nights or so, talking, social like, with something, always something, to talk about. Stands to reason if we found out what the damn thing is there'd be nothing to talk about, so there!"

"Well, damn it to hell!" rumbled a bull voice. "I don't think it's nothin'!"

Tom Carmody.

Tom Carmody standing, as always, in shadow. Out on the porch, just his eyes staring in, his lips laughing at you dimly, mocking. His laughter got inside Charlie like a hornet sting. Thedy had put him up to it, Thedy was trying to undermine Charlie's social life, she was!

"Nothin'," repeated Carmody, harshly, "in that jar but a bunch of old jelly-fish from Sea Cove, a rottin' and stinkin' fit to whelp!"

"You mightn't be jealous, Cousin Carmody?" asked Charlie, slow.

"Haw!" snorted Carmody. "I just come aroun' ta watch you dumb cyppers jaw about nuthin'. I gits a kick outa it. You notice I never set foot inside or took part. I'm goin' home right now. Any body wanna come along with me?"

He got no offer of company. He laughed again, as if this were a bigger joke, how so many people could be so dumb, and Thedy was raking her palms with angry nails back of the room. Charlie felt a twinge of unexpected fear at this.

Carmody, still laughing, rapped off the porch with his high-heeled boots and the sound of crickets took him away.

Granny Carnation gummed her pipe. "Like I was saying before the storm: that thing on the shelf, why couldn't it be sort of—all things? Lots of things. What they call a—gimmle—"

"Symbol?"

"That's it. Symbol. Symbol of all the nights and days in the dead canebrake. Why's it have to be *one* thing? Maybe it's *lots*."

And the talking went on for another hour, and Thedy slipped away into the night on the track of Tom Carmody, and Charlie began to sweat. They were up to something, those two. They were planning something. Charlie sweated warm all the rest of the evening . . . .

The meeting broke up late, and Charlie bedded down with mixed emotions. The meeting had gone off well, but what about Thedy and Tom Carmody?

Very late, with certain star coveys shuttled down the sky marking the time as after midnight, Charlie heard the shushing of the tall grass parted by her penduluming hips. Her heels tacked soft across the porch, into the house, into the bedroom.

She lay soundlessly in bed, cat eyes staring at him. He couldn't see them, but he could feel them staring.

"Charlie?"

He waited.

Then he said, "I'm awake."

Then she waited.

"Charlie?"

"What?"

"Bet you don't know where I been, bet you don't know where I been." It was a faint, derisive sing-song in the night.

He waited.

She waited again. She couldn't bear waiting long, though, and continued:

"I been to the carnival over in Cape City. Tom Carmody drove me. We—we talked to the carny-boss, Charlie, we did, we did, we *sure* did." And she sort of giggled to herself, secretly.

Charlie was ice cold. He stirred upright on an elbow.

She said, "We found out what it is in your jar, Charlie—" insinuatingly.

Charlie flumped over, hands to ears. "I don't wanna hear!"

"Oh, but you gotta hear, Charlie. It's a good joke. Oh, it's rare, Charlie," she hissed.

"Go—away," he said.

"Unh-unh! No. No, sir, Charlie. Why, no, Charlie-Honey. Not until I tell!"

"Go," he said in a low, firm voice, "away."

"Let me tell! We talked to that carny-boss, and he—he liked to die laughin', he said he sold that jar and what was in it to some, some—hick—for twelve bucks. And it ain't worth more'n two bucks at most!"

Laughter bloomed in the dark, right out of her mouth, an awful kind of laughter.

She finished it, snapping, quick:

"It's just junk, Charlie! Liquid rubber, papier-mache, silk, cotton, chemicals! That's all! Got a metal frame inside it! That's all! That's all it is, Charlie! That's all!" she shrilled in triumph.

"No, no!"

He sat up swiftly, ripping sheets apart in big fingers, roaring, tears coming bright on his cheeks.

"I don't wanna hear! Don't wanna hear!" he bellowed over and over.

She teased. "Wait'll everyone hears how fake it is! Won't they laugh! Won't they flap their lungs!"

He caught her wrists. "You ain't—gonna tell them?"

"Ouch! You hurt me!"

"You *ain't* gonna tell them."

"Wouldn't want me known as a liar, would you, Charles?"

He flung her wrists like white sticks into a well:

"Whyncha leave me alone? You dirty! Dirty jealous mean of everthing I do. I took shine off your nose when

I brung the jar home. You didn' sleep right 'til you ruined things!"

She laughed nastily. "Then I *won't* tell any body," she said.

He caught on to her. "You spoiled *my* fun. That's all that counted. It don't matter if you tell the rest. *I* know. And I'll never have no more fun. You and that Tom Carmody. Him laughin'. I wish I could stop him laughin'. He's been laughin' for years at me! Well, you just go tell the rest, the other people, now—might as well have your fun—!"

He strode angrily, grabbed the jar so it sloshed, and would have flung it on the floor, but he stopped, trembling, and let it down softly on the spindly table. He leaned over it, sobbing. If he lost this, the world was gone. And he was losing Thedy, too. Every month that passed she danced further away, sneering at him, funning him. For too many years her hips had been the pendulum by which he reckoned the time of his living. But other men, Tom Carmody, for one, were reckoning time from the same source.

Thedy was standing, waiting for him to smash the jar. Instead, he petted and stroked and gradually quieted himself over it. He thought of the long good evenings in the past month, those rich evenings of camaraderie, conversation moving about the room. That, at least, was good, if nothing else.

He turned slowly to Thedy. She was lost forever to him.

"Thedy, you didn't go to the carnival."

"Yes, I did."

"You're lyin'," he said, quietly.

"No, I'm not!"

"This—this jar *has* to have somethin' in it. Somethin' besides the junk you say. Too many people believe there's somethin' in it, Thedy. You can't change that. The carny-boss, if you talked with him, he lied." Charlie took a deep breath and then said, "Come here, Thedy."

"What you want?" she asked, sullenly.

"Come over here."

"No, I won't."

He took a step toward her. "Come here."

"Keep away from me, Charlie."

"Just want to show you something, Thedy." His voice was soft, low and insistent. "Here, kittie. Here kittie, kittie, kittie—HERE KITTIE!"

It was another night, about a week later. Gramps Medknowe and Granny Carnation came, followed by young Juke and Mrs. Tridden and Jahdoo the colored man. Followed by all the others, young and old, sweet and sour, creaking into chairs, each with his or her thought, hope, fear and wonder in mind. Each not looking at the shrine, but saying hello softly to Charlie.

They waited for the others to gather. From the shine of their eyes one could see that each saw something different in the jar, something of the life and the pale life after life, and the life in death and the death in life, each with his story, his cue, his lines, familiar, old but new.

Charlie sat alone.

"Hello, Charlie." Somebody glanced around, into the empty bedroom. "Where's your wife? Gone off again to visit her folks?"

"Yeah, she run off again to Tennessee. Be back in a couple weeks. She's the darndest one for runnin'. You know Thedy."

"Great one for ganntin' around, that woman."

Soft voices talking, getting settled, and then, quite suddenly, walking into the dark porch and shining his eyes in at the people—Tom Carmody.

Tom Carmody standing outside the door, knees sagging and trembling, arms hanging and shaking at his side, staring into the room. Tom Carmody not daring to enter. Tom Carmody with his mouth open, but not smiling. His lips wet and slack, not smiling. His face pale as chalk, as if it had been kicked with a boot.

Gramps looked up at the jar, cleared his throat and said,

"Why, I never noticed so definite before. It's got *blue* eyes."

"It always had blue eyes," said Granny Carnation.

"No," whined Gramps. "No, it didn't. They was brown last time we was here." He blinked upward. "And another thing—it's got brown hair. Didn't have brown hair *before!*"

"Yes, yes, it did," sighed Mrs. Tridden.

"No, it didn't!"

"Yes, it did!"

Tom Carmody, shivering in the summer night, staring in at the jar. Charlie, glancing up at it, rolling a cigarette, casually, at peace and calm, very certain of his life and thoughts. Tom Carmody, alone, seeing things about the jar he never saw before. *Everybody* seeing what they wanted to see; all thoughts running in a fall of quick rain:

"My baby! My little baby!" screamed the thought of Mrs. Tridden.

"A brain!" thought Gramps.

The colored man jigged his fingers. "Middibamboo Mama!"

A fisherman pursed his lips. "Jellyfish!"

"Kitten! Here kittie, kittie, kittie!" the thoughts drowned clawing in Juke's skull. "Kitten!"

"Everything and anything!" shrilled Granny's weazened thought. "The night, the swamp, the death, the pallid moist things of the sea!"

Silence, and then Gramps said, "I wonder. Wonder if it's a he—or a she—or just a plain old *it?*"

Charlie glanced up, satisfied, tamping his cigarette, shaping it to his mouth. Then he looked at Tom Carmody, who would never smile again, in the door. "I reckon we'll never know. Yeah, I reckon we won't." Charlie smiled.

It was just one of those things they keep in a jar in the tent of a sideshow on the outskirts of a little, drowsy town. One of those pale things drifting in alcohol plasma, forever dreaming and circling, with its peeled dead eyes staring out at you and never seeing you . . . .

THE LAKE

They cut the sky down to my size and threw it over the Michigan Lake, put some kids yelling on yellow sand with bouncing balls, a gull or two, a criticizing parent, and me breaking out of a wet wave, finding this world very bleary and moist.

I ran up on the beach.

Mama swabbed me with a furry towel. "Stand there and dry," she said.

I stood there, watching the sun take away the water beads on my arms. I replaced them with goose-pimples.

"My, there's a wind," said Mama. "Put on your sweater."

"Wait'll I watch my goose-bumps," I said.

"Harold," said Mama.

I put the sweater on and watched the waves come up and fall down on the beach. But not clumsily. On purpose, with a green sort of elegance. Even a drunken man could not collapse with such elegance as those waves.

It was September. In the last days when things are getting sad for no reason. The beach was so long and lonely with only about six people on it. The kids quit bouncing the ball because somehow the wind made them sad, too, whistling the way it did, and the kids sat down and felt autumn come along the endless shore.

All of the hot dog stands were boarded up with strips of golden planking, sealing in all the mustard, onion, meat odors of the long, joyful summer. It was like nailing summer into a series of coffins. One by one the places slammed their covers down, padlocked their doors, and the wind came and touched the sand, blowing away all of the million footprints of July and August. It got so that now, in September, there was nothing but the mark of my rubber tennis shoes and Donald and Delaus Schabold's feet, down by the water curve.

Sand blew up in curtains on the sidewalks, and the merry-go-round was hidden with canvas, all of the horses frozen in mid-air on their brass poles, showing teeth, galloping on. With only the wind for music, slipping through canvas.

I stood there. Everyone else was in school. I was not. Tomorrow I would be on my way west across the United States on a train. Mom and I had come to the beach for one last brief moment.

There was something about the loneliness that made

me want to get away by myself. "Mamma, I want to run up the beach aways," I said.

"All right, but hurry back, and don't go near the water."

I ran. Sand spun under me and the wind lifted me. You know how it is, running, arms out so you feel veils from your fingers, caused by wind. Like wings.

Mama withdrew into the distance, sitting. Soon she was only a brown speck and I was all alone.

Being alone is a newness to a twelve year old child. He is so used to people about. The only way he can be alone is in his mind. There are so many real people around, telling children what and how to do, that a boy has to run off down a beach, even if it's only in his head, to get by himself in his own world, with his own miniature values.

So now I was really alone.

I went down to the water and let it cool up to my stomach. Always before, with the crowd, I hadn't dared to look, to come to this spot and search around in the water and call a certain name. But now—

Water is like a magician. Sawing you in half. It feels as if you were cut half in two, part of you, the lower part, sugar, melting, dissolving away. Cool water, and once in a while a very elegantly stumbling wave that fell with a flourish of lace.

I called her name. A dozen times I called it.

"Tally! Tally! Oh, Tally!"

Funny, but you really expect answers to your calling

when you are young. You feel that what ever you may think can be real. And some times may be that is not so wrong.

I thought of Tally, swimming out into the water last May, with her pigtails trailing, blonde. She went laughing, and the sun was on her small twelve year old shoulders. I thought of the water settling quiet, of the life-guard leaping into it, of Tally's mother screaming, and of how Tally never came out . . . .

The life-guard tried to persuade her to come out, but she did not. He came back with only bits of water-weed in his big-knuckled fingers, and Tally was gone. She would not sit across from me at school any longer, or chase indoor balls on the brick streets on summer nights. She had gone too far out, and the lake would not let her return.

And now in the lonely autumn when the sky was huge and the water was huge and the beach was so very long, I had come down for the last time, alone.

I called her name over and over. Tally, oh, Tally!

The wind blew so very softly over my ears, the way wind blows over the mouths of sea-shells to set them whispering. The water rose, embraced my chest, then my knees, up and down, one way and another, sucking under my heels.

"Tally! Come back, Tally!"

I was only twelve. But I know how much I loved her. It was that love that comes before all significance of body and morals. It was that love that is no more bad than wind and sea and sand lying side by side forever. It was made of all the warm long days together at the beach, and the humming quiet days of droning education at the school. All the long autumn days of the years past when I had carried her books home from school.

Tally!

I called her name for the last time. I shivered. I felt water on my face and did not know how it got there. The waves had not splashed that high.

Turning, I retreated to the sand and stood there for half an hour, hoping for one glimpse, one sign, one little bit of Tally to remember. Then, I knelt and built a sand castle, shaping it fine, building it as Tally and I had often built so many of them. But this time, I only built half of it. Then I got up.

"Tally, if you hear me, come in and build the rest."

I walked off toward that far away speck that was Mama. The water came in, blended the sand-castle circle by circle, mashing it down little by little into the original smoothness.

Silently, I walked along the shore.

Far away, a merry-go-round jangled faintly, but it was only the wind.

The next day, I went away on the train.

A train has a poor memory; it soon puts all behind it. It forgets the cornlands of Illinois, the rivers of childhood, the bridges, the lakes, the valleys, the cottages, the hurts and the joys. It spreads them out behind and they drop back of a horizon.

I lengthened my bones, put flesh on them, changed my young mind for an older one, threw away clothes as they no longer fitted, shifted from grammar to high-school, to college books, to law books. And then there was a young woman in Sacramento. I knew her for a time, and we were married.

I continued my law study. By the time I was twenty-two, I had almost forgotten what the East was like.

Margaret suggested that our delayed honeymoon be taken back in that direction.

Like a memory, a train works both ways. A train can bring rushing back all those things you left behind so many years before.

Lake Bluff, population 10,000, came up over the sky. Margaret looked so handsome in her fine new clothes. She watched me as I felt my old world gather me back into its living. She held my arm as the train slid into Bluff Station and our baggage was escorted out.

So many years, and the things they do to people's faces and bodies. When we walked through the town together I saw no one I recognized. There were faces with echoes in them. Echoes of hikes on ravine trails. Faces with small laughter in them from closed grammar schools and swinging on metal-linked swings and going up and down on teeter-totters. But I didn't speak. I walked and looked and filled up inside with all those memories, like leaves stacked for autumn burning.

We stayed on two weeks in all, revisiting all the places together. The days were happy. I thought I loved Margaret well. At least I thought I did.

It was on one of the last days that we walked down by the shore. It was not quite as late in the year as that day so many years before, but the first evidences of desertion were coming upon the beach. People were thinning out, several of the hot dog stands had been shuttered and nailed, and the wind, as always, waited there to sing for us.

I almost saw Mama sitting on the sand as she used to sit. I had that feeling again of wanting to be alone. But I could not force myself to speak of this to Margaret. I only held onto her and waited.

It got late in the day. Most of the children had gone home and only a few men and women remained basking in the windy sun.

The life-guard boat pulled up on the shore. The life-guard stepped out of it, slowly, with something in his arms.

I froze there. I held my breath and I felt small, only twelve years old, very little, very infinitesimal and afraid. The wind howled. I could not see Margaret. I could see only the beach, the life-guard slowly emerging from the boat with a grey sack in his hands, not very heavy, and his face almost as grey and lined.

"Stay here, Margaret," I said. I don't know why I said it.

"But, why?"

"Just stay here, that's all—"

I walked slowly down the sand to where the life-guard stood. He looked at me.

"What is it?" I asked.

The life-guard kept looking at me for a long time and he couldn't speak. He put the grey sack down on the sand, and water whispered wet up around it and went back.

"What is it?" I insisted.

"She's dead," said the life-guard, quietly.

I waited.

"Funny," he said, softly. "Funniest thing I ever saw. She's been dead. A long time."

I repeated his words.

He nodded. "Ten years, I'd say. There haven't been any children drowned here *this* year. There were twelve children drowned here since 1933, but we recovered all of them before a few hours had passed. All except one, I remember. This body here, why it must be ten years in the water. It's not—pleasant."

I stared at the grey sack in his arms. "Open it," I said. I don't know why I said it. The wind was louder.

He fumbled with the sack. "The way I know it's a little girl, is because she's still wearing a locket. There's nothing much else to tell by—"

"Hurry, man, *open it!*" I cried.

"I better not do that," he said. Then perhaps he saw the way my face must have looked. "She was such a *little* girl—"

He opened it only part way. That was enough.

The beach was deserted. There was only the sky and the wind and the water and the autumn coming on lonely. I looked down at her there.

I said something over and over. A name. The life-guard looked at me. "Where did you find her?" I asked.

"Down the beach, that way, in the shallow water. It's a long long time for her, ain't it?"

I shook my head.

"Yes, it is. Oh God, yes it is."

I thought: people grow. I have grown. But she has not changed. She is still small. She is still young. Death does not permit growth or change. She still has golden hair. She will be forever young and I will love her forever, oh God, I will love her forever.

The life-guard tied up the sack again.

Down the beach, a few moments later, I walked by myself. I stopped, and looked down at something. This is where the lifeguard found her, I said to myself.

There, at the water's edge, lay a sand-castle, only half-built. Just like Tally and I used to build them. She half and I half.

I looked at it. I knelt beside the sand-castle and saw the little prints of feet coming in from the lake and going back out to the lake again and not ever returning.

Then—I knew.

"I'll help you to finish it," I said.

I did. I built the rest of it up very slowly, then I arose

and turned away and walked off, so as not to watch it crumble in the waves, as all things crumble.

I walked back up the beach to where a strange woman named Margaret was waiting for me, smiling . . . .

THE MAIDEN

She was wondrous fair. She filled his eyes and he looked at her continually and was in love with her. Tall she was, and beautiful, with the morning sun on her. Tall she was, and stately of limb, and she worked for him. He knew her every whim, he did. And he stroked her and made love to her, but stayed out of her reach. He knew what she could do to men she loved too well.

Not today, he thought, you'll not have me today, maiden fair, maiden strong, maiden quick and maiden fatale.

Sometimes, he would let the children play with her, but only when he was near to be certain they didn't fall into the bad habit of teasing her too far.

How many lovers had she had? No, that was wording it a bit strongly. She had few lovers, ever, but she loved *them.* Sadist that she was she loved anyone she could get hold of.

And now this night he went up the steps to her and sat down beside her and rolled over against her and placed his weary head upon her shoulder and looked up at the sky, loving her, and seeing the long line of her face.

Then—he tripped the trigger.

Her long blue razor-sharp blade, weighing one hundred pounds, sliced down along the oiled grooves of the drop, straight at his throat—bamm!—through—chopping off light, sound, odor, feeling, his head popped into the waiting wicker, a sexual spout of red blood jutted from his sundered neck; and the two of them, he and she of the blade, lay together in that scarlet orgasm even as the first star appeared . . . .

THE TOMBSTONE

Well, first of all there was the long trip, and the dust poking up inside her thin nostrils, and Walter, her Oklahoma husband, swaying his lean carcass in their model-T Ford, so sure of himself it made her want to spit; then they got into this big brick town that was strange as old sin, and hunted up a landlord. The landlord took them to a small room and unlocked the door.

There in the middle of the simple room sat the tombstone.

Leota's eyes got a wise look, and immediately she pretended to gasp, and thoughts skipped through her mind in devilish quickness. Her superstitions were something Walter had never been able to touch or take away from her. She gasped, drew back, and Walter stared at her with his droopy eyelids hanging over his shiny grey eyes.

"No, no," cried Leota, definitely. "I'm not moving in any room with any dead man!"

"Leota!" said her husband.

"What do you mean?" wondered the landlord. "Madam, you don't—"

Leota smiled inwardly. Of course she didn't really believe, but this was her only weapon against her Oklahoma man, so— "I mean that I won't sleep in no room with no corpse. Get him out of here!"

Walter gazed at the sagging bed wearily, and this gave Leota pleasure, to be able to frustrate him. Yes, indeed, superstitions were handy things. She heard the landlord saying, "This tombstone is the very finest grey marble. It belongs to Mr. Whetmore."

"The name carved on the stone is WHITE," observed Leota coldly.

"Certainly. That's the man's name for whom the stone was carved."

"And is he dead?" asked Leota, waiting.

The landlord nodded.

"There, you *see!*" cried Leota. Walter groaned a groan which meant he was not stirring another inch looking for a room. "It smells like a cemetery in here," said Leota, watching Walter's eyes get hot and flinty. The landlord explained:

"Mr. Whetmore, the former tenant of this room, was an apprentice marble-cutter, this was his first job, he used to tap on it with a chisel every night from seven until ten."

"Well—" Leota glanced swiftly around to find Mr. Whetmore. "Where is he? Did he die, too?" She enjoyed this game.

"No, he discouraged himself and quit cutting this stone to work in an envelope factory."

"Why?"

"He made a mistake." The landlord tapped the marble lettering. "WHITE is the name here. Spelled wrong. Should be WHYTE, with a Y instead of an I. Poor Mr. Whetmore. Inferiority complex. Gave up at the least little mistake and scuttled off."

"I'll be damned," said Walter, shuffling into the room and unpacking the rusty brown suitcases, his back to Leota. The landlord liked to tell the rest of the story:

"Yes, Mr. Whetmore gave up easily. To show you how touchy he was, he'd percolate coffee mornings, and if he spilled a teaspoonful it was a catastrophe—he'd throw it all away and not drink coffee for days! Think of that! He got very sad when he made errors. If he put his left shoe on first, instead of his right, he'd quit trying and walk barefooted for ten or twelve hours, on cold mornings, even. Or if someone spelled his name wrong on his letters, he'd replace them in the mail-box marked NO SUCH PERSON LIVING HERE. Oh, he was a great one, was Mr. Whetmore!"

"That don't paddle us no further up-crick," pursued Leota grimly. "Walter, what're you commencing?"

"Hanging your silk dress in this closet; the red one."

"Stop hanging, we're not staying."

The landlord blew out his breath, not understanding how a woman could grow so dumb. "I'll explain once more. Mr. Whetmore did his home work here; he hired a truck which carried this tombstone here one day while I was out shopping for a turkey at the grocery, and when I walked back—tap-tap-tap—I heard it all the way downstairs—Mr. Whetmore had started chipping the marble. And he was so proud I didn't dare complain. But he was so awful proud he made a spelling mistake and now he ran off without a word, his rent is paid all the way till Tuesday, but he didn't want a refund, and now I've got some truckers with a hoist who'll come up first thing in the morning. You won't mind sleeping here one night with it, now will you? Of course not."

The husband nodded. "You understand, Leota? Ain't no dead man under that rug." He sounded so superior, she wanted to kick him.

She didn't believe him, and she stiffened. She poked a finger at the landlord. "*You* want your money. And you, Walter, you want a bed to drop your bones on. Both of you are lying from the word 'go'!"

The Oklahoma man paid the landlord his money tiredly, with Leota tongueing him. The landlord ignored her as if she were invisible, said good-night and she cried "Liar!" after him as he shut the door and left them alone. Her husband undressed and got in bed and said, "Don't stand there staring at the tombstone, turn out the light. We been traveling four days and I'm bushed."

Her tight criss-crossed arms began to quiver over her

thin breasts. "None of the three of us," she said, nodding at the stone, "will get any sleep."

Twenty minutes later, disturbed by the various sounds and movements, the Oklahoma man unveiled his vulture's face from the bedsheets, blinking stupidly. "Leota, you still up? I said, a long time ago, for you to switch off the light and come sleep! What are you doing there?'

It was quite evident what she was about. Crawling on rough hands and knees, she placed a jar of fresh-cut red, white and pink geraniums beside the headstone, and another tin-can of new-cut roses at the foot of the imagined grave. A pair of shears lay on the floor, dewy with having snipped flowers in the night outside a moment before.

Now she briskly whisked the colorful linoleum and the worn rug with a midget whisk broom, praying so her husband couldn't hear the words, but just the murmur. When she rose up, she stepped across the grave carefully so as not to defile the buried one, and in crossing the room she skirted far around the spot, saying, "There, that's done," as she darkened the room and laid herself out on the whining springs which sang in tune with her husband who now asked, "What in the Lord's name!" and she replied, looking at the dark around her, "No man's going to rest easy with strangers sleeping right atop him. I made amends with him, flowered his bed so he won't stand around rubbing his bones together late tonight."

Her husband looked at the place she occupied in the dark, and couldn't think of anything good enough to say, so he just swore, groaned, and sank down into sleeping.

Not half an hour later, she grabbed his elbow and turned him so she could whisper swiftly, fearfully into one of his ears, like a person calling into a cave: "Walter!" she cried. "Wake up, wake up!" She intended doing this all night, if need be, to spoil his superior kind of slumber.

He struggled with her. "What's wrong?"

"Mr. White! Mr. White! He's starting to haunt us!"

"Oh, go to sleep!"

"I'm not fibbing! Listen to him!"

The Oklahoma man listened. From under the linoleum, sounding about six feet or so down, muffled, came a man's sorrowful talking. Not a word came through clearly, just a sort of sad mourning.

The Oklahoma man sat up in bed. Feeling his movement, Leota hissed, "You heard, you heard?" excitedly. The Oklahoma man put his feet on the cold linoleum. The voice below changed into a falsetto. Leota began to sob. "Shut up, so I can hear," demanded her husband, angrily. Then, in the heart-beating quiet, he bent his ear to the floor and Leota cried, "Don't tip over the flowers!" and he cried, "Shut up!" and again listened, tensed. Then he spat out an oath and rolled back under the covers. "It's only the man downstairs," he muttered.

"That's what I mean. Mr. White!"

"No, not Mr. White. We're on the second floor of an

apartment house, and we got neighbors down under. Listen." The falsetto downstairs talked. "That's the man's wife. She's probably telling him not to look at another man's wife! Both of them probably drunk."

"You're lying!" insisted Leota. "Acting brave when you're really trembling fit to shake the bed down. It's a haunt, I tell you, and he's talking in voices, like Gran'ma Hanlon used to do, rising up in her church pew and making queer tongues all mixed, like a black man, an Irishman, two women and tree frogs, caught in her craw! That dead man, Mr. White, hates us for moving in with him tonight, I tell you! Listen!"

As if to back her up, the voices downstairs talked louder. The Oklahoma man lay on his elbows, shaking his head hopelessly, wanting to laugh, but too tired.

Something crashed.

"He's stirring in his coffin!" shrieked Leota. "He's mad! We got to move outa here, Walter, or we'll be found dead tomorrow!"

More crashes, more bangs, more voices. Then, silence. Followed by a movement of feet in the air over their heads.

Leota whimpered. "He's free of his tomb! Forced his way out and he's tromping the air over our heads!"

By this time, the Oklahoma man had his clothing on. Beside the bed, he put on his boots. "This building's three floors high," he said, tucking in his shirt. "We got neighbors overhead who just come home." To Leota's weeping he had this to say, "Come on. I'm taking you upstairs to meet them people. That'll prove who they are. Then we'll walk downstairs to the first floor and talk to that drunkard and his wife. Get up, Leota."

Someone knocked on the door.

Leota squealed and rolled over and over making a quilted mummy of herself. "He's in his tomb again, rapping to get out!"

The Oklahoma man switched on the lights and unlocked the door. A very jubilant little man in a dark suit, with wild blue eyes, wrinkles, gray hair and thick glasses danced in.

"Sorry, sorry," declared the little man. "I'm Mr. Whetmore. I went away. Now I'm back. I've had the most astonishing stroke of luck. Yes, I have. Is my tombstone still here?" He looked at the stone a moment before he saw it. "Ah, yes, yes, it is! Oh, hello." He saw Leota peering from many layers of blanket. "I've some men with a roller-truck, and, if you don't mind, we'll move the tombstone out of here, this very moment. It'll only take a minute."

The husband laughed with gratitude. "Glad to get rid of the damned thing. Wheel her out!"

Mr. Whetmore directed two brawny workmen into the room. He was almost breathless with anticipation. "The most amazing thing. This morning I was lost, beaten, dejected—but a miracle happened." The tombstone was loaded onto a small coaster truck. "Just an hour ago, I heard, by chance, of a Mr. White who had just died of pneumonia. A Mr. White, mind you, who spells his name with an I instead of a Y. I have just contacted his wife, and she is delighted that the stone is all prepared. And Mr. White not cold more than sixty minutes, and spelling his name with an I, just think of it. Oh, I'm so happy!"

The tombstone, on its truck, rolled from the room, while Mr. Whetmore and the Oklahoma man laughed, shook hands, and Leota watched with suspicion as the commotion came to an end. "Well, that's now all over," grinned her husband as he closed the door on Mr. Whetmore, and began throwing the canned flowers into the sink and dropping the tin cans into a waste-basket. In the dark, he climbed into bed again, oblivious to her deep and solemn silence. She said not a word for a long while, but just lay there, alone-feeling. She felt him adjust the blankets with a sigh. "Now we can sleep. The damn old thing's took away. It's only ten-thirty. Plenty of time for sleep." How he enjoyed spoiling her fun.

Leota was about to speak when a rapping came from down below again. "There! There!" she cried, triumphantly, holding her husband. "There it is again, the noises, like I said. Hear them!"

Her husband knotted his fists and clenched his teeth. "How many times must I explain. Do I have to kick you in the head to make you understand, woman! Let me alone. There's nothing—"

"Listen, listen, oh, listen," she begged in a whisper.

They listened in the square darkness.

A rapping on a door came from downstairs.

A door opened. Muffled and distant and faint, a woman's voice said, sadly, "Oh, it's you, Mr. Whetmore."

And deep down in the darkness underneath the suddenly shivering bed of Leota and her Oklahoma husband, Mr. Whetmore's voice replied: "Good evening again, Mrs. White. Here. I brought the stone."

THE SMILING PEOPLE

It was the sensation of silence that was the most notable aspect of the house. As Mr. Greppin came through the front door the oiled silence of the door opening and swinging close behind him was like an opening and shutting dream, a thing accomplished on rubber pads, bathed in lubricant, slow and unmaterialistic. The double carpet in the hall, which he himself had so recently laid, gave off no sound from his movements. And when the wind shook the house late of nights there was not a rattle of eave or tremor of loose sash. He had, himself, checked the storm windows. The screen doors were securely hooked with bright new, firm hooks, and the furnace did not knock but sent a silent whisper of warm wind up the throats of the heating system that sighed ever so quietly, moving the cuffs of his trousers as he stood, now, warming himself from the bitter afternoon.

Weighing the silence with the remarkable instruments of pitch and balance in his small ears, he nodded with satisfaction that the silence was so unified and finished. Because there *had* been nights when rats had walked between wall-layers and it had taken baited traps and poisoned food before the walls were mute. Even the grandfather clock had been stilled, its brass pendulum hung frozen and gleaming in its long cedar, glass-fronted coffin.

They were waiting for him in the dining room.

He listened. They made no sound. Good. Excellent, in fact. They had learned, then, to be silent. You had to teach people, but it was worth while—there was not a stir of knife or fork from the dining table. He worked off his thick grey gloves, hung up his cold armour of overcoat and stood there with an expression of urgency and indecisiveness . . . . thinking of what had to be done.

Mr. Greppin proceeded with familiar certainty and economy of motion into the dining room, where the four individuals seated at the waiting table did not move or speak a word. The only sound was the merest allowable pad of his shoes on the deep carpet.

His eyes, as usual, instinctively fastened upon the lady heading the table. Passing, he waved a finger near her cheek. She did not blink.

Aunt Rose sat firmly at the head of the table, and if a mote of dust floated lightly down out of the ceiling spaces, did her eye trace its orbit? Did the eye revolve in its shellacked socket, with glassy cold precision? And if the dust mote happened upon the shell of her wet eye did the eye batten? Did the muscles clinch, the lashes close?

No.

Aunt Rose's hand lay on the table like cutlery, rare and fine and old; tarnished. Her bosom was hidden in a salad of fluffy linen. The breasts had not been exhumed for years; either for love or child-suckling. They were mummies wrapped in cerements and put away for all time. Beneath the table her stick legs in high button shoes went up into a sexless pipe of dress. You felt that the legs terminated at the skirt line and from there on she was a department store dummy, all wax and nothingness. You felt that her husband, years ago, must have handled her in just such a way as one handled window mannequins, and she responded with the same chill waxen movements, with as much enthusiasm and response as a mannequin; and the husband, beaten off with no blows and no words, had turned over under the bedding and lain trembling with a feeding passion for many nights and then, finally, silently, taken to evening walks and little places across town, beyond the ravine, where a pink curtained window glowed with fresher electricity and a young lady answered when he tapped the bell.

So here was Aunt Rose, staring straight at Mr. Greppin, and—he choked out a laugh and clapped hands derisively shut—there were the first hints of a dust moustache gathering across her upper lip!

"Good evening, Aunt Rose," he said, bowing. "Good

evening, Uncle Dimity," he said, graciously. "No, not a *word,*" he held up his hand. "Not a word from any of you." He bowed again. "Ah, good evening, cousin Lila, and you, cousin Lester."

Lila sat upon his left, her hair like golden shavings from a tube of lathed brass. Lester, opposite her, told all directions with *his* hair. They were both young, he fourteen, she sixteen. Uncle Dimity, their father (but "father" was a nasty word!) sat next to Lila, placed in this secondary niche long long ago because Aunt Rose said the window draft might get his neck if he sat at the head of the table. Ah, Aunt Rose!

Mr. Greppin drew the chair under his tight-clothed little rump and put a casual elbow to the linen.

"I've something to say," he said. "It's very important. This has gone on for weeks now. It can't go any further. I'm in love. Oh, but I told you that long ago. On the day I made you all smile. Remember?"

The eyes of the four seated people did not blink, the hands did not move.

Greppin became introspective. The day he had made them smile. Two weeks ago it was. He had come home, walked in, looked at them and said, "I'm to be married!"

They had all whirled with expressions as if someone had just smashed the window.

"You're to be *what*!" cried Aunt Rose.

"To Alice Jane Bellerd!" he had said, stiffening somewhat.

"Congratulations," said Uncle Dimity. "I *guess,*" he

added, looking at his wife. He cleared his throat. "But isn't it a little early, son?" He looked at his wife again. "Yes. Yes, I think it *is* a little early. I wouldn't advise it yet, not just yet, no."

"The house is in a terrible way," said Aunt Rose. "We won't have it fixed for a year yet."

"That's what you said last year and the year before," said Mr. Greppin. "And anyway," he said, bluntly, "this is *my* house."

Aunt Rose's jaw had clamped at that. "After all these years, for us to be bodily thrown out, why I—"

"You won't be thrown out, don't be idiotic!" said Greppin, furiously.

"Now, Rose—" said Uncle Dimity in a pale tone.

Aunt Rose dropped her hands. "After all I've done—"

In that instant Greppin had known they would *have* to go, all of them. First he would make them silent, then he would make them smile, then, later, he would move them out like luggage. He couldn't bring Alice Jane into a house full of grims such as these, where Aunt Rose followed wherever you went even when she wasn't following you, and the children performed indignities upon you at a glance from their maternal parent, and the father, no better than a third child, carefully rearranged his advice to you on being a bachelor. Greppin stared at them. It was their fault that his loving and living was all wrong. If he did something about them—then his warm, luminous dreams of soft bodies glowing with an anxious perspiration of love might become tangible and near. Then he would have the house for himself and—and Alice Jane. Yes, Alice Jane.

Aunt, Uncle and cousins would have to go. Quickly. If he told them to go, as he had often done, twenty years might pass as Aunt Rose gathered sun-bleached sachets and Edison phonographs. Long before then, Alice Jane herself would be moved and gone.

Greppin looked at them as he picked up the carving knife.

Greppin's head snapped with tiredness. He flicked his eyes open. Eh? Oh, he had been drowsing, thinking.

All *that* had occurred two weeks ago. Two weeks ago this very night that conversation about marriage, moving, Alice Jane, had come about. Two weeks ago it had been. Two weeks ago he had made them smile.

Now, recovering from his reverie, he smiled around at the silent and motionless figures. They smiled back in a peculiarly pleasing fashion.

"I hate you. You are an old bitch," he said to Aunt Rose, directly. "Two weeks ago I wouldn't have dared to say that. Tonight, ah, well—" He lazed his voice, turning. "Uncle Dimity, let *me* give *you* a little advice, old man—"

He talked small talk, picked up a spoon, pretended to eat peaches from an empty dish. He had already eaten downtown in a restaurant, pork, potatoes, pie, coffee. But now he made dessert eating motions because he enjoyed this little act. He made as if he were chewing.

"So—tonight you're finally, once and for all, moving

out. I've waited two weeks, thinking it all over. In a way, I guess I've kept you here this long because I wanted to keep an eye on you. Once you're gone, I can't be sure—" And here his eyes gleamed with fear. "You might come prowling around, making noises at night, and I couldn't stand that. I can't ever have noises in this house, not even when Alice moves in . . . ."

The double carpet was thick and soundless underfoot, reassuring.

"Alice wants to move in day after tomorrow. We're getting married."

Aunt Rose winked evilly, doubtfully, at him.

"Ah!" he cried, leaping up. Then, staring, he sank down, mouth convulsing. He released the tension in him, laughing. "Oh. I see. It was a fly." He watched the fly crawl with slow precision on the ivory cheek of Aunt Rose and dart away. Why did it have to pick that instant to make her eye appear to blink, to doubt? "Do you doubt I ever will marry, Aunt Rose? Do you think me incapable of marriage, of love and love's duties? Do you think me immature, unable to cope with a woman and her methods? Do you think me a child, only day dreaming? Well!" He calmed himself with an effort, shaking his head. "Man, man," he argued to himself, "it was only a fly. And does a fly make doubt of love, or did you make it into a fly and a wink? Damn it!" He pointed at the four of them. "I'm going to fix the furnace hotter. In an hour I'll be moving you out of the house once and for all. You comprehend? Good. I see you do."

Outside, it began to rain, a cold nuzzling downpour that drenched the house. A look of irritation came to Greppin's face. The rain sound was one thing he couldn't stop, the one thing that couldn't be helped. No way to buy new hinges or lubricants or hooks for that. You might tent the housetop with lengths of cloth to soften the sound, mightn't you? That'd be going a bit far. No. No way of preventing the rain sounds.

He wanted silence now, where he had never wanted it in his life so much. Each sound was a fear. So each sound had to be muffled, gotten to and eliminated.

The drum of rain was like the knuckles of an impatient man on a surface. He lapsed again into remembering.

He recalled the rest of it. The rest of that hour on that day two weeks ago when he had made them smile . . . .

He had taken up the carving knife, prepared to cut the bird upon the table. As usual, the family had been gathered, all wearing their solemn, puritanical masks. If the children smiled the smiles were stepped on like nasty bugs by Aunt Rose.

Aunt Rose criticized the angle of Greppin's elbows as he cut the bird. The knife, she made him understand also, was not sharp enough. Oh, yes, the sharpness of the knife. At this point in his memory he stopped, roll-tilted his eyes, and laughed. Dutifully, then, he had crisped the knife on the sharpening rod, and again set upon the fowl. He had severed away much of it in some minutes before he slowly looked up at their solemn, critical faces, like puddings with agate eyes, and after staring at them a moment, as if discovered with a naked woman instead of a naked-limbed partridge, he lifted the knife and yelled hoarsely, "Why in God's name can't you, *any* of you, ever smile? I'll *make* you smile!"

He raised the knife a number of times like a magician's wand.

And, in a short interval—behold! *all* of them smiled!

He broke that memory in half, crumpled it, balled it, tossed it down. Rising briskly, he went to the hall, down the hall to the kitchen, and from there down the dim stairs into the cellar where he opened the furnace door and built the fire steadily and expertly into wonderful flame.

Walking upstairs again he looked about. He'd have cleaners come and clean the empty house, redecorators pull down the dull drapes and hoist new shimmery banners up. New thick Oriental rugs purchased for the floors would subtly insure the silence he desired and would need at least for the next month, if not for the entire year.

He put his hands to his ears. What if Alice Jane made noise moving about the house? Some noise, somehow, some place!

Then, he laughed. It was quite a joke. That problem was already solved. He need fear no noise from Alice. It was all absurdly simple. He would have all the pleasure of Alice Jane and none of the dream-destroying distractions and uncomfortables.

There was one other addition needed to the quality of silence. Upon the tops of the doors that the wind sucked shut with a bang at frequent intervals he would install modern air-compression brakes, those kind they have on library doors that hiss gently as their levers seal.

He passed through the dining room. The figures had not moved from their tableau. Their hands remained affixed in familiar positions, and their indifference to him was not impoliteness.

He climbed the hall stairs to change his clothing, preparatory to the task of moving the family. Taking the links from his fine cuffs he swung his head to one side.

Music.

First, he paid it no mind. Then, slowly, his face lifting to the ceiling, the color drained from his cheeks.

At the very apex of the house the music sounded, note by note, tone following tone, and it terrified him.

Each tone came like a plucking of one single harp thread. In the complete silence the small sound of it was made larger until it grew out of proportion to itself, gone mad with all this soundlessness to stretch about in.

The door opened in an explosion from his hands, the next thing his feet were trying the stairs to the third level of the house, the banister twisted in a long polished snake under his tightening, relaxing, sliding, reaching-up, pulling hands! The steps went under to be replaced by longer, higher, darker steps. He had started the game at the bottom with a slow stumbling. Now he was running with full impetus and if a wall had suddenly confronted him he'd not have stopped for it until he saw blood on it and fingernail scratches where he tried to pass through.

He felt like a mouse running in a great clear space of a bell. High in the bell sphere the one harp thread hummed. It drew him on, caught him up with an umbilical of sound, gave his fear sustenance and life, mothered him. Fears passed between mother and groping child. He sought to shear away the connection with his hands, could not. He fell, as if someone'd given a heave on the cord, wriggling.

Another clear threaded tone. And *another*.

"No, keep quiet!" he shouted. "There can't be noise in *my* house. Not since two weeks ago. I said there'd be no more noise. So there can't be—it's impossible! Keep quiet!"

He burst upward into the attic.

Relief can be hysteria.

Rain-drops, falling from a vent in the roof, struck shattering upon a tall cut-glass Swedish flower vase, with resonant tone.

He destroyed the vase with one violent kick.

Putting on an old shirt and old pair of pants in his room, he chuckled. The music was gone, the vent plugged, the vase in a thousand pieces, the silence again insured.

There are silences and silences. Each with its own identity. There were summer night silences, which weren't silences at all, but layer on layer of insect chorals and the sound of electric lamps swaying in lonely small orbits on lonely country roads, casting out feeble rings of illumination upon which the night fed—summer night silence which, to be a silence, demanded an indolence and a neglect and an indifference upon the part of the listener. Not a silence at all! And there was a winter silence, but it was an encoffined silence, ready to burst free at the first nod of spring; things had a compressed, a not-for-long feel, the silence made a sound unto itself, the freezing was so complete it made chimes of everything or detonations of a single breath or word you spoke at midnight on the diamond air. No, it was not a silence worthy of the name. There were also other silences. For instance—a silence between two lovers, when there need be no words. Color came in his cheeks, he shut his eyes. It was a most pleasant silence, even if not complete, because women were always spoiling it by complaining of some little pressure or lack of pressure. He smiled. But with Alice Jane even *that* was eliminated. He had seen to everything. *Everything* was perfect.

Whispering.

He hoped the neighbors hadn't heard him shrieking like a fool.

A faint whispering.

Now, about silences . . . . The best silence was one conceived in every aspect by an individual, himself, so that there could be no bursting of crystal bonds, no electric-insect hummings; the human mind could cope with each sound, each emergency, until such a complete silence was achieved that one could hear one's cells adjust in one's hand.

A whispering.

He shook his head. There was no whispering. There could be none in *his* house. Sweat began to seep down his body, his jaw loosened, his eyes were turned free in their sockets.

Whisperings. Low rumors of talk.

"I tell you I'm getting married," he said, weakly, loosely.

"You're lying," said the whispers.

His head fell forward on its neck as if hung, chin on chest.

"Her name is Alice Jane—" he mouthed it between soft, wet lips and the words were formless. One of his eyes began to jitter its lid up and down as if blinking out a code to some unseen guest. "You can't stop me from loving her. I love her—"

Whispering.

He took a blind step forward.

The cuff of his pants leg quivered as he reached the floor grille of the ventilator. A hot rise of air hollowed his cuffs. Whispering.

The furnace.

He was on his way downstairs when someone knocked on the front door.

He leaned against it. "Who is it?"

"Mr. Greppin?"

Greppin drew in his breath. "Yes?"

"Will you let us in, please?"

"Who is it?"

"The police," said the man outside.

"What do you want? I'm just sitting down to supper!"

"Just want a talk with you. The neighbors phoned. Said they hadn't seen your Aunt and Uncle for two weeks. Heard a noise awhile ago—"

"I assure you every thing is all right." He forced a laugh.

"Well, then," continued the voice outside, "we can talk it over in friendly style if you'll only open the door."

"I'm sorry," insisted Greppin. "I'm tired and hungry, come back tomorrow. I'll talk to you then, if you want."

"I'll have to *insist*, Mr. Greppin."

They began to beat against the door.

Greppin turned automatically, stiffly, walked down the hall past the cold clock, into the dining room, without a word. He seated himself without looking at any one in particular and then he began to talk, slowly at first, then more rapidly.

"Some pests at the door. You'll talk to them, won't you, Aunt Rose? You'll tell them to go away, won't you, we're eating supper? Everyone else go on eating and look pleasant and they'll go away, if they do come in. Aunt Rose, you *will* talk to them, won't you? And now that things are happening I have something to tell you." A few hot tears fell for no reason. He looked at them as they soaked and spread in the white linen, vanishing.

"I don't know any one named Alice Jane Bellerd. I *never* knew any one named Alice Jane Bellerd! It was all—all—I don't know. I said I loved her and wanted to marry her to get around somehow to make you smile. Yes, I said it because I planned to make you smile, that was the only reason. I'm never going to have a woman, I always knew for years I never would have. Will you please pass the potatoes, Aunt Rose?"

The front door splintered and fell. A heavy, softened rushing filled the hall. Men broke into the dining room.

A hesitation.

The police inspector hastily removed his hat.

"Oh, I beg your pardon," he apologized. "I didn't mean to intrude upon your supper, I—"

The sudden halting of the police was such that their movement shook the room. The movement catapulted the bodies of Aunt Rose and Uncle Dimity straight away to the carpet, where they lay, their throats severed in a half moon from ear to ear—which caused them, like the children seated at the table, to have what was the horrid illusion of a smile under their chins; ragged smiles that welcomed in the late arrivals and told them everything with a simple grimace . . . .

THE EMISSARY

He knew it was autumn again, because Torry came romping into the house bringing the windy crisp cold smell of autumn with him. In every black curl of his dog-hair he carried autumn. Leaf flakes tangled in his dark ears and muzzle, dropping from his white vest, and off his flourished tail. The dog smelled just like autumn.

Martin Christie sat up in bed and reached down with one pale small hand. Torry barked and displayed a generous length of pink, rippling tongue, which he passed over and along the back of Martin's hand. Torry licked him like a lollypop. "Because of the salt," declared Martin, as Torry leaped upon the bed.

"Get down," warned Martin. "Mom doesn't like you up here." Torry flattened his ears. "Well . . ." Martin relented. "Just for a while, then."

Torry warmed Martin's thin body with his dog warmness.

Martin relished the clean dog smell and the litter of fallen leaves on the quilt. He didn't care if Mom scolded. After all, Torry was new-born. Right out of the stomach of autumn Torry came, reborn in the firm sharp cold.

"What's it like outside, Torry? Tell me."

Lying there, Torry would tell him. Lying there, Martin would know what autumn was like; like in the old days before sickness had put him to bed. His only contact with autumn now was this brief chill, this leaf-flaked fur; the compact canine representation of summer gone—this autumn-by-proxy.

"Where'd you go today, Torry?"

But Torry didn't have to tell him. He knew. Over a fall-burdened hill, leaving a pad-pattern in the brilliantly piled leaves, down to where the kids ran shouting on bikes and roller skates and wagons at Barstow's Park, that's where Torry ran, barking out his canine delight. And down into the town where rain had fallen dark, earlier; and mud furrowed under car wheels, down between the feet of week-end shoppers. That's where Torry went.

And wherever Torry went, then Martin could go; because Torry would always tell him by the touch, feel, consistency, the wet, dry, or crispness of his coat. And, lying there holding Torry, Martin would send his mind out to retrace each step of Torry's way through fields, over the shallow glitter of the ravine creek, darting across the marbled spread of the graveyard, into the wood, over the meadows; where all the wild, laughing autumn sports went on, Martin could go now through his emissary.

Mother's voice sounded downstairs, angrily.

Her short angry walking came up the hall steps.

Martin pushed. "Down, Torry!"

Torry vanished under the bed just before the bedroom door opened and Mom looked in, blue eyes snapping. She carried a tray of salad and fruit juices, firmly.

"Is Torry here?" she demanded.

Torry gave himself away with a few rumps of his tail against the floor.

Mom set the tray down impatiently. "That dog is more trouble. Always upsetting things and digging places. He was in Miss Tarkins' garden this morning, and dug a big hole. Miss Tarkins is mad."

"Oh." Martin held his breath. There was silence under the bed. Torry knew when to keep quiet.

"And it's not the only time," said Mom. "This is the third hole he's dug this week!"

"Maybe he's looking for something."

"Something fiddlesticks! He's just a curious nuisance. He can't keep that black nose out of anything. *Always* curious!"

There was a hairy pizzicato of tail under the bed. Mom couldn't help smiling.

"Well," she ended, "if he doesn't stop digging in yards, I'll have to keep him in and not let him run."

Martin opened his mouth wide. "Oh, no, Mom! Don't do that! Then I wouldn't know—anything. He *tells* me."

Mom's voice softened. "Does he, son?"

"Sure. He goes around and comes back and tells what happens, tells everything!"

Mom's hand was spun glass touching his head. "I'm glad he tells you. I'm glad you've got him."

They both sat a moment, considering how worthless the last year would've been without Torry. Only two more months, thought Martin, of being in bed, like the doctor said, and he'd be up and around.

"Here, Torry!"

Jangling, Martin locked the special collar attachment around Torry's neck. It was a note, painted on a tin square:

"MY NAME IS TORRY. WILL YOU VISIT MY MASTER, WHO IS SICK? FOLLOW ME!"

It worked. Torry carried it out into the world every day.

"Will you let him out, Mom?"

"Yes, if he's good and stops his digging!"

"He'll stop; won't you, Torry?"

The dog barked.

You could hear the dog yipping far down the street and away, going to fetch visitors. Martin was feverish and his eyes stood out in his head as he sat, propped up, listening, sending his mind rushing along with the dog, faster, faster. Yesterday Torry had brought Mrs. Holloway from Elm Avenue, with a story book for a present; the day before Torry had sat up, begged at Mr. Jacobs, the jeweler.

Mr. Jacobs had bent and near-sightedly deciphered the tag message and, sure enough, had come shuffling and waddling to pay Martin a little how-do-you-do.

Now, Martin heard the dog returning through the smoky afternoon, barking, running, barking again.

Footsteps came lightly after the dog. Somebody rang the downstairs bell, softly. Mom answered the door. Voices talked.

Torry raced upstairs, leaped on the bed. Martin leaned forward excitedly, his face shining, to see who'd come upstairs this time. Maybe Miss Palmborg or Mr. Ellis or Miss Jendriss, or—

The visitor walked upstairs, talking to Mom. It was a young woman's voice, talking with a laugh in it.

The door opened.

Martin had company.

Four days passed in which Torry did his job, reported morning, afternoon and evening temperatures, soil consistencies, leaf colors, rain levels, and, most important of all, brought visitors.

Miss Haight, again, on Saturday. She was the young, laughing, handsome woman with the gleaming brown hair and the soft way of walking. She lived in the big house on Park Street. It was her third visit in a month.

On Sunday it was Reverend Vollmar, on Monday Miss Clark and Mr. Hendricks.

And to each of them Martin explained his dog. How in spring he was odorous of wild-flowers and fresh earth;

in summer he was baked, warm, sun-crisp; in autumn, now, a treasure trove of gold leaves hidden in his pelt for Martin to explore out. Torry demonstrated this process for the visitors, lying over on his back, waiting to be explored.

Then, one morning, Mom told Martin about Miss Haight, the one who was so handsome and young and laughed.

She was dead.

Killed in an auto accident in Glen Falls.

Martin held onto his dog, remembering Miss Haight, thinking of the way she smiled, thinking of her bright eyes, her closely cropped chestnut hair, her slim body, her quick walk, her nice stories about seasons and people.

So now she was dead. She wasn't going to laugh or tell stories any more. That's all there was to it. She was dead.

"What do they do in the graveyard, Mom, under the ground?"

"Nothing."

"You mean they just lay there?"

"Lie there," corrected Mom.

"*Lie* there . . . ?"

"Yes," said Mom, "that's all they do."

"It doesn't sound like much fun."

"It's not supposed to be."

"Why don't they get up and walk around once in awhile if they get tired of lying there?"

"I think you've said enough, now," said Mom.

"I just wanted to know."

"Well, now you know."

"Sometimes I think God's pretty silly."

"Martin!"

Martin scowled. "You'd think He'd treat people better than throw dirt in their faces and tell them to lay still for keeps. You'd think He'd find a better way. What if I told Torry to play dead-dog? He does it awhile, but then he gets sick of it and wags his tail or blinks his eyes, or pants, or jumps off the bed, and walks around. I bet those graveyard people do the same, huh, Torry?"

Torry barked.

"That will *do!*" said Mom, firmly. "I don't like such talk!"

The autumn continued. Torry ran across forests, over the creek, prowling through the graveyard as was his custom, and into town and around and back, missing nothing.

In mid-October, Torry began to act strangely. He couldn't seem to find anybody to come visit Martin. Nobody seemed to pay attention to his begging. He came home seven days in a row without bringing a visitor. Martin was deeply despondent over it.

Mom explained it. "Everybody's busy. The war, and all. People have lots to worry over besides little begging dogs."

"Yeah," said Martin, "I guess so."

But there was more than that to it. Torry had a funny gleam in his eyes. As if he wasn't really trying, or didn't care, or—something. Something Martin couldn't figure out. Maybe Torry was sick. Well, to heck with visitors. As long as he had Torry, everything was fine.

And then one day Torry ran out and didn't come back at all.

Martin waited quietly at first. Then—nervously. Then—anxiously.

At supper time he heard Mom and Dad call Torry. Nothing happened. It was no use. There was no sound of paws along the path outside the house. No sharp barking in the cold night air. Nothing. Torry was gone. Torry wasn't coming home—ever.

Leaves fell past the window. Martin sank on his pillow, slowly, a pain deep and hard in his chest.

The world was dead. There was no autumn because there was no fur to bring it into the house. There would be no winter because there would be no paws to dampen the quilt with snow. No more seasons. No more time. The go-between, the emissary, had been lost in the wild thronging of civilization, probably hit by a car, or poisoned, or stolen, and there was no time.

Sobbing, Martin turned his face to his pillow. There was no contact with the world. The world was dead.

Martin twisted in bed and in three days the Hallowe'en pumpkins were rotting in trash cans, masks were burnt in incinerators, the bogeys were stacked away on shelves until next year. Hallowe'en was withdrawn, impersonal, untouchable. It had simply been one evening when he had heard horns blowing off in the cold autumn stars, people yelling and thumping windows and porches with soap and cabbages. That was all.

Martin stared at the ceiling for the first three days of November, watching alternate light and dark shift across it. Days got shorter, darker, he could tell by the window. The trees were naked. The autumn wind changed its tempo and temperature. But it was just a pageant outside his window, nothing more. He couldn't get at it.

Martin read books about the seasons and the people in that world that was now non-existent. He listened each day, but didn't hear the sounds he wanted to hear.

Friday night came. His parents were going to the theatre. They'd be back at eleven. Mrs. Tarkins, from next door, would come over for awhile until Martin got sleepy, and then she would go home.

Mom and Dad kissed him goodnight and walked out of the house into the autumn. He heard their footsteps go down the street.

Mrs. Tarkins came over, stayed awhile and then when Martin confessed to being tired, she turned out all the lights and went back home.

Silence, then. Martin just lay there and watched the stars moving slowly across the sky. It was a clear, moonlit evening. The kind when he and Torry had once run together across the town, across the sleeping graveyard, across the ravine, through the meadows, down the shadowed streets, chasing phantasmal childish dreams.

Only the wind was friendly. Stars don't bark. Trees

don't sit up and beg. The wind, of course, did wag its tail against the house a number of times, startling Martin.

Now it was after nine o'clock.

If only Torry would come home, bringing some of the world with him. A burr or a rimed thistle, or the wind in his ears. If only Torry would come home.

And then, way off somewhere, there was a sound.

Martin arose in his covers, trembling. Starlight was reflected in his small eyes. He threw back the covers and tensed, listening.

There, again, was the sound.

It was so small it was like a needle-point moving through the air miles and miles away.

It was the dreamy echo of a dog—barking.

It was the sound of a dog coming across meadows and fields, down dark streets, the sound of a dog running and letting his breath out to the night. The sound of a dog circling and running. It came and went, it lifted and faded, it came forward and went back, as if it was being led by someone on a chain. As if the dog was running and somebody whistled under the chestnut trees and the dog ran back, circled, and darted again for home.

Martin felt the room revolve under him, and the bed tremble with his body. The springs complained with metal, tining voices.

The faint barking continued for five minutes, growing louder and louder.

Torry, come home! Torry, come home! Torry, boy, oh Torry, where've you been? Oh, Torry, Torry!

Another five minutes. Nearer and nearer, and Martin kept saying the dog's name over and over again. Bad dog, wicked dog, to go off and leave him for all these days. Bad dog, good dog, come home, oh, Torry, hurry home and tell me about the world! Tears fell and dissolved into the quilt.

Nearer now. Very near. Just up the street, barking. Torry!

Martin held his breath. The sound of dog feet in the piled dry leaves, down the path. And now—right outside the house, barking, barking, barking! Torry!

Barking to the door.

Martin shivered. Did he dare run down and let the dog in, or should he wait for Mom and Dad to come home? Wait. Yes, he must wait. But it would be unbearable if, while he waited, the dog ran away again. No, he would go down and release the lock and his own special dog would leap into his arms again. Good Torry!

He started to move from bed when he heard the other sound. The door opened downstairs. Somebody was kind enough to have opened the door for Torry.

Torry had brought a visitor, of course. Mr. Buchanan, or Mr. Jacobs, or perhaps Miss Tarkins.

The door opened and closed and Torry came racing upstairs and flung himself, yipping, on the bed.

"Torry, where've you been, what've you done all this week?"

Martin laughed and cried all in one. He grabbed the dog and held him. Then he stopped laughing and crying, suddenly. He just stared at Torry with wide, strange eyes.

The odor arising from Torry was—different.

It was a smell of earth. Dead earth. Earth that had lain cheek by jowl with unhealthy decaying things six feet under. Stinking, rancid earth. Clods of decaying soil fell off Torry's paws. And—something else—a small withered fragment of—*skin?*

Was it? Was it! WAS IT!

What kind of message was this from Torry? What did such a message mean? The stench—the ripe and awful cemetery earth.

Torry was a bad dog. Always digging where he shouldn't dig. Torry was a *good* dog. Always making friends so easily. Torry took to liking everybody. He brought them home with him.

And now this latest visitor was coming up the stairs. Slowly. Dragging one foot after the other, painfully, slowly, slowly, slowly.

"Torry, Torry—where've you *been!*" screamed Martin.

A clod of rank crawling soil dropped from the dog's chest.

The door to the bedroom moved inward.

Martin had company.

THE TRAVELER

Father looked into Cecy's room just before dawn. She lay upon her bed. He shook his head uncomprehendingly and waved at her.

"Now, if you can tell me what good she does, lying there," he said, "I'll eat the crepe on my mahogany box. Sleeping all night, eating breakfast, and then lying on top her bed all day."

"Oh, but she's so helpful," explained Mother, leading him down the hall away from Cecy's slumbering pale figure. "Why, she's one of the most adjustable members of the Family. What good are your brothers? Most of them sleep all day and do nothing. At least Cecy is *active*."

They went downstairs through the scent of black candles; the black crepe on the banister, left over from the Homecoming some months ago and untouched, whispering as they passed. Father unloosened his tie, exhaustedly. "Well, we work nights," he said. "Can we help it if we're—as you put it—old-fashioned?"

"Of course not. Everyone in the Family can't be modern." She opened the cellar door; they moved down into darkness arm in arm. She looked over at his round white face, smiling. "It's really very lucky I don't have to sleep *at all*. If you were married to a night-sleeper, think what a marriage it would be! Each of us to our own. None of us the same. All wild. That's how the Family goes. Some times we get one like Cecy, all mind; and then there are those like Uncle Einar, all wing; and then again we have one like Timothy, all even and calm and normal. Then there's you, sleeping days. And me, awake all and all of my life. So Cecy shouldn't be too much for you to understand. She helps me a million ways each day. She sends her mind down to the green-grocers for me, to see what he sells. She puts her mind inside the butcher. That saves me a long trip if he's fresh out of good cuts. She warns me when gossips are coming to visit and talk away the afternoon. And, well, there are six hundred other things—!"

They paused in the cellar near a large empty mahogany box. He settled himself into it, still not convinced. "But if she'd only contribute more," he said. "I'm afraid I'll have to ask her to find some sort of work."

"Sleep on it," she said to him. "Think it over. You may change your mind by sunset."

She was closing the lid down on him. "Well," he said, thoughtfully. The lid closed.

"Good morning, dear," she said.

"Good morning," he said, muffled, enclosed, within the box.

The sun rose. She hurried upstairs to make breakfast.

Cecy Elliott was the one who Traveled. She seemed an ordinary eighteen year old. But then none of the Family looked like what they were. There was naught of the fang, the foul, the worm or wind-witch to them. They lived in small towns and on farms across the world, simply, closely re-aligning and adapting their talents to the demands and laws of a changing world.

Cecy Elliott awoke. She glided down through the house, humming. "Good morning, Mother!" She walked down to the cellar to recheck each of the large mahogany boxes, to dust them, to be certain each was tightly sealed. "Father," she said, polishing one box. "Cousin Esther," she said, examining another, "here on a visit. And—" she rapped at a third, "Grandfather Elliott." There was a rustle inside like a piece of papyrus. "It's a strange, cross-bred family," she mused, climbing to the kitchen again. "Night siphoners and flume-fearers, some awake, like Mother, twenty-five hours out of twenty-four; some asleep, like me, 59 minutes out of 60. Different species of sleep."

She ate breakfast. In the middle of her apricot dish she saw her mother's stare. She laid the spoon down. Cecy said, "Father'll change his mind. I'll show him how fine I can be to have around. I'm family insurance; he doesn't understand. You wait."

Mother said, "You were inside me awhile ago when I argued with Father?"

"Yes."

"I thought I felt you looking out my eyes," the mother nodded.

Cecy finished and went up to bed. She folded down the blankets and clean cool sheets, then laid herself out atop the covers, shut her eyes, rested her thin white fingers on her small bosom, nodded her slight, exquisitely sculptured head back against her thick gathering of chestnut hair.

She started to Travel.

Her mind slipped from the room, over the flowered yard, the fields, the green hills, over the ancient drowsy streets of Mellin Town, into the wind and past the moist depression of the ravine. All day she would fly and meander. Her mind would pop into dogs, sit there, and she would feel the bristly feels of dogs, taste ripe bones, sniff tangy-urined trees. She'd hear as a dog heard. She forgot human construction completely. She'd have a dog frame. It was more than telepathy, up one flue and down another. This was complete separation from one body environment into another. It was entrance into tree-nozzling dogs, men, old maids, birds, children at hopscotch, lovers on their morning beds, into workers asweat with shoveling, into unborn babies' pink, dream-small brains.

Where would she go today? She made her decision, and went!

When her mother tiptoed a moment later to peek

into the room, she saw Cecy's body on the bed, the chest not moving, the face quiet. Cecy was gone already. Mother nodded and smiled.

The morning passed. Leonard, Bion and Sam went off to their work, as did Laura and the manicuring sister; and Timothy was dispatched to school. The house quieted. At noon time the only sound was made by Cecy Elliott's three young girl-cousins playing Tisket Tasket Coffin Casket in the back yard. There were always extra cousins or Uncles or grand-nephews and night-nieces about the place; they came and went; water out a faucet, down a drain.

The Cousins stopped their play when the tall loud man banged on the front door and marched straight in when Mother answered.

"That was Uncle Jonn!" said the littlest girl, breathless.

"The one we hate?" asked the second.

"What's he want?" cried the third. "He looked mad!"

"*We're* mad at *him*, that's what," explained the second, proudly. "For what he did to the Family sixty years ago, and seventy years ago and twenty years ago."

"Listen!" They listened. "He's run upstairs!"

"Sounds like he's cryin'."

"Do grown-ups cry?"

"Sure, silly!"

"He's in Cecy's room! Shoutin'. Laughin'. Prayin'. Cryin'. He sounds mad, and sad, and fraidy-cat, all together!"

The littlest one made tears, herself. She ran to the

cellar door. "Wake up! Oh, down there, wake up! You in the boxes! Uncle Jonn's here and he might have a cedar stake with him! I don't want a cedar stake in my chest! Wake up!"

"Shh," hissed the biggest girl. "He hasn't a stake! You can't wake the Boxed People, anyhow. Listen!"

Their heads tilted, their eyes glistened upward, waiting.

"Get off the bed!" commanded Mother, in the doorway. Uncle Jonn bent over Cecy's slumbering body. His lips were mis-shaped. There was a wild, fey and maddened focus to his green eyes.

"Am I too late?" he demanded, hoarsely, sobbing. "Is she gone?"

"Hours ago!" snapped Mother. "Are you blind? She might not be back for days. Sometimes she lies there a week. I don't have to feed the body, she finds sustenance from whatever or whoever she's in. Get away from her!"

Uncle Jonn stiffened, one knee pressed on the springs.

"Why couldn't she wait?" he wanted to know, frantically, looking at her, his hands feeling her silent pulse again and again.

"You heard me!" Mother moved forward curtly. "She's not to be touched. She's got to be left as she is. So if she comes home she can get back in her body exactly right."

Uncle Jonn turned his head. His long hard red face was pocked and senseless, deep black grooves crowded the tired eyes.

"Where'd she go? I've *got* to find her."

Mother talked like a slap in the face. "I don't know. She has favorite places. You might find her in a child running along a trail in the ravine. Or swinging on a grape vine. Or you might find her in a crayfish under a rock in the creek, looking up at you. Or she might be playing chess inside an old man in the court-house square. You know as well as I she can be anywhere." A wry look came to Mother's mouth. "She might be vertical inside me now, looking out at you, laughing, and not telling you. This might be her talking and having fun. And you wouldn't know it."

"Why—" He swung heavily around, like a huge pivoted boulder. His big hands came up, wanting to grab something. "If I *thought*—"

Mother talked on, casual quiet. "Of course she's *not* in me, here. And if she was there'd be no way to tell." Her eyes gleamed with a delicate malice. She stood tall and graceful, looking upon him with no fear. "Now, suppose you explain what you want with her?"

He seemed to be listening to a distant bell, tolling. He shook his head, angrily, to clear it. Then he growled. "Something . . . inside me . . ." He broke off. He leaned over the cold, sleeping body. "Cecy! come back, you hear! You can come back if you want!"

The wind blew softly through the high willows outside the sun-drifted windows. The bed creaked under his shifted weight. The distant bell tolled again and he was listening to it, but Mother could not hear it. Only he heard the drowsy summer-day sounds of it, far far away. His mouth opened obscurely:

"I've a thing for her to do to me. For the past month I've been kind of going—insane. I get funny thoughts. I was going to take a train to the big city and talk to a psychiatrist but he wouldn't help. I know that Cecy can enter my head and exorcise those fears I have. She can suck them out like a vacuum cleaner, if she wants to help me. She's the only one can scrape away the filth and cobwebs and make me new again. That's why I need her, you understand?" he said, in a tight, expectant voice. He licked his lips. "She's *got* to help me!"

"After all you've done to the Family?" said Mother.

"I did nothing to the Family!"

"The story goes," said Mother, "that in bad times, when you needed money, you were paid a hundred dollars for each of the Family you pointed out to the law to be staked through the heart."

"That's unfair!" he said, wavering like a man hit in the stomach. "You can't prove that. You lie!"

"Nevertheless, I don't think Cecy'd want to help you. The Family wouldn't want it."

"Family, Family!" He stomped the floor like a huge, brutal child. "Damn the Family! I won't go insane on their account! I need help, God damn it, and I'll get it!"

Mother faced him, her face reserved, her hands crossed over her bosom.

He lowered his voice, looking at her with a kind of evil shyness, not meeting her eyes. "Listen to me, Mrs.

Elliott," he said. "And you, too, Cecy," he said to the sleeper. "If you're there," he added. "Listen to this." He looked at the wall clock ticking on the far, sun-drenched wall. "If Cecy isn't back here by six o'clock tonight, ready to help clean out my mind and make me sane, I'll—I'll go to the police." He drew himself up. "I've got a list of Elliotts who live on farms all around and inside Mellin Town. The police can cut enough new cedar stakes in an hour to drive through a dozen Elliott hearts." He stopped, wiped the sweat off his face. He stood, listening.

The distant bell began to toll again.

He had heard it for days. There was no bell, but he could hear it ringing. It rang now, near, far, close, away. Nobody else could hear it save himself.

He shook his head. He shouted to cover the sound of those bells, shouted at Mrs. Elliott. "You heard me?"

He hitched up his trousers, tightened the buckle clasp with a jerk, walked past Mother to the door.

"Yes," she said. "I heard. But even I can't call Cecy back if she doesn't want to come. She'll arrive eventually. Be patient. Don't go running off to the police—"

He cut her. "I can't wait. This thing of mine, this noise in my head's gone on eight weeks now! I can't stand it much longer!" He scowled at the clock. "I'm going. I'll try to find Cecy in town. If I don't get her by six—well, you know what a cedar stake's like . . . ."

His heavy shoes pounded away down the hall, fading down the stairs, out of the house. When the noises were all gone, the mother turned and looked, earnestly, painfully, down upon the sleeper.

"Cecy," she called, softly, insistently. "Cecy, come home!"

There was no word from the body. Cecy lay there, not moving, for as long as her mother waited.

Uncle Jonn walked through the fresh open country and into the streets of Mellin Town, looking for Cecy in every child that licked an ice-pop and in every little white dog that padded by on its way to some eagerly anticipated nowhere.

The town spread out like a fancy graveyard. Nothing more than a few monuments, really—edifices to lost arts and pastimes. It was a great meadow of elms and deodars and hackmatack trees, laid out with wooden walks you could haul into your barn at night if the hollow sound of walking people irked you. There were tall old maiden houses, lean and narrow and wisely wan, in which were spectacles of colored glass, upon which the thinned golden hair of age-old bird nests sprouted. There was a drug shop full of quaint wire-rung soda fountain stools with plywood bottoms, and the memorious clear sharp odor that used to be in drug stores but never is any more. And there was a barber emporium with a red-ribboned pillar twisting around inside a chrysalis of glass in front of it. And there was a grocery that was all fruity shadow and dusty boxes and the smell of an old Armenian woman, which was like the odor of a rusty penny. The town lay under the deodar and mellow-leaf trees, in no hurry, and somewhere in the town was Cecy, the one who Traveled.

Uncle Jonn stopped, bought himself a bottle of Orange Crush, drank it, wiped his face with his handkerchief, his eyes jumping up and down, like little kids skipping rope. I'm afraid, he thought. I'm afraid.

He saw a code of birds strung dot-dash on the high telephone wires. Was Cecy up there laughing at him out of sharp bird eyes, shuffling her feathers, singing at him? He suspicioned the cigar store Indian. But there was no animation in that cold, carved, tobacco-brown image.

Distantly, like on a sleepy Sunday morning, he heard the bells ringing in a valley of his head. He was stone blind. He stood in blackness. White, tortured faces drifted through his inturned vision.

"Cecy!" he cried, to everything, everywhere. "I know you can help me! Shake me like a tree! Cecy!"

The blindness passed. He was bathed in a cold sweating that didn't stop, but ran like a syrup.

"I know you can help," he said. "I saw you help Cousin Marianne years ago. Ten years ago, wasn't it?" He stood, concentrating.

Marianne had been a girl shy as a mole, her hair twisted like roots on her round ball of head. Marianne had hung in her skirt like a clapper in a bell, never ringing when she walked; just swithering along, one heel after another. She gazed at weeds and the sidewalk under her toes, she looked at your chin if she saw you at all—and never got as far as your eyes. Her mother despaired of Marianne's ever marrying or succeeding.

It was up to Cecy, then. Cecy went into Marianne like fist into glove.

Marianne jumped, ran, yelled, glinted her yellow eyes. Marianne flickered her skirts, unbraided her hair and let it hang in a shimmery veil on her half-nude shoulders. Marianne giggled and rang like a gay clapper in the tolling bell of her dress. Marianne squeezed her face into many attitudes of coyness, merriment, intelligence, maternal bliss, and love.

The boys raced after Marianne. Marianne got married.

Cecy withdrew.

Marianne had hysterics; her *spine* was gone!

She lay like a limp corset all one day. But the habit was in her now. Some of Cecy had stayed on like a fossil imprint on soft shale rock; and Marianne began tracing the habits and thinking them over and remembering what it was like to have Cecy inside her, and pretty soon she was running and shouting and giggling all by herself; a corset animated, as it were, by a memory!

Marianne had lived joyously thereafter.

Standing with the cigar store Indian for conversation, Uncle Jonn now shook his head violently. Dozens of bright bubbles floated in his eyeballs, each with tiny, slanted, microscopic eyes staring in, in at his brain.

What if he never found Cecy? What if the plain winds had borne her all the way to Elgin? Wasn't that where she dearly loved to bide her time, in the asylum for the insane, touching their minds, holding and turning their confetti thoughts?

Far-flung in the afternoon distance a great metal whistle sighed and echoed, steam shuffled as a train cut across valley trestles, over cool rivers through ripe cornfields, into tunnels like finger into thimble, under arches of shimmering walnut trees. Jonn stood, afraid. What if Cecy was in the cabin of the engineer's head, now? She loved riding the monster engines across country far as she could stretch the contact. Yank the whistle rope until it screamed across sleeping night land or drowsy day country.

He walked along a shady street. Out of the corners of his eyes he thought he saw an old woman, wrinkled as a dried fig, naked as a thistle-seed, floating among the branches of a hawthorne tree, a cedar stake driven into her breast.

Somebody screamed!

Something thumped his head. A blackbird, soaring skyward, took a lock of his hair with it!

He shook his fist at the bird, heaved a rock. "Scare me, will you!" he yelled. Breathing rawly, he saw the bird circle behind him to sit on a limb waiting another chance to dive for hair.

He turned slyly from the bird.

He heard the whirring sound.

He jumped about, grabbed up. "Cecy!"

He had the bird! It fluttered, squalled in his hands.

"Cecy!" he called, looking into his caged fingers at the wild black creature. The bird drew blood with its bill.

"Cecy, I'll crush you if you don't help me!"

The bird shrieked and cut him.

He closed his fingers tight, tight, tight.

He walked way from where he finally dropped the dead bird and did not look back at it, even once.

He walked down into the ravine that ran through the very center of Mellin Town. What's happening now, he wondered. Has Cecy's mother phoned people? Are the Elliotts afraid? He swayed drunkenly, great lakes of sweat bursting out under his armpits. Well, let *them* be afraid awhile. He was tired of being afraid. He'd look just a little longer for Cecy and then go to the police!

On the creek bank, he laughed to think of the Elliotts scurrying madly, trying to find some way around him. There was no way. They'd have to make Cecy help him. They couldn't afford to let good old Uncle Jonn die insane, no, sir.

B-b-shot eyes lay deep in the water, staring roundly up at him.

On blazing hot summer noons, Cecy had often entered into the soft-shelled greyness of the mandibled heads of crayfish. She had often peeked out from the black egg eyes upon their sensitive filamentary stalks and felt the creek sluice by her, steadily, and in fluid veils of coolness and captured light. Breathing out and in the particles of stuff that floated in water, holding her horny, lichened claws before her like some elegant salad utensils, swollen and scissor-sharp. She watched the giant strides of boy feet progressing toward her through the creek bottom, heard the faint, water-thickened shout of boys searching for crayfish, jabbing their pale fingers down, tumbling rocks aside, clutching and tossing frantic flippery animals into open metal cans where scores of other crayfish scuttled like a basket of waste-paper come to life.

She watched pale stalks of boy legs poise over her rock, saw the nude loin-shadows of boy thrown on the sandy muck of the creek floor, saw the suspenseful hand hovered, heard the suggestive whisper of a boy who's spied a prize beneath a stone. Then, as the hand plunged, the stone rolled, Cecy flirted the borrowed fan of her inhabited body, kicked back in a little sand explosion and vanished downstream.

On to another rock she went to sit fanning the sand, holding her claws before her, proud of them, her tiny glass-bulb eyes glowing black as creek-water filled her bubbling mouth, cool, cool, cool . . . .

The realization that Cecy might be this close at hand, in any live thing, drove Uncle Jonn to a mad fury. In any squirrel or chipmunk, in a disease germ, even, on his aching body, Cecy might be existing. She could even enter amoebas . . . .

On some sweltering summer noons, Cecy would live in an amoeba, darting, vacillating, deep in the old tired, philosophical dark waters of a kitchen well. On days when the world high over her, above the unstirred water, was a dreaming nightmare of heat printed on each object of the land, she'd lie somnolent, quivering and cool and distant, settling in the well-throat. Up above, trees were like images burned in green fire. Birds were like bronze stamps you inked and punched on your brain. Houses steamed like manure sheds. When a door slammed it was like a rifle shot. The only good sound on a simmering day was the asthmatic suction of well water drawn up into a porcelain cup, there to be inhaled through an old skelatinous woman's porcelain teeth. Overhead, Cecy could hear the brittle clap of the old woman's shoes, the sighing voice of the old woman baked in the August sun. And, lying lowermost and cool, sighting up up through the dim echoing tunnel of well, Cecy heard the iron suction of the pump handle pressed energetically by the sweating old lady; and water, amoeba, Cecy and all rose up the throat of the well in sudden cool disgorgement out into the cup, over which waited sun-withered lips. Then, and only then, did Cecy withdraw, just as the lips came down to sip, the cup tilted, and porcelain met porcelain . . .

Jonn stumbled, fell flat into the creek water!

He didn't rise, but sat dripping stupidly.

Then he began crashing rocks over, shouting, seizing upon and losing crayfish, cursing. The bells rang louder in his ears. And now, one by one, a procession of bodies that couldn't exist, but seemed to be real, floated by on the water. Worm-white bodies, turned on their backs, drifting like loose marionettes. As they passed, the tide bobbed their heads so their faces rolled over, revealing the features of the typical Elliott family member.

He began to weep, sitting there in the water. He had wanted Cecy's help, but now how could he expect to deserve it, acting a fool, cursing her, hating her, threatening her and the Family?

He stood up, shaking himself. He walked out of the creek and up the hill. There was only one thing to do now. Plead with individual members of the Family. Ask them to intercede for him. Have them ask Cecy to come home, quickly.

In the undertaking parlor on Court Street, the door opened. The undertaker, a short, well-tonsored man with a moustache and sensitively thin hands, looked up. His face fell.

"Oh, it's *you,* Uncle Jonn," he said.

"Nephew Bion," said Jonn, still wet from the creek, "I need your help. Have you seen Cecy?"

"Seen her?" said Bion Elliott. He leaned against the marble table where he was working on a body. He laughed. "God, don't ask me *that!*" he snorted. "Look at me, close. Do you know me?"

Jonn bristled. "You're Bion Elliott, Cecy's brother, of course!"

"Wrong." The undertaker shook his head. "I'm Cousin Ralph, the butcher! Yes, the *butcher.*" He tapped his head. "Here, inside, where it counts, I'm Ralph. I was working in my refrigerator a moment ago over at the butcher shop when suddenly Cecy was inside me. She borrowed my mind, like a cup of sugar. And brought me over here just now and sifted me down into Bion's body. Poor Bion! What a joke!"

"You're—you're *not* Bion!"

"No, ah, no, dear Uncle Jonn. Cecy probably put Bion in *my* body! You see the joke? A meat-cutter exchanged for a meat-cutter! A dealer in cold-cuts traded for another of the same!" He quaked with laughter. "Ah, that Cecy, what a child!" He wiped happy tears from his face. "I've stood here for five minutes wondering what to do. You know something? Undertaking isn't hard. Not much harder than fixing pot-roasts. Oh, Bion'll be mad. His professional integrity. Cecy'll probably trade us back, later. Bion never was one to take a joke on himself!"

Jonn looked confused. "Even *you* can't control Cecy?"

"God, no. She does what she does. We're helpless."

Jonn wandered toward the door. "Got to find her somehow," he mumbled. "If she can do this to you, think how she'd help me if she wanted . . . ." The bells rang louder in his ears. From the side of his eyes he saw a movement. He whirled and gasped.

The body on the table had a cedar-stake driven through it.

"So long," said the undertaker to the slammed door. He listened to the sound of Jonn's running feet, fading.

The man who staggered into the police station at five that afternoon was barely able to stand up. His voice was a whisper and he retched as if he'd taken poison. He didn't look like Uncle Jonn any more. The bells rang all the time, all the time, and he saw people walking behind him, with staked chests, who vanished whenever he turned to look.

The sheriff looked up from reading a magazine, wiped his brown moustache with the back of one claw-like hand, took his feet down off a battered desk and waited for Uncle Jonn to speak.

"I want to report a family that lives here," whispered Uncle Jonn, his eyes half-shut. "A wicked family, living under false pretenses."

The sheriff cleared his throat. "What's the family's name?"

Uncle Jonn stopped. "What?'

The sheriff repeated it, "What's the family's name?"

"Your voice," said Jonn.

"What about my voice?" said the sheriff.

"Sounds familiar," said Jonn. "Like—"

"Who?" asked the sheriff.

"Like Cecy's mother! That's who you sound like!"

"Do I?" asked the sheriff.

"That's who you are inside! Cecy changed you, too, like she changed Ralph and Bion! I can't report the Family to you, now, then! It wouldn't do any good!"

"Guess it wouldn't," remarked the sheriff, implacably.

"The Family's gotten around me!" wailed Uncle Jonn.

"Seems that way," said the sheriff, wetting a pencil on his tongue, starting on a fresh crossword puzzle. "Well, good day to you, Jonn Elliott."

"Unh?"

"I said 'Good day'."

"Good day." Jonn stood by the desk, listening. "Do you—do you *hear* anything?"

The sheriff listened. "Crickets?"

"No."

"Frogs?"

"No," said Uncle Jonn. "Bells. Just bells. Holy church bells. The kind of bells a man like me can't stand to hear. Holy church bells."

The sheriff listened. "No. Can't say as I hear 'em. Say, be careful of that door there; it slams."

The door to Cecy's room was knocked open. A moment later, Uncle Jonn was inside, moving across the floor. The silent body of Cecy lay on the bed, not moving. Behind him, as Jonn seized Cecy's hand, her mother appeared.

She ran to him, struck him on head and shoulders till he fell back from Cecy. The world swelled with bell sounds. His vision blacked out. He groped at the mother, biting his lips, releasing them in gasps, eyes streaming.

"Please, please tell her to come back," he said. "I'm sorry. I don't want to hurt any one any more."

The mother shouted through the clamor of bells. "Go downstairs and wait for her there!"

"I can't hear you," he cried, louder. "My head." He held his hands to his ears. "So loud. So loud I can't stand it." He rocked on his heels. "If only I knew where Cecy was—"

Quite simply, he drew out a folded pocket knife,

unfolded it. "I can't go on—" he said. And before the mother moved he fell to the floor, the knife in his heart, blood running from his lips, his shoes looking senseless one atop the other, one eye shut, the other wide and white.

The mother bent down to him. "Dead," she whispered, finally. "So," she murmured, unbelievingly, rising up, stepping away from the blood. "So he's dead at last." She glanced around, fearfully, cried aloud.

"Cecy, Cecy, come home, child, I need you!"

A silence, while sunlight faded from the room.

"Cecy, come home, child!"

The dead man's lips moved. A high clear voice sprang from them.

"Here! I've been here for days! I'm the fear he had in him; and he never guessed. Tell Father what I've done. Maybe he'll think me worthy now . . . ."

The dead man's lips stopped. A moment later, Cecy's body on the bed stiffened like a stocking with a leg thrust suddenly into it, inhabited again.

"Supper, mother," said Cecy, rising from bed.

THE SMALL ASSASSIN

Just when the idea occurred to her that she was being murdered she could not tell. There had been little subtle signs, little suspicions for the past month; things as deep as sea tides in her, like looking at a perfectly calm stretch of cerulean water and liking it and wanting to bathe in it, and finding, just as the tide takes your body into it, that monsters dwell just under the surface, things unseen, bloated, many-armed, sharp-finned, malignant and inescapable.

A room floated around her in an effluvium of hysteria. Sharp instruments hovered and there were voices and people in sterile white masks.

My name, she thought. My name; what is it?

Alice Leiber. It came to her. David Leiber's wife. But it gave her no comfort. She was alone with these silent whispering white people and there was great pain and nausea and death-fear in her.

I am being murdered before their eyes. These doctors, these nurses don't realize what hidden thing has happened to me. David doesn't know. Nobody knows except me and—the killer, the small assassin, the little murderer.

I am dying and I can't tell them how. They'd laugh and call me one in delirium. They'll see the murderer and hold him and like him and they won't think him responsible for my death. Here I am, in front of God and man, dying, and there is no one to believe my story, everyone to doubt me, comfort me with lies, bury me in ignorance, mourn me and salvage my murderer.

Where is David? she wondered. In the outer room, smoking one cigarette after another, listening to the long tickings of the very slow clock?

Sweat exploded from all of her body at once, and with it a crying and agonizing. Now. Now! Try and kill me, she screamed. Try, try, but I won't die! I won't!

There was a hollow in her. A vacuity. Suddenly there was no pain. Exhaustion. Blackness. It was over. It was all over. Oh, God. She plummeted rapidly down and struck against a black nothingness which gave way to another nothing and another nothing and another and still another . . . .

Footsteps. Gentle, approaching footsteps. The sound of people trying to be quiet.

Far away, a voice said, "She's asleep. Don't disturb her."

An odor of tweeds, a pipe, a certain shaving lotion. She knew David was standing over her. And beyond him the immaculate odor of Dr. Jeffers.

She did not open her eyes. "I'm awake," she said, quietly. It was a surprise, a relief to be able to speak, to not be dead.

"Alice," someone said, and it was David beyond her closed eyes, his hands holding one of her tired ones.

Would you like to meet the murderer, David? she thought. That's who you're here to see now, aren't you? I hear your voice asking to see him, so there's nothing but for me to point him out to you.

David stood over her. She opened her eyes. The room came into focus. Moving a weak hand she pulled aside a coverlet.

The murderer looked up at David Leiber with a small red-faced, blue-eyed calm. Its eyes were deep and sparkling.

"Why!" cried David Leiber, smiling. "Why, he's a *fine* baby!"

Dr. Jeffers was waiting for David Leiber the day he showed up at the hospital to take his wife and new child home. He motioned Leiber into a chair in his office, gave him a cigar, lit one for himself, sat on the edge of his desk, puffing solemnly for a long moment. Then he cleared his throat, looked David Leiber straight in the eye and said, "Your wife doesn't like her child, Dave."

"What!"

"It's been a hard thing for her. The whole thing.

She'll need a lot of love in this next year. I didn't say much at the time, but she was hysterical in the delivery room. The strange things she said. I won't repeat them. All I'll say is that she feels alien to the child. Now, this may simply be a thing we can clear up with one or two questions." He sucked on his cigar another moment, then said, "Is this child a 'wanted' child, Dave?"

"Why do you ask?"

"It's vital."

"Yes. Yes, it is a 'wanted' child. It was planned. We planned it together. Alice was so happy, a year ago, when—"

"Mmm—that makes it more difficult. Because if the child was unplanned, it would be a simple case of a mother who hates the idea of motherhood. That doesn't fit Alice." Dr. Jeffers took his cigar from his lips, rubbed his hand across his jaw, tongued the inside of his cheek. "It must be something else, then. Perhaps something buried in her childhood that's coming out now. Or it might be the simple temporary doubt and distrust of any mother who's gone through the unusual pain and near-death that Alice has. If so, then a little time should heal that. I thought I'd tell you, though, Dave. It'll help you be easy and tolerant with her. If she says anything about—well—about wishing the child had been born dead, smooth it over, will you, son? And if things don't get along, the three of you drop in on me. I'm always glad to see old friends, eh? Here, take another cigar along for—ah—for the baby."

*

It was a bright spring afternoon. Their car hummed along wide, tree-lined boulevards. Blue sky, flowers, a warm wind. Dave talked a lot, lit his cigar, talked some more. Alice answered directly, softly, relaxing a bit more as the trip progressed. But she held the baby not tightly enough or warmly enough or motherly enough to satisfy the queer ache in Dave's mind. She seemed to be merely carrying a porcelain figurine.

He tried joviality. "What'll we name him?" he asked.

Alice Leiber watched green trees slide by. "Let's not name him yet," she said. "I'd rather wait until we get an exceptional name for him. Don't blow smoke in his face." Her sentences ran together with no distinction of tone between one or the other. The last statement held no motherly reproof, no interest, no irritation. She just mouthed it and it was said.

The husband, disquieted, dropped the cigar from the window. "Sorry," he said.

The baby rested in the crook of its mother's arm, shadows of sun and tree changing its face over and again. His blue eyes opened like fresh blue spring flowers. Moist noises came from the tiny, pink, elastic mouth.

Alice gave her baby a quick glance. Her husband felt her shiver against him.

"Cold?" he asked.

"A chill. Better raise the window, David."

It was more than a chill. He rolled the window thoughtfully up.

*

Suppertime.

Candles flickered odd dances of light-shadow about the large, amply-furnished dining room. There was good familiarity in eating together again for both of them; friendliness and relaxation in passing salt or sharing the last biscuit, or commenting on flavors.

David Leiber had brought the child from the nursery, propped him at a tiny, bewildered angle, supported by many pillows, in a newly purchased high-chair.

Alice watched her knife and fork move. "He's not high-chair size," she said.

"Fun having him here, anyway," said Leiber, feeling fine. "Everything's fun. At the office, too. Orders up to my nose. If I don't watch myself I'll make another fifteen thousand this year. Hey, look at Junior, will you? Drooling all down his chin!" He reached over to dab at the baby's chin with his napkin. From the corner of his eye he realized that Alice wasn't even watching. He finished the job.

"I guess it wasn't very interesting," he said, back again at his food. A minor irritation rose in him, disregarding all self-argument. "But one would think a mother'd take some interest in her own child, wouldn't one?"

Alice jerked her chin up. "Don't speak that way. Not in *front of him!* Later, if you must."

"Later?" he cried. "In front of, in back of, what's the difference?" He quieted suddenly, swallowed, was sorry. "All right. Okay. I know how it is."

After dinner she let him carry the baby upstairs. She didn't tell him to; she *let* him.

Coming down, he found her standing by the radio, listening to music she wasn't hearing. Her eyes were closed, her whole attitude one of wondering, self-questioning. She started when he appeared.

Suddenly, she was at him, against him, soft, quick; the same. Nothing different. Her lips found him, kept him. He was stunned by her. He laughed, unexpectedly, and deeply. Something cold in him thawed and melted; like fear of winter melting at spring, his fear went now. Now that the baby was gone, upstairs, out of the room, she began to breathe again, live again. She was free. And this in itself made a subtle worry in him, but he let it go, enjoyed her being against him. She was whispering, rapidly, endlessly.

"Thank you, thank you, darling. For being yourself, always. Yourself, you, and nobody and nothing else! Dependable, so very dependable!'

He had to laugh. "My father told me, 'son, provide for your family!'"

Wearily, she rested her dark, shining hair against his neck. "You've overdone it. Sometimes I wish we were just the way we were when we were first married. No responsibilities, nothing but ourselves. No—no babies."

She took him too eagerly by the hand, a flushed strangeness in her white face, unnaturally intense. It seemed there were many things for her to say and she couldn't, so she said the next best thing, a fair substitute.

"A third element's come in. Before, it was just you and I. We protected each other, and now we protect the baby, but get no protection from it. Do you understand? Lying in the hospital I had time to think a lot of things. The world is evil—"

"Is it?" he said.

"Yes. It is. But laws protect us from it. And when there aren't laws, then love does the protecting. You're protected from my hurting you, by my love. You're vulnerable to me, of all people, but love shields you. I feel no fear of you, because love cushions all your irritations, unnatural instincts, hatreds and immaturities. But—what about the baby? It's too young to know love, or a law of love, or anything, until we teach it."

"We'll teach it, then."

"And in the meantime be vulnerable to it!"

"Vulnerable? To a baby?" He held her away from him and laughed gently at her.

"Does a baby know the difference between rights and wrongs?" she asked.

"No. But it'll learn."

"But a baby is so new, so amoral, so conscience-free," she argued. She stopped. Her arms dropped from him and she turned swiftly. "That noise? What was it?"

Leiber looked around the room. "I didn't hear—"

She stared at the library door. "In there," she said, slowly.

Leiber crossed the room and opened the door and switched the library lights on and off. "Not a thing," he said, and came back to her. "You're worn. To bed with you; *right now*."

Turning out the lights together, they walked quietly up the soundless hall stairs, not speaking. At the top she apologized. "My wild talk, darling. Forgive me. I'm just exhausted."

He understood, and said so.

She paused, undecided, by the nursery door. Then she fingered the brass knob sharply, walked in. He watched her approach the crib much too carefully, look down, and stiffen as if she'd been struck in the face. "David!"

Leiber stepped forward, reached the crib, and looked down.

The baby's face was bright red and very moist. The little pink mouth gestured. Bright blue eyes stared as if being strangled outward. Small red hands weaved in the air.

"Oh, he's just been crying," said Leiber.

"Has he?" Alice Leiber grasped the crib-railing to hold herself erect. "I didn't *hear* him crying."

"The door was closed."

"Is that why he breathes so hard, why his face is red?"

"Sure. Poor little guy. Crying all alone in the dark. He can sleep in our room tonight, just in case he cries."

"You'll spoil him," his wife said.

Leiber felt her eyes follow as he rolled the crib into their bedroom. He undressed silently, sat on the edge of the bed. Suddenly he lifted his head, swore under his breath, snapped his fingers. "Damn it. Forgot to tell you. Have to fly to Chicago Friday."

"Oh, David." She seemed a little lost girl. "So soon?"

"I've put this trip off for two months, and now it's so critical I just *have* to make it."

"I'm afraid to be alone."

"We'll have the new cook here by Friday. She'll be here all the time. All you have to do is call. I'll only be away a little while."

"But I'm afraid. I don't know of what. You wouldn't believe me if I told you. I guess I'm crazy."

He was in bed now. She darkened the room; he heard her walk around the bed, throw back crisp sheets, slide in. He smelled the warm woman smell of her next to him. He said, "If you want me to wait a few extra days, perhaps I could—"

"No," she said, unconvinced. "You go. I know it's important. It's just that I keep thinking about what I told you. Laws and love and protection. Love protects you from me. But, the baby—" She took a breath. "*What* protects you from him, David?"

Before he could answer, before he could tell her how silly it was, speaking of infants, she switched on the bed light, abruptly.

"Look," she said, pointing.

The baby lay wide awake in its crib, staring straight at him, with deep, sharp, blue eyes. The eyes closed.

The lights went out again. She trembled against him.

"It's not nice, being afraid of the thing you birthed." Her whisper lowered, became harsh, fierce, swift. "He tried to kill me! He lies there, listens to us talking, waiting for you to go away so he can try to kill me again! I swear it!"

Sobs broke from her he could not stop by holding her. "Please," he kept saying, soothing her. "Stop it, stop it. Please."

She cried in the dark for a long time. Very late she relaxed, shakingly, against him. Her breathing came soft, warm, regular, her body twitched its worn reflexes and she slept.

He drowsed.

And just before his eyes lidded wearily down, sinking into the deep sleep tides, he heard a strange little sound of awareness and awakeness in the room.

The sound of moist, small, pinkly elastic lips.

The baby.

And then—sleep.

In the morning, the sun blazed. Alice smiled.

David Leiber dangled his watch over the crib. "See, baby? Something bright. Something pretty. Sure. Sure. Something bright. Something pretty."

Alice smiled. She told him to go ahead, fly to Chicago, she'd try to be a brave girl, no need to worry. She'd take care of baby. Oh, yes, she'd take care of *him*, all right. This last she said with a peculiar emphasis, which David Leiber ignored.

The airplane went east with Leiber. There was a lot of sky, a lot of sun and clouds and then Chicago came running over the horizon. Leiber was dropped into the rush of ordering, planning, banqueting, making the rounds, telephoning, arguing in conference, downing coffee in scalding gulps between times. But he wrote letters each day and sent telegrams that said brief, nice, direct things to Alice, and baby.

On the evening of his sixth day away from home he received the long distance phone call. Los Angeles.

"Alice?"

"No, Dave. This is Jeffers, speaking."

"Doctor!"

"Hold onto yourself, son. Alice is sick. You'd better get the next plane home. It's pneumonia. I'll do everything I can, boy. If only it wasn't so soon after the baby. She needs strength."

Leiber dropped the phone into its cradle. He got up, with no feet under him, and no hands and no body. The hotel room blurred and fell apart.

"Alice," he said, blindly, starting for the door.

The airplane went west and California came up, and out of the twisting circular metal of propellors came a vibratingly sudden materialization of Alice lying in bed, Dr. Jeffers standing in the sunlight at a window, and the reality of Leiber feeling his feet walking slowly, becoming more real and more real, until, when he reached her bed, everything was whole, intact, a reality.

Nobody spoke. Alice smiled, faintly. Jeffers talked, but only a little of it got through to David.

"Your wife's too good a mother, son. She worried more about your baby than about herself . . . ."

A muscle in Alice's cheek flattened out, taut, then.

Alice began to talk. She talked like a mother should, now. Or did she? Wasn't there a trace of anger, fear, repulsion in her voice? Dr. Jeffers didn't notice it, but *he* wasn't looking for it.

"The baby wouldn't sleep," said Alice. "I thought he was sick. He just lay in his crib, staring. Late at night, he'd cry. Loud. He cried all night and all night. I couldn't quiet him. I couldn't sleep."

Dr. Jeffers nodded. "Tired herself right into pneumonia. But she's full of sulfa drug now, and she's on the safe side."

Leiber felt ill. "The baby, what about *him*?"

"Chipper as ever; healthy as a cock."

"Thanks, doctor."

The doctor took leave, walked down the stairs, opened the front door faintly, and was gone. Leiber listened to him go.

"David!"

He turned to her whisper.

"It was the baby, again," she said. "I try to lie to myself—convince myself I'm a fool. But the baby knew I was weak from the hospital. So he cried all night. And when he wasn't crying he'd be *too quiet*. If I switched the light on he'd be there, staring at me."

Leiber jerked inside. He remembered seeing the baby, awake in the dark, himself. Awake very late at night when babies should sleep. He pushed it aside. It was crazy.

Alice went on. "I was going to kill the baby. Yes, I

was. When you'd been gone only an hour on your trip I went to his room and put my hands about his neck, and I stood there, for a long time, thinking, afraid. Then I put the covers up over his face and turned him over on his face and pressed him down and left him that way and ran out of the room."

He tried to stop her.

"No let me finish," she said, hoarsely, looking at the wall. "When I left his room I thought, it's simple. Babies die every day of smothering. No one'll ever know. But when I came back to see him dead, David, he was alive! Yes, alive, turned over on his back, alive and smiling and breathing. And I couldn't touch him again after that. I left him there and I didn't come back, not to feed him or look at him or do anything. Perhaps the cook tended to him. I don't know. All I know is that his crying kept me awake and I thought all through the night, and walked around the rooms and now I'm sick." She was almost finished now. "The baby lies there and thinks of ways to kill me. Simple ways. Because he knows that I know so much about him. I have no love for him, there is no protection between us, there never will be again."

She was through. She collapsed inward on herself and finally slept. David Leiber stood for a long while over her, not able to move. His brain was frozen in his head, not a cell of it stirred.

*

The next morning there was only one thing to do. He did it. He walked into Dr. Jeffers' office and told him the whole thing, and listened to Jeffers' tolerant replies:

"Let's take this thing slowly, son. It's quite natural for mothers to hate their children, some times. We have a label for it—ambivalence. The ability to hate, while loving. Lovers hate each other, frequently. Children detest their mothers—"

Leiber interrupted. "I never hated *my* mother."

"You won't admit it, naturally. People hate admitting hatred for loved ones."

"So Alice hates her baby."

"The best way to put it is that she has an obsession. She's gone a step further than plain, ordinary ambivalence. A Caesarian operation brought the child into the world, and almost took Alice out of it. She blames the child for her near-death and her pneumonia. She's projecting her troubles, blaming them on the handiest object she can use as a source of blame. We *all* do it. We stumble into a chair and curse the furniture, not our own clumsiness. We miss a golf-stroke and damn the turf or our club, or the make of ball. If our business fails we blame the gods, the weather, our luck. All I can tell you is what I told you before. Love her. Finest medicine in the world. Find little ways of showing your affection, give her security. Find ways of showing her how harmless and innocent the child is. Make her feel that the baby was *worth* the risk. After awhile, she'll settle down, forget about death, and begin to love the child. If she doesn't come around in the next month or so, ask me and I'll recommend a good psychiatrist. Go on along now, and take that look off your face."

When summer came, things seemed to settle and become easy. Leiber worked, immersed himself in office detail, but never forgot to be thoughtful of his wife. She, in turn, took long walks, gained strength, played an occasional light game of badminton. She rarely burst out emotionally any more. She seemed to have rid herself of her fears.

Except on one certain midnight when a sudden summer wind swept around the house, warm and swift, shaking the trees like so many shining tamborines. Alice wakened, trembling, and slid over into her husband's arms, and let him console her, and ask her what was wrong.

She said, "Something's here in the room, watching us."

He switched on the light. "Dreaming again," he said. "You're better, though. Haven't been scared for a long time."

She sighed as he clicked off the light again, and suddenly she slept. He held her, considering what a sweet, weird creature she was, for about half an hour.

He heard the bedroom door sway open a few inches.

There was nobody at the door. No reason for it to come open. The wind had died.

He waited. It seemed like an hour he lay silently, in the dark.

Then, far away, wailing like some small meteor dying in the vast inky gulf of space, the baby began to cry in his nursery.

It was a small, lonely sound in the middle of the stars and the dark and the breathing of this woman in his arms and the wind beginning to sweep through the trees again.

Leiber counted to fifty. The crying continued.

Finally, carefully disengaging Alice's grip, he slipped from bed, put on his slippers, robe, and tiptoed out of the room.

He'd go downstairs, he thought tiredly, and fix some warm milk, bring it up, and—

The blackness dropped out from under him. His foot slipped and plunged. Slipped on something soft. Plunged into nothingness.

He thrust his hands out, caught frantically at the railing. His body stopped falling. He held. He cursed.

The "something soft" that had caused his feet to slip, rustled and thumped down a few steps and stopped. His head rang. His heart hammered at the base of his throat, thick and shot with pain.

Why do careless people leave things strewn about a house? He groped carefully with his fingers for the object that had almost spilled him headlong down the stairs.

His hand froze, startled. His breath went in. His heart held one or two beats.

The thing he held in his hand was a toy. A large

cumbersome, patchwork doll he had brought as a joke, for—

For the baby.

Alice drove him to work the next day.

She slowed the car half way down-town; pulled to the curb and stopped it. Then she turned on the seat and looked at her husband.

"I want to go away on a vacation. I don't know if you can make it now, darling, but, if not, please let me go alone. We can get someone to take care of the baby, I'm sure. But I just have to get away. I thought I was growing out of this—this *feeling*. But I haven't. I can't stand being in the room with him. He looks up at me as if he hates me, too. I can't put my finger on it; all I know is I want to get away before something happens."

He got out on his side of the car, came around, motioned to her to move over, got in. "The only thing you're going to do is see a good psychiatrist. And if he suggests a vacation, well, okay. But this can't go on; my stomach's in knots all the time." He started the car. "I'll drive the rest of the way."

Her head was down, she was trying to keep back tears. She looked up when they reached his office-building. "All right. Make the appointment. I'll go talk to anyone you want, David."

He kissed her. "Now, you're talking sense, lady. Think you can drive home okay?"

"Of course, silly."

"See you at supper, then. Drive carefully."

"Don't I always? 'Bye."

He stood on the curb, watching her drive off, the wind taking hold of her long dark, shining hair. Upstairs, a minute later, he phoned Jeffers, got an appointment arranged with a reliable neuropsychiatrist. That was *that*.

The day's work went uneasily. Things seemed to tangle and he kept seeing Alice all the time, mixed into everything he looked at. So much of her fear had come over into him. She actually had *him* convinced that the child was somewhat unnatural.

He dictated long, uninspired letters. He checked some shipments downstairs. Assistants had to be questioned, and kept going. At the end of the day he was all exhaustion, and nothing else. His head throbbed. He was very willing to go home.

On the way down in the elevator he wondered, what if I told Alice about that toy—that patchwork doll—I stumbled over on the stairs last night? Lord, wouldn't *that* send her off into hysterics! No, I won't ever tell her about that. After all, it was just one of those accidents.

Daylight lingered in the sky as he drove home in a taxi. In front of his Brentwood place he paid the driver and walked slowly up the cement walk, enjoying the light that was still in the sky and the trees. The white colonial front to the house looked unnaturally silent and uninhabited, and then, quietly, he remembered that this was Thursday, and the few hired help they were able to obtain from time to time, were all gone for the day. It was cook's day off, too, and he and Alice would have to scriven for themselves or eat on the Strip somewhere.

He took a deep breath of air. A bird sang behind the house. Traffic moved on the boulevard a block away. He turned the key in the door. The knob turned under his fingers, oiled, silent.

The door opened. He stepped in, put his hat on the chair with his briefcase, started to shrug out of his coat, when he looked up.

Late sunlight streamed down the stair-well from the window at the top of the house. Where the sunlight landed it took on the bright color of the patchwork doll sprawled in a grotesque angle at the bottom of the stairs.

But he paid no attention to the patchwork doll.

He could only look, and not move, and look again at Alice.

Alice lay in a broken, grotesque, pallid gesturing and angling of her thin body. She was lying at the bottom of the stairs, like a crumpled doll who doesn't want to play any more, ever.

Alice was dead.

The house remained quiet, except for the sound of his heart.

She was dead.

He held her head in his hands, he felt of her fingers. He held her body. But she wouldn't live. She wouldn't even try to live. He said her name, out loud, many times, and he tried, once again, by holding her to him, to give her back some of the warmth she had lost, but that didn't help.

He stood up. He must have made a phone call. He didn't remember. He found himself, suddenly, upstairs. He opened the nursery door and walked inside and stared blankly at the crib. His stomach was sick. He couldn't see very well.

The baby's eyes were closed, but his face was red, moist with perspiration, as if he'd been crying long and hard.

"She's dead," said Leiber to the baby. "She's dead."

Then he started laughing low and soft and continuous for a long time until Dr. Jeffers walked in out of the night-time and slapped him again and again across his cheeks.

"Snap out of it! Pull yourself together, son!"

"She fell down the stairs, doctor. She tripped on a patchwork doll and fell. I almost slipped on it the other night, myself. And now—"

The doctor shook him.

"Doc, doc, doc," said Leiber, hazily. "Funny thing. Funny. I—I finally thought of a name for the baby."

The doctor said nothing.

Leiber put his head back in his trembling hands and spoke the words. "I'm going to have him christened next Sunday. Know what name I'm giving him? I'm—I'm going to call him—*Lucifer*!"

It was eleven at night. A lot of strange people had come and gone through the house, taking the essential flame with them—Alice.

David Leiber sat across from the doctor in the library.

"Alice wasn't crazy," he said, slowly. "She had good reason to fear the baby."

Jeffers exhaled. "Now you're following in her pattern. She blamed the child for her sickness, now *you* blame it for her death. She stumbled on a *toy*, remember that. You can't blame the child."

"You mean Lucifer?"

"Stop calling him Lucifer!"

Leiber shook his head. "Alice heard things at night. Things moving in the halls. As if someone spied on us. You want to know what those noises were, doctor? I'll tell you. They were made by the baby! Yes, *my* son! Four months old, creeping around the dark halls at night, listening to us talk. Listening to *every word*!" He held to the sides of the chair. "And if I turned the lights on, a baby is a small object. It can conveniently hide behind furniture, a door, against a wall—below eye-level."

"I want you to stop this!" demanded Jeffers.

"Let me say what I think or I'll go crazy. When I went to Chicago, who was it kept Alice awake, tiring her, weakening her into pneumonia? The baby! And when Alice didn't die, then he tried killing me. It was simple; leave a toy doll on the stairs, then cry in the night until your father rouses up, tired of listening to you cry, and goes downstairs to fetch you warm milk, and stumbles. A crude trick, but effective. It didn't get me. But it killed Alice quite dead."

David Leiber stopped long enough to light a cigarette.

"I should have caught on. I'd turn on the lights in the middle of the night, many nights, and the baby'd be lying there, eyes wide. Most babies sleep constantly, all the time. Not *this* one. He stayed awake—thinking."

"Babies don't think," countered Jeffers.

"He stayed awake doing whatever he *could* do with his brain, then. What in hell do we know about a baby's brain? He had every reason to hate Alice; she suspected him for what he was—certainly not a normal child. Something—different. What do you know of babies, doctor? The general knowledge, yes. You know, of course, how babies kill their mothers at birth. Why? In resentment at being forced into a lousy world like this one!"

Leiber leaned toward the doctor, tiredly. "It all ties up. Suppose that a few babies out of all the millions born are instantaneously able to move, see, hear, think, like many animals and insects can. Many insects are self-sufficient when born. In a few days most mammals and birds are adjusted. Little man-children take years to speak, faltering around on rubbery legs.

"But, suppose one child in a million is—strange? Born perfectly aware, able to think, instinctively. Wouldn't it be a perfect set-up, a perfect blind for anything the baby might want to do? He could pretend to be ordinary, weak, crying, ignorant. With just a *little* expenditure of energy he could crawl about a darkened house, listening. And how easy to place obstacles at the top of stairs. How easy to cry all night and tire a mother into pneumonia.

How easy, right at birth, to be so close to the mother that *a few deft maneuvers might cause peritonitis*!"

"For God's sake!" Jeffers was on his feet. "That's a repulsive thing to say!"

"It's a repulsive thing I'm speaking of. How many mothers have died at the birth of their children? How many have suckled strange little improbabilities who cause death one way or another? Strange, red little creatures with brains that function in a scarlet darkness we can't even guess at. Elemental little brains, aswarm with racial memory and hatred and raw cruelty, with no more thought than self-preservation. And self-preservation in this case consisted of eliminating a mother who realized what a horror she had birthed. I ask you, doctor, what is there in the world more selfish than a baby? Nothing! Nothing is so self-centered, unsocial, selfish, nothing!"

Jeffers scowled and shook his head, helplessly, and shrugged.

Leiber dropped his cigarette down, weakly. "I'm not claiming any great strength for the child. Just enough to crawl around a little, a few months ahead of schedule. Just enough to listen all the time. Just enough to cry late at night. That's enough, more than enough."

Jeffers tried ridicule. "Call it murder, then. And murder must have a motivation. Name a motivation for the child."

Leiber was ready with the answer. "What is more at peace, more dreamfully happy, content, at ease, at rest, fed, comforted, unbothered than an unborn child?

Nothing. It floats in a sleepy dark effluvium of timeless wonder and warm nourishment and silence. All is an enclosed dream. Then, suddenly, it is asked to give up its berth, is forced to vacate, propelled out into a noisy, uncaring, selfish, swift and merciless world where it is asked to shift for itself, to hunt, to feed from the hunting, to seek after a vanishing love that once was its unquestionable right, to meet confusion instead of inner silence and conservative slumber! And the newborn *resents* it! Resents it with all the soft, small fibres of its miniature body. Resents the raw cold air, the huge spaces, the sudden departure from familiar things. And in the tiny filament of brain the only thing that the child knows is selfishness and hatred because the spell has been rudely shattered. And who is responsible for this disenchantment, this rude breakage of the spell? The mother. And so the new child has someone to hate, and hate with all the tiny fabric of its mind. The mother has cast it out, rejected it. And the father is no better, kill him, too! He's responsible in *his* way!"

Jeffers interrupted. "If what you say is true, then every woman in the world would have to look on her newborn as something to dread, something to wonder about, to shudder at."

"And why not? Hasn't the child a perfect alibi? He has a thousand years of accepted medical belief to protect him. By all natural accounts he is helpless, not responsible. The child is born hating. And things grow worse, instead of better. At first the baby gets a certain amount of attention and mothering. But then as time passes, things change. When very new, a baby has great power. Power to make parents do silly things when it cries or sneezes, jump when it makes a noise. As the years pass, the baby feels even that little power slipping rapidly, forever away from it, never to return. Why shouldn't it grasp for all the power it can have, why shouldn't it jockey for position while it has all the advantages? In later years it would be too late to express its hatred. *Now* would be the time to strike. And later, this child, secretly aware, becoming more aware each and every day, would learn new things—about position, money, security. The child would see that through money it might eventually provide itself with a self-built womb of comforts, warmth, and aloneness. And naturally, then, it might pay to destroy the father whose insurance policies for twenty thousand dollars are made out to the wife and baby. Again, I admit the baby isn't old enough for *that* motivation yet. Money is something beyond it. But *hatred* is not. The money angle might come later, not now. But it would come from the same desire, the desire to return to warm comfort and let-aloneness."

Leiber's voice was very soft, very low.

"My little boy baby, lying in his crib nights, his face moist and red and out of breath. From crying? No. From climbing tediously, achingly slow, out of his crib, from crawling long distances through darkened hallways. My little boy baby. I want to kill him."

The doctor handed him a water glass and some pills.

"You're not killing anyone. You're going to sleep for twenty-four hours. Sleep'll change your mind. Take this."

Leiber drank down the pills and let himself be led upstairs to his bedroom, crying, and felt himself being put to bed.

The doctor said good night and left the house.

Leiber, alone, drifted toward sleep.

He heard a noise. "What's—what's *that?*" he demanded, feebly.

Something moved in the hall.

David Leiber slept.

The next morning, Dr. Jeffers drove up to the Leiber house. It was a good morning, and he was here to tell Leiber to get out into the country for a rest. Leiber would still be asleep upstairs. Jeffers had given him enough sedative to knock him out for at least fifteen hours.

He rang the doorbell. No answer. The servants hadn't returned, it was too early. Jeffers tried the front door, found it open, stepped in. He put his medical kit on the nearest chair.

Something white moved out of view at the top of the stairs. Just a suggestion of a movement. Jeffers hardly noticed it.

The odor of gas was in the house.

Jeffers ran up the stairs, crashed into Leiber's bedroom.

Leiber lay on the bed, not moving, and the room billowed with gas, which hissed from a released jet at the base of the wall near the door. Jeffers twisted it off, then forced up all the windows, and ran back to Leiber's body.

The body was cold. It had been dead quite a few hours.

Coughing violently, the doctor hurried from the room, eyes watering. Leiber hadn't turned the gas on himself. He *couldn't* have. Those sedatives had knocked him out, he wouldn't have wakened until noon. It wasn't suicide. Or was there the faintest possibility?

Jeffers stood in the hall for five minutes. Then he walked to the door of the nursery. It was shut. He opened it. He walked inside and over to the crib.

The crib was empty.

He stood swaying over the crib for half a minute, then he said something to nobody in particular.

"The nursery door blew shut. You couldn't get back into your crib where it was safe. You didn't plan on the door blowing shut. A little thing like a slammed door can ruin the best of plans. I'll find you somewhere in the house, hiding, pretending to be something you are not." The doctor looked dazed. He put his hand to his head and smiled palely. "Now I'm talking like Alice and David talked. But, I can't take any chances. I'm not sure of anything, but I can't take any chances."

He walked downstairs, opened his medical bag upon the chair, took something out of it and held it in his hands.

Something rustled down the hall. Something very small and very quiet. Jeffers turned rapidly.

"I had to operate to bring you into this world. Now I guess I can operate to take you out of it . . . ."

He took half a dozen, quick, sure steps forward into the hall. He raised his hand into the sunlight.

"See, baby! Something bright—something pretty!"

A scalpel.

THE CROWD

Mr. Spallner put his hands over his face.

There was the feeling of movement in space, the beautifully tortured scream, the impact and tumbling of the car with wall, through wall, over and down like a toy, and him hurled out of it. Then—silence.

The crowd came running. Faintly, where he lay, he heard them running. He could tell their ages and their sizes by the sound of their numerous feet over the summer grass and on the lined sidewalk, and over the asphalt street, and picking through the cluttered bricks to where his car hung half into the night sky, still spinning its wheels with a senseless centrifuge.

Where the crowd came from he didn't know. He struggled to remain aware and then the crowd faces hemmed in upon him, hung over him like the large glowing leaves of down-bent trees. They were a ring of shifting, compressing, changing faces over him, looking down, looking down, reading the time of his life or death by his face, making his face into a moon-dial, where the moon cast a shadow from his nose out upon his cheek to tell the time of breathing or not breathing any more ever.

How swiftly a crowd comes, he thought, like the iris of an eye compressing in out of nowhere.

A siren. A police voice. Movement. Blood trickled from his lips and he was being moved into an ambulance. Someone said, "Is he dead?" And someone else said, "No, he's not dead." And a third person said, "He won't die, he's not going to die." And he saw the faces of the crowd beyond him in the night, and he knew by their expressions that he wouldn't die. And that was strange. He saw a man's face, thin, bright, pale; the man swallowed and bit his lips, very sick. There was a small woman, too, with red hair and too much red on her cheeks and lips. And a little boy with a freckled face. Others' faces. An old man with a wrinkled upper lip, an old woman, with a mole upon her chin. They had all come from—where? Houses, cars, alleys, from the immediate and the accident-shocked world. Out of alleys and out of hotels and out of street-cars and seemingly out of nothing they came.

The crowd looked at him and he looked back at them and did not like them at all. There was a vast wrongness to them. He couldn't put his finger on it. They were far worse than this machine-made thing that happened to him now.

The ambulance doors slammed. Through the windows he saw the crowd looking in, looking in. That crowd that always came so fast, so strangely fast, to form a circle, to peer down, to probe, to gawk, to question, to point, to disturb, to spoil the privacy of a man's agony by their frank curiosity.

The ambulance drove off. He sank back and their faces still stared into his face, even with his eyes shut.

The car wheels spun in his mind for days. One wheel, four wheels, spinning, spinning, and whirring, around and around.

He knew it was wrong. Something wrong with the wheels and the whole accident and the running of feet and the curiosity. The crowd faces mixed and spun into the wild rotation of the wheels.

He awoke.

Sunlight, a hospital room, a hand taking his pulse.

"How do you feel?" asked the doctor.

The wheels faded away. Mr. Spallner looked around.

"Fine—I guess."

He tried to find words. About the accident. "Doctor?"

"Yes?"

"That crowd—was it last night?"

"Two days ago. You've been here since Thursday. You're all right, though. You're doing fine. Don't try and get up."

"That crowd. Something about wheels, too. Do accidents make people, well, a—little off."

"Temporarily, some times. It wears off."

He lay staring up at the doctor. "Does it hurt your time sense?"

"Panic sometimes does."

"Makes a minute seem like an hour, or maybe an hour seem like a minute?"

"Yes."

"Let me tell you then." He felt the bed under him, the sunlight on his face. "You'll think I'm crazy. I was driving too fast, I know. I'm sorry now. I jumped the curb and hit that wall. I was hurt and numb, I know, but I still remember things. Mostly—the crowd." He waited a moment and then decided to go on, for he suddenly knew what it was that bothered him. "The crowd got there too quickly. Thirty seconds after the smash they were all standing over me and staring at me . . . it's not right they should run that fast, so late at night . . . ."

"You only think it was thirty seconds," said the doctor. "It was probably three or four minutes. Your senses—"

"Yeah, I know—my senses, the accident. But I was conscious! I remember one thing that puts it all together and makes it funny, God, so damned funny. The wheels of my car, upside down. The wheels were still spinning when the crowd got there!"

The doctor smiled.

The man in bed went on. "I'm positive! The wheels were spinning and spinning fast—the front wheels! Wheels don't spin very long, friction cuts them down. And these were really spinning!"

"You're confused," said the doctor.

"I'm not confused. That street was empty. Not a soul in sight. And then the accident and the wheels still spinning and all those faces over me, quick, in no time. And the way they looked down at me, I *knew* I wouldn't die. . . ."

"Simple shock," said the doctor, walking away into the sunlight.

They released him from the hospital two weeks later. He rode home in a taxi. People had come to visit him during his two weeks on his back, and to all of them he had told his story, the accident, the spinning wheels, the crowd. They had all laughed with him concerning it, and passed it off.

He leaned forward and tapped on the taxi window. "What's wrong?"

The cabbie looked back. "Sorry, boss. This is one helluva town to drive in. Got an accident up ahead. Want me to detour?"

"Yes. No, no! Wait. Go ahead. Let's—let's take a look."

The cab moved forward, honking.

"Funny damn thing," said the cabbie. "Hey, *you!* Get that fleatrap out the way!" Quieter. "Funny thing—more damn people. Nosy people."

Mr. Spallner looked down and watched his fingers tremble on his knee. "You noticed that, too?"

"Sure," said the cabbie. "All the time. There's always a crowd. You'd think it was their own mother got killed."

"They come running awfully fast," said the man in the back of the cab.

"Same way with a fire or an explosion. Nobody around. Boom. Lotsa people around. I dunno."

"Ever seen an accident—at night?"

The cabbie nodded. "Sure. Don't make no difference. There's always a crowd."

The wreck came in view. A body lay on the sidewalk. You knew there was a body even if you couldn't see it. Because of the crowd. The crowd with its back toward him as he sat in the rear of the cab. With its back toward him. He opened the window and almost started to yell. But he didn't have the nerve. If he yelled they might turn around.

And he was afraid to see their *faces*.

"I seem to have a penchant for accidents," he said, in his office. It was late afternoon. His friend sat across the desk from him, listening. "I got out of the hospital this morning and first thing on the way home, we detoured around a wreck."

"Things run in cycles," said Morgan.

"Let me tell you about my accident."

"I've heard it. Heard it all."

"But it was funny, you must admit."

"I must admit. Now how about a drink."

They talked on for half an hour or more. All the while they talked, at the back of Spallner's brain a small watch ticked, a watch that never needed winding. It was the memory of a few little things. Wheels and faces.

At about five thirty there was a hard metal noise in the street. Morgan nodded and looked out and down. "What'd I tell you? Cycles. A truck and a cream-colored Cadillac. Yes, yes."

Spallner walked to the window. He was very cold and as he stood there, he looked at his watch, at the small minute hand. One two three four five seconds—people running—eight nine ten eleven twelve—from all over, people came running—fifteen sixteen seventeen eighteen seconds—more people, more cars, more horns blowing. Curiously distant, Spallner looked upon the scene as an explosion in reverse, the fragments of the detonation sucked back to the point of impulsion. Nineteen, twenty, twenty-one seconds and the crowd was there. Spallner made a gesture down at them, wordless.

The crowd had gathered so *fast*.

He saw a woman's body a moment before the crowd swallowed it up.

Morgan said. "You look lousy. Here. Finish your drink."

"I'm all right, I'm all right. Let me alone. I'm all right. Can you see those people? Can you see any of them? I wish we could see them closer."

Morgan cried out, "Where in hell are *you* going?"

Spallner was out the door, Morgan after him, and

down the stairs, as rapidly as possible. "Come along, and hurry."

"Take it easy, you're not a well man!"

They walked out onto the street. Spallner pushed his way forward. He thought he saw a red-haired woman with too much red color on her cheeks and lips.

"There!" He turned wildly to Morgan. "Did you see her?"

"See *who?*"

"Damn it; she's gone. The crowd closed in!"

The crowd was all around, breathing and looking and shuffling and mixing and mumbling and getting in the way when he tried to shove through. Evidently the red-haired woman had seen him coming and run off.

He saw another familiar face! A little freckled boy. But there are many freckled boys in the world. And, anyway, it was no use, before Spallner reached him, this little boy ran away and vanished among the people.

"Is she dead?" a voice asked. "Is she dead?"

"She's dying," someone else replied. "She'll be dead before the ambulance arrives. They shouldn't have moved her. They shouldn't have moved her."

All the crowd faces—familiar, yet unfamiliar, bending over, looking down, looking down.

"Hey, mister, stop pushing."

"Who you shovin', buddy?"

Spallner came back out, and Morgan caught hold of him before he fell. "You damned fool. You're still sick.

Why in hell'd you have to come down here?" Morgan demanded.

"I don't know, I really don't. They moved her, Morgan, someone moved her. You should never move a traffic victim. It kills them. It kills them."

"Yeah. That's the way with people. The dumb saps."

Spallner arranged the newspaper clippings carefully.

Morgan looked at them. "What's the idea? Ever since your wreck you think every traffic scramble is part of you. What are these?"

"Clippings of motor car crackups, and photos. Look at them. Not at the cars," said Spallner, "but at the crowds around the cars." He pointed. "Here. Compare this photo of a wreck in the Wilshire District with one in Westwood. No resemblance. But now take this Westwood picture and align it with one taken in the Westwood District ten years ago." Again he motioned. "This woman is in both pictures."

"Coincidence. The woman happened to be there once in 1936, again in 1946."

"A coincidence once, maybe. But twelve times over a period of ten years, when the accidents occurred as much as three miles from one another, no. Here." He dealt out a dozen photographs. "She's in *all* of these!"

"Maybe she's perverted."

"She's more than that. How does she *happen* to be there so quickly after each accident? And why does she wear the same clothes in pictures taken over a period of a decade?"

"I'll be damned, so she *is*."

"And, last of all, why was she standing over *me* the night of my accident, two weeks ago!"

They had a drink. Morgan went over the files. "What'd you do, hire a clipping service while you were in the hospital to go back through the newspapers for you?" Spallner nodded. Morgan sipped his drink. It was getting late. The street lights were coming on in the streets below the office. "What does all this add up to?"

"I don't know," said Spallner, "except that there's a universal law about accidents. *Crowds gather*. They *always* gather. And people, like you and I, have wondered from year after year, why they gathered so quickly, and *how*. *I* know the answer. Here it is!"

He flung the clippings down. "It frightens me."

"These people—mightn't they be thrill-hunters, perverted sensationalists with a carnal lust for blood and morbidity?"

Spallner shrugged. "Does that explain their being at *all* the accidents? Notice, they stick to certain territories. A Brentwood accident will bring out one group. A Huntington Park another. But there's a norm for faces, a certain percentage appear at each wreck."

Morgan said, "They're not *all* the same faces, are they?"

"Naturally not. Accidents draw normal people, too, in the course of time. But these, I find, are always the *first* ones there."

"Who are they? What do they want? You keep hinting

and never telling. Good Lord, you must have some idea. You've scared yourself and now you've got me jumping."

"I've tried getting *to* them, but someone always trips me up, I'm always too late. They slip into the crowd and vanish. The crowd seems to offer protection to some of its members. They see me coming."

"Sounds like some sort of clique."

"They have one thing in common, they always show up together. At a fire or an explosion or on the sidelines of a war, at any public demonstration of this thing called death. Vultures, hyenas or saints, I don't know which they are, I just don't know. But I'm going to the police with it, this evening. It's gone on long enough. One of them shifted that woman's body today. They shouldn't have touched her. It killed her."

He placed the clippings in a brief-case. Morgan got up and slipped into his coat. Spallner clicked the brief-case shut. "Or, I just happened to think of it . . . ."

"What?"

"Maybe they *wanted* her dead."

"Why?"

"Who knows. Come along?"

"Sorry. It's late. See you tomorrow. Luck." They went out together. "Give my regards to the cops. Think they'll believe you?"

"Oh, they'll believe me all right. Good night."

Spallner took it slow driving down-town.

"I want to get there," he told himself, "alive."

He was rathered shocked, but not surprised, somehow, when the truck came rolling out of an alley straight at him. He was just congratulating himself on his keen sense of observation and talking out what he would say to the police department in his mind when the truck smashed into his car. It wasn't really his car, that was the disheartening thing about it. In a preoccupied mood he was tossed first this way and then that way, while he thought, what a shame, Morgan has gone and lent me his extra car for a few days until my other car is fixed, and now here I go again. The windshield hammered back into his face. He was forced back and forth in several lightning jerks. Then all motion stopped and all noise stopped and only pain filled him up.

He heard their feet running and running and running. He fumbled with the car door. It clicked. He fell out upon the pavement drunkenly and lay, ear to the asphalt, listening to them coming. It was like a great rainstorm, with many drops, heavy and light and medium, touching the earth. He waited a few seconds and listened to their coming and their arrival. Then, weakly, expectantly, he rolled his head up and looked.

The crowd was there.

He could smell their breaths, the mingled odors of many people sucking and sucking on the air a man needs to live by. They crowded and jostled and sucked and sucked all the air up from around his gasping face until he tried to tell them to move back, they were making him live in a vacuum. His head was bleeding very badly.

He tried to move and he realized something was *wrong* with his spine. He hadn't felt much at the impact, but his spine *was* hurt. He didn't dare move.

He couldn't speak. Opening his mouth, nothing came out but a gagging.

Someone said, "Give me a hand. We'll roll him over and lift him into a more comfortable position."

Spallner's brain burst apart.

"No! Don't move me!"

"We'll move him," said the voice, casually.

"You idiots, you'll kill me, don't!"

But he could not say any of this out loud. He could only think it.

Hands took hold of him. They started to lift him. He cried out and nausea choked him up. They straightened him out into a ramrod of agony. Two men did it. One of them was thin, bright, pale, alert, a young man. The other man was very old and had a wrinkled upper lip.

He had seen their faces before.

A familiar voice said, "Is—is he dead?"

Another voice, a memorable voice, responded, "No. Not yet. But he will be dead before the ambulance arrives."

It was all a very silly, mad plot. Like every accident. He squealed hysterically at the solid wall of faces. They were all around him, these judges and jurors with the faces he had seen before. Through his pain he counted their faces.

The freckled boy. The old man with the wrinkled upper lip.

The red-haired, red-cheeked woman. An old woman with a mole on her chin.

"I know what you're here for," he thought. "You're here just as you're at all accidents. To make certain the right ones live and the right ones die. That's why you lifted me. You knew it would kill. You knew I'd live if you left me alone.

"And that's the way it's been since time began, when crowds gather. You murder much easier, this way. Your alibi is very simple; you didn't know it was dangerous to move a hurt man. You didn't mean to hurt him."

He looked at them, above him, and he was curious as a man under deep water looking up at people on a bridge. "Who are you? Where do you come from and how do you get here so soon? You're the crowd that's always in the way, using up good air that a dying man's lungs are in need of, using up space he should be using to lie in, alone. Tramping on people to make sure they die, that's you. I know *all* of you."

It was like a polite monologue. They said nothing. Faces. The old man. The red haired woman.

Someone picked up his briefcase. "Whose is this?" they asked.

"It's mine! It's evidence against all of you!"

Eyes, inverted over him. Shiny eyes under tousled hair or under hats.

Faces.

Somewhere—a siren. The ambulance was coming.

But, looking at the faces, the construction, the cast,

the form of the faces, Spallner knew it was too late. He read it in their faces. They *knew*.

He tried to speak. A little bit got out:

"It—looks like I'll—be joining up with you. I—guess I'll be a member of your—group—now."

He closed his eyes then, and waited for the coroner.

REUNION

Every Monday morning the clugging clamor on the back-porch, the quaking of the house in every ancient beam and joint, signified that the ritual of clothes-washing had begun.

The clothes would lie in brilliant mounds, sorted out, ready to be dispatched into the cauldron where the metal clunkers went up and down with an *eeeeeee aawwww eeeeeee aawwww* noise, and the sound of much thrashing water. Within that electrified machine the surgings would be incredible, as the clothes swam about, were submerged by merciless attacks of the plungers. They seemed alive, floundering empty sleeves, bobbing their deserted necks and showing, without so much as a blush, their under-skirts. The mad bubbling continued into late afternoon. Then the wind snapped regiments of materials on wire lines under the blossoming apple trees.

It was Malcolm Briar's duty to fetch soap chips from the cellar, gather spilled clothes-pins, and keep his mouth shut, being careful not to raise dust to spoil the wind-flapped linens. Malcolm scuttled about the yard, obedient to every shrill instruction of his Aunt Opie, but secretly rebelling against her ordinances.

So here it was—a particular Monday. Aunt Opie, her mouth chocked with clothes-pins, wiped the lines clean with a rag and began hanging clothes. But Malcolm, seizing the first chance, sought refuge in the attic of their old house on Oak Street; this very same house where his mother and father had lived before their deaths.

He heard Aunt Opie shrilling down in the yard. Her voice was like the pump handle's creak in the kitchen.

"Mal! Oh, Mal! Mal!"

Mal surveyed his kingdom below through a small hole in the dusty attic window. Aunt Opie called again, "Mal!"

Mal giggled. She would never find him up here. This was the Robber's Roost. None could enter save those who rapped and swiftly whispered, "Hing-a-ding-a-rock-in-my-shoe!"

About him was the collected paraphernalia of fifty years of living and dying. All the implements, the unnecessaries, the frills, the knick-knacks collected, shelved and tucked away by aging humans when they no longer served a purpose.

Small tinker-toys of babes now grown into cynics with their own babies. High-chairs gathering dust, offering seating space for fat, lazy old spiders who sat greyly and rarely considered the task of spinning a regular web.

Neat stacks, leaned against the odorous walls, were family pictures: Mom and Dad, Grandma and Grandpa, great-grandparents, cousins, and his brother David, who had died aged seven.

The great brown trunk with the metal hasps on it. If you blew your breath and wiped the hasps they would gleam like sudden brass stars in the attic night. And if you pulled up on the hasps, the trunk mouth gaped open and the odor of millennial moth-balls would spring outward into your nostrils. With it would come the odor that memory imparts to a room, an odor all its own.

Here, Mal was happiest.

Downstairs, where Uncle Walter sat a pallid thin old insect of an invalid, with his feet from day to day in boiling waters and ice waters, and his breath like old meat, it was not fun. Years had pushed Aunt Opie into an irrevocably stern mould; her whale-bone corset tightened in her shape, just as Uncle Walter had tightened in her life.

"Mal!"

Mal listened. He heard the washing-machine's ominous thunder still alive down below in the sunlit world, and if you listened closer, the hacking cough of Uncle Walter busy with his throat.

Inserting small hands into the clothes stacked inside one ancient trunk, Mal found, first of all, his baby clothes. Suits that he had once worn himself, before that part of him that was younger, smaller and uneducated, had died. For it was like dying, seeing these clothes—it seemed impossible he could ever have inhabited them. Now hc was eleven and could not hope to retrogress to those squalling days, and he was amazed that he had survived being so infinitesimal!

Discarding those, Mal next seized upon his brother's clothes. A fine grey little suit, with a grey cap that had fitted snugly to David's handsome head, he imagined. But now David could not use it; he was captured in wood, like a fly in amber, prisoned deep in Rose Lawn cemetery for the next thirty thousand years. On Memorial Day Mal would walk upon David's spot at that cemetery, give him a fistful of daisies and wait for David to say thank you.

Next, Dad's old walking cane. Inscriptions on it from some mystical lodge. Next to it an old rubber football nose-guard, Dad had worn over his face when he was in college.

"Dad, Dad, what were you like? What were you like?"

Dad was a picture in an oaken frame; a young, handsome man with twinkling eyes and a high clutching collar.

Mother wore her hair in a soft pompadour and showed her teeth which were small, feminine—like white kernels of close-set corn.

Just pictures. Clothes, jewelry, things collected in a misshapen attic.

Here a net blouse, time-yellowed, worn by Mother

perhaps to a card-party, or to play Mah-Jong, or to see John Barrymore in *Hamlet,* maybe.

"Mom, Mom!" he said. "Where are you? What were *you* like?"

Tears rolled in soft streaks down his face. His crying was mellowed by the very understanding garret, which had seen all things, even tears, shelved, forgotten, and gathering dust.

Mal was hungry.

Lunch time. The rollers of Uncle Walter's wheel-chair rolled soft rubber through the hall three stories below. Momentarily, the pound of the washing machine was snapped into silence.

Replacing the clothes, stacking the memories neatly back into place, hasping the trunk, wiping his eyes, Mal descended softly down stairs to acknowledge the threats and tongue-lashings that would accompany his lunch.

"Oh, *there* you, are, Malcolm!"

After lunch, when Uncle Walter had retreated to his room to snore away the hot afternoon, Mal helped snatch clothes from the line and put them before an iron in the kitchen that would hiss if you spit on it. Aunt Opie ironed all day, with his cooperation. Early evening he'd be allowed an hour's play with neighborhood kids "until it gets dark, then come straight home, and don't go near the river!"

Mal sat dangling his legs.

"Go and play!" snapped Aunt Opie, putting the iron

away at last. "Don't sit there, fiddling. You make me nervous. You're an awful waste of flesh, honestly!"

"Am I, Aunt Opie?"

"You are! Underfoot, underfoot!"

"Guess I'm not much use," he said, staring straight ahead, not moving. "Why are people born, anyway, Aunt Opie?"

"To keep undertakers busy. Now go and play."

"I'm too tired."

"Go up to bed, then."

"I'm too tired to go to bed."

"That's a silly thing to say."

The screen door slammed behind him.

"Don't slam the door, Mal!"

He walked slowly across the porch.

"And don't scuff your shoes. You'll wear down the heels!"

Snap.

The next instant he was upstairs. He didn't remember the moment when the decision had come like the sun falling in his lap. He didn't recall charging up to his room. He found himself now, crying without tears, assembling before himself on his bed all of his worldly accumulations.

Marbles, hankies, shirts, shoes, pencils, books, wires, slings, feathers, codes, stones, ribbons: all of it he pushed into huge brown paper sacks.

The sun was setting as he let himself out of his room. In a few minutes Aunt Opie'd blow her silver whistle—

the shiny one with the marble inside that fluttered like a captive bird when blown upon—and call his name.

"Mal!"

There. She was calling now.

"Mal!"

He climbed rickety stairs in almost total darkness to enter the thick hot and ancient, but friendly, smell of the attic.

"Mal!"

Aunt Opie's voice, so far away it was a dream. The other world, below, no longer existed. It was put away, buried under stout timbers.

Mal buried his clothes deep in the nearest trunk, deep down into the years, where all things that will never be used again are buried. His shirts by his father's and his brother's shirts, his small cap by David's cap, his shoes side by side with mother's silver dance slippers. His trinkets splashed down into the cache of all time's trinkets.

He carried Dad and Mom's pictures to a tiny hole in the dirty attic window where a light beam entered, so small it was almost like web spun from the machinery of a golden spider. The beam picked out one final smile from Mom, one last understanding twinkle of Dad's eyes.

The light beam vanished.

The smile and the twinkle hung in mid-air, in the dark, after-images in Mal's eyes.

"Mom! Dad, what were you like? Wouldn't you like to see how I turned out?" A long pause. "Huh?" A long pause. "Wouldn'tcha?" A long pause. "Mom." A long pause. "Dad?"

Something shifted in the dark.

"I wanna be here—with you," he said.

There was so much of them here. All their things. If he could put them together—may be he could make them whole again. Maybe they'd *live!*

It was true! Deep in these trunks every sweat droplet ever shed by Dad, every molecule of flesh that had ever slipped from his fingers, a cell of skin, a fragment of fingernail, was preserved! The coats contained the good animal sweat of Dad, expelled and absorbed, kept in summer and winter. All intact! The clothing *was* Dad! People are like reptiles, shedding skin. In small shards and bits. They'd be here, those unseeable bits! All in the trunks. Here and now! Dad! Here and now! Mom! David, too!

Mal put his hands on the trunk rims, excitedly. He'd stay here, forever, never go down stairs. He'd stay here, be one of *them,* waste away into vanishing, until he was no more than a picture stacked against the wall, a bundle of folded clothes, a scatter of odd toys.

This was only the start of adventure. Why, he hadn't really lived yet, at all. That'd come as each hour passed and he groped nearer toward the reality of Mom and Dad and David!

He trembled like a single candle-flame in a draft. He was almost extinguished by the violent storm inside himself.

Sorting out all Mom's things, he examined them. Thread by thread, button by button, caressing and kissing and understanding them. He put her picture amidst them. Her jewels, her bracelets, her imitation pearls, and a few dried compacts of musty cosmetics.

With her symbols, like a milk-pale young sorcerer, laying them in designs on the attic timbers, chanting on them in a childish piping, perhaps he could summon back one or all of those loved ones from their three coffin-like trunks! Each containing the accumulated symbols of three people whom he had never seen.

He threw wide all three trunks at once.

"Mal!"

Early morning. A week later. Maybe a month. Maybe even ten years, or fifteen.

"Mal!"

Aunt Opie shouted on the green lawn and blew the silvery whistle. Despairing, she thumped into the house, perhaps to pluck up the phone.

If she called the police, well, Mal didn't care. He sat up here, laughing while things evolved toward the final phase. Things were working right. He had no fears, nothing but a calm, certain assurance that everything would be fine.

Already, he was part of the discarded things. One of those useless objects, as Aunt Opie had labeled him, best thrown in the garret, framework for spiders to make tapestry on. He was fitting in, sinking through the dark, becoming a shadow, like Mom and Dad. Just a picture, just clothes, baubles and toy memory. It would take a little time, that was all.

He had not eaten. Hunger was not in him, nor room for hunger. It was simply enough to be up here. His face must be filthy black by now, his clothes in a horrible state, his body in a thinned, neglected condition. Just a bit longer . . . .

He watched the hours crawl by like bright animals.

He got more sensitive to the place. He heard things, moving. He smelled odors of—perfume? He—*saw* things. Now, at *last!* The fulfilment! Dad and Mom and David and he! One large, rollicking family!

From the odors, the flakes of skin, the perspirations and colognes imbedded in pyramids of clothing, from the photographs, from the furniture they had sat in, from books in yellow piles, now came Dad and Mom and David! To meet him, join hands, kiss him, welcome, hold him, laugh with him, dance and whirl in circles!

"Dad, Mom! I'm so glad to *see* you! To *really* see you! I knew if I kept trying, I'd do it! It's magic! Are you really here? Mom, Dad!"

They were there.

Mal felt tears of happiness warm on his face.

And then the darkness was split down the middle by a great knife of fresh day light.

Mal screamed.

The door leading up into the attic was thrown back. Coming up the daylight was the stern stiff figure of Aunt Opie!

"Mal! Mal, is that *you*? Mal? Are you up here?'

Again Mal screamed.

"Mom, Dad, wait! Don't go away! Mom, Dad, David!"

Daylight infested the attic. Mal rolled upon the floor in a tangled skein of clothes and baubles. Aunt Opie darted forward.

"Have you been up here for four days? Worrying us *that* long! Mercy God Almighty, Malcolm Briar, look at you! *Look* at you! LOOK AT YOU!"

She grabbed him, twisted him toward the door. Daylight stung his eyes. He stumbled.

"Walter!" cried Aunt Opie. "Come see where I found him!"

It was insane, the last of it all. No matter how Mal screamed, babbled, cried out, carried on, or tried to attack Aunt Opie, her mind was made up.

Spring cleaning.

The attic was emptied of all its dark treasure. The baubles were thrown heartlessly into the incinerator. The pictures were sold for their valuable frames.

But impossible of all impossibilities, was the washing machine churning, churning on the back porch. Inside the washing machine all the writhing clothes that had belonged to Mom, Dad and David! Churning, jumping, frothing, shuddering. Dad's shirts. Mom's blouses. David's play-suits!

All of the magic, the memory, the symbolism being washed, churned, beaten, soaked, twisted and laved out by the merciless metal plungers and the acid soap and the slushing water!

All of the perspiration of long ago, the sweet immortal perfume damned by lysol and water. All the tiny flakes of living and memory now cleansed, put asunder and drowned!

And the clothes, as they came, one by one from the machine, hung like empty corpses, no more to live, no more life to them, on the line beneath the blossoming apple trees, swaying in a slow, hot wind.

Mal collapsed, writhing in Aunt Opie's hard fingers. He screamed and screamed, crying out his heart and his lungs and weakly sobbing into an insane hysteria.

"Mom, Dad, David, don't go away! Don't, oh, don't!"

Sinking into a nauseated darkness, the last sound he heard was the merciless thrashing, plunging, gurgling of the washing machine, killing, stomping, pounding, *down and around and down . . . .* !

THE HANDLER

Mr. Benedict came out of his little house. He stood on the porch, painfully shy of the sun and inferior to people. A little dog trotted by with clever eyes; so clever that Mr. Benedict could not meet its gaze. A small child peered through the wrought iron gate around the graveyard, near the church, and Mr. Benedict winced at the pale penetrant curiosity of the child.

"You're the funeral man," said the child.

Cringing within himself, Mr. Benedict did not speak.

"You own the church?" asked the child, finally.

"Yes," said Mr. Benedict.

"And the funeral place?"

"Yes," said Mr. Benedict bewilderedly.

"And the yards and the stones and the graves?" wondered the child.

"Yes," said Mr. Benedict, with some show of pride.

And it was true. An amazing thing it was. A stroke of business luck really, that had kept him busy and humming nights over long years. First he had landed the church and the churchyard, with a few green-mossed tombs, when the Baptist people moved uptown. Then he had built himself a fine little mortuary, in Gothic style, of course, and covered it with ivy, and then added a small house for himself, way in back. It was very convenient to die for Mr. Benedict. He handled you in and out of buildings with a minimum of confusion and a maximum of synthetic benediction. No need of a funeral procession! declared his large ads in the morning paper. Out of the church and into the earth, slick as a whistle. Nothing but the finest preservatives used!

The child continued to stare at him and he felt like a candle blown out in the wind. He was so very inferior. Anything that lived or moved made him feel apologetic and melancholy. He was continually agreeing with people, never daring to argue or shout or say no. Whoever you might be, if Mr. Benedict met you on the street he would look up your nostrils or perceive your ears or examine your hairline with his little shy, wild eyes and never look you straight in your eyes and he would hold your hand between his cold ones as if your hand was a precious gift as he said to you:

"You are definitely, irrevocably, believably correct."

But, always, when you talked to him, you felt he never heard a word you said.

Now, he stood on his porch and said, "You are a sweet

little child," to the little staring child, in fear that the child might not like him.

Mr. Benedict walked down the steps and out the gate, without once looking at his little mortuary building. He saved that pleasure for later. It was very important that things took the right precedence. It wouldn't pay to think with joy of the bodies awaiting his talents in the mortuary building. No, it was better to follow his usual day after day routine. He would let the conflict begin.

He knew just where to go to get himself enraged. Half of the day he spent traveling from place to place in the little town, letting the superiority of the living neighbors overwhelm him, letting his own inferiority dissolve him, bathe him in perspiration, tie his heart and brain into trembling knots.

He spoke with Mr. Rodgers, the druggist, idle, senseless morning talk. And he saved and put away all the little slurs and intonations and insults that Mr. Rodgers sent his way. Mr. Rodgers always had some terrible thing to say about a man in the funeral profession. "Ha, ha," laughed Mr. Benedict at the latest joke upon himself, and he wanted to cry with miserable violence. "There you are, you cold one," said Mr. Rodgers on this particular morning. "Cold one," said Mr. Benedict. "Ha, ha!"

Outside the drug-store, Mr. Benedict met up with Mr. Stuyvesant, the contractor. Mr. Stuyvesant looked at his watch to estimate just how much time he dared waste on Benedict before trumping up some appointment. "Oh, hello, Benedict," shouted Stuyvesant. "How's business?

I bet you're going at it tooth and nail. Did you get it? I said, I bet you're going at it tooth and—" "Yes, yes," chuckled Mr. Benedict vaguely. "And how is your business, Mr. Stuyvesant?" "Say, how do your hands get so cold, Benny old man? That's a cold shake you got there. You just get done embalming a frigid woman? Hey, that's not bad. You heard what I said?" roared Mr. Stuyvesant, pounding him on the back. "Good, good!" cried Mr. Benedict, with a fleshless smile. "Good day."

On it went, person after person. Mr. Benedict, pummeled on from one to the next, was the lake into which all refuse was thrown. People began with little pebbles and then when Mr. Benedict did not ripple or protest, they heaved a stone, a brick, a boulder. There was no bottom to Mr. Benedict, no splash and no settling. The lake did not answer.

As the day passed he became more helpless and enraged with them, and he walked from building to building and had more little meetings and conversations and hated himself with a very real, masochistic pleasure. But the thing that kept him going most of all was the thought of the night pleasures to come. So he inflicted himself again and again with these stupid, pompous bullies and bowed to them and held his hands like little biscuits before his stomach, and asked no more than to be sneered at.

"There you are, meat-chopper," said Mr. Flinger, the delicatessen man. "How are all your corned beeves and pickled brains?"

Things worked to a crescendo of inferiority. With a final kettle-drumming of insult and terrible self-effacement, Mr. Benedict, seeking wildly the correct time from his wrist watch, turned and ran back through the town. He was at his peak, he was all ready now, ready to work, ready to do what must be done, and enjoy himself. The awful part of the day was over, the good part was now to begin! He ran eagerly up the steps to his mortuary.

The room waited like a fall of snow. There were white hummocks and pale delineations of things recumbent under sheets in the dimness.

The door burst open.

Mr. Benedict, framed in a flow of light, stood in the door, head back, one hand upraised in dramatic salute, the other hand upon the doorknob in unnatural rigidity.

He was the puppet-master come home.

He stood a long minute in the very center of his theatre. In his head applause, perhaps, thundered. He did not move, but lowered his head in abject appreciation of this kind kind applauding audience.

He carefully removed his coat, hung it up, got himself into a fresh white smock, buttoned the cuffs with professional crispness, then washed his hands together as he looked around at his very good friends.

It had been a fine week; there were any number of family relics lying under the sheets, and as Mr. Benedict stood before them he felt himself grow and grow and tower and stretch over them.

"Like Alice!" he cried to himself in surprise. "Taller,

taller. Curiouser and curiouser!" He flexed his hands straight out and up.

He had never gotten over his initial incredulity when in the room with the dead. He was both delighted and bewildered to discover that here he was master of peoples, here he might do what he wished with men, and they must, by necessity, be polite and cooperative with him. They could not run away. And now, as on other days, he felt himself released and resilient, growing, growing like Alice. "Oh, so tall, oh, so tall, so very tall . . . until my head . . . bumps . . . the ceiling."

He walked about among the sheeted people. He felt the same he did when coming from a picture show late at night, very strong, very alert, very certain of himself. He felt that everyone was watching him as he left a picture show, and that he was very handsome and very correct and brave and all the things that the picture hero was, his voice oh, so resonant, persuasive, and he had the right lilt to his left eyebrow and the right tap with his cane—and sometimes this movie-induced hypnosis lasted all the way home and persisted into sleep. Those were the only two times in his living he felt miraculous and fine, at the picture show, or here—in his own little theatre of the cold.

He walked along the sleeping rows, noting each name on its white card.

"Mrs. Walters. Mr. Smith. Miss Brown. Mr. Andrews. Ah, good afternoon, one and all!"

"How are you today, Mrs. Shellmund?" he wanted to

know, lifting a sheet as if looking for a child under a bed. "You're looking splendid, dear lady."

Mrs. Shellmund had never spoken to him in her life; she'd always gone by like a large white statue with roller skates hidden under her skirts, which gave her an elegant gliding, imperturbable rush.

"My dear Mrs. Shellmund," he said, pulling up a chair and regarding her through a magnifying glass. "Do you realize, my lady, that you have a sebaceous condition of the pores? You were quite waxen in life. Pore trouble. Oil and grease and pimples. A rich rich diet, Mrs. Shellmund, there was your trouble. Too many frosties and spongie cakes and cream candies. You always prided yourself on your brain, Mrs. Shellmund, and thought I was like a dime under your toe, or a penny, really. But you kept that wonderful priceless brain of yours afloat in parfaits and fizzes and limeades and sodas and were so very superior to me that now, Mrs. Shellmund, here is what shall happen . . . ."

He did a neat operation on her. Cutting the scalp in a circle, he lifted it off, then lifted out the brain. Then he prepared a cake-confectioner's little sugar-bellows and squirted her empty head full of little whipped cream and crystal ribbons, stars and frollops, in pink, white and green, and on top he printed in a fine pink scroll SWEET DREAMS and put the skull back on and sewed it in place and hid the marks with wax and powder. "So there," he said, finished.

He walked on to the next table.

"Good afternoon, Mr. Wren. Good afternoon. And how is the master of the racial hatreds today, Mr. Wren? Pure, white, laundered Mr. Wren. Clean as snow, white as linen, Mr. Wren, you are. The man who hated Jews and Negroes. Minorities, Mr. Wren, minorities." He pulled back the sheet. Mr. Wren stared up with glassy cold eyes. "Mr. Wren, look upon a member of a minority. Myself. The minority of inferiors, those who speak not above a whisper, those afraid of talking aloud, those frightened little nonentities, mice. Do you know what I am going to do with you, Mr. Wren? First, let us draw your blood from you, intolerant friend." The blood was drawn off. "Now—the injection of, you might say, embalming fluid."

Mr. Wren, snow-white, linen-pure, lay with the fluid going in him.

Mr. Benedict laughed.

Mr. Wren turned black; black as dirt, black as night. The embalming fluid was—ink.

"And hello to *you*, Edmund Worth!"

What a handsome body Worth had. Powerful, with muscles pinned from huge bone to huge bone, and a chest like a boulder. Women had grown speechless when he walked by, men had stared with envy and hoped they might borrow that body some night and ride home in it to the wife and give her a nice surprise. But Worth's body had always been his own, and he had applied it to those tasks and pleasures which made him a conversational topic among all people who enjoyed sin.

"And now, here you are," said Mr. Benedict, looking down at the fine body with pleasure. For a moment he was lost in memory of his own body in his own past.

He had once tried strangling himself with one of those apparati you nail in a doorway and chuck under your jawbone and pull yourself up on, hoping to add an inch to his ridiculously short frame. To counteract his deadly pale skin he had lain in the sun, but he boiled and his skin fell off in pink leaflets, leaving only more pink, moist, sensitive skin. And what could he do about the eyes from which his mind peered, those close-set, glassy little eyes and the tiny wounded mouth? You can repaint houses, burn trash, move from the slum, shoot your mother, buy new clothes, get a car, make money, change all those outer environmentals for something new. But what's the brain to do when caught like cheese in the throat of a mouse? His own environment thus betrayed him; his own skin, body, color, voice gave him no chance to extend out into that vast bright world where people tickled ladies' chins and kissed their mouths and shook hands with friends and traded aromatic cigars.

Thinking in this fashion, Mr. Benedict stood over the magnificent body of Edmund Worth.

He severed Worth's head, put it in a coffin on a small satin pillow, facing up, then he placed one hundred ninety pounds of bricks in the coffin and arranged some pillows inside a black coat and a white shirt and tie to look like the upper body, and covered the whole with a blanket of blue velvet, up to the chin. It was a fine illusion.

The body itself he placed in a refrigerating vault.

"When I die, I shall leave specific orders, Mr. Worth, that my head be severed and buried, joined to your body. By that time I will have acquired an assistant willing to perform such a rascally act, for money. If one cannot have a body worthy of love in life, one can at least gain such a body in death. Thank you."

He slammed the lid on Edmund Worth.

Since it was a growing and popular habit in the town for people to be buried with the coffin lids closed over them during the service, this gave Mr. Benedict great opportunities to vent his repressions on his hapless guests. Some he locked in their boxes upside down, some face down, or making obscene gestures. He had the most utterly wondrous fun with a group of old maiden ladies who were mashed in an auto on their way to an afternoon tea. They were famous gossips, always with heads together over some choice bit. What the onlookers at the triple funeral did not know (all three casket lids were shut) was that, as in life, all three were crowded into one casket, heads together in eternal, cold, petrified gossip. The other two caskets were filled with pebbles and shells and ravels of gingham. It was a nice service. Everybody cried. "Those three inseparables, at last separated," everybody sobbed.

"Yes," said Mr. Benedict, having to hide his face in his grief.

Not lacking for a sense of justice, Mr. Benedict buried one rich man stark naked. A poor man he buried wound in gold cloth, with five dollar gold pieces for buttons and twenty dollar coins on each eyelid. A lawyer he did not bury at all, but burnt him in the incinerator—his coffin contained nothing but a pole-cat, trapped in the woods one Sunday.

An old maid, at her service one afternoon, was the victim of a terrible device. Under the silken comforter, parts of an old man had been buried with her. There she lay, insulted by cold organs, being made cold love to by hidden hands, hidden and planted other things. The shock showed on her face, somewhat.

So Mr. Benedict moved from body to body in his mortuary that afternoon, talking to all the sheeted figures, telling them his every secret. The final body for the day was the body of one Merriwell Blythe, an ancient man afflicted with spells and comas. Mr. Blythe had been brought in for dead several times, but each time had revived in time to prevent premature burial.

Mr. Benedict pulled back the sheet from Mr. Blythe's face.

Mr. Merriwell Blythe fluttered his eyes.

"Ah!" and Mr. Benedict let fall the sheet.

"You!" screamed the voice under the sheet.

Mr. Benedict fell against the slab, suddenly shaken and sick.

"Get me up from here!" cried the voice of Mr. Merriwell Blythe.

"You're alive!" said Mr. Benedict, jerking aside the sheet.

"Oh, the thing's I've heard, the things I've listened to the last hour!" wailed the old man on the slab, rolling his eyes about in his head in white orbits. "Lying here, not able to move, and hearing you talk the things you talk! Oh, you dark dark thing, you awful thing, you fiend, you monster, get me up from here. I'll tell the mayor and the council and everyone, oh, you dark dark thing! You defiler and sadist, you perverted scoundrel, you terrible man, wait'll I tell, I tell on you!" shrieked the old man, frothing. "Get me up from here!" "No!" said Mr. Benedict, falling to his knees. "Oh, you terrible man!" sobbed Mr. Merriwell Blythe. "To think this has gone on in our town all these years and we never knew the things you did to people! Oh, you monstrous monster!" "No," whispered Mr. Benedict, trying to get up, falling down, palsied and in terror. "The things you *said,*" accused the old man in dry contempt. "The things you do!" "Sorry," whispered Mr. Benedict.

The old man tried to rise. "Don't!" said Mr. Benedict, and held onto him. "Let go of me!" said the old man. "No," said Mr. Benedict. He reached for a hypodermic and stabbed the old man in the arm with it. "You!" cried the old man, wildly, to all the sheeted figures. "Help me!" He squinted blindly at the window, at the churchyard below with the leaning stones. "You, out there, too, under the stones, help! Listen!" The old man fell back, whistling and frothing. He knew he was dying. "All, listen," he babbled. "He's done this to me, and you, and you, all of you, he's done too much, too long. Don't take it! Don't, don't let him do any more to anyone!" The old man licked away the stuff from his lips, growing weaker. "Do something to him!"

Mr. Benedict stood there, shocked, and said, "They can't do anything to me. They can't. I say they can't."

"Out of your graves!" wheezed the old man. "Help me! Tonight, or tomorrow or soon, but jump up and fix him, oh, this horrible man!" And he wept many tears.

"How foolish," said Mr. Benedict numbly. "You're dying and foolish." Mr. Benedict could not move his lips. His eyes were wide. "Go on and die, now, quickly."

"Everybody up!" shouted the old man. "Everybody out! Help!"

"Please don't talk anymore," said Mr. Benedict. "I really don't like to listen."

The room was suddenly very dark. It was night. It was getting late. The old man raved on and on, getting weaker. Finally, smiling, he said, "They've taken a lot from you, horrible man. Tonight, they'll do something."

The old man died.

People say there was an explosion that night in the graveyard. Or rather, a series of explosions, a smell of strange things, a movement, a violence, a raving. There was much light and lightning, and a kind of rain, and the church bells hammered and slung about in the belfry, and stones toppled, and thing swore oaths, and things flew through the air, and there was a chasing and a screaming, and many shadows and all the lights in the mortuary blazing on, and things moving inside and outside in swift jerks and shamblings, windows broke, doors were torn from hinges, leaves from trees, iron gates clattered, and in the end there was a picture of Mr. Benedict running about, running about, vanishing, the lights out, suddenly, and a tortured scream that could only be from Mr. Benedict himself.

After that—nothing. Quiet.

The town people entered the mortuary the next morning. They searched the mortuary building and the church, and then they went out into the graveyard.

And they found nothing but blood, a vast quantity of blood, sprinkled and thrown and spread everywhere you could possibly look, as if the heavens had bled profusely in the night.

But not a sign of Mr. Benedict.

"Where could he be?" everybody wondered.

"How should *we* know?" everybody replied, confounded.

And then they had the answer.

Walking through the graveyard they stood in deep tree shadows where the stones, row on row, were old and time-erased and leaning. No birds sang in the trees. The sunlight which finally managed to pierce the thick leaves, was like a light bulb illumination, weak, frail, unbelievable, theatrical, thin.

They stopped by one tombstone. "Here, now!" they exclaimed.

Others paused and bent over the greyish, moss-flecked stone, and cried out.

Freshly scratched, as if by feebly, frantic, hasty fingers (in fact, as if scratched by fingernails, the writing was that new) was the name: MR. BENEDICT.

"Look over here!" someone else cried. Everybody turned. "This one, this stone, and this one, and this one, too!" cried the villager, pointing to five other gravestones.

Everybody hurried around, looking and recoiling.

Upon each and every stone, scratched by fingernail scratchings, the same message appeared:

MR. BENEDICT—

The town people were stunned.

"But that's impossible," objected one of them, faintly. "He *couldn't* be buried under *all* these gravestones!"

They stood there for one long moment. Instinctively they all looked at one another nervously in the silence and the tree darkness. They all waited for an answer. With fumbling, senseless lips, one of them replied, simply:

"*Couldn't* he?"

THE COFFIN

There was any amount of banging and hammering for a number of days; deliveries of metal parts and oddments which Mr. Charles Braling took into his little workshop with a feverish anxiety. He was a dying man; a badly dying man and he seemed to be in a great hurry, between racking coughs and spittlings, to piece together one last invention.

"What are you doing?" inquired his younger brother, Richard Braling. He had listened with increasing difficulty and much curiosity for a number of days to that banging and rattling about, and now he stuck his head through the work-room door.

"Go far far away and let me alone," said Charles Braling, who was seventy, trembly and wet-lipped most of the time. He trembled nails into place and trembled a hammer down with a weak blow upon a large timber and then struck a small metal ribbon down into an intricate machine, and, all in all, was having a carnival of labor.

Richard looked on, bitter-eyed, for a long moment. There was a hatred between them. It had gone on for some years and now was neither any better or any worse for the fact that Charlie was dying. Richard was delighted to know of the impending death, if he thought of it at all. But all this busy fervor of his old brother's stimulated him.

"Pray tell," he said, not moving from the door.

"If you must know," snarled old Charles, fitting in an odd thingumabob on the box before him. "I'll be dead in another week and I'm—I'm building my own coffin!"

"A coffin, my dear Charlie. That doesn't *look* like a coffin. A coffin isn't that complex. Come on now, what are you up to?"

"I tell you it's a coffin! An odd coffin, yes, but nevertheless," the old man shivered his fingers around in the large box, "—nevertheless a coffin!"

"But it would be easier to buy one."

"Not one like this! You couldn't buy one like this any place, ever. Oh, it'll be a real fine coffin, all right."

"You're obviously lying." Richard moved forward. "Why, that coffin is a good twelve feet long. Six feet longer than normal size!"

"Oh, yes?" The old man laughed quietly.

"And that transparent top; who ever heard of a coffin lid you can see through? What good is a transparent lid to a corpse?"

"Oh, just never you mind at all," sang the old man heartily. "La!" And he went humming and hammering about the shop.

"This coffin is terribly thick," shouted the young brother over the din. "Why, it must be five feet thick; how utterly unnecessary!"

"I only wish I might live to patent this amazing coffin," said old Charlie. "It would be a god-send to all the poor peoples of the world. Think how it would eliminate the expenses of most funerals. Oh, but, of course, you don't know how it would do that, do you? How silly of me. Well, I shan't tell you. If this coffin could be mass-produced—expensive at first, naturally—but then when you finally got them made in vast quantities, gah, but the money people would save."

"To hell with you!" And the younger brother stormed out of the shop.

It had been an unpleasant life. Young Richard had always been such a bounder he never had two coins to clink together at one time; all of his money had come from old brother Charlie, who had the indecency to remind him of it at all times. Richard spent many hours with his hobbies; he dearly loved piling up bottles with French wine labels, in the garden. "I like the way they glint," he often said, sitting and sipping, sipping and sitting. He was the only man in the county who could hold the longest grey ash on a fifty cent cigar for the longest recorded time. And he knew how to hold his hands so his diamonds jangled in the light. But he had not bought the wine, the diamonds, the cigars—no! They were all gifts. He was never allowed to buy anything himself. It was always brought to him and given to him. He had to ask for everything, even writing paper. He considered himself quite a martyr to have put up with taking things from that rickety old brother for so long a time. Everything Charlie ever laid his hand to turned to money; everything Richard had ever tried in the way of a leisurely career had failed.

And now, here was this old mole of a Charlie whacking out a new invention which would probably bring Charlie additional specie long after his bones were slotted in the earth!

Well, two weeks passed.

One morning the old brother toddled upstairs and stole the insides out of the electric phonograph. Another morning he raided the gardener's greenhouse. Still another time he received a delivery from a medical company. It was all young Richard could do to sit and hold his long grey cigar ash steady while these murmuring excursions took place.

"I'm finished!" cried old Charlie on the fourteenth morning, and dropped dead.

Richard finished out his cigar, and, without showing his inner excitement, he laid down his cigar with its fine long whitish ash, two inches long, a real record, and arose.

He walked to the window and watched the sunlight playfully glittering among the fat beetle-like champagne bottles in the garden.

He looked toward the top of the stairs where old dear brother Charlie lay peacefully sprawled against the banister. Then he walked to the phone and perfunctorily dialed a number.

"Hello, Green Lawn Mortuary? This is the Braling residence. Will you send around a wicker, please? Yes. For Brother Charlie. Yes. Thank you. Thank you."

As the mortuary people were taking brother Charles out in their wicker they received instructions. "Ordinary casket," said young Richard. "No funeral service. Put him in a pine coffin. He would have preferred it that way—simple. Good bye."

"Now!" said Richard, rubbing his hands together. "We shall see about this 'coffin' built by dear Charlie. I do not suppose he will realize he is not being buried in his 'special' box. Ah."

He entered the downstairs shop.

The coffin sat before some wide-flung French windows, the lid shut, complete and neat, all put together like the fine innards of a Swiss watch. It was vast, and it rested upon a long long table with rollers beneath for easy maneuvering.

The coffin interior, as he peered through the glass lid, was six feet long. There must be a good three feet of false body at both head and foot of the coffin, then. Three feet at each end which, covered by secret panels that he must find some way of opening, might very well reveal—exactly what?

Money, of course. It would be just like Charlie to suck

his riches into his grave with himself, leaving Richard with not a cent to buy a bottle with. The old bastard!

He raised the glass lid and felt about, but found no hidden buttons. There was a small sign studiously inked on white paper, thumbtacked to the side of the satin lined box. It said:

THE BRALING ECONOMY CASKET. Copyright, April, 1946.

Simple to operate. Can be used again and again by morticians and families with an eye to the future.

Richard snorted thinly. Who did Charlie think he was fooling?

There was more writing:

DIRECTIONS: SIMPLY PLACE BODY IN COFFIN.

What a fool thing to say. Put body in coffin! Naturally! How else would one go about it? He peered intently and finished out the directions:

SIMPLY PLACE BODY IN COFFIN—AND MUSIC WILL START.

"It can't be—" Richard gaped at the sign. "Don't tell me all this work has been for a—" He went to the open door of the shop, walked out upon the tiled terrace and called to the gardener in his green-house. "Rogers!" The gardener stuck his head out. "What time is it?" asked Richard. "Twelve o'clock, sir," replied Rogers. "Well, at twelve fifteen, you come up here and check to see if everything is all right, Rogers," said Richard. "Yes, sir," said the gardener. Richard turned and went back into the shop. "We'll find out—" he said, quietly.

There would be no harm in lying in the box, testing it. He noticed small ventilating holes in the sides. Even if the lid were closed down there'd be air. And Rogers would be up in a moment or two. SIMPLY PLACE BODY IN COFFIN—AND MUSIC WILL START. Really, how naive of old Charlie! Richard hoisted himself up.

He was like a man getting into a bath-tub. He felt naked and watched over. He put one shiny shoe into the coffin and crooked his knee and eased himself up and made some little remark to nobody in particular, then he put in his other knee and foot and crouched there, as if undecided about the temperature of the bath-water. Edging himself about, chuckling softly, he lay down, pretending to himself (for it was fun pretending) that he was dead, that people were dropping tears on him, that candles were fuming and illuminating and that the world was stopped in mid-stride because of his passing. He put on a long pale expression, shut his eyes, holding back the laughter in himself behind pressed, quivering lips. He folded his hands and decided they felt waxen and cold.

Whirr. Spung! Something whispered inside the box-wall. *Spung!*

The lid slammed down on him!

From outside, if one had just come into the room, one would have imagined a wild man was kicking, pounding, blathering, and shrieking inside a closet! There was a sound of a body dancing and cavorting. There was a thudding of flesh and fists. There was a squeaking and a kind of wind from a frightened man's lungs. There was a rustling like paper and a shrilling as of many pipes simultaneously played. Then there was a real fine scream. Then—silence.

Richard Braling lay in the coffin and relaxed. He let loose all his muscles. He began to chuckle. The smell of the box was not unpleasant. Through the little perforations he drew more than enough air to live on, comfortably. He need only push gently up with his hands, with none of this kicking and screaming and the lid would open. One must be calm. He flexed his arms.

The lid was locked.

Well, still there was no danger. Rogers would be up in a minute or two. There was nothing to fear.

The music began to play.

It seemed to come from somewhere inside the head of the coffin. It was green music. Organ music, very slow and melancholy, typical of Gothic arches and long black tapers. It smelled of earth and whispers. It echoed high between stone walls. It was so sad that one almost cried listening to it. It was music of potted plants and crimson and blue stained glass windows. It was late sun at twilight and a cold wind blowing. It was a dawn with only fog and a far away fog-horn moaning.

"Charlie, Charlie, Charlie, you old fool you! So this is your odd coffin!" Tears of laughter welled into Richard's eyes. "Nothing more than a coffin which plays its own dirge. Oh, my sainted Grandma!"

He lay and listened critically, for it was beautiful music and there was nothing he could do until Rogers came up and let him out. His eyes roved aimlessly, his fingers tapped soft little rhythms on the satin cushions. He crossed his legs idly. Through the glass lid he saw sunlight shooting through the French windows, dust particles dancing on it. It was a lovely blue day.

The sermon began.

The organ music quieted and a gentle voice said:

"We are gathered together, those who loved and those who knew the deceased, to give him our homage and our due—"

"Charlie, bless you, that's *your* voice!" Richard was delighted. "A mechanical funeral, by God. Organ music and lecture. And Charlie giving his own oration for himself!"

The soft voice said, "We who knew and loved him are grieved at the passing of—"

"What was *that*?" Richard raised himself, startled. He didn't quite believe what he had heard. He repeated it to himself just the way he had heard it:

"We who knew and loved him are grieved at the passing of Richard Braling."

That's what the voice had said.

"Richard Braling," said the man in the coffin. "Why, *I'm* Richard Braling."

A slip of the tongue, naturally. Merely a slip. Charlie had meant to say "Charles" Braling. Certainly. Yes. Of course. Yes. Certainly. Yes. Naturally. Yes.

"Richard was a fine man," said the voice, talking on. "We shall see no finer in our time."

"My name again!"

Richard began to move about uneasily in the coffin. Why didn't Rogers come?

It was hardly a mistake, using that name twice. Richard Braling. Richard Braling. We are gathered here. We shall miss— We are grieved. No finer man. No finer in our time. We are gathered here. The deceased. Richard Braling. *Richard* Braling.

Whirrrr. Spung!

Flowers! Six dozen bright blue, red, yellow, sun-brilliant flowers leaped up from behind the coffin on concealed springs!

The sweet odor of fresh cut flowers filled the coffin. The flowers swayed gently before his amazed vision, tapping silently on the glass lid. Others sprang up until the coffin was banked with petals and color and sweet odors. Gardenias and dahlias and daffodils, trembling and shining.

"Rogers!"

The sermon continued.

"—Richard Braling, in his life, was a connoisseur of great and good things—"

The music sighed, rose and fell, distantly.

"Richard Braling savored of life, as one savors of a rare wine, holding it upon the lips—"

A small panel in the side of the box flipped open. A swift bright metal arm snatched out. A needle stabbed Richard in the thorax, not very deeply. He screamed. The needle shot him full of a colored liquor before he could seize it. Then it popped back into a receptacle and the panel snapped shut.

"Rogers!"

A growing numbness. Suddenly he could not move his fingers or his arms or turn his head. His legs were cold and limp.

"Richard Braling loved beautiful things. Music. Flowers," said the voice.

"Rogers!"

This time he did not scream it. He could only think it. His tongue was motionless in his anaesthetized mouth.

Another panel opened. Metal forceps issued forth on steel arms. His left wrist was pierced by a huge sucking needle.

His blood was being drained from his body.

He heard a little pump working somewhere.

"—Richard Braling will be missed among us—"

The organ sobbed and murmured.

The flowers looked down upon him, nodding their bright-petalled heads.

Six candles, black and slender, rose up out of hidden receptacles, and stood behind the flowers, flickering and glowing.

Another pump started to work. While his blood drained out one side of his body, his right wrist was punctured, held, a needle shoved into it, and the second pump began to force formaldehyde into him.

Pump, pause, *pump*, pause, *pump*, pause, *pump*, pause.

The coffin moved.

A small motor popped and chugged. The room drifted by on either side of him. Little wheels revolved. No pallbearers were necessary. The flowers swayed as the casket moved gently out upon the terrace under a blue clear sky.

Pump, pause. *Pump,* pause.

"Richard Braling will be missed—"

Sweet soft music.

Pump, pause.

"Ah, sweet mystery of life, at last—" Singing.

"Braling, the gourmet—"

"Ah, at last I have the secret of it all—"

Staring, staring, his eyes egg-blind, at the little card out of the corners of his eyes: *The Braling Economy Casket* . . . .

DIRECTIONS: SIMPLY PLACE BODY IN COFFIN—AND MUSIC WLL START.

A tree swung by overhead. The coffin rolled gently through the garden, behind some bushes, carrying the voice and the music with it.

"Now it is the time when we must consign this part of this man to the earth—"

Little shining spades leaped out of the sides of the casket.

They began to dig.

He saw the spades toss up dirt. The coffin settled. Bumped, settled, dug, bumped and settled, dug, bumped and settled again.

Pulse, pause, *pulse,* pause. *Pump,* pause, *pulse, pump,* pause.

"Ashes to ashes, dust to dust—"

The flowers shook and jolted. The box was deep. The music played.

The last thing Richard Braling saw was the spading arms of the Braling Economy Casket reaching up and pulling the hole in after it.

"Richard Braling, Richard Braling, Richard Braling, Richard Braling, Richard Braling . . . ."

The record was stuck.

Nobody minded. Nobody was listening.

INTERIM

The rustle went through the land from one end to the other; and the land was not very large—being bounded on the east and west by poplars, sycamores and great oaks and shrubs, and held on north and south by wrought iron and mortared brick. From one end of this land to the other, shortly before dawn, the rustling traveled. One bird, about to sing, silenced itself, and there was a kind of dim pulsing and a whispering under the earth.

The coffins, each a womb for silent, stiffened contents, each deep, each separate, were being slowly and certainly beat upon. The lids and sides of the deep boxes gave off slow, even, muffled beats. The earth bore each sound on and on. It started at one dark box and the code beat and beat, passing on to the next box where a new, tired dry hand would repeat the message slowly and tiredly.

So it went, until the deep-buried ones all heard and slowly began to understand.

After a time it was like a great heart beating under the earth. The systolic murmuring continued as the sun readied itself beyond the horizon. The bird upon the tree crooked its bead-eyed head, waiting. The heart beat on.

"Mrs. Lattimore."

Slowly and painfully the beating spelled out the name.

(She was the one buried up on the north end, under the moss-tree, a year ago, just before the planned birth of her child, remember her? *so* pretty, she was!)

"Mrs. Lattimore."

The heart-beat pounded, dim and far under the compressed sod.

"Have," asked the heart-beat sluggishly. "You," asked the heart-beat tiredly. "Heard," it asked. "What," it asked. "Is happening," it continued. "To her?" it concluded.

The heart-beat paused dramatically. And the thousand cold contents of a thousand deep boxes waited for the answer to the slow, slow, beating question.

The sun hung just beyond the far blue hills. The stars shone coldly.

Then, evenly, quietly, slowly, beat after beat, systolic thudding upon thudding, the answer to the question sounded. The land trembled with it, and repeated it, again and again, pounding and pounding away into a shocked and buried silence.

"Mrs. Lattimore."

The pulsing deep under.

"Will have."

Slowly, slowly.

"Her child today."

And then a quick, amazing staccato, as of a thousand hands battering the lids in questioning hysteria:

"What'll it possibly be like? How can this thing be? What will it resemble? Why? Why? Why!"

The pounding faded. The sun rose.

Deep under, as the bird sang, deep under the stone where Mrs. Lattimore's name appeared, there was a scrabbling and a twisting and a strange sound from her buried, earth-moist box.

JACK-IN-THE-BOX

Let us imagine a Jack-in-the-box, stuffed, compressed in upon its coiled body, its head hard against a locked lid. Oh, how the springs ache to relax, to fling the Jack out of the box, bang! but no, all is tension and imprisonment. The lid stays locked thirteen years on the little trapped animal. The animal within does not know of the World, but senses it is there; not with eye, or ear, or flesh, nor by nostril, but by a sense that grew simply because the little animal has been jailed so long. Anyway, here is the boxed Jack, coiled and tightened and neurotic, head crushed to locked lid, waiting and waiting and waiting to be shot out, as from a cannon.

Edwin stood looking out the window. He could not see beyond the trees. The trees surrounded the house and the house surrounded Edwin. If he tried to find another

World beyond, why the trees grew thicker in an instant, almost, to still this odd and silly notion of his.

Edwin stared out the window this way each morning.

Behind him, he heard Mother's waiting, nervous breath as she drank her breakfast coffee. She rang the emptied cup with her spoon. "Edwin, stop staring. Come eat!"

"No," he said, not knowing why.

There was a stiffened rustle. Mother turned to him as if she'd been slapped. "What do you *mean?* Breakfast's ready, isn't it? Or is the window better?"

"It's better, it's better," he said. He pressed the window with his nose, eyes feverish for some life, *out there*. For thirteen years he had looked for life beyond the trees, seen none. He'd heard only vague noises. "It's *better,*" he whispered, once again.

But finally he turned and went to eat the tasteless apricots and toast. He and Mother, alone, just like five thousand other mornings. Thirteen years of breakfasts and no movement beyond the trees and a growing curiosity.

The two of them ate silently.

She was the pale woman you saw in old houses in third floor cupola windows, each morning at nine, each afternoon at one and four, each evening at eight, and, also, if you happened to be passing at three in the morning, these she would be, in her window, silent and white, high and alone and quiet. It was like passing a deserted greenhouse in which one last wild white blossom lifted its head to the moonlight.

And her child, Edwin, was the thistle you unpodded with a breath of your mouth in thistle-time. His hair was silken and his eyes were of a constant blue and feverish temperature. He had a haunted look. He looked as if he slept poorly. He might fly all apart like a packet of ladyfinger firecrackers if you said the right word.

So here they were at breakfast. He with his fever in him, she with hers forever dead in her, save for occasional sparkles.

Now she began to talk, slowly at first, then very rapidly and angrily, almost spitting at him. "Why must you disobey every morning?" She cried at him. "I don't want you staring out, I don't want it, do you hear? What do you want? Do you want to see Them?" she cried, her fingers twitching. She was blazingly lovely, like an angry white flower. "Do you want to see the Beasts that run down paths and crush people like strawberries! Is *that* it?"

Yes, he thought, I'd like to see the Beasts, horrible as they are.

He said nothing.

"Do you want to go *out there?*" she asked, sharply. "Do you want to go out there like your Father did before you were born and be killed, be run down by one of those terrible Beasts on the road, is *that* what you want! *Answer* me!"

He looked at the floor. "No, Ma'm."

"Isn't it enough your Father died that way? Isn't it enough that They killed him? Why should you want to have anything to do with those terrible Things? How many times must I tell you?" She motioned toward the door. "Of course, if you really *want* to die—go ahead. *Be* killed."

She quieted at last, but her fingers kept flexing. "Your Father built this World, every part of it. It was good enough for him and it should be enough for you. There's nothing beyond those trees but death and I won't have you poking your nose out. This *is* the World, remember. There's no other worth bothering with!"

He nodded miserably.

"Don't do it again," she said. She ate for a few seconds and then looked up. "You're forgiven. It's silly to think there could possibly be anything worth seeing beyond the trees. Smile now, and finish your toast."

He ate softly, with the window reflected where he could stare secretly at it, upon his spoon. After a long time he glanced up.

"Mom?" he asked, carefully.

"Yes?" She was wary.

"What's—?" He couldn't say it. He swallowed. "What's—dying? You talk about it all the time. Is it a—*feeling*?"

"To those who have to live on after someone else, a very *bad* feeling, yes." She stood up, warningly. "Stop chattering; you'll be late for school. Run!"

He kissed her as he ran by with his books. "Bye!"

"Say hello to Teacher for me!" she cried after him.

*

He fled from her like a bullet from a gun. Up endless staircases. Along passages and through halls, past windows that cascaded down dark gallery walls like waterfalls. Up and up through the layer cake of the World, with the thick frosting of Oriental rugs between and the bright candles on top.

From one high staircase he looked down through four intervals of World.

The Lowlands of kitchen, dining room, living room. The two Middle Lands of music, play, pictures, and locked, forbidden rooms. And then, *here*—he turned and stared about—the Highlands of adventure, picnic, school. Here he roamed, skipped, sang lonely child songs on the long brisk journey to his Teacher.

This was the World. Father (or God, as Mother often called him) had raised its mountains of wall-papered plaster long ago. There were foothills of stairs, forested with banisters. This was Father-God's World; in which star firmaments shone at the flick of a wall switch. And the sun was Mother, and Mother was the sun, the center about which all the World steadfastly revolved. And Edwin, like a small dark meteor, tore through all the carpeted and tapestried spaces of the World. You saw him coming and going on vast staircases, on hikes and explorations.

This *was* the World, enchanted square countries between boundaries of nailed lath and polished wood. Unknown lands and wild lands and some lands hidden.

Sometimes he and Mom picnicked in the Highlands, spread snow linens on red-tuffed Persian scrolled lawns, upon the crimson carpeting of a meadow in a top plateau of the house were ancient portraits of dissatisfied peoples looked dimly down upon their eating and their revels. They drew water from silver taps in hidden tiled niches, and crashed the tumblers against the wall in dual demonstration. They played Hide and Seek and she found him rolled like a mummy in a window curtain on the fourth level. Once he got lost and wandered for hours in insane countries of dust and sheeted furniture and echoes. But she found him at last and took him back down through the layers and stratas of countries, to the familiar Parlor land where each dust particle was exact and familiar as a snow flake.

He ran up a stair.

There were doors to knock on, a thousand thousand doors, most of them locked and forbidden. There were bottom-tempting banisters to slide on. And there were Picasso ladies and Dali gentlemen who screamed silently at him from their canvas asylums, their golden eyes fierce, when he dawdled.

"These sorts of Things live *out there,*" his mother told him one day, pointing to the Dali-Picasso people in their frames.

He stuck his tongue at them now, and ran quickly past.

He stopped running.

One of the forbidden doors stood open.

Sunlight slanted through it and warmed and excited him.

He put out his hand to the knob, and stood twisting

it. He looked in. Beyond the door, a spiral staircase screwed around and up into sun and silence. His eyes darted up like birds, flying and twining on the circular stair into forbidden, sun-mellowed heights.

He flung his books down without even thinking and ran in and climbed the stairs up and around and up around until his knees ached and his breath fountained in and out, and his head banged like a bell with the effort, and at last he reached the terrible summit of the climb and stood in a sun-drenched tower to look out upon a *new* World!

"It's there!" he gasped, running from window to window in exultant discovery. "It's there!"

He was above the sombre tree barrier. For the first time in thirteen enclosed years he was high over the windy chestnuts and elms and as far as his eye could stretch he saw green and green grass and green trees and white ribbons on which beetles ran, and the other half of the world was blue and endless, with a sun in it like a navel, like an incredible deep blue room. It was so vast he felt as if he were falling, and screamed, and held onto the tower ledge, and beyond the trees, beyond the white ribbons where the beetles ran he saw things like fingers sticking up, but he didn't see any Picasso-Dali creatures, but he did see little red-white-and-blue handkerchiefs blowing in a slow wind on high white poles.

He was going to be sick. Great whitenesses moved across the eternal blue room over him and birds flew like bullets, shrilling.

Turning, he almost fell flat down the stairs.

Slamming the forbidden door at the bottom he heard the lock snap tight. He fell against the door.

"You'll go blind," he told himself, hysterically, hands to eyes. "You shouldn't have seen. You'll go blind!"

In the hall, gasping, staring, he waited for the blindness.

A minute later he stared from an ordinary Highlands window, and saw only his *own* familiar World. The high wall of elms, chestnuts and hickories, the stone fence in the vast garden below. He had always taken the forest to be a wall beyond which was nothing but terror, nothingness, and Beings. Now he knew his World didn't end with the wall. There was more to the World than the Continent of Kitchen, the Parlor Archipelago, the Peninsula of Learning, the Music Hall (he could hear mother brightly speaking each of these clever names for places!).

He tried the locked door again.

Had he really gone up? Or was it a dream? Had he seen that half green, half blue vastness?

What if God had seen him now? Edwin trembled at the thought. God, who'd built this house, timber on timber. God, who had smoked a mysterious black pipe and had a shiny magic cane to walk with. God, who had made Edwin and the World, and who might be watching, even now.

He looked around. "I can still see," he told himself, thankfully. "I can still *see*."

*

Nine thirty, a good half hour late, he rapped at the School.

The door swung open.

"Good morning, Teacher."

Teacher Granleigh stood inside.

"You're late, Edwin."

"I'm sorry."

Teacher was unchanged. She wore the tall grey thick-clothed monk's robe, the cowl up over her head. She wore the silver spectacles and the grey gloves. "Come in," she said.

Beyond her the land of books burned in colors from the hearth. There were walls bricked with books, and a hearth wide enough to stand in without bumping your head, and a blazing log for heat.

The door closed behind the aching boy.

God had been here. Once He had sat at that desk, there. Once He'd walked this floor, touched these books. God had stuffed that pipe with tobacco bits and puffed it. God had stood looking out that window. This was God's room, and it smelled of Him; rubbed wood, tobacco-leather and silver spurs.

Edwin's face became a pale and peaceful thing.

Here, his heart slowed. Here, he relaxed. Teacher's voice sang like a little harp, telling of God, the old days, and the World when it had shaken with God's determination and trembled at his wit. Teacher told of the days when the World skeleton was freshly blueprinted by His fingers, a pencil slash here, a loud, decisive word there, an argument, and, finally, timber rising, nail, plaster, paper and crystal. God's fingerprints still lay on little pencils under glass. Teacher never touched them. The fingerprints must be left intact! she said.

Here, in the Highlands, Edwin learned what was expected of him and his body. He was to grow into a Presence. He was to fit the odors of God and the voice of God, he was one day to stand tall and dark and very malignantly pale by that window and make the house boom with his shout. He was to be God, himself, and nothing was to stop this. Not the sky or the trees or the Things beyond the trees.

Teacher moved like a vapour in the room.

"Why were you late, Edwin?"

"I don't know."

"I'll ask you again," she said. "Why were you late?"

"Because." He looked at the floor so as not to see her. "I found a door. It was open. One of the forbidden ones."

"A door!" Teacher Granleigh sank into a large carved chair, concerned, her glasses flashing lights off them.

Her eyes had suddenly grown intense, as if she didn't understand, or was afraid to understand.

Edwin felt drops of sweat collecting in the hollows of his eyes. "Yes. I went in!" he said, swiftly, to get the pain over.

"I won't hurt you," she said. "I won't hurt you," she insisted. "Just tell me which door, where, it must be locked."

They had always been friends. Was the friendship over? Had he spoiled things? He felt like crying.

"The door by the Dali-Picasso people. There was sunlight and steps and I climbed up, I'm sorry, I'm sorry," he said in deep misery. "Don't tell Mother, please, please!"

She sat lost in her chair, her face vanishing deep back into the hollow of her grey cowl, the glasses making only a faint glitter. "And what did you see?" she asked.

"A big blue room."

"Did you?"

"And a green one. And ribbons!" He tried to make it sound unimportant to himself, but there was no stopping the eagerness and wonder behind the words.

"Ribbons?"

"Ribbons with bugs running on them. Like those little ladybugs that crawl on my hand."

"*And* bugs running on the ribbons," she repeated it, as if that was the last straw.

It made him sad, her voice. She sounded as if she'd lost a precious something. He wanted to make her happy.

"But I didn't stay long," he said, eagerly. "I came right down and slammed the door and locked it myself and won't go up again!"

"You won't?" Her lips, faintly moved in the shadowed cowl, were doubtful.

"No'm."

"But now you've seen," she said wearily, "and you'll want to see more."

"Mam?"

She shook her head. Then she leaned forward and

asked a question to which she wanted a negative answer, he could tell by her tone: "And—did you *like* what you saw?"

"Mam?"

"The blue room, the blue room, child, did you like it?"

"I don't know." He fidgeted, trying not to think. Then he thought of a solution, a way out. "I was scared."

She relaxed visibly. "Were you?"

"Yes'm, It was *big!*"

"It is big, Edwin, too big, uncomfortable, not like *this* world, and it's very uncertain, Edwin, remember."

"Yes'm," he said, wistfully.

"But why did you climb the stairs when you knew they were behind a forbidden door?"

He knew the answer, but hid it, trembling. "I don't know."

"There *must* be a reason."

The fire bloomed and withered and bloomed on the hearth and she waited ten long seconds. And finally he went to the little hiding place in his mind and took out the reason and without looking at teacher said, very low, "Mom."

"Your mother? She makes you—unhappy?"

"I don't know, oh, I don't know," he wailed. It was going to be good to cry, to tell someone, to get it over with and rest. "She—she," he gasped, and drew his knees tight to his bosom, misery embraced. "She's all funny, all funny."

"Nervous?"

"Yes, yes,"

"Touchy, unbearable, tight, tense, is that it?"

The words were correct buttons, pushed. He let go.

"Yes!" It was a sin to admit such things of mother and he wailed and covered his face, got his hands all wet and sticky, biting and crying on them. But he wasn't saying the words, now, she said them, and all he had to do was agree between sobs. "Yes, yes, oh, yes!"

"She runs about, funny, does she? And snaps at you and holds onto you, too tight? And sometimes—you want to be alone?"

Yes, to all of them! It was very sad, he loved mother dearly!

"That's what makes you want to run away by yourself? because she demands all your thoughts and every thing you do?"

Teacher was a million years old. "We learn," she said to herself, wearily. Rousing fitfully from her chair she walked with a slow swaying, grey robes awhisper, to a pen and paper on the desk and wrote words out. "We learn, Oh God, but slowly, and with much pain. We think we do things right, and all the time we're killing the plan." She looked up at him swiftly. He was caught with wet-rimmed, curious eyes.

"You're growing up?" she said, not as a question, but as a heavy statement of circumstance. She finished the note. "Take this to your mother. It tells her to let you have two full hours to yourself every afternoon, to prowl where you wish. Except—out *there.*" She stopped. "Are you listening to me, child?"

He wiped away the tears. "Teacher. Did Mom lie to me? I mean about out there, and the Things?"

"Look at me," she said. He looked. She moved her cowl ever so little. "I've been your friend, and never beaten you, as your mother sometimes has had to. Both of us are here to help you understand. We don't want you destroyed as God was destroyed."

Color from the hearth washed her face.

Edwin gasped.

She looked familiar. The lines were erased by the firelight and she was revealed.

She looked like his mother!

His heart leaped against his ribs.

She noticed him. "What were you going to say?"

"The fire," he looked at the fire and back at her face and the cowl jerked away from his gaze, the face vanished in blackness. "You look like Mom. I guess I'm funny."

She walked swiftly to the books on the shelves, took one down. "You know women look alike," she said, fumbling with it. "Forget it." She breathed harshly. "Here." She brought him a book. "Read from the first chapter of the Diary."

Edwin read. The fire rumbled and sucked itself brilliantly up the flue, the grey cowl settled and nodded and quieted, the face in it like a clapper in a solemn bell. The firelight ignited the little animal lettering on the shelved books. Those books from which pages had been razored and torn and censored, from which certain lines had been inked or erased, from which all pictures had been ripped, some books glued shut, or locked in bronze straps, because Edwin might see, read, understand. He read from the Diary:

"In the Beginning there was God. Who created the World with all its corridors and rooms and lands. With His hands he formed for his pleasure his loving wife and much later the child Edwin who was to be a God himself, after a number of years . . . ."

Teacher nodded and Edwin read on.

Down the banisters, breathless, he slid into the Parlor.

"Mom!"

She lay in a plump maroon chair, very like bone china. She was breathing hard as if she'd been running, and perspiring.

"Mom, you're wet!"

"Oh, hello," she said, looking at him as if it was his fault she had been running and was wet. "Nothing, nothing." Then she took him and kissed his cheeks. "Forgive me, darling. I'm a weasel. I have a great surprise for you. Your birthday is coming!"

"So soon? But it's only been ten months."

"Tomorrow it is, anyway. Do us wonders. I *say* so. Anything *I say* is true, my dear."

"And we open another room?" Dazed.

"The fourteenth room! Fifteenth room next year, and so on to your twenty-first birthday when we'll open the most important room and you'll be man of the House, God, Father, Head of the World!"

"Whee!" He tossed his books.

They laughed. It echoed and shook crystals in all the continents.

Edwin lay on his moonlit bed. Beyond his open window was the World's edge. Beyond was the blue world and the green where the Wicked Killers lived.

Tomorrow, his birthday. Why? Was he a good boy? No. Why, then? Because things were—nervous. Yes. That was it. Because they needed his birthday to cheer and calm them.

He sensed that the birthdays would come swifter, sooner from now on. The house was knotting up. Things were tight, like fists. Mom laughed too high and too much and there was a wild light in her eyes.

Would Teacher be invited? No! Mom and she'd never met. "Why not, Mom?" "Because," said Mom. "Don't you want to meet Mom, Teacher?" "Some day," said Teacher.

Where'd teacher go nights? To one of the secret rooms? Out into *there*. He looked at the wall of trees. Hardly.

His eyes closed.

Last year, when things had got nervous, Mom had advanced his birthday then, too.

Some night, he dreamed, I'll go to the Highlands and see if Teacher's really there *all* the time.

Think of something else. God. God building this Land.

Think of the hour of His death when the metal thing on the concrete road crushed and killed Him because it was jealous of Him.

Oh, how the World must have *rocked* with His passing.

One day, I'll be God. Mom says so.

He slept.

In the morning, bright voices below. In and out doors they moved. Edwin listened against the door that was bolted from outside; it was always bolted on festive days until the voices stopped below. Edwin scowled. *Whose* voices? They must be God's workers. They couldn't be Dali People from out there! Mom hated them with perfumed fury. Silence.

"Happy Birthday!"

Mom danced him about the party table. Cakes and ices and strawberries and hams and beefs and pink drinks in tall glasses and his name on a snowy white cake and his age in red numbers. He was stunned.

"Where'd it come from?"

"Where all food comes from," sang Mom, cryptically, swirling her green party gown. She plinked the piano in the music room and sang him Happy Birthday to You, Happy Birthday, Dear Edwin, Happy Birthday To—

Wild fanatical joy. Down with the drinks and on with the dance. She was afraid to stop.

With a silver key she unlocked the fourteenth, forbidden door. Hold your breath!

The door slid into the wall.

Disappointment. This fourteenth birthday room was hardly worth looking at. On his sixth birthday it had been the school in the Highlands. Seventh birthday? The playroom in the Lowlands. Eighth? The music room. Ninth: the kitchen all glittery chrome. Tenth birthday—the phonograph room where angels sang from moving discs. Eleventh: the garden room, a grass plot with a carpet that really *grew*, and had to be cut instead of swept. Twelfth and thirteenth birthdays, the wonders of Mom's cosmetic room and a new room for himself. Now, keenly disappointed, he looked into the fourteenth room. A dim brown closet. They stepped in.

Mom laughed. "You don't know how magic it is. Shut the door."

Hastily she poked red buttons on one wall.

"Mother!" he screamed.

The wall slid down. The room moved.

She soothed him. "Hush, darling."

Horrified, he watched the wall sink down into the floor, taking the door with it. Another door appeared and then another. The room stopped. Mother pointed at the strange new door. "Open it."

He opened it and stood paralyzed.

"Where's the parlor? How'd we get here? This is the Highlands!"

"We flew! From now on, once a week, you'll fly to school instead of taking the long way round."

"Oh, Mother, Mother!"

They idled deliciously in the sweet grass of the garden, sipping wide saucers of apple cider, their elbows on crimson silk cushions, their feet, with the shoes kicked off, wriggling in the tickly dandelions. Mom jumped three times when she heard a Monster roaring beyond the trees. One of those Monsters that had run down and killed God. "I'll protect you," said Edwin. "Thank you," she said, with polite uneasiness.

Beyond the trees, Chaos waited. Metal beasts shouted mating calls. Mom shivered, convulsed her sequin shawl with her fingers. Once, they sighted a chromium bird thing flying through the blue rift in the trees, humming.

From the garden, a double path ran into oblivion, between trees. Down it, mother whispered tensely over her cider, the beasts snuffled at night, waiting to mash Edwin.

"See?" she pointed. "Their droppings."

He saw the oily pools like molasses between the double tracks.

Crackle, crackle, crackle. The birthday ended like cellophane burnt to nothing.

At sunset in the Parlor security, mother inhaled champagne with her tiny, seedling nostrils and her little eye of a mouth. She hiccupped with a soft flourish of her breasts. Drowsy wild, she herded the cider-sober Edwin to his room, and a moment later on her way downstairs dropped a champagne bottle two flights.

He undressed in wonder. This year. Next. And which room two years, three years from now? The beasts. Being mashed. God. Killed. What was killed? What was death? Was death a feeling? Did God enjoy it? Was death a journey?

Below, another champagne bottle shattered.

Morning was a cool smell in the room. Downstairs, food was probably manifesting in a finger-snap on the table.

Edwin washed and dressed. He outlined the day in his mind. Breakfast, school, lunch, an hour in the music room at the piano, phonograph for an hour, then perhaps an hour or two with the electrical games that shot back at him and Mom, then tea in the Outlands. Then— He remembered the note. He picked it up. He'd forgotten to give it to Mom. He'd give it to her now. She'd have to let him run around the World by himself from tea-time until supper. Then, this evening, he might go up to School again where he and Teacher prowled the censored library together and he'd puzzle which words and thoughts about that world out there had been censored from his eyes.

He opened the door. There was an unusual silence in the World. He expected to find Mom gay, happy, relaxed, waiting for him. The hall was empty.

Down through the dells of the World a vapour hung like a light, unmoving veil. There was a silence which no footstep broke; the hills were quiet, the silver founts did not pulse in the first sunlight, and the balustrade lifted its sinuous neck up up the stairs like some prehistoric monster, to peer into his room . . . .

He walked downstairs to the parlor.

From the parlor, he walked to the dining room.

"Good morning, Mother."

Mother slept in her shining green dress on the floor, a glass still clasped in one hand. The hearth was littered with glass bits, nearby.

"Mother?"

Her face was pale, relaxed, and she enjoyed some dream.

Not wanting to disturb her he sat at the table and was shocked to find it empty. All his life there'd been food on it, but not this morning. He looked blankly at it.

Earlier, he'd heard a beast baying outside the kitchen door. Insistently. Why?

He went to Mother.

"Mother, wake up, wake up."

She paid no attention. She'd had spells before of stubbornness, but now she would not move.

"Shall I go to school? I'm hungry."

He sat on the chair for half an hour waiting for the food to appear like magic. It didn't.

"Well," he said, finally. "You just sleep, mother. I'm going up to school."

The Highlands were gloomy and shadowed. The white glass suns that shone in the ceilings no longer glowed. It was a day of sullen fog in the World; up the dark corridors, on the soft, silent stairs, through dim, dusty rooms Edwin wandered, a sense of overwhelming wrongness seizing on him. Things were changing.

He rapped and rapped again at the School door. The door drifted in, whining, of its own accord.

The school was dark. The hearth stones were cold; no fire hid in its cavern to throw shadows on the high ceiling. The blinds were drawn at the windows. The books sat upon the shelves. There was not a sound.

"Teacher?"

He drew the blinds.

"Teacher Granleigh?"

Everything was flat and empty. A faint colony of dust particles trickled down a melancholy shaft of sunlight that fell upon the floor.

Edwin put out his hands as if to normalize things. He wanted the fire to crack open like a popcorn kernel, blooming to life. He shut his eyes to give Teacher time to appear. He opened them and was stupefied at what he saw on the desk.

Neatly folded was the grey cowl and the grey robe, atop which gleamed the silver spectacles, and one grey glove. He touched them. One grey glove was gone. There were also two pieces of some greasy chalk that made a mark on the back of his hand when he used it.

He drew back, staring at Teacher's empty robe, the glasses, the greasy chalk. His hand fell upon a doorknob in a door which had always been locked, on the far side of the room. The door swung open, revealing another of those small, moving rooms.

"Teacher?" He walked into it. The door slid shut.

Pressing a button made it move and with it moved a

slow awful coldness, of fear, of silence, of the World grown so very quiet. Teacher gone, and mother—sleeping. Down sank the room, purring like a cat, then it clashed some machinery, and another room opened before him as he pushed the door. He stepped out.

The dining room!

Behind him was not a door, but a tall, six foot bookcase from which he'd emerged. Edwin blinked rapidly.

And Mother lay sleeping, untouched, uncaring, upon the floor. And folded under her, barely showing, he noticed for the first time, was one of Teacher's soft grey gloves.

He stood over her, staring down at the grey glove.

After awhile he began to whimper.

The table was bare. He shouted for it to fill with food. It did not. He called to Mother. She didn't move. He ran back up to the Highlands again and the hearth was still cold, Teacher's robe still lay folded and empty, and one grey glove was missing. He waited. Teacher didn't come. He ran back down the Lowlands, crying now. He sat by Mother and talked with her and felt the grey glove. The afternoon came and he was hungry.

The idea of hunger and loneliness engulfed him.

Teacher must be out in the Outlands somewhere, now. If he found her, he'd bring her back to wake mother so everything would be fine!

Through the kitchen, out back, he found late afternoon light and the beasts hooting beyond the rim of the

World. He clung to the garden wall, not daring to let go, and then when nothing threatened, and sunlight warmed him as the hearth fire often had, he felt better. He heard the wind blow softly in the trees. He walked on the path. His feet slipped on the beast droppings and he stared far down the tunnel between the trees. Did he dare go beyond, out there?

"Teacher?"

He walked along the beast spoor a few yards.

"Teacher!"

Over his shoulder lay his World and its very new silence. From a distance he heard noises, sounds, beyond the trees. His mouth widened and his eyes squinted fiercely. He walked some more, pausing, then going on. Behind, he was startled to see his World diminish. How small! Why? It had always been so large! He called again and again, and everything was new. Smells filled his nose, colors and shapes and sizes filled his eyes.

If I go beyond the trees I'll die, he thought. Mom said so. What's dying? What is it anyway, what's it like? Is it another room? A blue one? A green one? There's a big green one, ahead. Oh, Mother, Teacher.

His feet hurried, increased their pace, knowing not why. The legs that carried him were no longer his own; his voice, his yelling, belonged to something new. The path rushed under him, the Universe behind dwindled and vanished. He began to laugh . . . .

*

The policeman scratched his head and looked at the pedestrian.

"These kids. Honest to God, I can't figure them."

"How's that?" asked the pedestrian.

The policeman thought it over. "A second ago a little boy ran by. He laughed and cried all at the same time. He jumped up and down and *touched* things. Things like bushes and trees and little pieces of paper, and fire hydrants and dogs, and people. Things like sidewalks and gates and parked cars. Why, Christ, he even touched *me* to see if *I* was here, and he looked at the sky, all running tears, and he kept yelling something funny."

"What did he yell?" asked the pedestrian.

"He kept yelling, 'I'm dead, I'm dead, I'm glad I'm dead, I'm dead, I'm dead, it's *good* to be dead, I'm dead, I'm dead, I'm *glad* I'm dead!' One of them new kid's games, I guess."

THE SCYTHE

Quite suddenly there was no more road. It ran down the valley like any other road, between slopes of barren stony ground and live oak trees, and then past a broad field of wheat standing alone in the wilderness. It came up beside the small white house that belonged to the wheat field and then just faded out, as though there was no more use for it.

It didn't matter much, because just there the last of the gas was gone. Drew Erickson braked the ancient car to a stop and sat there, not speaking, staring at his big rough farmer's hands.

Molly spoke, without moving where she lay in the corner beside him. "We must of took the wrong fork back yonder."

Drew nodded.

Molly's lips were almost as white as her face. Only

they were dry where her skin was damp with sweat. Her voice was flat, with no expression in it.

"Drew," she said. "Drew, what are we a-goin' to do now?"

Drew stared at his hands. A farmer's hands, with the farm blown out from under them by the dry hungry wind that never got enough good loam to eat.

The kids in the back seat woke up and pried themselves out of the dusty litter of bundles and bedding. They poked their heads over the back of the seat and said,

"What are we stoppin' for, Pa? Are we gonna eat now, Pa? Pa, we're awful hungry. Can we eat now, Pa?"

Drew closed his eyes. He hated the sight of his hands.

Molly's fingers touched his wrist. Very light, very soft. "Drew—maybe in the house there they'd spare us somethin' to eat?"

A white line showed around his mouth. "Beggin'," he said harshly. "Ain't none of us ever begged before. Ain't none of us ever goin' to."

Molly's hand tightened on his wrist. He turned and saw her eyes. He saw the eyes of Susie and little Drew, looking at him.

Slowly all the stiffness went out of his neck and his back. His face got loose and blank, shapeless like a thing that has been beaten too hard and too long. He got out of the car and went up the path to the house. He walked uncertainly, like a man who is sick, or nearly blind.

The door of the house was open. Drew knocked three

times. There was nothing inside but silence, and a white window curtain moving in the slow hot air.

He knew it before he went in. He knew there was death in the house. It was that kind of silence.

He went through a small clean living room and down a little hall. He wasn't thinking anything. He was past thinking. He was going toward the kitchen, unquestioning, like an animal.

Then he looked through an open door and saw the dead man.

He was an old man, lying out on a clean white bed. He hadn't been dead long; not long enough to lose the last quiet look of peace. He must have known he was going to die, because he wore his grave clothes—an old black suit, brushed and neat, and a clean white shirt and a black tie.

A scythe leaned against the wall beside the bed. Between the old man's hands there was a blade of wheat, still fresh. A ripe blade, golden and heavy in the tassel.

Drew went into the bedroom, walking soft. There was a coldness on him. He took off his broken, dusty hat and stood by the bed, looking down.

The paper lay open on the pillow beside the old man's head. It was meant to be read. Maybe a request for burial, or to call a relative. Drew scowled over the words, moving his pale, dry lips.

"To him who stands beside me at my death bed: Being of sound mind, and alone in the world as it has been decreed, I, John Buhr, do give and bequeath this farm, with all pertaining

to it, to the man who is to come. Whatever his name or origin shall be, it will not matter. The farm is his, and the wheat; the scythe, and the task ordained thereto. Let him take them freely, and without question—and remember that I, John Buhr, am only the giver, not the ordainer. To which I set my hand and seal this third day of April, 1938. (Signed) John Buhr. Kyrie eleison!"

Drew walked back through the house and opened the screen door. He said, "Molly, you come in. Kids, you stay in the car."

Molly came inside. He took her to the bedroom. She looked at the will, the scythe, the wheat-field moving in a hot wind outside the window. Her white face tightened up and she bit her lips and held on to him. "It's too good to be true. There must be some trick to it."

Drew said, "Our luck's changin', that's all. We'll have work to do, stuff to eat, somethin' over our heads to keep rain off." He touched the scythe. It gleamed like a half moon. Words were scratched on its blade. *"Who wields me—wields the world."* It didn't mean much to him, right at that moment.

"Drew," Molly asked, staring at the old man's clasped hands. "Why—why's he holdin' that wheat-stalk so hard in his fingers?"

Just then the heavy silence was broken by the sound of the kids scrambling up the front porch. Molly gasped.

They lived in the house. They buried the old man on a hill and said some words over him and came back down and swept the house and unloaded the car and had something to eat because there was food, lots of it, in the kitchen, and they did nothing for three days but fix the house and look at the land and lie in the good beds and then look at one another in surprise that all this was happening this way and their stomachs were full and there was even a cigar for him to smoke in the evenings.

There was a small barn behind the house and in the barn a bull and three cows, and there was a well-house, a spring-house, under some big trees that kept it cool. And inside the well-house were big sides of beef and bacon and pork and mutton, enough to feed a family five times their size for a year, two years, maybe three. There was a churn and a box of cheeses there, and big metal cans for the milk.

On the fourth morning Drew Erickson lay in bed looking at the scythe and he knew it was time for him to work because there was ripe grain in the long field, he had seen it with his eyes, and he did not want to get soft. Three days sitting were enough for any man. He roused himself in the first fresh smell of dawn and took the scythe and held it before him as he walked out into the field. He held it up in his hands and swung it down.

It was a big field of grain. Too big for one man to tend and yet one man had tended it.

At the end of the first day of work, he walked in with the scythe riding his shoulder quietly, and there was a look on his face of a puzzled man. It was a wheat field the like of which he had never seen. It ripened only in separate clusters, each set off from the others. Wheat shouldn't do that. He didn't tell Molly. Nor did he tell her the other things about the field. About how, for instance, the wheat rotted within a few hours after he cut it down. Wheat shouldn't do that, either. He was not greatly worried. After all, there was food at hand.

The next morning the wheat he had left rotting, cut down, had taken hold and come up again in little green sprouts, with tiny roots, all born again.

Drew Erickson rubbed his chin, wondered what and why and how it acted that way and what good it would be to him, he couldn't sell it. A couple of times during the day he walked far up in the hills to where the old man's grave was, just to be sure the old man was there, maybe with some notion he might get an idea there about the field. He looked down and saw how much land he owned. The wheat stretched three miles in one direction toward the mountains, and was about two acres wide, patches of it in seedlings, patches of it golden, patches of it green, patches of it fresh cut by his hand. But the old man said nothing concerning this; there were a lot of stones and dirt in his face now. The grave was in the sun and the wind and silence. So Drew Erickson walked back down to use the scythe, curious, enjoying it because it seemed important. He didn't know just why, but it was. Very, very important.

He couldn't just let the wheat stand. There were always new patches of it ripened and in his figuring out loud to no one in particular he said, "If I cut the wheat for the next ten years, just as it ripens up, I don't think I'll pass the same spot twice. Such a damn big field." He shook his head. "That wheat ripens just *so*. Never too much of it so I can't cut *all* the ripe stuff each day. That leaves nothin' but green grain. And the next mornin', sure enough, another patch of ripe stuff . . . ."

It was damned foolish to cut the grain when it rotted as quick as it fell. At the end of the week he decided to let it go a few days.

He lay in bed late, just listening to the silence in the house that wasn't anything like death silence, but a silence of things living well and happily.

He got up, dressed, and ate his breakfast slowly. He wasn't going to work. He went out to milk the cows, stood on the porch smoking a cigarette, walked about the backyard a little and then came back in and asked Molly what he had gone out to do. "Milk the cows," she said. "Oh, yeah," he said, and went out again. He found the cows waiting and full and milked them and put the milk cans in the spring house, but thought of other things. The wheat. The scythe.

All through the morning he sat on the back porch rolling cigarettes. He made a toy boat for little Drew and one for Susie and then he churned some of the milk into butter and drew off the buttermilk, but the sun was in his head, aching. It burned there. He wasn't hungry for lunch. He kept looking at the wheat and the wind bending and tipping and ruffling it. His arms flexed, his fingers, resting on his knee as he sat again on the porch, made a kind of grip in the empty air, itching. The pads of his palms itched and burned. He stood up and wiped his hands on his pants and sat down and tried to roll another cigarette and got mad at the mixings and threw it all away with a muttering. He had a feeling as if a third arm had been cut off of him, or he had lost something of himself. It had to do with his hands and his arms.

He heard the wind whisper in the field.

By one o'clock he was going in and out of the house, getting underfoot, thinking about digging an irrigation ditch but all the time really thinking about the wheat and how ripe and beautiful it was, aching to be cut.

"Damn it to hell!"

He strode into the bedroom, took the scythe down off its wall-pegs. He stood holding it. He felt cool. His hands stopped itching. His head didn't ache. The third arm was returned to him. He was intact again.

It was instinct. Illogical as lightning striking and not hurting. Each day the grain must be cut. It *had* to be cut. Why? Well, it just *did*, that was all. He laughed at the scythe in his big hands. Then, whistling, he took it out to the ripe and waiting field and did the work. He thought himself a little mad. Hell, it was an ordinary enough wheat-field, really, wasn't it? Almost.

The days loped away like gentle horses.

Drew Erickson began to understand his work as a sort of dry ache and hunger and need. Things built in his head.

One noon, Susie and little Drew giggled and played

with the scythe while their father ate lunch in the kitchen. He heard them. He came out and took it away from them. He didn't yell at them. He just looked very concerned and locked the scythe up after that when it wasn't being used.

He never missed a day, scything.

Up. Down. Up, down, and across. Back and up and down and across. Cutting. Up. Down.

Up.

Think about the old man and the wheat in his hands when he died.

Down.

Think about this dead land, with wheat living on it.

Up.

Think about the crazy patterns of ripe and green wheat, the way it grows!

Down.

Think about . . . .

The wheat whirled in a full yellow tide at his ankles. The sky blackened. Drew Erickson dropped the scythe and bent over to hold his stomach, his eyes running blindly. The world reeled.

"I've killed somebody!" he gasped, choking, holding to his chest, falling to his knees beside the blade. "I've killed a lot—"

The sky revolved like a blue merry-go-round at the county fair in Kansas. But no music. Only a ringing in his ears.

*

Molly was sitting at the blue kitchen table peeling potatoes when he blundered into the kitchen, dragging the scythe behind him.

"Molly!"

She swam around in the wet of his eyes.

She sat there, her hands fallen open, waiting for him to finally get it out.

"Get the things packed," he said, looking at the floor.

"Why?"

"We're leaving," he said, dully.

"We're leaving?" she said.

"That old man. You know what he did here? It's the wheat, Molly, and this scythe. Every time you use the scythe on the wheat a thousand people die. You cut across them and—"

Molly got up and put the knife down and the potatoes to one side and said, understandingly, "You're tired. We traveled a lot and haven't eaten good until the last month here, and you been workin' every day and you're tired—"

"I hear voices, sad voices, out there. In the wheat," he said. "Tellin' me to stop. Tellin' me not to kill them!"

"Drew!"

He didn't hear her. "The field grows crooked, wild, like a crazy thing. I didn't tell you. But it's wrong."

She stared at him. Her eyes were blue glass, nothing else.

"You think I'm crazy," he said. "But wait 'til I tell you. Oh, God, Molly, help me; I just killed my mother!"

"Stop it!" she said, firmly.

"I cut down one stalk of wheat and I killed her, I felt her dyin', that's how I found out just now—"

"Drew!" Her voice was like a crack across the face with the back of her fist, angry and afraid now. "Shut up!"

He mumbled. "Oh . . . Molly . . ."

The scythe dropped from his hands, clamored on the floor. She picked it up with a snap of anger and set it in one corner. "Ten years I been with you," she said. "Sometimes we had nothin' but dust and prayers in our mouths. Now, all this good luck sudden, and you can't bear up under it!"

She brought the Bible from the living room.

She rustled its pages over. They sounded like the wheat rustling in a small, slow wind. "You sit down and listen," she said.

A sound came in from the sunshine. The kids, laughing in the shade of the large live oak beside the house.

She read from the Bible, looking up now and again to see what was happening to Drew's face.

She read from the Bible each day after that. The following Wednesday, a week later, when Drew walked down to the distant town to see if there was any General Delivery mail, there was a letter.

He came home looking two hundred years old.

He held the letter out to Molly and told her what it said in a cold, uneven voice,

"—mother passed away—one o'clock Tuesday afternoon—her heart—"

*

All that Drew Erickson had to say was, "Get the kids in the car, load it up with food. We're goin' on to California."

"Drew," said his wife, holding the letter.

"You know yourself," he said, "this is poor grain land. Yet look how ripe it grows. I ain't told you, all the things. It ripens in patches, a little each day. It ain't right. And when I cut it, it rots! And next mornin' it comes up without any help, growin' again! Last Tuesday, a week ago, when I cut the grain it was like rippin' my own flesh. I heard somebody scream! It sounded just like—my mother. And now, today, this letter."

She said, "We're stayin' here."

"Molly."

"We're stayin' here, where we're sure of eatin' and sleepin' and livin' decent and livin' long. I'm not makin' skeletons of my children again, ever."

The sky was blue through the windows. The sun slanted in touching half of Molly's calm face, shining one eye bright blue. Four or five water drops hung and fell from the kitchen faucet slowly, shining, before Drew sighed. The sigh was husky and resigned and tired. He nodded, looking away, "All right," he said. "We'll stay."

He picked up the scythe weakly. The words on the metal leaped up with a sharp glitter:

WHO WIELDS ME—WIELDS THE WORLD!

"We'll stay . . . ."

*

Next morning he walked to the old man's grave. There was a single fresh sprout of wheat growing in the center of it. The same sprout, reborn, that the old man had held in his hands weeks before.

He talked to the old man, getting no answers.

"You worked the field all your life because you *had* to, and one day you came across your own life growin' there. You knew it was yours. You cut it. And you went home, put on your grave clothes, and your heart gave out and you died. That's how it was, wasn't it? And you passed the land on to me, and when I die, I'm supposed to hand it over to someone else."

Drew's voice had awe in it. "How long a time has this been goin' on? With nobody knowin' about this field and its use except the man with the scythe . . . ?"

Quite suddenly he felt very old. The valley seemed ancient, mummified, secretive, dried and bent and powerful. When the Indians danced on the prairie it had been here, this field. The same sky, the same wind, the same wheat. And, before the Indians? Some Cro-Magnon, gnarled and shag-haired, wielding a crude wooden scythe, perhaps, prowling down through the living wheat . . . .

Drew returned to work. Up, down. Up, down. Obsessed with the idea of being the wielder of *the* scythe. He, himself! It burst upon him in a mad, wild surge of strength and horror.

Up! WHO WIELDS ME! Down! WIELDS THE WORLD!

He had to accept the job with some sort of philosophy. It was simply his way of getting food and housing for his family. They deserved eating and living decent, he rationalized, after all these years.

Up and down. Each grain a life he neatly cut into two pieces. If he planned it carefully—he looked at the wheat with an inquisitive look to his eyes—why, he and Molly and the kids could live forever!

Once he found the place where the grain grew that was Molly and Susie and little Drew he would never cut it. They'd be immortal!

Just then, as if at a signal, it hit him.

Molly, and little Drew, and Susie.

Right there, before him. Their grains of wheat.

Another sweep of the scythe and he'd slice them away.

Molly, Drew, Susie. He was certain. Trembling, he knelt and looked at the three grains. They glowed at his touch.

He groaned with relief. What if he had cut them down, never guessing? He blew out his breath and got up and took the scythe and stood back away from the three small grains.

Molly thought it awfully strange when he came home early and kissed her on the cheek, for no reason at all.

At dinner, Molly said, "You quit early today? Does—does the wheat still rot when it falls?"

He nodded and took more meat.

She said, "You ought to write to the Agriculture people and have them come look at it."

"No," he said.

"I was just suggestin'," she said.

His eyes dilated. "I got to stay here all my life. Can't nobody else mess with that wheat, they wouldn't know where to cut and not to cut. They might cut the wrong parts."

"What wrong parts?"

"Nothin'," he said, chewing slowly. "Nothin' at all."

He slapped his fork down, hard. "Who knows *what* they might want to do! Those gover'ment men! They might even—might even want to plow the whole field under!"

Molly nodded. "That's just what it needs," she said. "And start all over again, with new seed."

He didn't finish eating. "I'm not writin' any gover'ment, and I'm not handin' this field over to no stranger to cut, and that's that!" he said, and the screen door banged behind him.

He detoured around that place where the wheat grains of his children and his wife grew up in the sun, and used his scythe on the far end of the field where he knew he wouldn't cut them down by mistake.

But he no longer liked the work. At the end of an hour he had brought death to three of his old, loved friends in Missouri. Joe Spangeler, Bill March, Ole Johnson; he read their names in the cut grain and couldn't go on.

He locked the scythe in the cellar and threw the key away. He was done being the Reaper. Done for good and all!

*

He smoked his pipe in the evening, on the front porch, and told the kids stories to hear them laugh. But they didn't laugh much. They seemed withdrawn, tired and funny, like they weren't his children any more.

Molly complained of a headache, dragged around the house a little, and went to bed early and fell into a deep sleep. That was funny, too. Molly always stayed up late and was full of vinegar.

The wheat field rippled with moonlight on it, making it into a sea.

It wanted cutting. It didn't like this neglect. Certain grains needed cutting *now*. Drew Erickson sat, swallowing quietly, trying not to look at it.

What'd happen to the world if he never went in the field again? What'd happen to people ripe for death, who waited the coming of the scythe?

He'd wait and see.

Molly was breathing softly when he blew out the oil lamp and got to bed. He couldn't sleep. He heard the wind in the wheat, felt the hunger to do the work in his arms and fingers.

In the middle of the night he found himself walking in the field, the scythe in his hands. Walking like a crazy man, walking and afraid, half-awake. He didn't remember unlocking the cellar door, getting the scythe, but here he was in the moonlight, walking in the grain.

Among these grains there were many who were old, weary, wanting so very much to sleep. The long, quiet, moonless sleep.

The scythe held him, grew into his palms, forced him to walk.

Somehow, struggling, he got free of it. He threw it down, ran off into the wheat where he stopped and went down on his knees.

"I don't want to kill any more," he said. "If I work with the scythe I'll have to kill Molly and the kids. Don't ask me to do that!"

The stars only sat in the sky, shining.

Behind him, he heard a dull thumping sound.

Something shot up over the hill into the sky. It was like a living thing, with arms of red color, licking at the stars. Sparks fell into his face. The thick hot odor of fire came with it.

The house!

Crying out, he got sluggishly, hopelessly, to his feet, looking at the big fire.

The little white house with the live oaks was roaring up in one savage bloom of fire. Heat rolled over the hill and he swam in it and went down in it, stumbling, drowning over his head.

By the time he got down the hill there was not a shingle, bolt or threshold of it that wasn't alive with flame. It made blistering, crackling, fumbling noises.

No one screamed inside. No one ran around or shouted.

He yelled in the yard. "Molly! Susie! Drew!"

He got no answer. He ran close in until his eyebrows withered and his skin crawled hot like paper burning, crisping, curling up in tight little curls.

"Molly! Susie!'

The roof fell in. Brilliant skirts of sparks were tossed out by it.

The fire settled contentedly down to feed. Drew ran around the house a dozen times, all alone, trying to find a way in. Then he sat where the fire roasted his body and waited until all of the walls had sunken down with fluttering crashes, until the last ceilings bent, blanketing the floors with molten plaster and scorched lathing. Until the flames died and smoke coughed up and the new day came slowly and there was nothing but embering ashes and an acid smouldering.

Disregarding the heat fanning from the leveled frames, Drew walked into the ruin. It was still too dark to see much. Red light glowed on his sweating throat. He stood like a stranger in a new and different land. Here—the kitchen. Charred tables, chairs, the iron stove, the cupboards. Here—the hall. Here the parlor and then over here was the bedroom where—

Where Molly was still alive.

She slept among fallen timbers and angry-colored pieces of wire spring and metal.

She slept as if nothing had happened. Her small white hands lay at her sides, flaked with sparks. Her calm face slept with a flaming lath across one cheek.

Drew stopped and didn't believe it. In the ruin of her smoking bedroom she lay on a glittering bed of sparks, her skin intact, her breast rising, falling, taking air.

"Molly!"

Alive and sleeping after the fire, after the walls had roared down, after ceilings had collapsed upon her and flame had lived all about her.

His shoes smoked as he pushed through piles of fuming litter. It could have seared his feet off at the ankles, he wouldn't have known.

"Molly . . . ."

He bent over her. She didn't move or hear him, and she didn't speak. She wasn't dead. She wasn't alive. She just lay there with the fire surrounding her and not touching her, not harming her in any way. Her cotton nightgown was streaked with ashes, but not burnt. Her brown hair was pillowed on a tumble of red-hot coals.

He touched her cheek. It was cold. Cold in the middle of hell. Tiny breaths trembled her half-smiling lips.

"Molly, what's wrong? How did you . . .?"

Susie and her brother were there, too. Behind a veil of smoke he made out two smaller figures huddled in the middle of a stretch of crisped plaster, sleeping.

He carried all three of them out to the edge of the wheat field and tried to wake them. It was no use.

"Molly. Molly, wake up! Kids! Kids, wake up!'

They breathed and didn't move and went on sleeping.

"Kids, wake up! You're mother is—"

Dead? No, not dead. But—

He shook the kids as if they were to blame. They paid no attention, they were too busy with their dreams. He put them back down and stood over them, his face cut with lines. He *knew*.

He knew why they'd slept through the fire and continued to sleep now. He knew why Molly just lay there, never wanting to laugh again.

The power of the wheat and the scythe.

Their lives, scheduled to end yesterday, May 30th, 1938, had been prolonged simply because he refused to harvest the grain. They should have died in the fire. That's the way it was supposed to *be*. But since he had not cut their grain, nothing could hurt them. A house had flamed and fallen and still they lived. But there was nothing for them to do. They were caught halfway, not dead, not alive. Simply—waiting. And all over the world thousands more just like them, victims of accidents, fires, disease, suicide, waited, slept just like Molly and her children slept. Not able to die, not able to live. All because a man was afraid of harvesting the ripe grain. All because one man thought he could stop working with a scythe and never work with that scythe again.

He looked down upon the children. The job had to be done every day and every day, with never a stopping, but a going on, with never a pause, but always the harvesting, forever and forever and forever.

All right, he thought. By Christ, he'd show them! He'd *cut* the God-damned grain!

He didn't say goodbye to his family. He turned with a slow feeding anger and found the scythe and walked rapidly, then he began to trot, then he ran with long jolting strides into the field, raving, feeling the hunger in his arms, the hunger he nursed now with insane violence! Wheat whipped and flailed his legs. He pounded through it, shouting. He stopped.

"Molly!" he cried, and raised the blade and swung it down.

"Susie!" he cried again. "Drew!" And swung the blade down again.

Somebody screamed. It sounded like three people. He didn't turn to look at the fire-ruined house.

And then, sobbing wildly, with a fierce, unrelenting insanity of vengeance against fate in every muscle, he rose above the grain again and again and hewed to left and to right and to left and to right and to left and to right. Over and over and over! Slicing out huge scars in green wheat and ripe wheat, with no selection and no care, cursing, over and over, swearing, laughing, the blade swinging up in the rising sun and coming down in the sun with a singing whistle! Down!

Hitler marched into Austria.

The blade swung insanely.

Hitler marched into Czechoslovakia.

The blade sang, crimson wet.

Poland fell.

The grain leaped up, green, falling left and right.

Bombs shattered London, shattered Moscow, shattered Tokyo.

And the blade went on rising, crashing, severing with the hot fury of a man who has held and lost his loved ones and does not care what he does to the world.

Just a few short miles off the Main Highway, down

a rough dirt road that leads to nowhere, just a few short miles from the highway jammed with California-bound traffic.

Once in a while during the long years a jalopy gets off the main highway, pulls up steaming in front of the charred ruin of a little white house at the end of the dirt road, to ask instructions from a farmer who works insanely, unendingly, wildly, without ever stopping, night and day in the wheat field there.

But they get no help, no answer. The farmer in the field is too busy, even after all these years; too busy hewing and chopping the green wheat instead of the ripe wheat.

And Drew Erickson moves on with his scythe, with that hot mad light in his eyes. On and on and on . . . .

LET'S PLAY "POISON"

"We hate you!" cried the sixteen boys and girls rushing and crowding about Michael in the school room. Michael screamed. Recess was over, Mr. Howard, the teacher, was still absent from the filling room. "We hate you!" and the sixteen boys and girls, bumping and clustering and breathing, raised a window. It was three flights down to the side walk. Michael flailed.

They took hold of Michael and pushed him out the window.

Mr. Howard, their teacher, came into the room. "Wait a minute!" he shouted.

Michael fell three flights. Michael died.

Nothing was done about it. The police shrugged eloquently. These children were all eight or nine, they didn't understand what they were doing. So.

Mr. Howard's breakdown occurred the next day. He

refused, ever again, to teach! "But, why?" asked his friends. Mr. Howard gave no answer. He remained silent and a terrible light filled his eyes, and later he remarked that if he told them the truth they would think him quite insane.

Mr. Howard left Madison City. He went to live in a small nearby town, Green Bay, for seven years, on an income managed from writing stories and poetry.

He never married. The few women he approached always desired—children.

In the autumn of his seventh year of self-enforced retirement, a good friend of Mr. Howard's, a teacher, fell ill. For lack of a proper substitute, Mr. Howard was summoned and convinced that it was his duty to take over the class. Because he realized the appointment could last no longer than a few weeks, Mr. Howard agreed, unhappily.

"Sometimes," announced Mr. Howard, slowly pacing the aisles of the school room on that Monday morning in September, "sometimes, I actually believe that children are invaders from another dimension."

He stopped, and his shiny dark eyes snapped from face to face of his small audience. He held one hand behind him, clenched. The other hand, like a pale animal, climbed his lapel as he talked and later climbed back down to toy with his ribboned glasses.

"Sometimes," he continued, looking at William Arnold and Russell Newell, and Donald Bowers and Charlie Hencoop, "sometimes I believe children are little monsters thrust out of hell, because the devil could no longer cope with them. And I certainly believe that everything should be done to reform their uncivil little minds."

Most of his words ran unfamiliarly into the washed and unwashed ears of Arnold, Newell, Bowers and Company. But the tone inspired one to dread. The little girls lay back in their seats, against their pigtails, lest he yank them like bell-ropes, to summon the dark angels. All stared at Mr. Howard, as if hypnotized.

"You are another race entirely, your motives, your beliefs, your disobediences," said Mr. Howard. "You are not human. You are—children. Therefore, until such time as you are adults, you have no right to demand privileges or question your elders, who know better."

He paused, and put his elegant rump upon the chair behind the neat, dustless desk.

"Living in your world of fantasy," he said, scowling darkly. "Well, there'll be no fantasy here. You'll soon discover that a ruler on your hand is no dream, no faerie frill, no Peter Pan excitement." He snorted. "Have I frightened you? I have. Good! Well and good. You deserve to be. I want you to know where we stand. I'm not afraid of you, remember that. I'm not afraid of you." His hand trembled and he drew back in his chair as all their eyes stared at him. "Here!" He flung a glance clear across the room. "What're you whispering about, back there? Some necromancy or other?"

A little girl raised her hand. "What's necromancy?"

"We'll discuss that when our two young friends, Mr.

Arnold and Mr. Bowers, explain their whispers. Well, young men?"

Donald Bowers arose. "We don't like you. That's all we said." He sat down again.

Mr. Howard raised his brows. "I like frankness, truth. Thank you for your honesty. But, simultaneously, I do not tolerate flippant rebellion. You'll stay an hour after school tonight and wash the boards."

After school, walking home, with autumn leaves falling both before and after his passing, Mr. Howard caught up with four of his students. He rapped his cane sharply on the sidewalk. "Here, what are you children doing?"

The two startled boys and girls jerked as if struck upon their shoulders by his cane. "Oh," they all said.

"Well," demanded the man. "Explain. What were you doing here when I came up?"

William Arnold said, "Playing poison."

"Poison!" Their teacher's face twisted. He was carefully sarcastic. "Poison, poison, playing poison. Well. And how does one play poison?"

Reluctantly, William Arnold ran off.

"Come back here!" shouted Mr. Howard.

"I'm only showing you," said the boy, hopping over a cement block of the sidewalk. "How we play poison. Whenever we come to a dead man we jump over him."

"One does, does one?" said Mr. Howard.

"If you jump on a dead man's grave, then you're

poisoned and fall down and die," explained Isabel Skelton, much too brightly.

"Dead men, graves, poisoned," Mr. Howard said, mockingly. "Where do you get this dead man idea?"

"See?" said Clara Parris, pointing with her arithmetic. "On this square, the name of the two dead men."

"Ridiculous," retorted Mr. Howard, squinting down. "Those are simply the names of the contractors who mixed and laid the cement sidewalk."

Isabel and Clara both gasped wildly and turned accusing eyes to the two boys. "You said they were grave stones!" they cried, almost together.

William Arnold looked at his feet. "Yeah. They are. Well, almost. Anyway." He looked up. "It's late. I gotta go home. So long."

Clara Parris looked at the two little names cut into the sidewalk. "Mr. Kelly and Mr. Terrill," she read the names. "Then these aren't graves? Mr. Kelly and Mr. Terrill aren't buried here? See, Isabel, that's what I told you, a dozen times I did."

"You did not," sulked Isabel.

"Deliberate lies," Mr. Howard tapped his cane in an impatient code. "Falsification of the highest calibre. Good God, Mr. Arnold, Mr. Bowers, there'll be no more of this, do you understand?"

"Yes, sir," mumbled the boys.

"Speak up!"

"Yes, sir," they replied, again.

Mr. Howard swung off swiftly down the street. William

Arnold waited until he was out of sight before he said, "I hope a bird drops something right smack on his nose—"

"Come on, Clara, let's play poison," said Isabel, hopefully.

Clara pouted. "It's been spoiled. I'm going home."

"I'm poisoned!" cried Donald Bowers, falling to the earth and frothing merrily. "Look, I'm poisoned! Gahhh!"

"Oh," cried Clara, angrily, and ran away.

Saturday morning Mr. Howard glanced out his front window and swore when he saw Isabel Skelton making chalk marks on his sidewalk and then hopping about, making a monotonous sing-song with her voice.

"Stop that!"

Rushing out, he almost flung her to the pavement in his emotion. He grabbed her and shook her violently and let her go and stood over her and the chalk marks.

"I was only playing hopscotch," she sobbed, hands over her eyes.

"I don't care, you can't play it here," he declared. Bending, he erased the chalk marks with his handkerchief, muttering. "Young witch. Pentagrams. Rhymes and incantations, and all looking perfectly innocent, God, how innocent. You little *fiend*!" he made as if to strike her, but stopped. Isabel ran off, wailing. "Go ahead, you little fool!" he screamed, furiously. "Run off and tell your little cohorts that you've failed. They'll have to try some other way! They won't get around me, they won't, oh, no!"

He stalked back into his house and poured himself a stiff drink of brandy and drank it down. The rest of the day he heard the children playing kick-the-can, hide-and-seek, Over-Annie-Over, jacks, tops, mibs, and the sound of the little monsters in every shrub and shadow would not let him rest. "Another week of this," he thought, "and I'll be stark staring." He flung his hand to his aching head. "God in heaven, why weren't we all born adults?"

Another week, then. And the hatred growing between him and the children. The hate and the fear growing apace. The nervousness, the sudden tantrums over nothing, and then—the silent waiting, the way the children climbed the trees and looked at him as they swiped late apples, the melancholy smell of autumn settling in around the town, the days growing short, the night coming too soon.

"But they won't touch me, they won't *dare* touch me," thought Mr. Howard sucking down one glass of brandy after another. "It's all very silly anyhow, and there's nothing to it. I'll soon be away from here, and—them. I'll soon—"

There was a white skull at the window.

It was eight o'clock of a Thursday evening. It had been a long week, with the angry flares and the accusations. He had had to continually chase the children away from the water-main excavation in front of his house. Children loved excavations, hiding places, pipes and conduits and trenches, and they were ever ascramble over and on and down in and up out of the holes where the new pipes were being laid. It was all finished, thank the Lord, and tomorrow the work-men would shovel in the earth and tamp it down and put in a new cement sidewalk, and that would eliminate the children. But, right now—

There was a white skull at the window!

There could be no doubt that a boy's hand held the skull against the glass, tapping and moving it. There was a childish tittering from outside.

Mr. Howard burst from the house. "Hey, you!" He exploded into the midst of the three running boys. He leaped after them, shouting and yelling. The street was dark, but he saw the figures dart beyond and below him. He saw them sort of bound and could not remember the reason for this, until too late.

The earth opened under him. He fell and lay in a pit, his head taking a terrific blow from a laid water-pipe, and as he lost consciousness he had an impression as of an avalanche, set off by his fall, cascading down cool moist pellets of dirt upon his pants, his shoes, upon his coat, upon his spine, upon the back of his neck, his head, filling his mouth, his ears, his eyes, his nostrils . . . .

The neighbor lady with the eggs wrapped in a napkin, knocked on Mr. Howard's door the next day for five minutes. When she opened the door, finally, and walked in, she found nothing but specules of rug-dust floating in the sunny air, the big halls were empty, the cellar smelled of coal and clinkers, and the attic had nothing in it but a rat, a spider, and a faded letter. "Funniest thing," she said many times in the following years, "what ever happened to Mr. Howard."

And adults, being what they are, never observant, paid no attention to the children playing "Poison" on Oak Bay Street, in all the following autumns. Even when the children leaped over one particular square of cement, twisted about and glanced at the marks on it which read:

"M. HOWARD—R.I.P."

"Who's Mr. Howard, Billy?"

"Aw, I guess he's the guy who laid the cement."

"What does R.I.P. mean?"

"Aw, who knows? You're poison! you stepped on it!"

"Get along, get along, children; don't stand in Mother's path! Get along now!"

UNCLE EINAR

"It will take only a minute," said Uncle Einar's sweet wife.

"I refuse," he said. "And that takes me but a *second*."

"I've worked all morning," she said, holding to her slender back. "And you refuse to help? It's drumming for a rain."

"Let it rain," he cried, morosely. "I'll not be pierced by lightning just to air your clothes."

"But you're so quick at it," she buttered him. "Take you no time."

"Again, I refuse." His vast tarpaulin wings hummed nervously behind his indignant back.

She gave him a slender rope on which were tied one hundred fresh-washed clothes. He turned it in his fingers with a distaste on his mouth and in his eyes. "So it's come to this," he muttered, bitterly. "To this, to this, to this." He almost wept angry and acid tears.

"Don't cry; you'll wet them down again," she said. "Jump up, now, run them about and it'll be finished in a jiffy."

"Run them about," he said in mockery, both hollow and deep and terribly wounded. "I say: let it thunder, let it pour!"

"If it was a nice sunny day I wouldn't ask," she said, reasonably. "All my washing gone for nothing if you don't. They'll hang about the house—"

That *did* it. If it was anything he hated it was clothes flagged and festooned so a man had to creep under them on the way across a room. He jumped up. He boomed his vast green wings.

"But only as far as the pasture fence," he said.

"That's a darling!" She laughed with relief.

Whirl: and up he jumped, like a spring, and his wings chewed and loved the cool air. Before you'd say Uncle Einar Has Green Wings he roared low across the farmland from his house, trailing the line of clothes in a vast fluttering loop behind, drying them in the pounding concussion and back-wash from his wings!

"Catch!"

A minute later, back from the trip, he sailed the clothes, dry as popcorn, down on a series of clean blankets she'd laid for their landing spot.

"Thank you, my sweet!" she cried.

"Gahh!" he shouted, and flew off to settle under the apple tree and brood.

*

Uncle Einar's beautiful silk-like wings hung like sea-green sails behind him and whirred and whispered from his shoulders when he sneezed or turned around swiftly. He was one of the few ones in the Family whose talent was visible. All the other cousins and nephews and brothers of his in various lands, in little towns across the world, did unseen mental things or did things with their fingers or their teeth, or blew across the sky like leaves, or loped in forests like wolves. They lived in comparative safety from the normal humans. Not so a man with great green wings.

Not that he hated his wings. Far from it. In his youth he'd always flown nights. Nights were the times for winged men. Daylight held dangers, always had, always would, but night, ah, night, he had sailed over far lands and farther seas. With no danger to himself. It had been a rich full flying and an exhilaration.

But now he could not fly at night.

On his way home to some high mountain pass in Europe after a Homecoming among Family members in Mellin Town, Illinois (some years ago) he had drunk too much rich crimson wine. "I'll be all right," he had told himself, blearily, as he beat his long way under the morning stars, over the moon-dreaming country hills beyond Mellin Town. And then—crack out of the sky—

A high tension tower.

Like a netted duck! A great sizzling! His face was blown black by a blue sparkler of wire. He fended off the electricity with a terrific back-jumping percussion of his wings, and fell.

His hitting the moonlit meadow under the tower made a noise like a large telephone book dropped from a window.

Early the next morning, his dew-sodden wings shaking violently, he stood up. It was still dark. There was a faint bandage of dawn stretched across the middle east. Soon the bandage would stain and all flight would be restricted. There was nothing to do but take refuge in the forest and wait out the day in the deepest thicket until another night gave his wings a hidden movement in the sky.

In this fashion he met his wife.

During the day which was warm for November 1st in Illinois country, pretty young Brunilla Wexley was out to udder a lost cow, for she carried a silver pail in one hand as she sidled through thickets and pleaded cleverly to the unseen cow to please return home or burst her gut with unplucked milk. The fact that the cow would have most certainly come home when her teats really needed pulling did not concern Brunilla Wexley. It was a sweet excuse for forest-journeying, thistle-blowing, and dandelion-chewing; all of which Brunilla was doing as she stumbled upon Uncle Einar.

Asleep near a bush, he seemed a man under a green shelter.

"Oh," said Brunilla, with a fever. "A man. In a camp-tent."

Uncle Einar awoke. The camp-tent spread like a large green fan behind him.

"Oh," said Brunilla, the cow-searcher. "A man with wings."

That was how she took it. She was startled, yes, but she had never been hurt by anyone in her life so she wasn't afraid of anything and it was a fancy thing to see a winged man and she was proud to meet him. She began to talk to him and in an hour they were old friends, and in two hours she'd quite forgotten his wings were there. And he somehow confessed how he happened to be in this wood.

"Yes, I noticed you looked banged around," she said. "That right wing looks very bad. You'd best let me take you home and fix it. You won't be able to fly all the way to Europe on it, anyway. And who wants to live in Europe now days?"

He thanked her but he didn't quite see how he could accept.

"But I live alone," she said. "For, as you see, I'm quite ugly."

He insisted she was not.

"How kind of you," she said. "But I am, there's no fooling myself. My folks are dead, I've a farm, a big one, all to myself, quite far from Mellin Town, and I'm in need of talking company."

But wasn't she afraid of him? he asked.

"Proud and envious would be more near it," she said. "*May* I?" And she stroked his large green membraned veils with careful envy. He shuddered at the touch and put his tongue between his teeth.

So there was nothing for it, but that he come to her house and have an ointment on that bruise, and my! what a burn across his face, beneath his eyes! "Lucky you weren't blinded," she said. "How'd it happen?"

"High tension tower," he said, and they were at her farm, hardly noticing they'd walked a mile, looking at each other.

Well, a day passed, and another. And he thanked her at her door and said he must be going, he certainly appreciated the ointment and the care and the lodging. It was twilight and between now, six o'clock, and five the next morning, he must cross an ocean and a continent. "Thank you, and goodbye," he said, and started to fly off in the dusk and crashed right into a maple tree.

"Oh!" she screamed, and ran to his unconscious body.

That *did* it. When he waked the next hour he knew he'd fly no nights again. His delicate night-perception was gone. The winged telepathy that told him where towers, trees and wires stood across his path, the fine, clear vision and mentality that guided him 'twixt cliff, pole, and pine, all of it was gone. That crack across his face, the blue electrical sparkle, had sloughed off his sensitivity, perhaps forever.

"How'm I to fly back to Europe?" he groaned, pitifully.

"Oh," she said, looking coyly at the floor. "Who wants Europe?"

*

They were married. A distant relative, one of the Family, tied the bond. His name was Minister Elliott, and the family constantly delighted in knowing that one of the fey Elliotts was actually a preacher of the Christian gospel. It was good for much irony and much jesting. Anyway, Minister Elliott arrived from Mellin Town with Father and Mother Elliott, and Laura. The ceremony was brief, if a little inverted and dark and mildly different to Miss Brunilla, but it ended gayly. Uncle Einar stood with his fresh bride thinking that he didn't dare fly back to Europe in the day time, which was the only time he could safely see now, for fear of being seen and shot down; but it didn't matter now, for with Brunilla beside him, Europe had less and less fascination for him.

He didn't have to see very well to fly straight up, or come down. So it was only natural that on the night of their wedding he took Brunilla in his arms and flew right straight up into the clouds.

A farmer, five miles over, glanced at a low cloud about midnight, saw faint glows and crackles.

"Heat lightnin'," he said, spitting.

They didn't come down till next morning; with the dew.

The marriage took. She was so wing-proud of him, it lifted her to think she was the only woman in the world married to a winged man. "Who else could say it?" she asked her mirror. And the answer was: "No one!"

He, on the other hand, found great beauty behind her

face, great kindness and understanding. He made some changes in his diet to fit her thinking, and was careful with his wings about the house; knocked porcelains and spilled lamps were nerve-scrapers, he didn't do them. He also changed his sleeping habits, since he couldn't fly nights now anyhow. And she in turn fixed chairs so they were comfortable for his wings, put extra padding here or took it out there, and the things she said were the things he loved her for. "We're in our cocoons, all of us," she said. "See how ugly I am?" she said. "But one day I'll break out, spread wings as fine and handsome as you."

"You broke out long ago," he said.

She thought it over. "Yes," she had to admit. "I know just which day it was, too. In the woods when I looked for a lost cow and found a camp-tent!" And they laughed, and in that moment, even as she'd said, her beauty proved that their meeting had slipped her from her ugliness, like a sword from its case.

They had children. At first there was a fear, all on his part, that they'd be winged.

"Nonsense," she said. "I'd love it. Keep them out from under foot."

"Then," he exclaimed, holding her, "they'd be in your *hair!*"

"Ow," she cried.

Four children were born, three boys and a girl, who, for their energy, seemed to have wings. They popped up like toadstools in a few years and on hot summer days would ask Father to sit under the apple tree and fan them with his cooling wings and tell them wild starlit tales of youth and sky excursions. This, he did. And told them of the winds and cloud textures, and what a star feels like melting in your mouth, and the taste of high mountain air, and how it feels to be a pebble dropped from Mt. Everest, turning to a green bloom, flowering your wings just before striking the frosty bottom.

This was his marriage, then.

And today, six years later, here sat Uncle Einar, here he was, fustering under the apple tree, grown impatient and unkind; not because this was his desire, but because after the long wait, he was still unable to fly nights, his extra sense had never returned. Here he sat despondently in the yard, looking like nothing more than a summer sun-parasol, green and discarded, abandoned for the season by the reckless vacationers who once sought refuge under its spread shadow. Was he to sit here forever, afraid to fly by day because someone might see him? Was his only flight to be as a clothes-drier for his good wife, or a fanner of children on hot August noons? Ah! To think!

He hadn't minded it so much at first. There had been Brunilla and the new marriage and, for a time, the children to raise. But now he was beginning to fret again. He was no good. His one occupation had always been flying, running Family errands, quicker than storms. Why, in the old days, he'd been faster than the telegraph. Like a boomerang he'd whickled over hills and valleys and like a thistle landed. He had never wanted for money, there are always people willing to employ a winged man.

But now? Bitterness! His wings jittered behind him.

"Papa, fan us," said little Meg.

The children stood before him, looking up at his thought-dark face.

"No," he said.

"Fan us, papa," said Ronald.

"It's a cool March day and there'll soon be rain," said Uncle Einar.

"There's a wind blowing, papa, that's all. The wind'll blow alla clouds way," said Stephen, no bigger than a bee.

"Will you come watch us, papa?" asked Michael.

He grew into himself, like the fingers inside a fist.

"Run on, run on," he told them. "Let papa brood."

On this day he was shut of marriage, love, the children of the love, and the love of the children. Brunilla was hanging in the clothes upon the back porch. "You whipped them dry as toast," she called, delighted, trying to brighten him, for she liked pots, pans, and people's faces all polished and silvery, and his brooding of late was like a rust which was hard to get off surfaces. "You're welcome," he said, listlessly, thinking of old skies, night skies, star skies, moon skies, wind skies, cool skies, midnight and dawn skies, cloudy skies and all kinds of skies. Was it to be his fate to scull the pasturage from now on, so low for fear of being seen that he might break wing on the silo, or crack it on a kindling fence? Misery in a deep well!

"Come watch us, papa," pleaded Meg.

"It's March," said Ronald.

"So it is," said Uncle Einar. "The rump of winter, which blows a fury."

"And we're goin' to the Hill," said Michael, his eyes lighted like little globes. "With all the kids from town."

Uncle Einar chewed his hand, gently, on the edge. "What hill's that?"

"The Kite Hill, of course!" they sang together.

Now he looked at them.

Each held a large paper kite against their gasping bosoms, their faces sweating with anticipation and animal glowing. In their small fingers were balls of white twine. From the kites, colored red and blue and yellow and green, hung caudal appendages of cotton and silk strips.

"We'll fly our kites!" said Ronald. "Won't you come watch?"

"No," he said, sadly. "I'd be seen. You know I mustn't be seen by anyone or there'd be trouble."

"You could hide and watch from the woods. We want you to see." said Meg.

"The kites?" he said.

"Made 'em ourselves," said Michael proudly. "Just because we know how."

"How do you know how?"

"You're our father!" was the instant cry. "That's why!"

He looked from one to the second to the third, and the fourth. He sighed. "A kite festival, is it?"

"Yes, sir!"

"I'm going to win," said Meg.

"No, *I'm*!" Michael contradicted.

"Me, me!" piped Stephen.

"God up the chimney!" roared Uncle Einar, leaping up with a deafening kettledrum of his wings. "Children! Children, I love you, I love you most dearly!"

"Are you sick?" Michael wanted to know, backing off.

"No, by Heaven!" chanted Einar, flexing his wings to their greatest propulsion and plundering. Whoom! they whammed together like cymbals and the children fell flat, giggling, from the backwash! "I have it, I *have* it! I'm free again, free! Fire in the flue! Feather on the wind! Brunilla!" Einar called to the house. She stuck her head out. "I'm free!" he called to her, flushed and tall, on his toes. "Listen, Brunilla, I don't need the night any more! I can fly by day, now! I don't need the night! I'll fly *every* day and *any* day of the year from now on, and nobody'll know, and nobody'll shoot me down, and, and—but, God, I waste time, talking. Look!"

And as the shocked, worried members of his family watched he seized the cotton tail from one of the little kites, tied it to his belt near his rump, grabbed the twine ball and held one end between his teeth, gave the other end to his children, and up, up into the air he flew, away into the March wind!

And across the meadows and over the farms his children ran, letting out the string into the daylit sky, bubbling and stumbling, and Brunilla stood back upon the farm land where they lived and waved and laughed with release to know that from now on her family would be in joy, and the children marched to the far Kite Hill and stood there, the four of them, holding the ball of twine in their eager, proud fingers, each of them tugging and directing and pulling. The children from Mellin Town came running with *their* small kites to let up on the wind, and they saw the great green kite dipping and hovering in the sky and they exclaimed:

"Oh, oh, what a kite! What a kite! Oh, oh! I wish I had a kite like that! Oh, what a kite! Where'd you get it!"

"Our father made it!" cried Meg and Michael and Stephen and Ronald, and gave an exultant pull upon the twine and the humming, thundering kite in the sky flew and soared and made a great and magical exclamation mark across a cloud!

THE WIND

The phone rang at six thirty that evening. It was December, and already dark as Thompson picked up the phone.

"Hello."

"Hello, *Herb?*"

"Oh, it's you, Allin."

"Is your wife home, Herb?"

"Sure. Why?"

"Damn it."

Herb Thompson held the receiver quietly. "What's up? You sound funny."

"I wanted you to come over tonight."

"We're having company."

"I wanted you to spend the night. When's your wife going away?"

"That's next week," said Thompson. "She'll be in Ohio

for about nine days. Her mother's sick. I'll come over then."

"I wish you could come over tonight."

"Wish I could. Company and all, my wife'd kill me."

"I wish you could come over."

"What's it? the wind again?"

"Oh, no. No."

"Is it the wind?" asked Thompson.

The voice on the phone hesitated. "Yeah. Yeah, it's the wind."

"It's a clear night, there's not much wind."

"There's enough. It comes in the window and blows the curtains a little bit. Just enough to tell me."

"Look, why don't you come and spend the night here?" said Herb Thompson looking around the lighted hall.

"Oh, no. It's too late for that. It might catch me on the way over. It's a damned long distance, I wouldn't dare, but thanks, anyway. It's thirty miles, but thanks."

"Take a sleeping tablet."

"I've been standing in the door for the past hour, Herb. I can see it building up in the west. There are some clouds there and I saw one of them kind of rip apart. There's a wind coming, all right."

"Well, you just take a nice sleeping tablet. And call me any time you want to call. Later this evening if you want."

"Any time?" said the voice on the phone.

"Sure."

"I'll do that, but I wish you could come out. Yet I wouldn't want you hurt. You're my best friend and I wouldn't want that. Maybe it's best I face this thing alone. I'm sorry I bother you."

"Hell, what's a friend for? Tell you what you do, sit down and get some writing done this evening," said Herb Thompson, shifting from one foot to the other in the hall. "You'll forget about the Himalayas and the Valley of the Winds and this preoccupation of yours with storms and hurricanes. Get another chapter done on your next travel book."

"I might do that. Maybe I will, I don't know. Maybe I will. I might do that. Thanks a lot for letting me bother you."

"Thanks, hell! Get off the wire, now, you. My wife's calling me to dinner."

Herb Thompson hung up.

He went and sat down at the supper table and his wife sat across from him. "Was that Allin?" she asked. He nodded. "Him and his winds that blow up and winds that blow down and winds that blow hot and blow cold," she said, handing him his plate heaped with food.

"He did have a time in the Himalayas, during the war," said Herb Thompson.

"You don't believe what he said about that valley, do you?"

"It makes a good story."

"Climbing around, climbing up things. Why do men climb mountains and scare themselves."

"It was snowing," said Herb Thompson.

"Was it?"

"And raining and hailing and blowing all at once, in that valley. Allin's told me a dozen times. He tells it well. He was up pretty high. Clouds, and all. The valley made a noise."

"I *bet* it did," she said, sulkily.

"Like a lot of winds instead of just one. Winds from all over the world." He took a bite. "So says Allin."

"He shouldn't have gone there and looked, in the first place," she said. "You go poking around and first thing you know you get ideas. Winds start getting angry at you for intruding, and they follow you."

"Don't joke at him, he's my best friend," snapped Herb Thompson.

"It's all so silly!"

"Nevertheless, he's been through a lot. That storm in Bombay, later, and the hurricane in the Pacific islands two months after that. And that time, at Cornwall."

"I have no sympathy for a man who continually runs into wind storms and hurricanes, and then gets a persecution complex because of it."

The phone rang again.

"Don't answer it," she said.

"Maybe it's important."

"It's only Allin, again."

They sat there and the phone rang nine times and they didn't answer. Finally, it quieted. They finished dinner. Out in the kitchen, the window curtains gently moved in a small breeze from a slightly opened window.

The phone rang again.

"I can't let it ring," he said, and answered it. "Oh, hello, Allin."

"Herb! It's here! It got here!"

"You're too near the phone, back up a little."

"I stood in the open door and waited for it. I saw it coming down the highway, shaking all the trees, one by one, until it shook the trees just outside the house and it dived down toward the door and I slammed the door in its face!"

Thompson didn't say anything. He couldn't think of anything to say, his wife was watching him in the hall door.

"How interesting," he said, at last.

"It's all around the house, Herb. I can't get out now, I can't do anything. But I fooled it, I let it think it had me, and just as it came down to get me I slammed and locked the door! I was ready for it, I've been getting ready for weeks."

"Have you, now; tell me about it, Allin, old man," Herb Thompson played it jovially into the phone, while his wife looked on and his neck began to sweat.

"It began six weeks ago . . . ."

"Oh, yes? Well, well."

". . . I thought I had it licked. I thought it had given up following and trying to get me. But it was just waiting. Six weeks ago I heard the wind laughing and whispering around the corners of my house, out here. Just for an hour or so, not very long, not very loud. Then it went away."

Thompson nodded into the phone. "Glad to hear it, glad to hear it." His wife stared at him.

"It came back, the next night. It slammed the shutters and kicked sparks out the chimney. It came back five nights in a row, a little stronger each time. When I opened the front door, it came in at me and tried to pull me out, but it wasn't strong enough. Tonight it *is*."

"Glad to hear you're feeling better," said Thompson.

"I'm not better, what's wrong with you? Is your wife listening to us?"

"Yes."

"Oh, I see. I know I sound like a fool."

"Not at all. Go on."

Thompson's wife went back into the kitchen. He relaxed. He sat down on a little chair near the phone. "Go on, Allin, get it out of you, you'll sleep better."

"It's all around the house now, like a great big vacuum machine nuzzling at all the gables. It's knocking the trees around."

"That's funny, there's no wind *here*, Allin."

"Of course not, it doesn't care about you, only about me!"

"I guess that's one way to explain it."

"It's a killer, Herb, the biggest damnedest prehistoric killer that ever hunted prey. A big sniffling hound, trying to smell me out, find me. It pushes its big cold nose up to the house, taking air, and when it finds me in the parlor it drives its pressure there, and when I'm in the kitchen it goes there. It's trying to get in the windows, now, but I had them reinforced and I put new hinges on the doors, and bolts. It's a strong house. They built them strong in the old days. I've got all the lights in the house on, now. The house is all lighted up, bright. The wind followed me from room to room, looking through all the windows, when I switched them on. Oh!"

"What's wrong?"

"It just snatched off the front screen door!"

"I wish you'd come over here and spend the night, Allin."

"I can't! God, I can't leave the house. I can't do anything. I know this wind, Lord, it's big and it's smart. I tried to light a cigarette a moment ago, and a little draft sucked the match out. The wind likes to play games, it likes to taunt me, it's taking its time with me, it's got all night. And now! God, right now, one of my old travel books, on the library table, I wish you could see it. A little breeze from God knows what small hole in the house, has flipped the cover of the book open and the little breeze is—turning the pages one by one. I wish you could see it. There's my introduction. Do you remember the introduction to my Tibet book, Herb?"

"Yes."

"This book is dedicated to those who lost the game of elements, written by one who has seen, but who has always escaped."

"Yes, I remember."

"The lights have gone out!"

The phone crackled.

"The power lines just went down. Are you there, Herb!"

"I still hear you."

"The wind got jealous of all that light in my house, it tore the power lines down. The telephone will probably go next. Oh, it's a real party, me and the wind, I tell you! Just a second."

"Allin?" A silence. Herb leaned against the mouthpiece. His wife glanced in from the kitchen. Herb Thompson waited. "Allin?"

"I'm back," said the voice on the phone. "There was a draft from the door and I shoved some wadding under it to keep it from cooling my legs. I'm glad you didn't come out after all, Herb, I wouldn't want you in this mess. It just broke one of the living room windows and a regular gale is in the house, knocking pictures off the wall. Do you hear it?"

Herb Thompson listened. There was a wild sirening on the phone and a whistling and banging. Allin shouted over it. "Do you hear it?"

Herb Thompson swallowed drily. "I hear it."

"It wants me alive, Herb. It doesn't dare knock the house down in one fell blow. That'd kill me. It wants me alive, so it can pull me apart, finger by finger. It wants what's inside me. My mind, my brain. It wants my life-power, my psychic force, my ego. It wants intellect."

"My wife's calling me, Allin, I have to go wipe the dishes."

"It's a big cloud of vapors, winds from all over the

world. The same wind that ripped the Celebes a year ago, the same pampero that killed in Argentina, the typhoon that fed well in Hawaii, and the hurricane that knocked the coast of Africa early this year. It's part of all those storms I escaped. It followed me from the Himalayas because it didn't want me to know what I know of it, the Valley of the Winds where it gathers and plans its destruction. Something, a long time ago, gave it a start in the direction of life. I know its feeding grounds, I know where it is born and where parts of it expire. For that reason, it hates me, for I have written books against it, telling how to defeat it. It doesn't want me preaching any more. It wants to incorporate me into its huge body, give it knowledge. It wants me on its own side!"

"I have to hang up, Allin, my wife—"

"What?" A pause, the blowing of the wind in the phone, distantly. "What did you say?"

"Call me back in about an hour, Allin."

He hung up.

He went out to wipe the dishes. His wife looked at him and he looked at the dishes, rubbing them with a towel.

"What's it like out tonight?" he said.

"Nice. Not very chilly. Stars," she said. "Why?"

"Nothing."

The phone rang three times in the next hour. At eight o'clock the company arrived, Stoddard and his wife. They sat around until eight-thirty talking and then got out and set up the card table and began to play Black Jack.

Herb Thompson shuffled the cards over and over, with a clittering, shuttering effect and clapped them out, one at a time before the three other players. Talk went back and forth. He lit a cigar and made it into a fine grey ash at the tip, and adjusted his cards in his hand and on occasion lifted his head and listened. There was no sound outside the house. His wife saw him do this, and he cut it out immediately, and discarded a Jack of Clubs.

He puffed slowly on his cigar and they all talked quietly with occasionally small eruptions of laughter, and the clock in the hall sweetly chimed nine o'clock.

"Here we all are," said Herb Thompson, taking his cigar out and looking at it reflectively. "And life is sure funny."

"Eh?" said Mr. Stoddard.

"Nothing, except here we are, living our lives, and some place else on earth a billion other people live their lives."

"That's a rather naive statement."

"True, nevertheless. Life," he put his cigar back in his lips. "Is a lonely thing. Even with married people. Sometimes when you're in a person's arms you feel a million miles away from them."

"I like *that,*" said his wife.

"I didn't mean it that way," he explained, not with haste; because he felt no guilt, he took his time. "I mean we all believe what we believe and live our own little lives while other people live entirely different ones. I mean, we sit here in this room while a thousand people are dying. Some of cancer, some of pneumonia, some of tuberculosis. I imagine someone in the United States is dying right now in a motor crash."

"This isn't very stimulating conversation," said his wife.

"I mean to say, we all live and don't think about how other people think or live their lives or die. We wait until death comes *to* us. What I mean is here we sit, on our self-assured butt-bones, while, thirty miles away, in a big old house, completely surrounded by night and God-knows-what, one of the finest guys who ever lived is—"

"Herb!"

He puffed and chewed on his cigar and stared blindly at his cards. "Sorry." He blinked rapidly and bit his cigar. "Is it my turn?"

"It's your turn."

The playing went around the table, with a flittering of cards, murmurs, conversation, laughter. Herb Thompson sank lower into his chair and began to look ill.

The phone rang. Thompson jumped and ran to it and jerked it off the hook.

"Herb! I've been calling and calling."

"I couldn't answer, my wife wouldn't let me."

"What's it like at your house, Herb?"

"What do you mean, what's it like?"

"Has the company come?"

"Hell, yes, it has—"

"Are you talking and laughing and playing cards?"

"Christ, yes, but what has that got to do with—"

"Are you smoking your ten cent cigar?"

"God damn it, yes, but . . ."

"Swell," said the voice on the phone, enviously. "That sure is swell. I wish I could be there. I wish I didn't know the things I know. I wish lots of things."

"Are you all right?"

"So far, so good. I'm locked in the kitchen now. The front wall of the house just blew in. But I planned my retreat. When the kitchen door gives, I'm heading for the cellar. If I'm lucky I may hold out there until morning. It'll have to tear the whole damned house down to get to me, and the cellar floor is pretty solid. I have a shovel and I may dig—deeper . . . ."

It sounded like a lot of other voices on the phone.

"What's *that?*" Herb Thompson demanded, cold, shivering.

"That?" asked the voice on the phone. "Those are the voices of ten thousand killed in a typhoon, seven thousand killed by a hurricane, three thousand buried by a cyclone. Am I boring you? It's a long list. That's what the wind is, you know. It's a lot of spirits, a lot of people dead. The wind killed them and took their intellects, their spirits, to give itself intelligence. It took all their voices and made them into one voice. Interesting, isn't it? All those millions of peoples killed in the past centuries, twisted and tortured and taken from continent to continent on the backs and in the bellies of monsoons and whirlwinds. I get very poetic at a time like this."

The phone echoed and rang with voices and shouts and whinings.

"Come on back, Herb," said his wife, at the card table.

"That's how the wind gets more intelligent each year, it adds to its intellect, body by body, life by life, death by death."

"We're waiting for you, Herb," called his wife.

"Damn it!" he turned, almost snarling. "Wait just a moment, won't you!" Back to the phone. "Allin, if you want me to come out there now, I will, if you need help."

"Wouldn't think of it. This is a grudge fight, wouldn't do to have you in it. Well, I'd better hang up. The kitchen door looks very weak and I'll have to get into the cellar."

"Call me back, later?"

"Maybe, if I'm lucky. I don't think I'll make it this time. I slipped away and escaped in the Celebes that time, but I think it has me now. I hope I haven't bothered you too much, Herb."

"You haven't bothered anyone, damn it. Call me back."

"I'll try . . . ."

Herb Thompson went back into the card game. His wife glared at him. "How's Allin, your friend?" she asked. "Is he sober?"

"He's never taken a drink in his life," said Thompson, sullenly, sitting down. "I should have gone out there earlier."

"But he's called every night for six weeks and you've been out there at least ten nights to sleep with him and nothing was wrong."

"He needs help. He might hurt himself."

"You were just out there, two nights ago, you can't always be running after him."

"First thing in the morning I'll move him into a sanitarium. Didn't want to. He seems so reasonable, so sane."

They played out the games. At ten-thirty coffee was served. Herb Thompson drank his slowly, looking at the phone. I wonder if he's in the cellar now, he thought.

Herb Thompson walked to the phone, called long-distance, put through a call.

"I'm sorry," said the operator. "The lines are down in that district. When the lines are repaired, we will put your call through."

"Then the telephone lines *are* down!" cried Thompson, slamming down the phone. Turning, he ran down the hall, opened the closet, pulled out his hat and coat. "Excuse me," he shouted. "You *will* excuse me, won't you? I'm sorry," he said, to his amazed guests and his wife with the coffee urn in her hand. "Herb!" she cried at him. "I've got to get out there!" he said, in return. He slipped into his coat.

There was a soft, faint stirring at the door.

Everybody in the room tensed and straightened up.

"Who could that be?" asked his wife.

The soft stirring was repeated, very quietly.

Thompson hurried down the hall where he stopped, alert.

Outside, faintly, he heard laughter.

"I'll be damned," said Thompson. He put his hand on the doorknob, pleasantly shocked and relieved. "I'd know that laugh anywhere. It's Allin. He came on over in his car, after all. Couldn't wait until morning to tell me his confounded tall tales." Thompson chuckled weakly. "Probably brought some friends with him. Sounds like a lot of other people . . . ."

He opened the front door.

The porch was vacant.

Thompson showed no surprise, his face grew amusedly sly. He laughed. "Allin? None of your tricks now! Come on." He switched on the porch-light and peered out and around. "Where are you, Allin? Come on, now."

A little breeze blew into his face.

Thompson waited a moment, suddenly chilled to his marrow. He stepped out on the porch and looked uneasily about, very carefully.

A sudden wind caught and whipped his coat flaps, disheveled his hair. He thought he heard laughter again. The wind suddenly rounded the house and was a pressure everywhere at once, and then, storming for a full minute, passed on.

The wind died down, sad, mourning in the high trees, passing away; going back out to the sea, to the Celebes, to the Ivory Coast, to Sumatra and Cape Horn, to Cornwall and the Philippines. Fading, fading, fading.

Thompson stood there, cold. He went in and closed the door and leaned against it, and didn't move, eyes closed.

"What's wrong . . . ?" asked his wife.

THE NIGHT

You are a child in a small town. You are, to be exact, eight years old, and it is growing late at night. Late, for you, accustomed to bedding in at nine or nine-thirty; once in awhile perhaps begging Mom or Dad to let you stay up later to hear Sam and Henry on that strange radio that is popular in this year of 1927. But most of the time you are in bed and snug at this time of night.

It is a warm summer evening. You live in a small house on a small street in the outer part of town where there are few street lights. There is only one store open, about a block away; Mrs. Singer's. In the hot evening Mother has been ironing the Monday wash and you have been intermittently begging for ice-cream and staring into the dark.

You and your mother are all alone at home in the warm darkness of summer. Finally, just before it is time for Mrs. Singer to close her store, Mother relents and tells you:

"Run get a pint of ice-cream and be sure she packs it tight."

You ask if you can get a scoop of chocolate ice-cream on top, because you don't like vanilla, and mother agrees. You clutch the money and run barefooted over the warm evening cement sidewalk, under the apple trees and oak trees, toward the store. The town is so quiet and far off, you can only hear the crickets sounding in the spaces beyond the hot indigo trees that hold back the stars.

Your bare feet slap the pavement, you cross the street and find Mrs. Singer moving ponderously about her store, singing Yiddish melodies.

"Pint ice-cream?" she says. "Chocolate on top? Yes!"

You watch her fumble the metal top off the ice-cream freezer and manipulate the scoop, packing the cardboard pint chock full with "chocolate on top, yes!" You give the money, receive the chill, icy pack, and rubbing it across your brow and cheek, laughing, you thump barefootedly homeward. Behind you, the lights of the lonely little store blink out and there is only a street light shimmering on the corner, and the whole city seems to be going to sleep . . .

Opening the screen door you find Mom still ironing. She looks hot and irritated, but she smiles just the same.

"When will Dad be home from lodge-meeting?" you ask.

"About eleven-thirty or twelve," Mother replies. She

takes the ice-cream to the kitchen, divides it. Giving you your special portion of chocolate, she dishes out some for herself and the rest is put away, "For Skipper and your father when they come."

Skipper is your brother. He is your older brother. He's twelve and healthy, red-faced, hawk-nosed, tawny-haired, broad-shouldered for his years, and always running. He is allowed to stay up later than you. Not much later, but enough to make him feel it is worth while having been born first. He is over on the other side of town this evening to a game of kick-the-can and will be home soon. He and the kids have been yelling, kicking, running for hours, having fun. Soon he will come clomping in, smelling of sweat and green grass on his knees where he fell, and smelling very much in all ways like Skipper; which is natural.

You sit enjoying the ice-cream. You are at the core of the deep quiet summer night. Your mother and yourself and the night all around this small house on this small street. You lick each spoon of ice-cream thoroughly before digging for another, and Mom puts her ironing board away and the hot iron in its case, and she sits in the armchair by the phonograph, eating her dessert and saying, "My lands, it was a hot day today. It's still hot. Earth soaks up all the heat and lets it out at night. It'll be soggy sleeping."

You both sit there listening to the summer silence. The dark is pressed down by every window and door, there is no sound because the radio needs a new battery, and you have played all the Knickerbocker Quartet records and Al Jolson and Two Black Crows records to exhaustion; so you just sit on the hardwood floor by the door and look out into the dark dark dark, pressing your nose against the screen until the flesh of its tip is moulded into small dark squares.

"I wonder where your brother is?" Mother says after awhile. Her spoon scrapes on the dish. "He should be home by now. It's almost nine-thirty."

"He'll be here," you say, knowing very well that he will be.

You follow Mom out to wash the dishes. Each sound, each rattle of spoon or dish is amplified in the baked evening. Silently, you go to the living room, remove the couch cushions and, together, yank it open and extend it down into the double bed that it secretly is. Mother makes the bed, punching pillows neatly to flump them up for your head. Then, as you are unbuttoning your shirt, she says:

"Wait awhile, Doug."

"Why?"

"Because. I say so."

"You look funny, Mom."

Mom sits down a moment, then stands up, goes to the door, and calls. You listen to her calling and calling Skipper, Skipper, Skiiiiiiiiperrrrrrrr over and over. Her calling goes out into the summmer warm dark and never comes back. The echoes pay no attention.

Skipper. Skipper. Skipper.

Skipper!

And as you sit on the floor a coldness that is not ice-cream and not winter, and not part of summer's heat, goes through you. You notice Mom's eyes sliding, blinking; the way she stands undecided and is nervous. All of these things.

She opens the screen door. Stepping out into the night she walks down the steps and down the front sidewalk under the lilac bush. You listen to her moving feet.

She calls again. Silence.

She calls twice more. You sit in the room. Any moment now Skipper will reply, from down the long long narrow street:

"All right, Mom! All right, Mother! Hey!"

But he doesn't answer. And for two minutes you sit looking at the made-up bed, the silent radio, the silent phonograph, at the chandelier with its crystal bobbins gleaming quietly, at the rug with the scarlet and purple curlicues on it. You stub your toe on the bed purposely to see if it hurts. It does.

Whining, the screen door opens, and Mother says, "Come on, Shorts. We'll take a walk."

"Where to?"

"Just down the block. Come on. Better put your shoes on, though. You'll catch cold."

"No, I won't. I'll be all right."

You take her hand. Together you walk down St. James street. You smell lilacs in blossom; fallen apples lying crushed and odorous in the deep grass. Underfoot, the concrete is still warm, and the crickets are sounding louder against the darkening dark. You reach a corner, turn, and walk toward the ravine.

Off somewhere, a car goes by, flashing its lights in the distance. There is such a complete lack of life, light and activity. Here and there, back off from where you are walking toward the ravine you see faint squares of light where people are still up. But most of the houses, darkened, are sleeping already, and there are a few lightless places where the occupants of a dwelling sit talking low dark talk on their front porches. You hear a porch swing squeaking as you walk near.

"I wish your father was home," says Mother. Her large hand tightens around your small one. "Just wait'll I get that boy. I'll spank him within an inch of his life."

A razor strop hangs in the kitchen for this. You think of it, remember when Dad has doubled and flourished it with muscled control over your frantic limbs. You doubt Mother will carry out her promise.

Now you have walked another block and are standing by the holy black silhouette of the German Baptist Church at the Corner of Chapel street and Glen Rock. In back of the church a hundred yards away, the ravine begins. You can smell it. It has a dark sewer, rotten foliage, thick green odor. It is a wide ravine that cuts and twists across the town, a jungle by day, a place to let alone at night, Mother has often declared.

You should feel encouraged by the nearness of the German Baptist Church, but you are not—because the building is not illumined, is cold and useless as a pile of ruins on the ravine edge.

You are only eight years old, you know little of death, fear, or dread. Death is the waxen effigy in the coffin when you were six and Grandfather passed away—looking like a great fallen vulture in his casket, silent withdrawn, no more to tell you how to be a good boy, no more to comment succinctly on politics. Death is your little sister one morning when you awaken at the age of seven, look into her crib and see her staring up at you with a blind blue, fixed and frozen stare until the men came with a small wicker basket to take her away. Death is when you stand by her high-chair four weeks later and suddenly realized she'll never be in it again, laughing and crying and make you jealous of her because she was born. That is death.

But this is more than death. This summer night wading deep in time and stars and warm eternity. It is an essence of all thc things you will ever feel or see or hear in your life again, being brought steadily home to you all at once.

Leaving the sidewalk, you walk along a trodden, pebbled, weed-fringed path to the ravine's edge. Crickets, in loud full drumming chorus now, are shouting to quiver the dead. You follow obediently behind brave, fine, tall mother who is defender of all the universe. You feel braveness because she goes before, and you hang back a trifle for a moment, and then hurry on, too. Together, then, you approach, reach and pause at the very edge of civilization.

The ravine.

Here and now, down there in that pit of jungled blackness is suddenly all the evil you will ever know. Evil you will never understand. All of the nameless things are there. Later, when you have grown you'll be given names to label them with. Meaningless syllables to describe the waiting nothingness. Down there in the huddled shadow, among thick trees and trailed vines, lives the odor of decay. Here, at this spot, civilization ceases, reason ends, and a universal evil takes over.

You realize you are alone. You and your mother. Her hand trembles.

Her hand *trembles*.

Your belief in your private world is shattered. You feel Mother tremble. Why? Is she, too, doubtful? But she is bigger, stronger, more intelligent than yourself, isn't she? Does she, too, feel that intangible menace, that groping out of darkness, that crouching malignancy down below? Is there, then, no strength in growing up? no solace in being an adult? no sanctuary in life? no flesh citadel strong enough to withstand the scrabbling assault of midnights? Doubts flush you. Ice-cream lives again in your throat, stomach, spine and limbs; you are instantly cold as a wind out of December-gone.

You realize that all men are like this. That each person is to himself one alone. One oneness, a unit in a society, but always afraid. Like here, standing. If you should scream now, if you should holler for help, would it matter?

You are so close to the ravine now that in the instant of your scream, in the interval between someone hearing it and running to find you, much could happen.

Blackness could come swiftly, swallowing; and in one titanically freezing moment all would be concluded. Long before dawn, long before police with flashlights might probe the disturbed pathway, long before men with trembling brains could rustle down the pebbles to your help. Even if they were within five hundred yards of you now, and help *certainly* is, in three seconds a dark tide could rise to take all eight years of life away from you and—

The essential impact of life's loneliness crushes your beginning-to-tremble body. Mother is alone, too. She cannot look to the sanctity of marriage, the protection of her family's love, she cannot look to the United States Constitution or the City Police, she cannot look anywhere, in this very instant, save into her heart, and there she'll find nothing but uncontrollable repugnance and a will to fear. In this instant it is an individual problem seeking an individual solution. You must accept being alone and work on from there.

You swallow hard, cling to her. Oh, Lord, don't let her die, please, you think. Don't do anything to us. Father will be coming home from lodge-meeting in an hour and if the house is empty . . . ?

Mother advances down the path into the primeval jungle. Your voice trembles. "Mom. Skip's all right. Skip's all right. He's all right. Skip's all right."

Mother's voice is strained, high. "He always comes through here. I tell him not to, but those darned kids, they come through here anyway. Some night he'll come through and never come out again—"

Never come out again. That could mean anything. Tramps. Criminals. Darkness. Accident. Most of all—death.

Alone in the universe.

There are a million small towns like this all over the world. Each as dark, as lonely, each as removed, as full of shuddering and wonder. The reedy playing of minor key violins is the small towns' music, with no lights but many shadows. Oh the vast swelling loneliness of them. The secret damp ravines of them. Life is a horror lived in them at night, when at all sides sanity, marriage, children, happiness, are threatened by an ogre called Death.

Mother raises her voice into the dark.

"Skip! Skipper!" she calls. "Skip! Skipper!"

Suddenly, both of you realize there is something wrong. Something very wrong. You listen intently and realize what it is.

The crickets have stopped chirping.

Silence is complete.

Never in your life a silence like this one. One so utterly complete. Why should the crickets cease? Why? What reason? They have never stopped ever before. Not ever.

Unless. Unless—

Something is going to happen.

It is as if the whole ravine is tensing, bunching together

its black fibres, drawing in power from all about sleeping countrysides, for miles and miles. From dew-sodden forest and dells and rolling hills where dogs tilt heads to moons, from all around the great silence is sucked into one center, and you at the core of it. In ten seconds now, something will happen, something will happen. The crickets keep their truce, the stars are so low you can almost brush the tinsel. There are swarms of them, hot and sharp.

Growing, growing, the silence. Growing, growing the tenseness. Oh it's so dark, so far away from everything. Oh God!

And then, way way off across the ravine:

"Okay Mom! Coming, Mother!"

And again:

"Hi, Mom! Coming, Mom!"

And then the quick scuttering of tennis shoes padding down through the pit of the ravine as three kids come dashing, giggling. Your brother Skipper, Chuck Redman and Augie Bartz. Running, giggling.

The stars suck up like the stung antennae of ten million snails.

The crickets sing!

The darkness pulls back, startled, shocked, angry. Pulls back, losing its appetite at being so rudely interrupted as it prepared to feed. As the dark retreats like a wave on a shore, three kids pile out of it, laughing.

"Hi, Mom! Hi, Shorts! Hey!"

It smells like Skipper all right. Sweat and grass and

his oiled leather baseball glove.

"Young man, you're going to get a licking," declares Mother. She puts away her fear instantly. You know she will never tell anybody of it, ever. It will be in her heart though, for all time, as it is in your heart, for all time.

You walk home to bed in the late summer night. You are glad Skipper is alive. Very glad. For a moment there you thought—

Far off in the dim moonlit country, over a viaduct and down a valley, a train goes rushing along and it whistles like a lost metal thing, nameless and running. You go to bed, shivering, beside your brother, listening to that train whistle, and thinking of a cousin who lived way out in the country where that train is now; a cousin who died of pneumonia late at night years and years ago . . . . You smell the sweat of Skip beside you. It is magic. You stop trembling. You hear footsteps outside the house on the sidewalk, as Mother is turning out the lights. A man clears his throat in a way you recognize.

Mom says, "That's your father."

It is.

THERE WAS AN OLD WOMAN

"No, there's no leif arguing. I got my mind fixed. You run along with your silly wicker basket. Land, land, where you ever get notions like that? You just skit out of here and don't bother me, I got my tattin' and knittin' to do, and no never minds about tall dark gentlemen with fangled ideas."

The tall dark young man stood quietly, not moving. Aunt Tildy hurried on with her talk.

"You *heard* what I said, young man. If you got a mind to talk to me, well, you can talk, but meantime I hope you don't mind if I pour myself a bit of coffee. There. If you'd been a bit more polite, I mighta offered you some; but you stride in here high and mighty and you never rapped on the door or nothing. I don't like that kind of doing. You think you *own* the place."

Aunt Tildy fussed with her lap. "Land, now, where'd

I lay the yarn? I'm making myself a comforter. These winters get on mighty chill, I'll allow, and it ain't fittin' for a lady with bones like rice-paper to be settin' in a drafty old house like this without warmin' herself."

The tall dark man sat down.

"That's an antique chair, so be gentle on it," warned Aunt Tildy. "Now, if you wants to start again, tell me things you got to tell, I'll listen respectful. But keep your voice in your shoes and stop staring at me with funny lights in your eyes. Land, it gives me the collie-wobbles."

The bone-porcelain, flowered clock on the mantel finished chiming three. Out in the hall, grouped around the wicker basket, four men waited, quietly, hardly moving, as if they were frozen.

"Now, about that wicker basket," said Aunt Tildy. "It's past six feet long, and by the look of it, it ain't laundry. And those four men you walked in with, you don't need them to carry that basket—why, it's light as thistles. Eh?"

The dark young man was leaning forward on the antique chair. Something in his face suggested that the basket wouldn't be so light after awhile. There'd be something in it.

"Shaw, now." Aunt Tildy mused. "Now where've I seen a wicker like that before? Seems it was only a couple year ago. Seems to me—oh! Now I remembers. Certainly I do. It was when Mrs. Dwyer passed away next door."

Aunt Tildy set her coffee cup down, sternly. "So *that's* what you're up on? I thought you were workin' to sell me something. Just set until my little Emily trounces home from college this afternoon! I wrote her a note the other day. Not admittin', of course, that I wasn't feelin' quite ripe and pert, but sort of hintin' I want to see her again, it's been a bunch of weeks. She livin' in New York and all. Almost like my own daughter, Emily is.

"Now, she'll take care of you, young man. She'll shoo you out'n this parlor so quick it'll—"

The dark young man looked at her as if she were tired.

"No, I'm *not,*" snapped Aunt Tildy.

He weaved back and forth on the chair, half shutting his eyes, resting himself. Maybe she would like to rest, too? Nice rest.

"Great sons of Goshen on the Gilberry Dike! I got a hunderd comforters, two hunderds of sweaters and six hunderds of pot-holders in these fingers, no matter they're skinny! You run away and come back when I'm done, and maybe I'll talk to you." Aunt Tildy shifted subjects. "Let me tell you about Emily. She's such a sweet, fair child."

Aunt Tildy nodded thoughtfully. Emily. With hair like light yellow corn tassles, just as soft and sweet.

"I well remembers the day her mother died, twenty years ago, leavin' Emily to my house. That's why I'm mad at you and your wickers and such goings-on. Who ever heard of people dyin' for any good cause? Young man, I don't *like* it. Why, I remembers—"

Aunt Tildy paused, a brief pain of memory touched her heart. She remembered twenty-five years back, her father's voice in that old time fragment:

"Tildy," he'd said, "what are you going to do in life?

The way you act, men don't have much with you. Nothing permanent, I mean. You kiss and run. You don't settle down and marry and raise children."

"Papa," Tildy snapped right back at him, "I like laughin' and playin' and singin', but I'm not the marryin' kind. You know why?"

"Why?" asked Papa.

"I can't find a man with my philosophy, Papa."

"What 'philosophy's' that?"

"That death is silly! And it *is*. It took Mama when we needed her most. Now, do you call that intelligent?"

Papa looked at her and his eyes got wet and grey and bleak. He patted her shoulder. "You're always right, Tildy. But what can we do? Death comes to everybody."

"Fight back!" she cried. "Strike it under the belt! Fight it! Don't believe in it!"

"It can't be done," said Papa, sadly. "Each of us is all alone in the world."

"There's got to be a start somewhere, Papa. I'm startin' my own philosophy here and now," Tildy declared. "Why, it's just silly that people live a couple years and then are dropped like a wet seed in a hole and nothing sprouts but a smell. What good do they do that way? They lay there a million years, helpin' nobody. Most of them fine, nice and neat people, or at least tryin'."

So, after a few years, Papa died. Aunt Tildy remembered how she'd tried to talk him out of it, but he passed on anyway. Then she ran off. She couldn't stay with him after he was cold. He was a denial of her philosophy.

She didn't attend his burial. She didn't do anything but set up this antique shop on the front of this old house and live alone for years, that is until Emily came. Tildy didn't want to take the girl in. Why? Because Emily believed in dying. But her mother was an old friend, and Tildy had promised help.

"Emily," continued Aunt Tildy, to the man in black, "was the first body to live in this house with me in years. I never got married. I didn't like the idea of livin' with a man twenty-thirty years and then have him up and die on me. It'd shake my philosophy down like a tower of cards. I shied away from the world pretty much. I guess I got pretty persnickety at people if they ever so much as mentioned death."

The young man listened patiently, politely. Then he lifted his hand. He seemed to know everything, with the shine in his cheeks, without her opening her mouth. He knew about her and the last war, in 1917, when she never read a newspaper. He knew about the time when she beat a man on the head with her umbrella and drove him from her shop because he insisted on telling her about the Argonne battle!

Yes, and the dark young man, smiling at her from his seat on the antique chair, he knew about when radio came in, and how Aunt Tildy had stuck to her nice old phonograph records. Harry Lauder singing Roamin' In The Gloamin', Madame Schumann-Heink and lullabies. With no interruptions of news; calamities, murders, mortalities, poisonings, accidents, terrors. Music that was the same each day. As the years went, Aunt Tildy had tried to teach Emily her philosophy. But Emily's mind was made up about—certain things. She was nice enough to respect Aunt Tildy's way of thinking, and she never mentioned—morbid things.

All these things, the young man knew.

Aunt Tildy sniffed. "Think you're smart, huh? How you know all those things?" She shrugged. "Well, now, if you think you can come and talk me into that silly wicker basket, you're way off the trestle. You so much as lay a hand on me, I'll spit *right in* your face!"

The young man smiled. Aunt Tildy sniffed again.

"You don't have to simper like a sick dog at me. I'm too old to be made love at. That's all twisted dry, like an old tube of paint, and left behind in the years."

There was a noise. The mantel clock sounded three. Aunt Tildy fastened her eyes on it. Strange. It seemed to her that it had just sounded three once before, five minutes ago. She liked the old clock. Bone pale porcelain, gold angels dangling naked around the numeraled face of it. Nice tone. Like cathedral chimes made small and soft.

"Are you just goin' to sit there, young man?"

He was.

"Then, you won't mind if I take a nap. Just a little cat-nap. Now, don't you get up off that chair. You set right there. You set there and don't come creepin' around me, toddying. Just goin' to close my eyes for a wee spell. That's right. That's right . . . ."

Nice and quiet and restful time of day. No noise.

Silence. Just the clock ticking away, busy as termites in wood. Just the old room smelling of polished mahogany and oiled leather in the morris chair, and books sitting stiff on the shelves. So nice.

You aren't gettin' up from the chair, are you, mister? Better not. I got one eye open for you. Yes, indeed I have. Yes, I have. Oh. Ah. Hmm.

So feathery. So drowsy. So deep. Under water, almost. Oh, so nice.

Who's that movin' around in the dark with my eyes closed?

Who's that kissin' my cheek? You, Emily? No. No. Guess it was my thoughts. Only—dreamin'. Land, yes, that it is. Driftin' off, off, off . . . .

AH? WHAT SAY? OH!

"Just a moment while I put on my glasses. There!"

The clock chimed three again. Shame, old clock! Have to have it fixed.

The young man in the dark suit stood near the door. Aunt Tildy nodded her head.

"You leavin' so soon, young man? Good thing! Emily's comin' home and she'd fix you. Had to give up, didn't you? Couldn't convince me, could you? I'm mule-stubborn. You couldn't get me out of this house, nosirree. Well, young man, you needn't bother comin' back to try again."

The young man bowed with slow dignity.

He had no intention of coming again. Ever.

"Fine," declared Aunt Tildy. "I always told Papa I'd

win out. Why, I'm going to knit in this window the next thousand years. They'll have to chew the boards down around me to get me out."

The dark young man twinkled his eyes.

"Quit lookin' like the cat that ate the bird," cried Aunt Tildy. "Get out! And tote that old fool wicker box with you!"

The four men treaded heavily out the front door. Tildy studied the way they handled the wicker. It wasn't heavy, yet they staggered with its weight.

"Here, now!" She arose in tremulous indignation. "Did you steal some of my antiques? My books?" She glanced about concernedly. "No. The clocks? No. What you got in that wicker?"

The dark young man whistled jauntily, turning his back to her and walking along behind the four staggering men. At the door he pointed to the wicker, offered its lid to Aunt Tildy. In pantomime he wondered if she would like to open it and gaze inside.

"Curious? Me? Shaw, no! Get out! Get it outa here!" cried Tildy.

The dark young man tapped a hat onto his head, saluted her crisply goodbye.

"Goodbye!" said Tildy." Go away!"

The door slammed. That was better. Gone. Darned fool men with their maggoty ideas. No never minds about the wicker. If they stole something, she didn't care, long as they let her alone.

"Look," said Aunt Tildy, pleased. "Here comes Emily,

home from college. About time. Lovely girl. See how she walks. But, Land, she looks pale and funny today. Walking so slow. I wonder why. Looks worried, she does. Poor girl. Tired, maybe. I'll just hustle her up a coffee pot and a tray of cakes."

Emily tapped up the front steps. Aunt Tildy, rustling around, could hear the slow, deliberate steps. What *ailed* the girl? Didn't sound like she had no more spunk than a flue-lizard. The front door swung wide. Emily stood in the hall, holding to the brass door knob. Why didn't she come in? Funny girl.

"Emily?" called Aunt Tildy.

Emily shuffled into the parlor, head down.

"Emily! I been waiting for you! There was the darndest fool men just here with a wicker. Tryin' to sell me something I didn't want. Glad you're home. Makes it right cozy—"

Aunt Tildy realized that for a full minute Emily had been staring.

"Emily, what's wrong? Stop starin'. Here, I'll bring you a cup of coffee. *There*.

"Emily, why you backin' away from me?

"Emily, stop screamin', child! Don't scream, Emily! Don't! You keep screamin' that way, you go crazy. Emily, get up off the floor, get away from that wall. Emily! Stop cringin', child. I won't hurt you!

"Land, if it ain't one thing it's another.

"Emily, what's *wrong*, child . . . ?"

*

Emily groaned through her hands over her face.

"Child, child," pleaded Tildy. "Here, sip this water. Sip it, Emily. Ah, That's it."

Emily widened her eyes, saw something, then shut them, quivering, pulling into herself. "Aunt Tildy, Aunt Tildy, Aunt Tildy, Aunt—"

"Stop that!" Tildy slapped her. "What *ails* you?"

Emily forced herself to look up again.

She thrust her fingers out. They vanished inside Aunt Tildy.

"What fool notion!" cried Tildy. "Take your hand away! Take it, I say!"

Emily dropped aside, jerked her head, the golden hair shaking into shiny temblors. "You're not here, Aunt Tildy. You're gone. I'm dreaming."

"You're not dreamin'."

"You're dead!"

"Hush, baby."

"You *can't* be here."

"Lands of Goshen, Emily—"

She took Emily's hand. It passed clean through her. Instantly, Aunt Tildy raged straight up, stomping her foot.

"Why—why," she muttered angrily. "That—fibber! That liar! That sneak-thief!" Her thin hands knotted to wiry hard pale fists. "That dark, dark fiend! He stole it, he stole it! He toted it away, he did, oh he did, he did! Why, I—" She found no words. Wrath steamed in her. Her pale blue eyes were fire. She sputtered into an indignant silence. Then she turned to Emily. "Child, get up! I need you. Get up, now!"

Emily lay, shivering.

"Part of me's here!" declared Aunt Tildy. "By the Lord Harry, what's left will have to do. Momentarily. Fetch my bonnet!"

Emily confessed. "I'm—scared."

Tildy planted fists on hips. "Of *me?*"

"Yes."

"Why? I'm no booger! You known me most your life! Now's no time to snivel-sopp. You fetch up on your heels or I'll slap you flat across your nose!"

Emily rose in sobs, stood like something cornered, trying to decide which direction to bolt in.

"Where's your car, Emily?"

"Down at the garage—, ma'm."

"Good." Aunt Tildy hustled her through the front door. "Now—" Her sharp stare poked up and down the streets. "Which way's the mortuary?"

Emily held to the step rail, fumbling down. "What're you going to do, Aunt Tildy?"

"Do?" cried Tildy, tottering after her, jowls shaking in a thin, pale, fury. "Why, get my body back, of course! Get my body back! Go on!"

The car roared, Emily clenched to the steering-wheel, staring straight ahead at the curved, rain-wet streets. Aunt Tildy shook her parasol.

"Hurry, child, hurry! Hurry before they squirt juices in

my body and dice and cube it the way them persnickety morticians have a habit of doin'. They cut and sew it so it ain't no good to no one!"

"Oh, Auntie, Auntie, let me go, don't make me drive! It won't do any good, no good at all," sighed the girl.

"Humph!" was all the old woman would say. "Humph!"

"Here we are, Auntie," Emily said, pulling to the curb. She collapsed over the wheel, but Aunt Tildy was already popped from the car and trotting with mincing skirt up the mortuary drive, around back to where the shiny black hearse was unloading a wicker basket.

"You!" she directed her attack at one of the four men with the wicker. "Put down that basket!"

The four men paid little attention.

One said, "Step aside, lady. We're doing our job. Let us do it, please."

"That's my body tucked in there!" She brandished the parasol,

"That I wouldn't know anything about," said a second man. "Please don't block traffic, madame. This thing is heavy."

"Sir," she cried, wounded. "I'll have you know I weigh only 110 pounds!"

He looked at her casually. "I'm not interested in your hip measure, lady. I just wanna go home to supper. My wife'll kill me if I'm late."

The four of them forged ahead, Aunt Tildy in pursuit, down a hall, into a preparations room.

A white-smocked man awaited the wicker's arrival

with a rather pleased smile on his long eager-looking face. Aunt Tildy didn't care for the avidity of that face, or the entire personality of the man. The basket was deposited, the four men retreated.

The man in the white smock, evidently a mortician, glanced at Auntie and said:

"Madame, this is no fit place for a gentlewoman."

"Well," said Auntie, gratified. "Glad you feel that way. Them is my sentiments, neat, but I can't convince those fellows. That's exactly what I tried to tell that dark-clothed young man!"

The mortician puzzled. "What dark-clothed young man is that?"

"The one who came puddlin' around my house, that's who."

"No one of that description works for us."

"No matter. As you just so intelligently stated, this is no place for a gentle lady. I don't want me here. I want me home. I want me cookin' ham for Sunday visitors, it's near Easter. I got Emily to feed, sweaters to knit, clocks to wind—"

"You are quite philosophical, and philanthropical, no doubt of it, madame, but I have work. A body has arrived." This last, he said with apparent relish, and a winnowing of his knives, tubes, jars and instruments.

Tildy bristled. "You lay so much as a cuticle on that body, I'll thrash you!" Again, the parasol.

He laid her aside like a little old moth. "George," he called with a suave gentleness. "Escort this little lady out, please."

Aunt Tildy glared at the approaching George.

"Show me your back-side, goin' the other way!"

George took her wrists. "This way, please."

Tildy extricated herself. Easily. Her flesh sort of—slipped. It even amazed Tildy. Such an unexpected talent to develop at this late day.

"See?" she said, pleased with her ability. "You can't budge me. I want my body back!"

The mortician opened the wicker lid casually. Then, in a recurrent series of scrutinies he realized that the body inside was . . . it *seemed* . . . *could* it be? . . . maybe . . . yes . . . no . . . well, uh . . . it just *couldn't* be, but . . . "Ah," he exhaled, abruptly. He turned. His eyes were saucer-wide.

"Madame," he said, cautiously. "Eh—this lady here. She is—a—relative—of yours?"

"A very dear relation. Be careful of her."

"A twin sister, perhaps?" He grasped at a straw of dwindling logic, hopefully.

"No, you fool. Me, do you hear? *Me!*"

The mortician considered the idea. He shook his head. "No," he decided. "No. Things like this don't happen." He went on fumbling with his tools. "Show her away, George. Get help from the others. I can't work with a crank present."

The four men assembled and converged. Aunt Tildy was a lace fortress, arms crossed in defiance. "Won't budge," she said. She repeated this as she was evicted in consecutive moves, like a pawn on a chessboard, from preparations room to slumber room, to hall, to waiting chamber, to funeral parlor, where she made her last fight by sitting down on a chair in the very center of the vestibule. There were pews going back into grey silence, and a flower smell.

"You can't sit there, mam," said one of the men. "That's where the body rests for the service tomorrow."

"I'm sittin' right plumb here until I get what I want."

She sat, pale fingers fussing with her fussy throat lace, jaw set, one high-ankled, button-shoe tapping irritated rhythms. If a man got in whopping distance, she gave him a parasol whop. And when they touched her, now, she sort of—slipped away.

Mr. Carrington, Mortuary President, heard the disturbance in his office and came toddling down the aisle to investigate. "Here, here," he whispered to all of them, finger to mouth. "More respect, more respect. What is this? Oh. Madame, may I help you?"

She looked him up and down. "You may."

"How may I be of service, please?"

"Go in that room back there," directed Aunt Tildy.

"Yee-ess."

"And tell that eager young investigator to quit fiddlin' with my body. I'm a maiden lady. My moles, birthmarks, scars and other bric-a-brac, including the turn of my ankle, are my own secret. I don't want him pryin' and probin', cuttin' it or hurtin' it any way."

This was vague to Mr. Carrington, who hadn't correlated bodies yet. He looked at her, in blank helplessness.

"He's got me in there on his table, like a pigeon ready to be drawn and stuffed!" she told him.

Mr. Carrington hustled off to check. After fifteen minutes of waiting silence and horrified arguing, comparing notes with the mortician behind closed doors, Carrington returned, three shades whiter.

"Well?" said Auntie.

"Uh—that is. Most irregular. You can't—sit—there."

"Can't I?"

Carrington dropped his glasses, picked them up. "You're making it difficult for us."

"I am!" raged Auntie. "Saint Vitus in the mornin'! Looky here, Mister Blood and Bones or whatever, you tell that—"

"But he's already pumping the blood from the body."

"What!"

"Yes, yes, I assure you, yes. So, you just go away, now, there's nothing to be done. The blood's running and soon the body'll be all filled with nice fresh formaldehyde." He laughed nervously. "Our mortician is also performing a brief autopsy to determine cause of death."

Auntie jumped onto her feet, burning. "Cuttin' me, is he?"

"Y-yes."

"He can't do that; only coroners are allowed to do that!"

"Well, we sometimes allow a little—"

"March straight in and tell that Cut-em-up to pump all that fine New England blue blood right back into that fine-skinned body, and if he's taken anything out, for him to attach it back in so it'll function proper, and then turn that body, fresh as paint, over into my keepin'! You *hear!*"

"There's nothing I can do. Nothing."

"All right. Tell you *what*. I'm settin' here the next two hunderd year. You hear? And every time anyone comes near I'll spit ectoplasm right squirt up their left nostril!"

Carrington groped that thought around his weakening mind and emitted a groan. "You'll dislocate our business. You wouldn't do that."

Auntie smiled pleasantly. "*Wouldn't* I?"

Carrington ran up the dark aisle. In the distance he made a series of phone-calls. Half an hour later cars roared up in front of the mortuary. Three vice-presidents of the mortuary came down the aisle with their hysterical President.

"What seems to be the trouble?"

Auntie told them with a few well chosen infernalities.

They held a conference, meanwhile notifying the mortician to discontinue his homework, at least until such time as an agreement was reached. The mortician walked from his chamber and stood smiling amiably, smoking a big black cigar.

Auntie stared at the cigar.

"Where'd you put the *ashes?*" she cried, in horror.

The mortician only grinned imperturbably and puffed.

The conference broke up.

"Madame, in all fairness, you wouldn't force us out on the street to continue our services, would you?"

Auntie scanned the vultures. "Oh, I wouldn't mind at all."

Harrington wiped sweat from his jowls. "You can have your body back."

"Ha!" shouted Auntie. Then, with caution: "Intact?"

"Intact."

"No formaldehyde?"

"No formaldehyde."

"Blood in it?"

"Blood, my God, yes, blood, if only you'll take it and go!"

A prim nod. "Fair enough. Fix 'er up. It's a deal!"

Harrington snapped fingers at the mortician. "Don't *stand* there, you mental incompetent. Fix it up!"

"And be careful with that cigar butt," warned Tildy.

"Easy, easy," said Aunt Tildy. "Put the wicker basket down to the floor where I can step in it."

She didn't look at the body much. Her only comment was, "Natural lookin'." She let herself fall back into the wicker.

A biting sensation of arctic coldness, a great unlikely nausea, and a giddy whorling. Like two drops of matter fusing. Water trying to seep into concrete. Slow to do. Hard. Like a butterfly trying to squirm back into its discarded dry husk of flinty chrysalis!

The mortuary people watched Aunt Tildy's wriggles. Mr. Carrington was deeply concerned. He wrung his fingers and tried to assist with boosting and grunting moves of his hands and arms. The mortician, frankly skeptical, watched with idle, amused eyes.

Seeping into cold, long granite. Seeping into a frozen and ancient statue. Squeezing all the way.

"Come alive, damn ye!" shouted Aunt Tildy to herself. "Raise up a bit."

The body half rose, rustling in the dry wicker.

"Find your legs, woman!"

The body grabbled up, blindly groping.

"See!" shouted Aunt Tildy.

Light entered the webbed blind eyes.

"Feel!" urged Aunt Tildy.

The body felt the room warmth, the sudden reality of the preparations table on which to lean, panting.

"Move!"

The body took a creakingly unsteady step.

"Hear!" she snapped.

The noises of the place came into the dull ears. The harsh, expectant breath of the mortician, shaken; the whimpering Mr. Harrington; her own crackling voice.

"Walk!" cried she.

The body walked.

"Think!" Auntie said.

The old brain thought.

"Now—speak!" she ordered.

The body spoke, bowing to the morticians:

"Much obliged. Thank you."

"Now," she said, finally. "Cry!"

And she began to cry tears of utter happiness.

*

And now, any afternoon about four, if you want to visit Aunt Tildy, you just walk around to her antique shop and rap on the door. There's a big black funeral wreath on the door. But don't mind that. Aunt Tildy left it there. She has *some* sense of humor. You rap on the door. It's double-barred and triple-locked, and when you rap her voice shrills out at you:

"Is that the man in black?"

And you laugh and say no, no, it's only me, Aunt Tildy.

And she laughs and says, "Come in, quick!" and she whips the door open and slams it shut behind you so no man in black can ever slip in with you. Then she escorts you in and pours you your cup of coffee and shows you her latest knitted sweater. She's not as fast as she used to be, and can't see as good, but she gets on.

"And if you're 'specially good," Aunt Tildy declares, setting her coffee-cup to one side, "I'll give you a little treat."

"What's that?" visitors will ask.

"This," says Auntie, pleased with her little uniqueness, her little joke.

Then with modest moves of her fingers she will unfasten the white lace at her neck and chest and for a brief moment show what lies beneath.

The long blue scar where the autopsy was neatly sewn together.

"Not bad sewin' for a man," she allows. "Oh, some more coffee? *There.*"

THE DEAD MAN

"That's the man, right over there," said Mrs. Ribmoll, nodding across the street. "See that man perched on the tar barrel afront Mr. Jenkens' store? Well, that's him. They call him Odd Martin."

"The one that says he's dead?" cried Arthur.

Mrs. Ribmoll nodded. "Crazy as a weasel down a chimney. Carries on firm about how he's been dead since the flood and nobody appreciates it."

"I see him sitting there every day," cried Arthur.

"Oh, yes, he sits there, he does. Sits there and stares at nothing. I say it's a crying shame they don't throw him in jail!"

Arthur made a face at the man.. "Yah!"

"Never mind, he won't notice you. Most uncivil man I ever seen. Nothing pleases him." She yanked Arthur's arm. "Come on, sonny, we got shopping to do."

They walked on up the street past the barber shop. In the window, after they'd gone by, stood Mr. Simpson, snipping his blue shears and chewing his tasteless gum. He squinted thoughtfully out through the fly-specked glass, looking at the man sitting over there on the tar barrel. "I figure the best thing could happen to Odd Martin would be to get married," he figured. His eyes glinted slyly. Over his shoulder he looked at his manicurist, Miss Weldon, who was busy burnishing the scraggly fingernails of a farmer named Gilpatrick. Miss Weldon, at this suggestion, did not look up. She had heard it often. They were always ragging her about Odd Martin.

Mr. Simpson walked back and started work on Gilpatrick's dusty hair again. Gilpatrick laughed softly. "What woman would marry Odd? Some times I almost believe he *is* dead. He's got an awful odor to him."

Miss Weldon looked up at Mr. Gilpatrick's face and carefully cut his finger with one of her little scalpels. "Gol darn it!" He jumped. "Watch what you're doin', woman!"

Miss Weldon looked at him with calm little blue eyes in a small white face. Her hair was mouse-brown; she wore no makeup and talked to no one most of the time.

Mr. Simpson cackled and snicked his blue steel shears. "Hope, hope, hope!" he laughed like that. "Miss Weldon, she knows what she's doin', Gilpatrick. Just you be careful. Miss Weldon, she give a bottle of eau de cologne to Odd Martin last Christmas. It helped cover up his smell."

Miss Weldon laid down her instruments.

"Sorry, Miss Weldon," apologized Mr. Simpson. "I won't say no more."

Reluctantly, she took up her instruments again.

"Hey!" cried one of the four other men waiting in the shop. "There he goes *again!*" Mr. Simpson whirled, almost taking Gilpatrick's pink ear with him in his shears. "Come look, boys!"

Across the street the sheriff stepped out of his office door just then and he saw it happen, too. He saw what Odd Martin was doing.

Everybody came running from all the little stores.

The sheriff walked over and looked down into the gutter.

"Come on, now, Odd Martin, come on now," he shouted. He poked down into the gutter with his shiny black boot-tip. "Come on, get up! You're not dead. You're good as me. You'll catch your death of cold there with all them gum wrappers and cigar butts. Come on, get up!"

Mr. Simpson arrived on the scene and looked at Odd Martin lying there. "He looks like a bottle a milk."

"He's takin' up valuable parkin' space for cars, this bein' Friday mornin'," whined the sheriff. "And lots of people needin' the area. Here now, *Odd!* Hmm. Well . . . give me a hand here, boys."

They lifted the body up onto the sidewalk.

"Let him stay here," declared the sheriff, jostling around in his boots. "Just let him stay 'til he gets tired of layin'. He's done this a million times before. Likes the publicity. Vamoose, you kids!"

He sent a bunch of children skipping ahead of his cheek of tobacco.

Back in the barber shop, Simpson looked around. "Where's Miss Weldon? Unh." He looked through the window. "There she is, brushing him off again, while he lies there. Fixing his coat, buttoning it up. Here she comes back. Don't nobody fun with her, she resents it."

The barber clock said twelve and then one and then two and then three. Mr. Simpson kept track of it. "I make you a bet that Odd Martin lies over there 'til four o'clock," he said.

Someone else said, "I'll bet he's there until four thirty."

"Last time—" A snickering of the shears. "—he was there five hours. Nice warm day today. He may snooze there until six. I'll say six. Let's see your money, gents!"

The money was put on the shelf by the hair-ointments.

One of the younger men shaved a stick with his pen-knife. "It's sorta funny how we joke about Odd. Sometimes I wonder if we ain't really just scared of him, inside us. I mean, we won't let ourselves believe he's really dead. We don't dare believe it. We'd never get over it if we knew. So we make him a kinda joke. We let him lay around. He don't hurt nobody. He's just there. But I notice old sawbones Hudson's never really touched Odd's heart with his stethoscope. Scared of what he'd find, I bet."

"Scared of what he'd find!" Laughter. Simpson laughed and snished his shears. Two men with crusty beards laughed, a little too loud. The laughter didn't last long.

"Great one for jokin', you are!" they all said, slapping their gaunt knees.

Miss Weldon, she went on manicuring her clients.

"He's gettin' up!"

There was a general half-rising of all the bodies in the shop and a lot of neck twisting to watch Odd Martin gain his feet. "He's up on one knee, now up on the other, now someone's givin' him a hand."

"It's Miss Weldon. She sure got over there in a rush!"

"What time is it?"

"Four fifteen! You lose, Simp! Pay us!"

The bet was settled.

"That Miss Weldon's a queer beetle herself. Takin' after a man like Odd."

Simpson clicked his scissors. "Being an orphan, she's got quiet ways. She likes men who don't say much. Odd, he don't say hardly anything. Just the opposite of us crude, crude men, eh, fellows? We talk too much. Miss Weldon don't like our way of speakin'."

"There they go. The two of 'em. Miss Weldon and Odd Martin."

"Say, take a little more off around my ears, will you, Simp?"

Skipping down the street, bouncing a red rubber ball, came little Radney Bellows, his blonde hair flopping in a yellow fringe over his blue eyes. He bounced the ball abstractedly, tongue between lips, and the ball fell under Odd Martin's feet where he sat once more on the tar barrel. Inside the grocery, Miss Weldon was doing her supper shopping, putting soup cans and vegetable cans into a basket.

"Can I have my ball?" asked little Radney Bellows upward at the six feet, two inches of Odd Martin. No one was within hearing distance.

"Can you have your ball?" said Odd Martin haltingly. He turned it over inside his head, it appeared. His level, gray eyes shaped up Radney like one would shape up a little ball of clay. "You can have your ball, yes; take it."

Radney bent slowly and took hold of the bright red rubber globe and arose slowly, a secretive look in his eyes.

"I know something."

Odd Martin looked down. "You know something?"

Radney leaned forward. "You're *dead.*"

Odd Martin sat there.

"You're really dead," whispered little Radney Bellows. "But I'm the only one who really knows. I believe you, Mr. Odd. I tried it once myself. Dying, I mean. It's hard. It's work. I laid on the floor for an hour. But my stomach itched, so I scratched it, and the blood got up in my head and made me dizzy. Then—I quit. Why?" He looked at his shoes. "'Cause I had to go to the bathroom."

A slow, understanding smile formed in the soft pallid flesh of Odd Martin's long, bony face. "It *is* work. It isn't easy."

"Sometimes, I think about you," said Radney. "I see

you walk by my house. Nights. Sometimes two in the morning. I wake up. I know you're out walking around. I know I should look out, and I do, and, gee, there you are, walking and walking. Not going hardly any place."

"There's no place to go." Odd sat with his large, square, calloused hands on his knees. "I try thinking of some—place to—go—" He slowed, like a horse to a bit-pull "—but it's hard to think. I try and—try. Sometimes I almost know what to do, where to go. Then, I forget. Once I had an idea to go to a doctor and have him declare me dead, but, somehow—" his voice was slow and husky and low "—I never got there."

Radney looked straight at him. "If you want, I'll take you."

Odd Martin glanced leisurely at the setting sun. "No. I'm weary, tired, but I'll—wait. Now I've gone this far, I'm curious to see what happens next. After the flood that washed away my farm and all my stock and put me under water, like a chicken in a bucket, I filled up like you'd fill a thermos with water, and I came walking out of the flood, anyhow. But I knew I was dead. Late of nights I lay listening in my room, but there's no heartbeat in my ears or in my chest or in my wrists, though I lie still as a cold cricket. Nothing inside me but a darkness and a relaxation and an understanding. There must be a reason for me still walking, though. Maybe it was because I was still young when I died. Only twenty-eight, and not married yet. I always wanted to marry, never got around to it. Here I am, doing odd jobs around town, saving my money, 'cause I never eat, *heck, I can't* eat, and sometimes getting so discouraged and downright bewildered that I lie in the gutter and hope they'll take me and poke me in a pine box and lay me away for ripening. Yet, at the same time—I don't want that. I want a little more. I realize it whenever Miss Weldon walks by and I see the wind playing her hair like a little brown feather—" He sighed away into a pause.

Radney Bellows waited a minute, then cleared his throat and darted away, bouncing his ball. "See you later!"

Odd stared at the spot where Radney had been. Five minutes later he blinked. "Eh? Somebody here? Somebody speak?"

Miss Weldon came from the grocery with a basket of food.

"Like to walk me home, Odd?"

They walked along in a comfortable silence, she careful not to walk too fast, because he set his feet down carefully. The wind rustled in the cedars and in the elms and the maples all along the way. Several times his lips parted and he glanced aside at her, and then he shut his mouth tight and squinted ahead, as if looking at something a million miles off.

Finally, he said, "Miss Weldon?"

"Yes, Odd?"

"I been saving and saving my money. I've got quite a handsome sum. I don't spend much for anything, and—you'd be surprised," he said, sincerely. "I got about a thousand dollars. Maybe more. Some times I count it and get tired and I can't count no more. And—" He seemed baffled and a little angry with her, suddenly. "*Why* do you like me, Miss Weldon?" he demanded.

She looked a little surprised, then smiled up at him. It was almost a child look of liking she gave him. "Because. You're quiet. Because. You're not loud and mean. Like the men at the barber's. Because. I'm lonely, and you've been kind. Because you're the first one that ever looked at me. The others don't even see me, not once. They say I can't think. They say I'm senseless because I didn't finish sixth grade. But I'm so lonely, Odd, and talking to you means so much."

He held her small white hand, tight.

She moistened her lips. "I wish we could do something about the way people talk about you. I don't want to sound mean, but if you'd only stop telling them you're dead, Odd."

He stopped walking. "Then you don't believe me, either," he said, remotely.

"You're 'dead' for want of a good woman's cooking, for loving, for living decent, Odd. That's what you mean by 'dead'; nothing else!"

His gray eyes were deep and lost. "Is that what I mean?" He saw her eager, shiny face. "Yes, that's what I mean. You guessed it right. That's what I mean."

Their footsteps went along together, drifting in the wind, like leaves floating, and the night got darker and softer and the stars came out.

Two boys and two girls stood under a street lamp about nine o'clock that evening. Far away down the street someone walked along slowly, quietly, alone.

"There he is," said one of the boys. "*You* ask him, Tom."

Tom scowled uneasily. The girls laughed at him. Tom said, "Okay, but you come along."

Odd Martin walked along, pausing now and then to examine a fallen leaf with the tip of his shoe, turning and lifting it.

"Mr. Odd? Hey there, Mr. Odd!"

"Eh? Oh, hello."

"Mr. Odd, we—" Tom swallowed and looked around for assistance. "That is—we want you to—well—we want you to come to our party!"

A minute later, after looking at Tom's clean, soap-smelling face and seeing the pretty blue jacket his sixteen year old girl friend wore, Odd answered. "Thank you. But I don't know. I might forget to come."

"No, you wouldn't. You'd remember, because this is Hallowe'en!"

Tom's girl pulled his arm. "Let's go, Tom. Let's not have him. Let's not. Please. He won't do, Tom."

"Why won't he do?"

"He's—he's not scary enough."

Tom shook her off. "Let *me* handle this."

The girl pleaded. "Please, no. He's just a dirty old man. Bill can put candle-tallow on his fingers and those horrid porcelain teeth in his mouth and the green chalk marks under his eyes, and scare the ducks out of us.

We don't need *him!*" And she perked her rebellious head at Odd.

Odd Martin stood watching the leaves under his shoe-tips. He heard the stars sitting in the sky for ten minutes before he knew the four young folks were gone. A round dry laugh came in his mouth like a pebble. Children. Hallowe'en. Not scary enough. Bill'd do better. Candle-tallow and green chalk. Just an old man. He tasted the laughter, found it both strange and bitter.

Morning again. Radney Bellows flung his ball against the store front, caught it, flung it again. Someone hummed behind him. He turned. "Hi, Mr. Odd!"

Odd Martin, walking with green paper dollars in his fingers, counted them. He stopped on one spot and held himself in one position. His eyes were senseless.

"Radney," he cried out. "Radney!" His hands groped.

"Yes, sir, Mr. Odd!"

"Radney, where was I going? Just now, where was I going? Going somewhere to buy something for Miss Weldon! Here, Radney, help me!"

"Yes, sir, Mr. Odd." Radney ran and stood in his shadow.

A hand came down, money in it, seventy dollars of money. "Radney, run buy a dress for—Miss Weldon—" The hand opened, the money fell, the hand remained out, opening, making gasping, seeking moves, wrestling, wondering moves. There was numbed terror and longing and fear in Odd's face. "The place, I can't remember the place, oh God, help me remember. A dress, and a coat. For Miss Weldon, at—at—"

"Krausmann's Department Store?" said Radney.

"No."

"Fielder's?"

"No!"

"Mr. Leiberman's?"

"That's it! Leiberman! Here, here, Radney, run down to—"

"Leiberman's."

"—and get a new green dress for—Miss Weldon, and a coat. A new green dress with yellow roses painted on it. You get them and bring them to me here. Oh, Radney, wait."

"Yes, sir?"

"Radney—you think, maybe, I could clean up at your house?" asked Odd quietly. "I need a—a bath."

"Gee, I don't know, Mr. Odd. My folks'r funny. I don't know."

"That's all right, Radney. I understand. Run now!"

Radney ran on the double. Odd Martin stood in the sunlight, humming a tune in his mouth. Radney ran with the money past the barber shop; poked his head inside. Mr. Simpson stopped snipping Mr. Trumbull's hair and glared at him. "Hey!" cried Radney. "Odd Martin's humming a tune!"

"What tune?" asked Simpson.

"Goes like *this*," and Radney hummed it.

"Yee Gods Amaughty!" bellowed Simpson. "So *that's*

why Miss Weldon ain't here manicurin' this mornin'! That there tune's the Weddin' March!"

Radney rushed on. Pandemonium!

Shouting, laughter, a squishing and pattering of water. The back room of the barber emporium steamed and sweated. Everybody had his turn. Mr. Simpson heaved a bucket of hot water down over Odd Martin sitting in a galvanized tin tub. Mr. Trumbull banged and whisked Odd's pale back with a big beardy brush on a stick. Old man Gilpatrick doused him with a half quart of cow-soap, that bubbled and frothed and stank sweetly, and every once in awhile Shorty Phillips hit Odd with a jigger of eau de cologne. They all funned and ran around, slipping, in the steam. "Put some more on 'em!" More water. "Scrub with that brush, *you!*" The brush sizzled on Odd's spine. Mr. Simpson gunked in his throat, laughing: "Always said marriage is what you needed, Odd!" Somebody else said, "Congratulations!" and smacked Odd right square on his shoulder blades with a can of ice water. Odd Martin didn't even notice the shock. "You'll smell fine now!"

Odd sat blowing bubbles in one cupped hand. "Thanks. Thanks so much for helping. Thanks for scouring me. Thanks, I needed it."

Simpson put a hand over his own smiling mouth. "Nothing's too good for you, ya know that, Odd."

Someone whispered in the steamy background, "Imagine . . . her . . . him . . . and married . . . moron married . . . to an idiot . . . why . . ."

"Shut up, back there!" Simpson frowned.

Radney ran in. "Here's the green dress, Mr. Odd!"

An hour later they perched Odd in the barber chair. Someone had lent him a new pair of black shoes. Mr. Trumbull polished them vigorously, winking at everybody. Mr. Simpson snipped Odd's hair, took no money for it. "No, Odd, keep your money. This is all a weddin' present to you. Yes, sir." And he spat. Then he shook rose-water on Odd's scalp. "There. Moonlight and roses!"

Odd Martin looked around. "You won't tell nobody about this marriage," he asked, "until tomorrow? Me and Miss Weldon sort of want a marriage without the town poking fun. You see?"

"Sure, Odd," said Simpson, finishing the job. "Mum's the word. Where you goin' to live? You buyin' a farm?"

"Farm?" Odd stepped from the chair. Somebody'd lent him a nice new tan coat, and someone else'd pressed his pants sharp for him. He looked elegant. "Yes, I'm going over to buy the property now. Have to pay extra, but it's worth it. Extra. Come on, Radney." He paused at the door. "I bought a house out on the edge of town. I have to go make the payment on it now."

Simpson stopped him. "What's it like? You didn't have much money."

"It's a small house," said Odd, "but it'll do. Some folks built it awhile back, then moved away East somewhere. It was up for sale for only five hundred, so I got it. Miss Weldon and I are moving out there tonight, after our marriage. But don't tell nobody, please, until tomorrow."

"Sure thing, Odd. Sure thing."

Odd went away into the four o'clock light. Radney at his side, and the barber shop men fell down into chairs and grabbed their ribs and laughed.

The sun went down slow and the snipping of the shears continued, with the buzzing of flies, the clock ticking, and the men sitting around nodding their heads, showing their teeth, waving their hands, joking . . .

The next morning at breakfast, little Radney Bellows sat thoughtfully spooning his cereal. Father folded his newspaper across the table and looked at Mother. "Everybody in town's talking about the quiet elopement of Odd Martin and Miss Weldon," said Father. "People, looking for them, can't find them."

"Well," said Mother, "I heard he bought her a house."

"I heard that, too," admitted Father. "I phoned Carl Rogers this morning. He says he didn't sell any house to Odd. And Carl is the only real-estate dealer in town."

Radney Bellows swallowed more cereal. He looked at his father. "Oh, no, he's not the *only* real-estate dealer in town."

"What do you mean?" demanded Father.

"Nothing, except I looked out the window at midnight and I saw something."

"You saw *what?*"

"It was all moonlight. And you know what I saw? Well, I saw two people walking up the Elm Glade road. A man and a woman. A man in a nice new coat, and a woman in a green dress. Walking real slow. Holding hands." Radney took a breath. "And the two people were Mr. Odd Martin and Miss Weldon. And walking out the Elm Glade road there ain't any houses out that way at all. Only the Trinity Park Cemetery. And Mr. Gustavsson, in town, he sells tombs in the Trinity Park Cemetery. He's got an office in town. Like I said, Mr. Carl Rogers ain't the only real estate man in town. So—"

"Oh," snorted Father, irritably, "you were dreaming!"

Radney bent his head over his cereal and looked out from the corners of his eyes.

"Yes, sir," he said, finally, sighing. "I was only dreaming."

THE MAN UPSTAIRS

He remembered how carefully and expertly Grandmother would fondle the cold cut guts of the chicken and withdraw the marvels therein; the wet shining loops of meat-smelling intestine, the muscled lump of heart, the gizzard with the collection of seeds in it. How neatly and nicely Grandma would slit the chicken's breast and push her fat little hand in to deprive it of its medals. These would be segregated, some in pans of water, others in paper to be thrown to the dog later, perhaps. And then the ritual of taxidermy, stuffing the bird with watered, seasoned bread, and performing surgery with a swift, bright needle, stitch after pulled tight stitch.

But for all the miracle of surgery, the bird would never survive the operation. It was only transported immediately into a hell and poked and basted and cooked until such time as the other surgeons gathered at the festive board and took up their scalpels to attack.

This was one of the prime thrills of Douglas's eleven year old life span.

The knife collection, itself, was an intrigue.

It lay abed in the various squeaking drawers of the large wooden kitchen table. A magic table, from which Grandmama, admittedly a rather kindly, gentle-faced and white-haired old witch, would draw paraphernalia for her miracles. The knives seemed to be most important in the dissection and investigation of chicken and other like fowl.

Altogether, moving his small lips, Douglas counted twenty knives of varying shapes and sizes. And each was unfailingly polished into a sharp mirror in which he could find his red hair and freckles distorted brilliantly.

He was to be quiet while Grandmama worked over her split animals. You could stand across the table from her, your nose tucked over the edge, watching, but any loose boy talk might interfere with the spell. It was a wonder watching Grandma brandish silver shakers over the bird, supposedly sprinkling showers of mummy-dust and pulverized Indian bones, muttering mystical verses under her toothless breath.

Douglas at last gathered courage under him like a coiled spring and let fly with:

"Grammy, am I like that inside?" He pointed at the chicken.

"Like what, child?"

"Am I like *that,* inside?"

"Yes; a little more orderly and presentable, but just about the same—"

"And more *of* it," added Douglas, proud of his guts.

"Yes," said Grandma. "More of it."

"Grandpa has lots more than me. His sticks out in front so he can rest his elbows on it, Grammy."

Grandma laughed and shook her head.

Douglas said, "And Lucie Williams, down the street, she—"

"Hush, child!" cried Grandma.

"But she's got—"

"Never you mind what she's got! That's different. You just shush up about Lucie!"

"But why is *she* different?"

"A darning-needle dragon-fly is coming by some day soon and sew up your mouth," said Grandma, firmly.

Douglas retreated immediately, then thoughtfully came back with, "How do you *know* I've got insides like that, Grandma?"

"I just know, that's all. Go 'way now."

Scowling, Douglas thumped off to the living room, still bothered about the wealth of knowledge obtainable from adults lacking absolute proof. They were so *darn* right.

The house bell jangled.

Through the front door glass as he ran down the hall, Douglas saw a straw hat. He opened the door, irritated at the continuous again and again jangle of the bell.

"Good morning, child, is the lady of the house at home?"

Cold grey eyes in a long smooth walnut-colored face gazed upon him. The man was tall, thin, and carried a suitcase, a brief-case, an umbrella under one bent arm, gloves rich and thick and grey on his thin hands, and wore a horribly new straw hat.

Douglas backed up. "She's busy."

"I wish to rent her upstairs room, as advertised."

"We've got ten boarders in the house, and it's already rented, go away."

"Douglas!" Grandma was behind him suddenly, forging along the hall. "How do you do?" she said to the stranger. "Won't you step in? Go right on upstairs. Never mind this child."

"Quite all right." Unsmiling, the man stepped stiffly in. Douglas watched them ascend out of sight, heard Grandma detailing the conveniences of the upstairs room. A suitcase bumped down on the upstairs floor, and soon Grandma hurried down to take linens from the linen-closet, pile them on Douglas and send him scurrying up to the newly rented room.

Douglas paused at the room's threshold. It was transformed simply by the man being in the room a moment. The straw hat lay on the bed, the umbrella leaned stiff against one wall like a dead bat with dark wings tucked. Douglas blinked at the umbrella. The man stood in the center of the room, his suitcase at his feet.

"Here." Douglas decorated the bed with linens. "We eat at twelve sharp and if you don't come down the soup'll get cold. Grandma fixes it so it will, every time."

The man counted out ten pennies, tinkled them into Douglas's blouse pocket. "We shall be friends," he said.

It was funny, the man having nothing but pennies. Lots of them. No silver at all, no dimes, no quarters. Just new copper pennies.

Douglas thanked him. "I'll drop these in my dime bank when I get them changed into a dime."

"Saving money, young fellow?"

"Got six dollars and fifty cents. This makes sixty cents. For my camp trip in August."

"I must wash now," said the tall, strange man.

Once, at midnight, Douglas had awakened to hear a storm rumbling outside, the cold hard wind shaking the house, the rain driving against the windows. And then, a bolt of lightning had landed outside the window with a silent, terrific pounding. He remembered that fear. That fear of looking around at his room, seeing it strange and terrible in the instantaneous light.

It was the same, now, in this room. He stood looking at the stranger. This room was no longer the same, but changed indefinably, because this man, as quick as a lightning bolt, had shed his light about it. Douglas did not like it.

The door closed in his face.

The wooden fork came down, went up with mashed potatoes. Mr. Koberman, for that was his name, had brought the fork and the wooden knife and spoon with him when Grandma called lunch.

"Mrs. Spaulding," he had said, quietly. "My own cutlery; please use it. I will have lunch today, but from tomorrow on, only breakfast and supper."

Grandma bustled in and out, bearing steaming tureens of soup and beans and mashed potatoes to impress her new boarder, while Douglas sat rattling his silverware on his plate, because he had discovered it irritated Mr. Koberman.

"I know a trick," said Douglas. "Watch." He picked a fork tine with his fingernail. He pointed at various sectors of the table, like a magician. Where ever he pointed, the sound of the vibrating fork-tine emerged, like a metal elfin voice. Simply done, of course. He simply pressed the fork handle on the table-top, secretly. The vibration came from the wood like a sounding board. It looked like magic. "There, *there, and there*!" exclaimed Douglas, happily plucking the fork again. He pointed at Mr. Koberman's soup and the noise came from it.

Mr. Koberman's walnut-colored face was hard and firm and awful. He pushed the soup bowl away, his lips twisting, and fell back in his chair.

Grandma appeared.

"Why, what's wrong, Mr. Koberman?"

"I cannot eat the soup," he said.

"Why?"

Mr. Koberman glared at Douglas.

"Because I am full and can eat no more. Thank you."

Excusing himself, Mr. Koberman walked upstairs.

"What did you do, just then?" asked Grandma at Douglas, sharply.

"Nothing. Grammy, why does he eat with wooden spoons?"

"You're not to question! When do you go back to school, anyway?"

"Seven weeks."

"Oh, my land," said Grandma.

Half way to the second floor was a large, sun-filled window. It was framed by six inch panes of orange, purple, blue, red and green glass. Some panes were yellow, some a wondrous burgundy.

In the enchanted late afternoons, when the sun fell through to strike upon the landing and slide down the stair banister, Douglas stood entranced by this window, peering at the world through the multi-colored panes.

Now a blue world. Douglas pressed his nostrils against the blue pane, saw the blue-blue sky, the blue people and the blue street-cars and the trotting blue dogs.

Now—he shifted panes—there was an amber world. Two lemonish women glided by, looking like daughters of Fu Manchu. Douglas giggled. This pane made even the sunlight more purely golden, like taffy spilled on everything.

Douglas heard a noise above him. He knew Mr. Koberman stood outside his door, watching.

Not turning, Douglas observed. "All kinds of worlds. Blue ones, red ones, yellow ones. All different."

After a long pause, Mr. Koberman said, distractedly: "That is true. All kinds of worlds. Yes. All different."

The door closed. The hall was empty. Mr. Koberman had gone in.

Douglas shrugged and found a new pane.

"Oh! Everything's *pink*!"

It was simple as a rain-drop. Spooning his morning cereal, Douglas felt a simple, pure white flame of hatred stand inside him, burning with a steady, unflickering beauty. Upstairs, this morning, Mr. Koberman's door had been ajar, the room empty. He had looked in, with distaste.

It was Mr. Koberman's room now. Once it had been bright and flowery when Miss Sadlowe had lived there; full of nasturtiums and bright bolls of knitting cotton, bright pictures on the walls. When Mr. Caples had lived there it reflected him: his athletic vivacity, his tennis shoes on a chair, a disembodied sweater crumpled on the bed, wrinkled pants in the closet, cut-outs of pretty girls on the bureau, But, now . . .

Now the room was Koberman Land. Bare and clean and cold and everything microscopically set in place. Not a microbe or dust-mote or oxygen cell existed in the room without having an appointed and irrevocable station.

Douglas finished breakfast, feeding simultaneously on one part buttered toast, two parts hatred.

He walked up to the landing and stared out the colored glasses.

Mr. Koberman strolled by below, on the sidewalk, on his morning exercise. He walked straight, cane looped on arm half way to elbow, his straw hat glued to his head with patent oil.

Mr. Koberman was a blue man walking through a blue world with blue trees and blue flowers and—something else.

There was something about Mr. Koberman. Douglas squinted. The blue glass *did* things to Mr. Koberman. His face, his suit—

There was no time to fathom it. Mr. Koberman glanced up just then, saw Douglas, and raised his cane-umbrella as if to strike, then put it down swiftly and hurried to the front door.

"Young man," he said, coming up the stairs, "what were you doing?"

"Just looking."

"That's all, it is?"

"Yes, sir."

Mr. Koberman stood, fighting himself. The veins stood out on his face like small, grey wires. His eyes were deep black holes.

Saying nothing, he went downstairs for another walk around the block.

Douglas played in his sand-box in the backyard for half an hour. At about nine thirty he heard the crash and the shattering tinkle. He jumped up. He heard

Grandma's slippers scuffing in the hall, hurriedly, then scuffing back to the kitchen. The screen door *swannged* open, on its wire spring restrainer.

"Douglas!"

She held the old razor strop in her hand.

"I told you time and again never to fling your basketball against the house! Oh, I could just cry!"

"I been sitting right here," he protested.

"Come in here! See what you done!"

The great colored window panes were tumbled in a rainbow chaos on the upstairs landing. The basketball lay on the ruins.

Before Douglas could even begin telling his innocence, Grandma struck him seven stinging whops on his rump. Screaming, Douglas leaped like a fish, and wherever he landed he was whopped again! He sang an age old song to his wild dancing.

Much later, hiding his mind in a pile of sand in the sand-box, like an ostrich, Douglas nursed his pain. He knew who'd thrown that basketball to shatter the colored windows. A man with a straw hat and a stiff umbrella, and a cold, grey room. Yeah, yeah, yeah. He dribbled tears in the sand. Just wait. Just wait.

The thin, tinkling shuf-shuf-shuf noise was Grandma sweeping up the glittering debris. She brought it out back and cascaded it into the trash-bin. Blue, pink, white, yellow meteors of glass dropped brightly down. Grandma looked broken-hearted.

When she was gone, Douglas dragged himself over to

save out three pieces of the precious glass; pink and green and blue. He had an idea why Mr. Koberman disliked the colored windows. These—he clinked them in his fingers—would be worth saving.

Mr. Koberman worked nights and slept all day. Each morning at eight he arrived home, devoured a light breakfast, took a brief walk around the block, then climbed primly upstairs to sleep soundlessly throughout the day until six at night, when he came down to the huge supper with all the other boarders.

Mr. Koberman's sleeping habits made it necessary for Douglas to be quiet. Not being quiet by nature, frustration set in on him like a growing abscess.

Resultantly, when Grandma visited next door at Mrs. Eddy's or bought groceries at Mrs. Singer's, Douglas would vent his repressions by stomping up and down stairs beating upon a drum. Golf-balls, rolled slowly down the steps, were also delightful. Followed by a quick shuttling of the house killing Indians and flushing all the toilets three times in succession.

After three days, Douglas realized he was getting no complaints. On the fourth day, after Grandma was gone to the store, he yelled outside Mr. Koberman's door ten minutes straight, without criticism.

Then, and only then, did he dare to try the door, carefully, and open it.

The room was in half-light, the shades drawn. Mr. Koberman lay on top of the covers of his bed, in sleeping clothes, breathing gently, up and down. He didn't move. His face was motionless.

"Hello, Mr. Koberman."

The colorless walls echoed the man's regular breathing.

"Mr. Koberman, hello!"

Bouncing the golf-ball, Douglas advanced. No response. He yelled. Still no answer. Mr. Koberman lay like a papier-mache dummy, not complaining, his eyes shut.

"Mr. Koberman!"

Douglas searched the room with quick eyes. On the bureau rested the wooden eating utensils. This gave Douglas an idea. He ran and got a silver fork, came back. Picking the tines he held it close to the sleeping face.

Mr. Koberman winced. He twisted on his bed, groaning, muttering bitterly.

Response. Good. Swell.

Another ting of the fork. Mr. Koberman twitched in a nightmare of vibrations, but could not wake up. He didn't look as if he could, even if he wanted to.

Douglas remembered about the colored glass. He drew a pink shard from his pocket and stared through it at Mr. Koberman.

The clothes dissolved off of Mr. Koberman. The pink glass had something to do with it. Or maybe it was the clothes themselves, being *on* Mr. Koberman. Douglas licked his lips. He could see *inside* Mr. Koberman.

Mr. Koberman was—weird inside.

Very weird. Very interesting.

He was beginning to enjoy himself when the front door banged. Grandma was home.

Douglas had to come downstairs, frustrated, trying to look innocent.

When a slow heavy tread filled the hall, and a thick mahogany cane thumped in the cane-rack, that always meant Grandfather was home for the day. He arrived from his newspaper office each night, shortly ahead of the boarders, at five-fifteen, a copy of his own newspaper folded into his black coat-pocket along with a pink peppermint stick to be used expressly for spoiling Douglas' dinner-appetite.

Douglas ran to embrace the large stomach that was Grandpa's main defense against a vigorously long life-battle with circumstance. Grandpa, peering down over the cliff of that stomach, cried, "Hello, down there!"

Seated in the great Morris chair, his spectacles attached, Grandpa scanned the paper with a keen eye.

"Grandma cut chickens again today. It's fun watching," said Douglas.

Grandpa kept reading. "Chickens? Again? That's twice this week. She's the chickenest woman. You like to watch her cut 'em, eh? Cold blooded little pepper, Ha!"

Douglas felt the subterranean laughter explode down through the huge old bones, echo out on Grandpa's vibrant knee-cap.

"I'm just curious," said Douglas.

"You *are*," rumbled Grandpa, pursing his lips, scowling.

"I remember that day when the young lady was killed at the rail station. Didn't bother you a mite. You just walked over and looked at her, blood and all."

"But, why shouldn't I look?"

"Doesn't it make you sick?" Grandpa put the paper aside.

"No."

"Queer duck. Sensible, though. Stay that way, Dougie-boy. Fear nothing, ever in life. Life's full of things not worth fearing. Bodies are bodies and blood is blood. The only bad things are those we make in our minds. We teach each other fear. We learn certain reactions to certain stimuli. Death, for instance. Orientals deem it fairly fine and honorable to die. But some European cultures have trumped up sassafras about death being a dark horror. Why—"

He stopped, blinked, swallowed, and laughed.

"What *am* I saying? You don't understand one word—"

"Sure, I do. Go ahead, Gramps. It's fun."

"Funny duck. Your father raised you funny. But then, him being a military man, and you so close to him 'till you come here last year."

"I'm not funny. I'm just *me*."

"There—" Grandpa nodded, "you *have* a point! There's no norm among humans, not really. Certain cultural norms, perhaps, but individual norms, no, no."

This seemed like the moment ripened on the tree of time for picking. Douglas picked.

"Gramps, what if a man didn't have no heart, lungs or stomach?"

Grandpa was used to such questions. "Why, then, I guess he'd be dead."

"No, I don't mean that. I mean, what if he didn't have a heart or no lungs or no stomach but still walked around? Alive."

"That," rumbled Gramps, "Would be a miracle."

"Besides," said Douglas, swiftly. "I don't mean a—a miracle. I mean—what if he was all *different* inside? Not like me."

"Oh, I see. Umm. Well, he wouldn't be quite human then, would he, boy?"

"I guess not." Douglas stared at the watch-fobbed stomach. "Gramps. Gramps, you got a heart and a brain and lungs, Gramps?"

"I should live to tell you!"

"How do you *know*?"

"Uh—" Gramps stopped. "Well." He had to laugh. "Tell the truth, I don't know. Never seen them. Never been to a doctor, never had an x-ray. Might as well be potato-solid for all I know."

"How about me? Have *I* got a stomach?"

"You certainly *have*!" said Grandma, in the parlor entrance. "'Cause I feed it. And you've lungs, because you scream loud enough to wake the crumblees. And you've dirty hands, go wash them! Dinner's ready. Grandpa, come on. Douglas, git!"

She tinkled a little black lacquered metal bell in the hall.

In the rush of boarders streaming downstairs, Grandpa,

if he had intentions of questioning Douglas further about the weird conversation, lost his opportunity. If dinner delayed an instant more, Grandma and the potatoes would develop simultaneous lumps.

The other boarders, laughing and talking at the table, Mr. Koberman silent and sullen between them—this attitude being attributed to liver trouble by Grandma—were put into a silent stasis by Grandfather who cleared his throat and spoke about the recent deaths in the town.

"Save that for later, when we drink our coffee," said Grandma.

"It's certainly enough to make a newspaper editor prick up his ancient ears," said Grandpa, carefully eyeing them all. "That young Miss Larsson, lived over across the ravine, now. Found her dead three days ago for no reason, just funny kinds of tattoos all over her, and a facial expression would make Dante cringe. And that other young lady, what was her name? Whitely? She disappeared and never did come back."

"Those things happen alla time," said Mr. Peters, the garage mechanic, chewing. "Ever peek in the Missing Peoples' Bureau file? It's *that* long." He illustrated. "Can't tell *what* happens to most of 'em."

Grandma cut in. "Anyone want more dressing?" She ladeled liberal portions from the chicken's sad interior. Douglas watched, thinking about how that chicken had had two kinds of guts—God-made and Man-made.

Well, how about *three* kinds of guts?

Eh?

Why not?

Conversation continued merry about the mysterious death of so-and-so, and, oh yes, remember a week ago, Marion Barsumian died of heart failure, but maybe that didn't connect up, or did it, you're crazy, forget it, why talk about it at supper, on a full stomach? So.

Cigarettes fired, the diners idled lazily into the parlor, where Grandpa let somebody interrupt him on occasions when he needed breath.

"Never can tell," said the garage mechanic. "Maybe we got a vampire in town."

"In the year 1927? Oh, go on now."

"Sure. Kill 'em with silver bullets. Anything silver for that matter. I read it in a book somewhere, once. Sure, I did."

Douglas sat on the floor looking up at Mr. Koberman who ate with wooden knives and forks and spoons, and carried only copper pennies in his pocket.

"It'd be poor judgment," said Grandpa, "to call anything by a name. We don't even know what a hobgoblin or a vampire or a troll is. Could be a lot of things. You can't heave them into categories with labels, and say they'll act one way or another. That'd be silly. They're people, people who do things. Yes, that's the way to put it—people who *do* things."

"Good evening, everyone," said Mr. Koberman, and got up and went out for his evening walk to work.

The radio was turned on. Card games were played. Ice cream was bought and served later. Then, the good-nights, and into bed.

The stars, the moon, the wind, the clock ticking and the chiming of hours into dawn, the sun coming up, and here it was another morning, another day, and Mr. Koberman coming from his walk after breakfast. Douglas stood off like a small mechanism whirring and watching with carefully microscopic eyes.

At noon, Grandma went to the store to buy groceries.

Douglas yelled outside Mr. Koberman's door for a minute, and then tried to enter. This time the door was locked. He had to run get the pass-key.

Clutching the pass-key, and the pieces of colored glass nervously, he entered and closed the door and heard Mr. Koberman breathing deep. Douglas placed the blue glass fragment over his own eyes.

Looking through it, he found himself in a blue room, in a blue world different from the world he knew. As different as was the red world. Aquamarine furniture, cobalt bed-clothes, turquoise ceilings, and the sullen dark blue of Mr. Koberman's face and arms, and his blue chest rising, falling. Also—something else.

Mr. Koberman's eyes were wide open, staring at him with a hungry darkness. Douglas fell back, pulled the blue glass from his face. Mr. Koberman's eyes were shut. Blue glass again—open. Blue glass away—shut. Blue glass again—open. Away—shut. Funny. Douglas experimented, trembling. Through the glass the eyes seemed to peer hungrily, avidly through the closed lids, like little flashlights. Without the blue glass they seemed tight shut.

But it was the rest of Mr. Koberman's body . . .

Douglas must have stood amazed for five minutes. Thinking about blue worlds, red worlds, yellow worlds, side by side, living together like glass panes around the big white stair window. Side by side, the colored panes, the different worlds; Mr. Koberman had said so himself.

So this was why the windows had been broken. At least partially why.

"Mr. Koberman, wake up!"

No response.

"Mr. Koberman, where do you work at night? Mr. Koberman, where do you work?"

A little breeze stirred the blue window shade.

"In a red world or a green world or a yellow one, Mr. Koberman!"

Over everything was a blue glass silence.

"Wait there," said Douglas.

He walked out of the room, walked downstairs to the kitchen and pulled open the great squeaking drawers where all the knives lay gleaming. He picked out the sharpest, biggest one. Very calmly he walked into the hall, climbed back up the stairs again, opened the door to Mr. Koberman's room and closed it.

Grandma was busy fingering a pie-crust into a pan when Douglas entered the kitchen to put something on the table.

"Grandma, what's this?"

She glanced up briefly, over her glasses. "I don't know."

It was square, like a box, and elastic. It was bright orange in color. It had four square tubes, colored blue, attached to it. It smelled funny. Not good but yet not bad.

"Ever see anything like it, Grandma?"

"No."

"That's what *I* thought."

Douglas left it there, went out of the kitchen. Five minutes later he returned with something else. "How about *this*?"

It resembled a bright pink linked chain with a purple triangle at one end.

"Don't bother me," sniffed Grandma. "It's only a chain."

He went away. Next time he came with two hands full. A ring, a square, a pyramid, a rectangle—and other shapes. "This isn't all. Lots more where this came from."

Grandma said, "Yes, yes," in a far off tone, very busy.

"You were wrong, Grandma."

"About what?"

"About all people being the same inside."

"Stop talking nonsense."

"Where's my piggy-bank?" he asked.

"On the mantel."

"Thanks."

He tromped into the parlor, reached up for the piggy-bank.

Grandpa came home from the office at five-fifteen.

"Grandpa, come upstairs."

"Sure, son. Why?"

"Something to show you. It's not nice. But it's interesting."

Grandpa chuckled, followed his grandson's feet up to Mr. Koberman's room.

"Grandma mustn't know about this; she wouldn't like it," said Douglas. He pushed the door wide. "There."

Grandfather gasped.

Douglas remembered the last scene all the rest of his life. Standing over the naked body, the coroner and his assistants. Grandma, downstairs, asking somebody, "What's going on up there?" and Grandpa saying, shakily, "I'll take Douglas away on a long vacation so he can forget this whole ghastly affair. Ghastly, ghastly affair!"

Douglas said, "Why should it be bad? I don't see anything bad. I don't feel bad."

The coroner shivered and said: "Koberman's dead, all right."

His assistant sweated. "Did you see those *things* in the pan of water and in the wrapping paper?"

"Oh, my God, my God, yes, I saw them."

"Christ."

The coroner bent over Mr. Koberman's body. "This better be kept secret, boys. It wasn't murder. It was a mercy the boy acted. God knows what may have happened if he hadn't."

"What was Koberman—a vampire? a monster?"

"Maybe. I don't know. I don't know anything. Something—not human." The coroner moved his hands deftly over the suture.

Douglas was proud of his work. He'd gone to much trouble. He had watched Grandma carefully and remembered. Needle and thread and all. All in all, Mr. Koberman was as neat a job as any chicken ever popped into hell by Grandma.

"I heard the boy say that Koberman *lived* even after all those *things* were taken out of him. Kept on *living*. God."

"Did the boy say that?"

"He did."

"Then, what killed Koberman?"

The coroner drew a few strands of sewing thread from their bedding. "This—" he said.

Sunlight blinked coldly off a half-revealed treasure trove; six dollars and seventy cents worth of silver dimes inside Mr. Koberman's chest.

"I think Douglas made a wise investment," said the coroner, sewing the flesh back up over the "dressing" quickly.

THE NIGHT SETS

The sets stood behind high green plank walls. The sun burned and tautened the flaky canvasses in the day and the fog moistened and sagged the canvasses at night. In the Rue de la Paix was silence. In Piccadilly Circus small birds pecked at the crumbs left by an electrician during the filming of a picture some months ago. One could see where the rain had made the new-old buildings really old. Multiple technicians had worked many years to age these sets of Oslo, Vienna, Dneiperpetrovsk, Singapore, Dublin; and now time itself was taking over and making an art of the process.

It was late afternoon; long shadows and a coolness. It was spring, but the *papier-mache* trees did not thrust out their blossoms, they waited to be wired with beauty and lacquered by technicians. It was only half a spring. The sky was mellow but the earth was in need of some

Christ-like director who might strike the rocks with his riding crop and a properly wielded check-book, to cause pomps, colors and natural pageants to gush forth.

The man stood in the shadow, not doing anything. He leaned against a telephone pole with his hands down at his sides, no expression on his face.

Another man, a younger one, rounded a corner of the plaza near the Notre Dame Cathedral, wandered on down past an American Bank building, a mosque, a Spanish hacienda, and looked into every door, obviously searching, obviously concerned.

The two men confronted one another. The searcher fell back a pace, then ran forward. "Matt! You *are* here!" He stopped.

Matt, the man standing against the telephone pole, in shadow, did not speak, nor move, nor flicker an eyelid.

The younger man was bewildered and said, peering into the shadow, "Is that *you*, Matt?" doubtfully.

The man beside the telephone pole looked off into the distance. After a time he opened his lips a bit and said, "Hello."

"Matt, it's me, Paul! I didn't think of looking in this place. I thought of it only today. How long've you been here?"

"A long time," said Matt slowly, looking at the sky.

Paul put his hand out. "Since December?"

"Longer than that."

"December was when you disappeared."

"Longer than that," said the man in the shadow, quietly.

"But it couldn't be longer." The young Paul laughed tolerantly. "You weren't gone until December."

The man did not move from his position beside the pole. "You'd be surprised how long I've been here. I like it here."

"Well, you'll come home now. Vera's forgiven you."

"I'm home now."

"Vera'll be glad to see you."

"Who's she?"

"Come on along now, Matt."

The man in the shadow did not move. "Please take your hand off my elbow, Paul. I'm not going with you. I don't belong out there. I don't like anyone out there. I belong here. This is my home. I know everybody here."

"You're tired."

"I'm rested." Not once in the conversation had he looked at the younger man. "I'll be tired if you take me out there. I've never been so rested as I've been here."

"Aren't you lonely?"

"No. I was lonely with Vera and Tom and the others. I walked around with them and I always felt funny. You'd better go back with them, Paul."

"I came to get you, and I won't walk away now," said Paul, stubbornly.

"I guess I'll have to walk away then," said the man in the shadow. "Goodnight, Paul."

And when the man turned away in the shadow, the back half of him, the spine of him and the back of his neck showed nothing but a mass of little strutworks and braces which held together and gave substance to the *papier-mache* shell of his false frontworks.

He walked slowly off between the dark buildings.

CISTERN

It was an afternoon of rain, and lamps lighted against the grey. For a long while the two sisters had been in the dining room. One of them, Juliet, embroidered table-cloths; the youngest, Anna, sat quietly on the window-seat, staring out at the dark street and the dark sky, her brow against the pane.

Anna did not move her head, but her lips moved and after thinking a long moment, she said, "I never thought of that before."

"Of what?" asked Juliet.

"It just came to me. There's actually a city under a city. A dead city, right here, right under our feet."

Juliet poked her needle in and out the white cloth. "Come away from the window. That rain's done something to you."

"No, really. Didn't you ever think of the cisterns

before? They're all through the town, there's one for every street and you can walk in them without bumping your head and they go everywhere and finally go down to the sea," said Anna, fascinated with the rain on the asphalt pavement out there and the rain falling from the sky and vanishing into sewer mouths at each corner of the distant cross-section. "Wouldn't you like to live in a cistern?"

"I *would* not!"

"But wouldn't it be fun; I mean, very secret, to live in the cistern and peek up at people through the slots and see them and them not see you? It's a nice goose-pimply, rainy-day feeling like when you were a child and played hide-and-seek and nobody found you and there you were in their midst all the time, all sheltered and hidden and warm and excited. I'd *like* that. I like to fool people. That's what it must be like to live in the cistern."

Juliet looked slowly up from her work. "You *are* my sister, aren't you, Anna? You *were* born, weren't you? Sometimes, the way you talk, I think mother found you under a tree one day and brought you home and planted you in a pot and grew you to this size and there you are, and you'll never change."

Anna didn't reply, so Juliet went back to her needle. There was no color in the room; neither of the two sisters added any color to it. Anna held her head to the window for five minutes. Then she looked like she had made a decision, she looked way off into the distance and said, "I guess you'd call it a dream. While I've been here, the last hour, I mean. Thinking. Yes, it was a dream."

Now it was Juliet's turn not to answer.

Anna whispered. "All this water put me to sleep awhile, I guess, and then I began to think about the rain and where it came from and where it went and how it went down those little slots in the curb, and then I thought about deep under and suddenly there *they* were. A man, and a—woman. Down in that cistern, under the road."

"What would they be doing there?" asked Juliet.

Anna said, "Must they have a reason?"

"No, not if they're insane, no," said Juliet, "in that case no reasons are necessary, there they are in their cistern and let them stay."

"But they weren't just *in* the cistern," said Anna, knowingly, her head to one side, her eyes moving under the half-down lids. "No, they were in love, these two."

"For heaven's sake," said Juliet, "did they crawl down there to make love?"

"No, they've been there for years and years," said Anna.

"You can't tell me they've been in that cistern for years, living together," protested Juliet.

"Did I say they were alive?" asked Anna, surprised. "Oh, but no. They're *dead*."

The rain scrambled in wild pushing pellets down the window. Drops came and joined with others and made streaks.

"Oh," said Juliet.

"Yes," said Anna, pleasantly. "Dead. He's dead and she's dead." This seemed to satisfy her, it was a nice discovery and she was proud of it. "He looks like a very lonely man who never traveled in all his life."

"How do you know?"

"He looks like the kind of man who never traveled, but wanted to. You know by his eyes. Traveling eyes in a sick body."

"You know what he looks like, then?"

"Yes. Very ill and very handsome. You know how it is with a man made handsome by illness? Illness brings out the bones in the face."

"And he's dead?" asked the older sister.

"For five years." Anna talked slowly, with her eyelids rising and lowering in gentle pulsations, as if she were about to tell a long story and knew it and wanted to work into it slowly, and then faster and then faster, until the very momentum of the story would carry her on, with her eyes wide and her lips parted. But now it was slowly, with only a slight fever to the telling. "Five years ago this man was walking along a street and he knew he'd been walking the same street on many nights and he'd go on walking them, so he came to a man-hole cover, one of those big iron waffles in the center of the street, and he heard the river rushing under his feet, under the metal cover, rushing toward the sea, toward other places and things." She put out her right hand. "And he bent slowly and lifted up the cistern lid and looked down at the rushing foam and the water, and he thought of someone he wanted to love and couldn't, and then he swung himself down in on the iron rungs and walked down them until he was all gone save his hand drawing the lid shut after him and the rain hit on the lid for all the rest of the night . . . ."

"And what about her?" asked Juliet, busy. "When'd she die?"

"I'm not sure. She's new. She's just dead, now. But she *is* dead. Beautifully, beautifully dead." She admitted the image she had in her mind. "It takes death to make a woman really beautiful, and it takes death by drowning to make her most beautiful of all. Then all the stiffness is taken out of her and her hair hangs upon the water like a drift of smoke. And her arms and legs and her fingers move in the water with such slow purposelessness and she's very water-elegant and water-graceful. There's not a clumsy move in her as she hangs in the water. She turns every once in awhile to read passing newspapers with unseeing eyes." Anna nodded her head, amusedly. "All the schools and etiquettes and teachings in the world can't make a woman move with this dreamy ease, supple and ripply, and fine." She tried to show how fine, how ripply, how graceful, with her broad, coarse hand, but it was more a jerking than a lazy gesture. She put her hand down and did not try to show how again for another full five minutes.

"He's been waiting for her, for five years. But she didn't know where he was, until now. So there they are, and will be, from now on! In the wet season they'll live. But, in the dry seasons, that's sometimes months, they'll have long rest periods, they'll lie in little hidden niches, under the drains, like those Japanese water flowers, all dry and compact and old and quiet."

Juliet got up and turned on yet another little lamp in the corner of the dining room. "I wish you wouldn't talk about it."

Anna laughed. "But let me tell you about how it starts, how they come to life, when the rainy season comes. I've got it all worked." She bent forward, held onto her knees, intensely interested, staring at the street and the rain and the cistern mouths. "There they are, down under, dry and quiet, and up above the sky gets electrical and powdery and the clouds look dark and soon the rain comes down!" She threw back her dull, grey-brown hair with one hand. "At first all the upper world is pellets. Street cars run by all pimply. Then there's lightning and the thunder and the dry season is over, and the little pellets run along the gutters and get big and fall into the drains. They take gum-wrappers and cigarettes and theatre tickets with them, and bus-transfers!"

"Come away from that window, now."

Anna made a square with her hands and imagined things. "I know just what it's like under the pavement, in the big square cistern. It's huge. It's all empty from the weeks with nothing but sunshine. It's empty and it echoes if you talk. The only sound you can hear standing down there is an auto passing above. Far up above. The whole cistern is like a dry hollow camelbone in a desert, waiting. I bet the whole floor of the canal is pasted and mashed flat with old circus banners and newspapers about 1936 and 1940 and the war and the movie star who died."

She lifted her hand, pointing, as if she herself were down in the cistern, waiting.

"Now—a little trickle. It comes down on the floor. It's like something was hurt and bleeding up in the outer world. There's some thunder! Or was it a truck going by?"

She spoke a little more rapidly now, but held her body very relaxed against the window with the rain streaking the glass, breathing out and in the next words she wanted to say:

"It seeps down. Then, in all the other hollows come other seepages. Little twines and snakes. Tobacco-stained water. It makes puddles. Then it—moves. It joins others. It makes snakes and then one big constrictor which rolls along on the flat-papered floor, with a majestic movement. From everywhere, from the north and south, from other streets, other streams come and they join and make one hissing and shining of coils.

"The cistern's full, from wall to wall, and it turns toward the ocean and the gravity pull of the ocean! There are little tidal swirls. And ten thousand drains drop down all kinds of undigested water, paper and muck. And the water gets into those two little dry niches I told you about. It rises slowly around those two dry people lying like Japanese water-flowers there, dead."

She clasped her hands, slowly, working finger into finger, interlacing.

"The water soaks into them. First, it lifts the woman's hand. In a little move. Her hand's the only live part of her. Then her arm lifts and one foot. And her hair—" She touched her own hair as it hung about her shoulders. "—unloosens and opens out like a flower in the water. Her shut eyelids are blue . . . ."

The room got darker, Juliet sewed on, and Anna talked and told all she saw in her mind. She told how the water rose and took the woman with it, unfolding her out and loosening her and standing her full upright in the cistern, the dead woman not caring. "The water is interested in the woman, and she lets it have its way. All morals come from outside *to* her. After a long time of lying still, and being stiff, she's ready to live again, any life the water wants her to have."

Somewhere else, the man stood up in the water also. And Anna told of that, and how the water carried him slowly, drifting, and her, drifting, until they met each other.

"The water opens their eyes. Now they can see but not see each other. They circle, not touching yet." Anna made a little slow circle of her head, eyes closed. "They watch each other and the only muscles they've got are made by the water. They glow with some kind of phosphorus. They smile.

"They—touch hands."

Anna hesitated, took in a long breath, lingered over

the thought, putting the tips of her right hand against the fingers of her left.

"The tide—*makes* them touch. They bump. They go away. They bump again. It's gentle. First, hands. Then, feet. Then—bodies."

At last, Juliet, stiffening, put down her sewing and stared at her sister, across the grey, rain-silent room.

"They circle," whispered Anna, softly, slowly, her fingers trailing in the air. "They bump, gently. They turn. Twist. Their heads bump and their lips bump softly. A lot of times, and their long white bodies bump and bump gently."

"Anna!"

"They float over and they float under each other. The tide comes and puts them together. Then, away again. Back and forth." She showed how with her hands. "It's a perfect kind of love, with no ego to it, only two bodies, moved by the water, which makes it clean and all right. It's not wicked, this way."

"It's bad you're saying it!" cried her sister.

"No, it's all right," insisted Anna, turning for an instant. "They're not 'thinking,' are they? They're just so deep down and quiet and not caring. Like children in a bath."

She took her right hand and held it over her left hand very slowly and gently, quavering and interweaving them for one another. The rainy window, with the dull autumn light penetrating, put a movement of light and running water on her fingers, made them seem submerged, fathoms deep in grey water, running one about the other as she finished her little dream:

"Him, tall and quiet, his hands open," She showed with a gesture how tall and how easy he was in the water. "Her, small and quiet and relaxed." She drifted the hands in a slow pressure one upon the other. "Both of them so wonderful about it, not hurrying, knowing that they've all the time in the world." The two hands hung in mid-air, her face fascinated over them. She looked at her sister, leaving her hands just that way. "Love's always better when it's long and careful and not rushed. They can be long and careful here, because no one sees them, there's no one to yell at them or criticize. Nobody can walk in on them. Except little bits of paper floating, or a magazine. And—why, even if somebody did happen in on them—they're dead!"

She seemed very pleased to have rediscovered this aspect of the situation. She looked at her white hands. "They're dead, with no place to go, and no one to tell them. They just wouldn't pay attention if people looked at them and said 'Look! A man and a woman, no clothing on, in the water, isn't that awful!'" She laughed softly. "They'd just go on being in the water, circling each other carelessly, no matter how people talked or stared, no matter which people, mothers or fathers, even, or sisters." She jerked her head at her sister. "Remember that child rhyme? how'd it go? 'Scoldings don't hurt, Lickings don't last, And kill me you dassn't!' Only with this man and this woman it's 'Resurrect us you dassn't!' They'd have to be resurrected, have to be made alive before any one could tell them they were wicked and wrong. And nobody could do that, it's too late. That's the beauty of it!

"So there they are, with nothing applying to them and no worries, very secret and hidden under the earth in the cistern waters, going around and about. They touch their hands and lips and when they come into a cross-street outlet of the cistern the tide rushes them together and they burn cold in the water!" She clapped her hands together. "They're crushed against a wall. They stay that way, one against the other, for maybe an hour, with the tide moving them in little fine moves and everything beautiful. Then, later . . ." She disengaged her hands. ". . . maybe they travel together, hand in hand, bobbling and floating, carefree and relaxed, down all the streets, doing little crazy upright dances when they're caught in sudden swirls, her like white fire, him the same." She whirled her hands about; a drenching of rain spatted the window. "And they go down to the sea, all across the town, past cross-drain and cross-drain, street and street. Genesee Avenue, Crenshaw, Edmond Place, Washington, Motor City, Ocean Side and then the ocean and the traveling. They can go anywhere they want, all over the earth, on a deep siphon, and come back later, to the cistern inlet and swim back up under the town, under a dozen tobacco shops and four dozen liquor stores, and six dozen groceries and ten theatres, a rail junction, Highway 101, under the walking feet of thirty thousand people who don't even know or think of the cistern."

Anna's voice drifted and dreamed and grew quiet again.

"And then—the day passes and the thunder goes away upon the street. The rain stops. The rainy season's over. The tunnels drip and stop. The tide goes down." Shc seemed disappointed, sad it was over. "The river runs out to the ocean. The man and woman feel the water leave them slowly to the floor. They settle." She lowered her hands in little bobblings toward her lap, watching them fixedly, longingly. "Their feet touch and their feet lose the life the water has given them from outside. Their knees touch, and their hips and now the water lays them down, side by side, and drains away and the tunnels are drying. There are just little puddles and wet papers. And there they lie. With little, contented smiles. They don't move and they're not ashamed. Like two children they lie there with the water all gone and their skin drying. They barely touch. Up above, in the world, the sun comes out. There they lie, in the darkness, sleeping, until the next time. Until the next rain."

Her hands were now upon her lap, palms up and open. "Nice man, nice woman," she murmured. She bowed her head over them and shut her eyes tight.

Suddenly, Anna sat up and glared at her sister. "Do you know who the man is?" she shouted, bitterly.

Juliet did not reply, she had watched, stricken, for the past five minutes while this thing went on. Her mouth was twisted and pale. Anna almost screamed:

"The man is Frank, that's who he is! And *I'm* the woman!"

"Anna!"

"Yes, it's Frank, down there!"

"But Frank's been gone for years, and certainly not down there, Anna!"

Now, Anna was talking to nobody, and to everybody, to Juliet, to the window, the wall, the street. "Poor Frank," she cried. "I know that's where he went. He couldn't stay anywhere in the world. His mother spoiled him for all the world! So he saw the cistern and saw how secret and fine it was, and how it went down to the ocean and everywhere in the world, and it was like going back to his mother's womb where it was nice and secret and nobody criticized. Oh, poor Frank. And poor Anna, poor me, with only a sister. God, Julie, how'd we get this way and why didn't I take Frank when he was here! But if I had held onto him he'd have been revolted and so would I, and Frank would have been shocked and frightened and run off like a little boy, and I'd have hated him if he had touched me. Christ, Julie, what good *are* we!"

"Stop it, this minute, do you hear, this minute!"

"It's rained three days, and all the time I sat here, and thought. And when I got the idea of Frank, down there, I knew it was the place for him, and when I turned on the faucet in the kitchen I heard him calling from deep in the cistern, up the long metal piping, calling and calling. And when I bathed this morning he looked out from the little grille in the tube and saw me. I soaped myself to hide myself! I saw his eye shining behind the grille!"

"A soap bubble," said Juliet frantically.

"No, an eye."

"A drop of water."

"No, Frank's eye!"

"A piece of metal, a nut or a bolt."

"Frank's lovely, seeing eye!"

"Anna!"

Anna slumped down into the corner, by the window, one hand up on it, and wept silently. A few minutes later she heard her sister say, "Are you finished?"

"What?"

"If you're done, come help me finish this, I'll be forever at it."

Anna raised her head, all pale, all expressionless. Juliet looked upon her with gentle impatience. An impatience so gently all-pervading one could not fight it. There was nothing to get hold of, or fight. It was just a continuing, gentle, tolerant impatience, year on year, year on year.

Anna rose and glided to her sister. "What do you want me to do?" she sighed.

"This and this," said Juliet, showing her. "All right," said Anna, and took it and sat by the cold window timing the rain, and moving her fingers with the needle and thread but knowing how dark the street now was, and how dark the room, and how hard to see the round metal top of the cistern now, there were just little midnight gleams and glitters out there in the black black late afternoon. Lightning crackled over the sky, in a web.

Half an hour passed. Juliet drowsed in her chair across

the room, removed her glasses, placed them down with her work and for a moment rested her head back and dozed. Perhaps thirty seconds later, she heard the front door open violently, heard the wind come in, heard the footsteps run down the walk, turn, and hurry along the black street.

"What?" asked Juliet, sitting up, fumbling for her glasses. "Who's there? Anna, did someone come in the door?" She stared at the empty window-seat where Anna had been. "Anna!" she cried. She sprang up and ran out into the hall.

The front door stood open, rain fell through it in a fine mist.

"She's only gone out for a run," said Juliet, standing there, trying to peer into the wet blackness. "She'll be right back. *Won't* you be right back, Anna dear? Anna, answer me, you *will* be right back, won't you, my dear sister?"

Outside, the cistern lid rose and slammed down.

The rain whispered on the street and fell upon the dropped shut lid all the rest of the night.

THE NEXT IN LINE

It was a little caricature of a town square. In it were the following fresh ingredients: a candy-box of a band-stand where men stood on Thursday and Sunday nights exploding music; fine, green-patinaed bronze-copper benches all scrolled and flourished; fine blue and pink tiled walks—blue as women's newly-lacquered eyes, pink as women's hidden wonders; and fine French-clipped trees in the shapes of exact hatboxes. The whole, from your hotel window, had the fresh ingratiation and unbelievable fantasy one might expect of a French village in the nineties. But no, this was Mexico! and this a plaza in a small colonial Mexican town, with a fine State Opera House (in which movies were shown for two pesos admission: RASPUTIN AND THE EMPRESS, THE BIG HOUSE, MADAME CURIE, LOVE AFFAIR, MAMA LOVES PAPA).

Joseph came out on the sun-heated balcony in the morning and knelt by the grille, pointing his little box-brownie. Behind him, in the bath, the water was running and Marie's voice came out:

"What're you doing?"

He muttered. "—a picture." She asked again. He clicked the shutter, stood up, wound the spool inside, squinting, and said, "Took a picture of the town square. God, didn't those men shout last night? I didn't sleep until two thirty. We would have to arrive when the local Rotary's having its whingding."

"What're our plans for today?" she asked.

"We're going to see the mummies," he said.

"Oh," she said. There was a long silence.

He came in, set the camera down, and lit himself a cigarette.

"I'll go up and see them alone," he said. "If you'd rather."

"No," she said, not very loud. "I'll go along. But I wish we could forget the whole thing. It's such a lovely little town."

"Look here!" he cried, catching a movement from the corner of his eyes. He hurried to the balcony, stood there, his cigarette smoking and forgotten in his fingers. "Come quick, Marie!"

"I'm drying myself," she said.

"Please, hurry," he said, fascinated, looking down into the street.

He heard the movement behind him, and then the

odor of soap and water-rinsed flesh, wet towel, fresh cologne; Marie was at his elbow. "Stay right there," she cautioned him, "so I can look without exposing myself. I'm stark. What *is* it?"

"Look!" he cried.

A procession traveled along the street. One man led it, with a package on his head. Behind him came women in black rebozos, chewing away the peels of oranges and spitting them on the cobbles; little children at their elbows, men ahead of them. Some ate sugar canes, gnawing away at the outer bark until it split down and they pulled it off in great hunks to get at the succulent pulp, the juicy sinews on which to suck. In all, there were fifty people.

"Joe," said Marie behind him, holding his arm.

It was no ordinary package the first man in the procession carried on his head, balanced delicately as a chicken-plume. It was covered with silver satin and silver fringe and silver rosettes. And he held it gently with one brown hand, the other hand swinging free.

This was a funeral and the little package was a coffin.

He watched his wife from one side of his face.

She was the color of fine, fresh milk. The pink color of the bath was gone. Her heart had sucked it all down to some hidden vacuum in her. She held fast to the French doorway and watched the traveling people go, watched them eat fruit, heard them talk gently, laugh gently. She forgot she was naked.

He said, "Some little girl or boy gone to a happier place."

"Where are they taking—her?"

She did not think it unusual, her choice of the feminine pronoun. Already she had identified herself with that tiny fragment of decay parceled like an unripe variety of fruit. Now, in this moment, she was being carried up the hill within compressing dark, a stone in a peach, silent and terrified, the touch of the father against the coffin material outside; gentle and noiseless and firm inside.

"To the graveyard, naturally; that's where they're taking her," he said, the cigarette making a casual filter of smoke across his casual face.

"Not *the* graveyard?" she asked, looking at him earnestly.

"There's only one cemetery in these towns, you *know* that. They usually hurry it. That little girl has probably been dead only a few hours."

"A few hours—"

She turned away, quite ridiculous, quite naked, with only the towel supported by her limp, untrying hands. She walked toward the bed. "A few hours ago she was alive, and now—"

He went on, "Now they're hurrying her up the hill. The climate isn't kind to the dead here. It's hot and there's no embalming. They have to finish it quickly."

"But to *that* graveyard, that horrible place," she said, with a voice from a dream.

"Oh, the mummies," he said. "Don't let that bother you."

She sat on the bed, again and again stroking the towel laid across her lap. Her eyes were blind as the brown paps of her breasts. She did not see him or the room. She knew that if he snapped his fingers or coughed, she wouldn't even look up.

"They were eating fruit at her funeral, and laughing," she said.

"It's a long climb to the cemetery."

She shuddered. A convulsive moving, like a fish trying to free itself from a deep swallowed hook. She lay back and he looked at her as one examines a poor sculpture; all criticism, all quiet and easy and uncaring. She wondered idly just how much his hands had had to do with the broadening and flattening and changement of her body. Certainly this was not the body he'd started with. It was past saving now. Like clay which the sculptor has carelessly impregnated with water, it was impossible to shape again. In order to shape clay you warm it with your hands, evaporate the moisture with heat. But there was no more passion, no more friction of the enjoyable sort between them. There was no warmth to bake away the aging moisture that collected and made pendant now her breasts and body. When the heat is gone, it is marvelous and unsettling to see how quickly a vessel stores self-destroying water in its fatty cells.

"I don't feel well," she said. She lay there, thinking it over. "I don't feel well," she said again, when he made no response. After another minute or two she lifted herself. "Let's not stay here another night, Joe."

"But it's a wonderful town."

"Yes, but we've seen everything." She got up. She

knew what came next. Gayness, false blitheness, false encouragement, everything quite false and hopeful. "We could go on to Patzcuaro. Make it in no time. You won't have to pack, I'll do it all myself, darling! We can get a room at the Don Posada there. They say it's a beautiful little town—"

"This," he remarked, "is a beautiful little town."

"Bougainvillea climb all over the buildings—" she said.

"These—" he pointed out some flowers at the window "—are bougainvillea."

"—and we'd fish, you like fishing," she said in bright haste. "And I'd fish, too, I'd learn, yes I would, I've always *wanted* to learn! And they say the Tarascan Indians there are almost Mongoloid in feature, and don't speak much Spanish, and from there we could go to Paracutin, that's near Uruapan, and they have some of the finest lacquered boxes there, oh, it'll be fun, Joe. I'll pack. You just take it easy, and—"

"Marie."

He stopped her with one word as she ran to the bath door.

"Yes?"

"I thought you said you didn't feel well?"

"I didn't. I don't. But, thinking of all those swell places—"

"We haven't seen one tenth of this town," he explained logically. "There's that statue of Morelos on the hill, I want a shot of that, and some of that French architecture up the street . . . we've traveled three hundred miles and we've been here one day and now want to rush off somewhere else. I've already paid the rent for another night . . . ."

"You can get it back," she said.

"Why do you want to run away?" he said, looking at her with an attentive simplicity. "Don't you like the town?"

"I simply adore it," she said, her cheeks white, smiling. "It's so green and pretty."

"Well, then," he said. "Another day. You'll love it. That's settled."

She started to speak.

"Yes?" he asked.

"Nothing."

She closed the bath room door. Behind it she rattled open a medicine box. Water rushed into a tumbler. She was taking some stuff for her stomach. He dropped his cigarette out the window.

He came to the bath room door.

"Marie, the mummies don't bother you, do they?"

"Unh-unh," she said.

"Was it the funeral, then?"

"Unh."

"Because, if you were really afraid, I'd pack in a moment, you know that, darling."

He waited.

"No, I'm not afraid," she said.

"Good girl," he said.

*

The graveyard was enclosed by a thick adobe wall, and at its four corners small stone angels tilted out on stony wings, their grimy heads capped with bird droppings, their hands gifted with amulets of the same substance, their faces unquestionably freckled.

In the warm smooth flow of sunlight which was like a depthless, tideless river, Joseph and Marie climbed up the hill, their shadows slanting blue behind them. Helping one another, they made the cemetery gate, swung back the Spanish blue iron grille and entered.

It was several mornings after the celebratory fiesta of El Dia de Muerte, the Day of the Dead, and ribbons and ravels of tissue and sparkle-tape still clung like insane hair to the raised stones, to the hand-carved, love-polished crucifixes, and to the above ground tombs which resembled marble jewel cases. There were statues frozen in angelic postures over gravel mounds, and intricately carved stones tall as men with angels spilling all down their rims, and tombs as big and ridiculous as beds put out to dry in the sun after some nocturnal accident. And within the four walls of the yard, inserted into square mouths and slots, were coffins, walled in, plated in by marble plates and plaster, upon which names were struck and upon which hung tin pictures, cheap peso portraits of the inserted dead. Thumb-tacked to the different pictures were trinkets they'd loved in life, silver charms, silver arms, legs, bodies, silver cups, silver dogs, silver church medallions, bits of red crepe and blue ribbon. On some places were painted slats of tin showing the dead rising to heaven in oil-tinted angels' arms.

Looking at the graves again, they saw the remnants of the death fiesta. The little tablets of tallow splashed over the stones by the lighted festive candles, the wilted orchid blossoms lying like crushed red-purple tarantulas against the milky stones, some of them looking horridly sexual, limp and withered. There were loop-frames of cactus leaves, bamboo, reeds and wild, dead morning-glories. There were circles of gardenias and sprigs of bougainvillea, desiccated. The entire floor of the yard seemed a ballroom after a wild dancing, from which the participants have fled; the tables askew, confetti, candles, ribbons and deep dreams left behind.

They stood, Marie and Joseph, in the warm silent yard, among the stones, between the walls. Far over in one corner a little man with high cheekbones, the milk color of the Spanish infiltration, thick glasses, a black coat, a grey hat and grey, unpressed pants and neatly laced shoes, moved about among the stones, supervising something or other that another man in overalls was doing to a grave with a shovel. The little man with glasses carried a thrice folded newspaper under his left arm and had his hands in his pockets.

"*Buenos diaz, senora y senor,*" he said, when he finally noticed Joseph and Marie and came to see them.

"Is this the place of *las mommias*?" asked Joseph. "They do exist, do they not?"

"*Si*, the mummies," said the man. "They exist and are here. In the catacombs."

"*Por favor*," said Joseph. "*Yo quiero veo las mommias, si?*"

"*Si, senor.*"

"*Me Espanol es mucho estupido, es muy malo*," apologized Joseph.

"No, no, senor. You speak well! This way, please."

He led between the flowered stones to a tomb near the wall shadows. It was a large flat tomb, flush with the gravel, with a thin kindling door flat on it, padlocked. It was unlocked and the wooden door flung back rattling to one side. Revealed was a round hole the circled interior of which contained steps which screwed into the earth.

Before Joseph could move, his wife had set her foot on the first step. "Here," he said. "Me first."

"No. That's all right," she said, and went down and around in a darkening spiral until the earth vanished her. She moved carefully, for the steps were hardly enough to contain a child's feet. It got dark and she heard the caretaker stepping after her, at her ears, and then it got light light again. They stepped out into a long white-washed hall twenty feet under the earth, into which light was allowed by geometric interstices of religious design. The hall was fifty yards long, ending on the left in a double door in which were set tall crystal panes and a sign forbidding entrance. On the right end of the hall was a large stack of white rods and round white stones.

"Oh, skulls and leg-bones," said Marie, interested.

"The soldiers who fought for Father Morelos," said the caretaker.

They walked to the vast pile. They were neatly put in place, bone on bone, like firewood, and on top was a mound of a thousand dry skulls.

"I don't mind skulls and bones," said Marie. "They're not human at all. There's nothing even vaguely human to them. I'm not scared of skulls and bones. They're like something insectivorous. Like stones or baseball bats or boulders. If a child was raised and didn't know he had a skeleton in him, he wouldn't think anything of bones, would he? That's how it is with me. Everything human has been scraped off *these*. There's nothing familiar left to be horrible. In order for a thing to be horrible it has to suffer a change you can recognize. This isn't changed. They're still skeletons, like they always were. The part that changed is gone, and so there's nothing to show for it. Isn't that interesting?"

He nodded.

She was quite brave now.

"Well," she said, "let's see the mummies."

"Here, senora," said the caretaker.

He took them far down the hall away from the stack of bones and when Joseph paid him a peso he unlocked the forbidden crystal doors and opened them wide and they looked into an even longer, dimly lighted hall in which stood the people.

*

They waited inside the door in a long line under the arch-roofed ceiling, fifty-five of them against one wall, on the left, fifty-five of them against the right wall, and five of them way down at the very end.

"Mister Interlocutor!" said Joseph, briskly.

They resembled nothing more than those preliminary erections of a sculptor, the wire frame, the first tendons of clay, the muscles, and a thin lacquer of skin. They were unfinished, all one hundred and fifteen of them.

They were parchment colored and the skin was stretched as if to dry, from bone to bone. The bodies were intact, only the watery humors had evaporated from them.

"The climate," said the caretaker. "It preserves them. Very dry."

"How long have they been here?" asked Joseph.

"Some one year, some five, senor, some ten, some seventy."

There was an embarrassment of horror. You started with the first man on your right, hooked and wired upright against the wall, and he was not good to look upon, and you went on to the woman next to him who was unbelievable and then to a man who was horrendous and then to a woman who was very sorry she was dead and in such a place as this.

"What are they doing here?" said Joseph.

"They are but standing around, senor."

"Yes, but why?"

"Their relatives did not pay the rent upon their graves."

"Is there a rent?"

"Si, senor. Twenty pesos a year. Or, if they desire the permanent interment, one hundred seventy pesos. But our people, they are very poor, as you must know, and one hundred seventy pesos is as much as many of them make in two years. So they carry their dead here and place them into the earth for one year, and the twenty pesos are paid, with fine intentions of paying each year and each year, but each year and each year after the first year they have a burro to buy or a new mouth to feed, or maybe three new mouths, and the dead, after all, are not hungry, and the dead, after all, can pull no plows; or there is a new wife or there is a roof in need of mending, and the dead, remember, can be in no beds with a man, and the dead, you understand, can keep no rain off one, and so it is that the dead are not paid up upon their rent."

"*Then* what happens? Are you listening, Marie?" said Joseph.

Marie counted the bodies. One, two, three, four, five, six, seven, eight. "What?" she said, quietly.

"Are you listening?"

"I think so. What? Oh, yes! I'm listening."

Eight, nine, ten, eleven, twelve, thirteen.

"Well, then," said the little man. "I call a *trabajando* and with his delicate shovel at the end of the first year he does dig and dig and dig down. How deep do you think we dig, senor?"

"Six feet. That's the usual depth."

"Ah, no, ah, no. There, senor, you would be wrong. Knowing that after the first year the rent is liable not to be paid, we bury the poorest two feet down. It is less work, you understand? Of course, we must judge by the family who own a body. Some of them we bury sometimes three, sometimes four feet deep, sometimes five, sometimes six, depending on how well the family is in money, depending on what the chances are we won't have to dig him from out his place a year later. And, let me tell you, senor, when we bury a man the whole six feet deep we are very certain of his staying. We have never dug up a six foot buried one yet, that is the accuracy with which we know the money of the people."

Twenty-one, twenty-two, twenty-three. Marie's lips moved with a small whisper.

"And the bodies which are dug up are down here placed against the wall, with the other *companeros*."

"Do the relatives know the bodies are here?"

"Si." The small man pointed. "This one, *yo veo?* It is new. It has been here but one year. His *madre y padre* know him to be here. But have they money? Ah, no."

"Isn't that rather gruesome on his parents?"

The little man was earnest. "They never think of it," he said.

"Did you hear *that*, Marie?"

"What?" Thirty, thirty-one, thirty-two, thirty-three, thirty-four. "Yes. They never think of it."

"What if the rent is paid again, after a lapse?" inquired Joseph.

"In that time," said the caretaker, "the bodies are reburied for as many years as are paid."

"Sounds like blackmail," said Joseph.

The little man shrugged, hands in pockets. "We must live."

"You are certain no one can pay the one hundred seventy pesos all at once," said Joseph. "So in this way you get them for twenty pesos a year, year after year, for maybe thirty years. If they don't pay you threaten to stand *mamacita* or little *nino* in the catacomb."

"We must live," said the little man.

Fifty-one, fifty-two, fifty-three.

Marie stood in the center of the long corridor, the standing dead on all sides of her.

They were screaming.

They looked as if they had leaped, snapped upright in their graves, clutched hands over their shriveled bosoms and screamed, jaws wide, tongues out, nostrils flared.

And been frozen that way.

All of them had open mouths. Theirs was a perpetual screaming. They were dead and they knew it. In every raw fibre and evaporated organ they knew it.

She stood listening to them scream.

They say dogs hear sounds humans never hear, sounds so many decibels higher than normal hearing that they seem non-existent.

The corridor swarmed with screams. Screams poured from terror-yawned lips and dry tongues, screams you couldn't hear because they were so high.

Joseph walked up to one standing body.

"Say 'ah,'" said Joseph.

Sixty-five, sixty-six, sixty-seven, counted Marie, among the screams.

"Here is an interesting one," said the proprietor.

They saw a woman with arms flung to her head, mouth wide, teeth intact, whose hair was wildly flourished, long and shimmery on her head. Her eyes were small pale white-blue eggs in her skull.

"Some times, this happens. This woman, she is a cataleptic. One day she falls down upon the earth, but is really not dead, for, deep in her, the little drum of her heart beats and beats, so dim one cannot hear. So she was buried in the graveyard in a fine inexpensive box . . . ."

"Didn't you know she was cataleptic?"

"Her sisters knew. But this time they thought her at last dead. And funerals are hasty things in this warm town."

"She was buried a few hours after her 'death'?"

"Si, the same. All of this, as you see her here, we would never have known, if a year later, her sisters, having other things to buy, refused the rent on her burial. So we dug very quietly down and loosed the box and took it up and opened the top of her box and laid it aside and looked in upon her—"

Marie stared.

This woman had wakened under the earth. She had torn, shrieked, clubbed at the box-lid with fists, died of suffocation, in this attitude, hands flung over her gaping face, horror-eyed, hair wild.

"Be pleased, senor, to find the difference between *her* hands and these other ones," said the caretaker. "Their peaceful fingers at their hips, quiet as little roses. Hers? Ah, hers! are jumped up, very wildly, as if to pound the lid free!"

"Couldn't rigor mortis do that?"

"Believe me, senor, rigor mortis pounds upon no lids. Rigor mortis screams not like this, nor twists nor wrestles to rip free nails, senor, or pry boards loose in an airless hysteria, senor. All these others are open of mouth, si, because they were not injected with the fluids of embalming, but theirs is a simple screaming of muscles, senor. This senorita, here, hers is the *muerte* horrible."

Marie walked, scuffling her shoes, turning first this way, then that. Naked bodies. Long ago the clothes had whispered away. The fat women's breasts were lumps of yeasty dough left in the dust. The men's loins were indrawn, withered orchids.

"Mr. Grimace and Mr. Gape," said Joseph.

He pointed his camera at two men who seemed in conversation, mouths in mid-sentence, hands gesticulant and stiffened over some long dissolved gossip.

Joseph clicked the shutter, rolled the film, focussed the camera on another body, clicked the shutter, rolled the film, walked on to another.

Eighty-one, eighty-two, eighty-three. Jaws down, tongues out like jeering children, eyes pale brown-irised in upclenched sockets. Hairs, waxed and prickled by sunlight, each sharp as quills imbedded on the lips, the cheeks, the eyelids, the brows. Little beards on chins and bosoms and loins. Flesh like drum-heads and manuscripts and crisp bread dough. The women, huge ill-shaped tallow things, death-melted. The insane hair of them, like nests made and unmade and remade. Teeth, each single, each fine, each perfect, in jaw. Eighty-six, eighty-seven, eighty-eight. A rushing of Marie's eyes. Down the corridor, flicking. Counting, rushing, never stopping. On! Quick! Ninety-one, ninety-two, ninety-three! Here was a man, his stomach open, like a tree hollow where you dropped your child love letters when you were eleven! Her eyes entered the hole in the space under his ribs. She peeked in. He looked like an Erector set inside. The spine, the pelvic plates. The rest was tendon, parchment, bone, eye, beardy jaw, ear, stupified nostril. And this ragged eaten cincture in his navel into which a pudding might be spooned. Ninety-seven, ninety-eight! Names, places, dates, things!

"This woman died in child-birth!"

Like a little hungry doll, the prematurely born child was wired, dangling, to her wrist.

"This was a soldier. His uniform still half on him—"

Marie's eyes slammed the furthest wall. After a back-forth, back-forth swinging from horror to horror, ricocheting from skull to skull, beating from rib to rib, staring with hypnotic fascination at paralyzed, loveless, fleshless loins, at men made into women by evaporation, at woman made into dugged swines. The fearful ricochet of vision, growing, growing, taking impetus from swollen breast to raving mouth, wall to wall, wall to wall, again, again, like a ball hurled in a game, caught in the incredible teeth, spat in a scream across the corridor to be caught in claws, lodged between thin teats, the whole standing chorus invisibly chanting the game on, on, the wild game of sight recoiling, rebounding, reshuttling on down the inconceivable procession, through a montage of erected horrors that ended finally and for all time when vision crashed against the corridor ending with one last scream from all present!

Marie turned and shot her vision far down to where the spiral steps walked up into sunlight. How talented was death. How many expressions and manipulations of hand, face, body, no two alike. They stood like tall naked pipes of a vast derelict calliope, their mouths cut into frantic vents. And now the great hand of mania descended upon all keys at once, and the long calliope screamed upon one, hundred-throated, unending scream.

Click, went the camera and Joseph rolled the film. Click went the camera and Joseph rolled the film.

Moreno, Morelos, Cantine, Gomez, Gutierrez, Villanousul, Ureta, Licon, Navarro, Iturbi, Jorge, Filomena, Nena, Manuel, Jose, Tomas, Ramona. This man walked and this man sang and this man had three wives; and this man died of this, and that of that, and the third from another thing, and the fourth was shot and the fifth was stabbed and the sixth fell straight down dead; and the seventh drank deep and died dead, and the eighth died in love, and the ninth fell from his horse, and the tenth coughed blood, and the eleventh stopped his heart, and the twelfth used to laugh much, and the thirteenth was a dancing one, and the fourteenth was most beautiful of all, the fifteenth had ten children and the sixteenth is one of those children as is the seventeenth; and the eighteenth was Tomas and did well with his guitar; the next three cut maise in their fields, had three lovers each; the twenty-second was never loved; the twenty-third sold tortillas, patting and shaping them each at the curb before the Opera House with her little charcoal stove; and the twenty-fourth beat his wife and now she walks proudly in the town and is merry with new men and here he stands bewildered by this unfair thing that has occurred, and the twenty-fifth drank several quarts of river with his lungs and was pulled forth in a net, and the twenty-sixth was a great thinker and his brain now sleeps like a burnt plum in his skull no bigger than a toe.

"I'd like a color shot of each and his or her name and how he or she died," said Joseph. "It would be an amazing, an ironical book to publish. The more you think, the more it grows on you. Their life histories and then a picture of each of them standing here."

He tapped each chest, softly. They gave off hollow sounds, like someone rapping on a door.

Marie pushed her way through screams that hung netwise across her path. She walked evenly, in the corridor center, not slow, but not too fast, toward the spiral stair, not looking to either side. Click went the camera behind her.

"You have room down here for more?" said Joseph.

"Si, senor. Many more."

"Wouldn't want to be next in line, on your waiting list."

"Ah, no, senor, one would not wish to be next."

"How are chances of buying one of these?"

"Oh, no, no, senor. Oh, no, no. Oh, no, senor."

"I'll pay you fifty pesos."

"Oh, no, senor, no, no, senor."

In the market, the remainder of candy skulls from the Death Fiesta were sold from flimsy little tables. Women hung with black rebozos sat quietly, now and then speaking one word to each other, the sweet sugar skeletons, the saccharine corpses and white candy skulls at their elbows. Each skull had a name on top in gold candy curlicue; Jose or Carmen or Ramon or Tena or Guiermo or Rosa. They sold cheap. The Death Festival was gone. Joseph paid a peso and got two candy skulls.

Marie stood in the narrow street. She saw the candy skulls and Joseph and the dark ladies who put the skulls in a sack.

"Not *really*," said Marie.

"Why not?" said Joseph.

"Not after just *now*," she said.

"In the catacombs?"

She nodded.

He said, "But these are good."

"They look poisonous."

"Just because they're skull-shaped?"

"No. The sugar itself looks raw, how do you know what kind of people made them, they might have the colic."

"My dear Marie, all people in Mexico have colic," he said.

"You can eat them both," she said.

"Alas, poor Yorick," he said, peeking into the bag.

They walked along a street that was held between high buildings in which were yellow window frames and pink iron grilles and the smell of tamales came from them and the sound of lost fountains splashing on hidden tiles and little birds clustering and peeping in bamboo cages and someone playing Chopin on a piano.

"Chopin, here," said Joseph. "How strange and swell." He looked up. "I like that bridge. Hold this." He handed her the candy sack while he clicked a picture of a red bridge spanning two white buildings with a man walking on it, a red serape on his shoulder. "Fine," said Joseph.

Marie walked looking at Joseph, looking away from him and then back at him, her lips moving but not speaking, her eyes fluttering, a little neck muscle under her chin like a wire, a little nerve in her brow ticking. She passed the candy bag from one hand to the other. She stepped up a curb, leaned back somehow, gestured, said something to restore balance, and dropped the sack.

"For Christ's sake!" Joseph snatched up the bag. "Look what you've done! Clumsy!"

"I should have broken my ankle," she said, "I suppose."

"These were the *best* skulls; both of them smashed; I wanted to save them for friends up home."

"I'm sorry," she said, vaguely.

"For God's sake, oh, damn it to hell," he scowled into the bag. "I might not find any more good as these. Oh, I don't *know*, I give up!"

The wind blew and they were alone in the street, he staring down into the shattered debris in the bag, she with the street shadows all around her, sun on the other side of the street, nobody about, and the world far away, the two of them alone, two thousand miles from anywhere, on a street in a false town behind which was nothing and around which was nothing but blank desert and circled hawks. On top the State Opera house, a block down, the golden Greek statues stood sun-bright and high, and in a beer place a shouting phonograph cried AY, MARIMBA . . . corazon . . . and all kinds of alien words which the wind stirred away.

Joseph twisted the bag shut, stuck it furiously in his pocket.

They walked back to the two-thirty lunch at the hotel.

He sat at the table with Marie, sipping Albondigas soup from his moving spoon, silently. Twice she commented cheerfully upon the wall murals and he looked at her steadily and sipped. The bag of cracked skulls lay on the table . . .

"Senora . . ."

The soup plates were cleared by a brown hand. A large plate of enchiladas was set down.

Marie looked at the plate.

There were sixteen enchiladas.

She put her fork and knife out to take one and stopped. She put her fork and knife down at each side of her plate. She glanced at the walls and then at her husband and then at the sixteen enchiladas.

Sixteen. One by one. A long row of them, crowded together.

She counted them.

One, two, three, four, five, six.

Joseph took one on his plate and ate it.

Six, seven, eight, nine, ten, eleven.

She put her hands on her lap.

Twelve, thirteen, fourteen, fifteen, sixteen. She finished counting.

"I'm not hungry," she said.

He placed another enchilada before himself. It had an interior clothed in a papyrus of corn tortilla. It was slender and it was one of many he cut and placed in his mouth and she chewed it for him in her mind's mouth, and squeezed her eyes tight.

"Eh?" he asked.

"Nothing," she said.

Thirteen enchiladas remained, like tiny bundles, like scrolls.

He ate five more.

"I don't feel well," she said.

"Feel better if you ate," he said.

"No."

He finished, then opened the sack and took out one of the half-demolished skulls.

"Not *here*?" she said.

"Why not?" And he put one sugar socket to his lips, chewing. "Not bad," he said, thinking the taste. He popped in another section of skull. "Not bad at all."

She looked at the name on the skull he was eating. *Marie*, it said.

It was tremendous, the way she helped him pack. In those newsreels you see men leap off diving boards into pools, only, a moment later when the reel is reversed, to jump back up in airy fantasy to alight once more safe on the diving board. Now, as Joseph watched, the suits and dresses flew into their boxes and cases, the hats were like birds darting, clapped into round, bright hat-boxes, the shoes seemed to run across the floor like mice to leap into valises. The suitcases banged shut, the hasps clicked, the keys turned.

"There!" cried she. "All packed!"

"In record time," he said.

She started for the door.

"Here, let me help," he said.

"They're not heavy," she said.

"But you *never* carry suitcases. You never have. I'll call a boy."

"Nonsense," she said, breathless with the weight of the valises.

A boy seized the cases outside the door. *"Senora, por favor!"*

"Have we forgotten anything?" He looked under the two beds, he went out on the balcony and gazed at the plaza, came in, went to the bathroom, looked in the cabinet and on the washbowl. "Here," he said, coming out and handing her something. "You forgot your wrist-watch."

"Did I?" She put it on and went out the door.

"I don't know," he said. "It's damn late in the day to be moving out."

"It's only three-thirty," she said. "Only three-thirty."

"I don't know," he said, doubtfully.

He looked around the room, stepped out, closed the door, locked it, went downstairs, jingling the keys.

She was outside in the car already, settled in, her coat folded on her lap, her gloved hands folded on the coat. He came out, supervised the loading of what luggage remained into the trunk receptacle, came to the front door and tapped on the window. She unlocked it and let him in.

"Well, here we *go*!" She cried with a laugh, her face rosy, her eyes frantically bright. She was leaning forward as if by this movement she might set the car rolling merrily down the hill. "Thank you, darling, for letting me get the refund on the money you paid for our room tonight. I'm sure we'll like it much better in Guadalajara tonight, thank you!"

"Yeah," he said.

Inserting the ignition keys he stepped on the starter.

Nothing happened.

He stepped on the starter again. Her mouth twitched.

"It needs warming," she said. "It was a cold night last night."

He tried it again. Nothing.

Marie's hands tumbled on her lap.

He tried it six more times. "Well," he said, lying back, ceasing.

"Try it again, next time it'll work," she said.

"It's no use," he said. "Something's wrong."

"Well, you've got to try it once more."

He tried it once more.

"It'll work, I'm sure," she said. "Is the ignition on?"

"Is the ignition on," he said. "Yes, it's *on*."

"It doesn't look like it's on," she said.

"It's on." He showed her by twisting the key.

"*Now*, try it," she said.

"There," he said, when nothing happened. "I *told* you."

"You're not doing it right; it almost caught that time," she cried.

"I'll wear out the battery, and God knows where you can buy a battery here."

"Wear it out, then. I'm sure it'll start next time!"

"Well, if you're so good, you try it." He slipped from the car and beckoned her over behind the wheel. "Go ahead."

She bit her lips and settled behind the wheel. She did

things with her hands that were like a little mystic ceremony, with moves of hands and body she was trying to overcome gravity, friction and every other natural law. She patted the starter with her toeless shoe. The car remained solemnly quiet. A little squeak came out of Marie's tightened lips. She rammed the starter home and there was a clear smell in the air as she fluttered the choke.

"You've flooded it," he said. "Fine! Get back over on your side, will you?"

He got three boys to push and they started the car downhill. He jumped in to steer. The car rolled swiftly, bumping and rattling. Marie's face glowed expectantly. "This'll start it!" she said.

Nothing started. They rolled quietly into the filling station at the bottom of the hill, bumping softly on the cobbles, and stopped by the tanks.

She sat there, saying nothing, except when the man came from the station her side was locked, the window up, and he had to come around on the husband's side to make his query.

The mechanic arose from the car engine, scowled at Joseph and they spoke together in Spanish, quietly.

She rolled the window down and listened.

"What's he say?" she demanded.

The two men talked on.

"What does he say?" she asked.

The dark mechanic waved at the engine, Joseph nodded and they conversed.

"What's wrong?" Marie wanted to know.

Joseph frowned over at her. "Wait a moment, will you. I can't listen to both of you."

"What's wrong!"

"The motor—"

The mechanic took Joseph's elbow. They said many words.

"What's he saying now?" she asked.

"He says—" said Joseph, and was lost as the Mexican took him over to the engine and bent him down in earnest discovery.

"How much will it cost?" she cried, out the window, around at their bent backs.

The mechanic spoke to Joseph.

"Fifty-five pesos," said Joseph.

"How long will it take?" said Marie.

Joseph asked the mechanic. The man shrugged and they argued for five minutes.

"How long will it take?" cried his wife.

The discussion continued.

The sun went down the sky. She looked at the sun upon the trees that stood high by the cemetery yard. The shadows rose and rose until the valley was enclosed and only the sky was clear and untouched and blue.

"Two days, maybe three," said Joseph, turning to Marie.

"Two days! Can't he fix it so we can just go on to the next town and have the rest done there?"

Joseph asked the man. The man replied.

Joseph said to his wife, "No, he'll have to do the entire job."

"Why, that's silly, it's so silly, he doesn't either, he doesn't really have to do it all, you tell him that, Joe, tell him that, he can hurry and fix it—"

The two men ignored her. They were talking earnestly again.

This time it was all in very slow motion. The unpacking of the suitcases. He did his own, she left hers by the door.

"I don't need anything," she said, leaving it locked.

"You'll need your nightgown," he said.

"I'll sleep naked," she said.

"Well, it isn't *my* fault," he said. "That damned car."

"You can go down and watch them work on it, later," she said. She sat on the edge of the bed. They were in a new room. She had refused to return to their old room. She said she couldn't stand it. She wanted a new room so it would seem they were in a new hotel in a new city. So this was a new room, with a view of the alley and the sewer system instead of the plaza and the drum-box trees. "You go down and supervise the work, Joe. If you don't, you know they'll take weeks!" She looked at him. "You should be down there now, instead of standing around."

"I'll go down," he said.

"I'll go down with you. I want to buy some magazines."

"You won't find any American magazines in a town like this."

"I can look, can't I?"

"Besides, we haven't much money," he said. "I don't want to have to wire my bank. It takes a god-awful time and it's not worth the bother."

"I can at least have my magazines," she said.

"Maybe one or two," he said.

"As many as I want," she said, feverishly, on the bed.

"For God's sake, you've got a million magazines in the car now. Post's, Collier's, Mercuries, Atlantic Monthlies, Barnaby, Superman! You haven't read half of the articles."

"But they're not new," she said. "They're not new, I've *looked* at them and after you've looked at a thing, I don't know—"

"Try *reading* them instead of looking at them," he said.

As they came downstairs night was in the plaza.

"Give me a few pesos," she said, and he gave her some. "Teach me to say about magazines in Spanish," she said.

"*Quiero una publicacion Americano,*" he said, walking swiftly.

She repeated it, stumblingly, and laughed. "Thanks."

He went on ahead to the mechanic's shop, and she turned in at the nearest *Farmacia Botica,* and all the magazines racked before her there were alien colors and alien names. She read the titles with swift moves of her eyes and looked at the old man behind the counter. "Do you have American magazines?" she asked in English, embarrassed to use the Spanish words.

The old man stared at her.

"Habla Ingles?" she asked.

"No, senorita."

She tried to think of the right words. "Quiero—no!" She stopped. She started again. "Americano—uh—magg-ah-zeen-as?"

"Oh, no, senorita!"

Her hands opened wide at her waist, then closed, like mouths. Her mouth opened and closed. The shop had a veil over it, in her eyes. Here she was and here were these small baked adobe people to whom she could say nothing and from whom she could get no words she understood, and she was in a town of people who said no words to her and she said no words to them except in blushing confusion and bewilderment. And the town was circled by desert and miles, and home was far away, far away in another life.

She whirled and fled.

Shop following shop she found no magazines save those giving bullfights in blood on their covers or murdered people or lace-confection priests. But at last three poor copies of the Post were bought with much display and loud laughing and she gave the vendor of this small shop a handsome tip.

Rushing out with the Posts eagerly on her bosom in both hands she hurried along the narrow walk, took a skip over the gutter, ran across the street, sang la-la, jumped onto the further walk, made another little scamper with her feet, smiled an inside smile, moving along swiftly, pressing the magazines tightly to her, half closing her eyes, breathing the charcoal evening air, feeling the wind watering past her ears.

Starlight tinkled in golden nuclei off the highly perched Greek figures atop the State theatre. A man shambled by in the shadow, balancing upon his head a basket. The basket contained bread loaves.

She saw the man and the balanced basket and suddenly she did not move and there was no inside smile, nor did her hands clasp tight the magazines. She watched the man walk, with one hand of his gently poised up to tap the basket any time it unbalanced, and down the street he dwindled, while the magazines slipped from Marie's fingers and scattered on the walk.

Snatching them up, she ran into the hotel and slipped going upstairs.

She sat in the room. The magazines were piled on each side of her and in a circle at her feet. She had made a little castle with portculli of words and into this she was withdrawn. All about her were the magazines she had bought and bought and looked at and looked at on other days, and these were the outer barrier, and upon the inside of the barrier, upon her lap, as yet unopened, but her hands were trembling to open them and read and read and read again with hungry eyes, were the three battered Post magazines. She opened the first page. She would go through them page by page, line by line, she decided. Not a line would go unnoticed, a comma unread, every little ad and every color would be fixed by her.

And—she smiled with discovery—in those other magazines at her feet were still advertisements and cartoons she had neglected—there would be little morsels of stuff for her to reclaim and utilize later.

She would read this first Post tonight, yes tonight she would read this first delicious Post. Page on page she would eat it and tomorrow night, if there was going to be a tomorrow night, but maybe there wouldn't be a tomorrow night here, maybe the motor would start and there'd be odors of exhaust and round hum of rubber tire on road and wind riding in the window and pennanting her hair—but, suppose, just suppose there would BE a tomorrow night here, in this room. Well, then, there would be two more Posts, one for tomorrow night, and the next for the next night. How neatly she said it to herself with her mind's tongue. She turned the first page.

She turned the second page. Her eyes moved over it and over it and her fingers unknown to her slipped under the next page and flickered it in preparation for turning, and the watch ticked on her wrist, and time passed and she sat turning pages, turning pages, hungrily seeing the framed people in the pictures, people who lived in another land in another world where neons bravely held off the night with crimson bars and the smells were home smells and the people talked good fine words and here she was turning the pages, and all the lines went across and down and the pages flew under her hands, making a fan. She threw down the first Post, seized on and rifled through the second in half an hour, threw that down, took up the third, threw that down a good fifteen minutes later and found herself breathing, breathing stiffly and swiftly in her body and out of her mouth. She put her hand up to the back of her neck.

Somewhere, a soft breeze was blowing.

The hairs along the back of her neck slowly stood upright.

She touched them with one pale hand as one touches the nape of a dandelion.

Outside, in the plaza, the street lights rocked like crazy flashlights on a wind. Papers ran through the gutters like sheep flocks. Shadows pencilled and slashed under the bucketing lamps now this way, now that, here a shadow one instant, there a shadow next, now no shadows, all cold light, now no light, all cold blue black shadow. The lamps creaked on their high metal hasps.

In the room her hands began to tremble. She saw them tremble. Her body began to tremble. Under the bright bright print of the brightest, loudest skirt she could find to put on especially for tonight, in which she had whirled and cavorted feverishly before the coffin-sized mirror, beneath the rayon skirt the body was all wire and tendon and excitation. Her teeth chattered and fused and chattered. Her lipstick smeared, one lip crushing another.

Joseph knocked on the door.

They got ready for bed. He had returned with the news that something had been done to the car and it would take time, he'd go watch them tomorrow.

"But don't knock on the door," she said, standing before the mirror as she undressed.

"Leave it unlocked then," he said.

"I want it locked. But don't rap. Call."

"What's wrong with rapping?" he said.

"It sounds funny," she said.

"What do you mean, funny?"

She wouldn't say. She was looking at herself in the mirror and she was naked, with her hands at her sides, and there were her breasts and her hips and her entire body, and it moved, it felt the floor under it and the walls and air around it, and the breasts could know hands if hands were put there, and the stomach would make no hollow echo if touched.

"For God's sake," he said. "Don't stand there admiring yourself." He was in bed. "What are you doing?" he said. "What're you putting your hands up that way for, over your face?"

He put the lights out.

She could not speak to him for she knew no words that he knew and he said nothing to her that she understood, and she walked to her bed and slipped in to it and he lay with his back to her in his bed and he was like one of these brown-baked people of this far away town upon the moon, and the real earth was off somewhere where it would take a starflight to reach it. If only he could speak with her and she to him tonight, how good the night might be, and how easy to breathe and how lax the vessels of blood in her ankles and in her wrists and the underarms, but there was no speaking and the night was ten thousand tickings and ten thousand twistings of the wretched blankets, and the pillow was like a tiny white warm stove undercheek, and the blackness of the room was a mosquito netting draped all about so that a turn entangled her in it. If only there was one word, one word between them. But there was no word and the veins did not rest easy in the wrists and the heart was a bellows forever blowing upon a little coal of fear, forever illumining and making it into a cherry light, again, pulse, and again, an ingrown light which her inner eyes stared upon with unwanting fascination. The lungs did not rest but were exercised as if she were a drowned person and she herself performing artificial respiration to keep the last life going. And all of these things were lubricated by the sweat of her glowing body, and she was glued fast between the heavy blankets like something pressed, smashed, redolently moist between the white pages of a heavy book.

And as she lay this way the long hours of midnight came when again she was a child. She lay, now and again thumping her heart in tambourine hysteria, then, quieting, the slow sad thoughts of bronze childhood when everything was sun on green trees and sun on water and sun on blonde child hair. Faces flowed by on merry-go-rounds of memory, a face rushing to meet her, facing her, and away to the right; another, whirling in from the left, a quick fragment of lost conversation, and out to the right. Around and round. Oh, the night was very long. She consoled herself by thinking of the car starting tomorrow, the throttling sound and the power sound and the road moving under, and she smiled in the dark with pleasure. But then, suppose the car did *not* start? She withered in the dark, like a burning, withering paper. All the folds and corners of her clenched in about her and tick tick tick went the wrist watch, tick tick tick and another tick to wither on . . . .

Morning. She looked at her husband lying straight and easy on his bed. She let her hand laze down at the cool space between the beds. All night her hand had hung in that cold empty interval between. Once she had put her hand out toward him, stretching, but the space was just a little too long, she couldn't reach him. She had snapped her hand back, hoping he hadn't heard the movement of her silent reaching.

There he lay now. His eyes gently closed, the lashes softly interlocked like clasped fingers. Breathing so quietly you could scarce see his ribs move. As usual, by this time of morning, he had worked out of his pajamas. His naked chest was revealed from the waist up. The rest of him lay under cover. His head lay on the pillow, in thoughtful profile.

There was a beard stubble on his chin.

The morning light showed the white of her eyes. They were the only things in the room in motion, in slow starts and stops, tracing the anatomy of the man across from her.

Each little hair was perfect on the chin and cheeks.

A tiny hole of sunlight from the window shade lay on his chin and picked out, like the spikes of a music box cylinder, each little hair on his face.

His wrists on either side of him had little curly black hairs, each perfect, each separate and shiny and glittering.

The hair on his head was intact, strand by dark strand, down to the roots. The ears were beautifully carved. The teeth were intact behind the lips.

"Joseph!" she screamed.

"Joseph!" she screamed again, flailing up in terror.

Bong! Bong! Bong! went the bell thunder across the street from the great tiled cathedral!

Pigeons rose in a papery white whirl, like so many magazines fluttered past the window! The pigeons circled the plaza, spiraling up. Bong! went the bells! Honk went a taxi horn! Far away down an alley a music box played CIELITO LINDO.

All these faded into the dripping of the faucet in the bath sink.

Joseph opened his eyes.

His wife sat on her bed, staring at him.

"I thought—" he said. He blinked. "No." He shut his eyes and shook his head. "Just the bells." A sigh. "What time is it?"

"I don't know. Yes, I do. Eight o'clock."

"Good God," he murmured, turning over. "We can sleep three more hours."

"You've got to get up!" she cried.

"Nobody's up. They won't be to work at the garage

until ten, you know that, you can't rush these people; keep quiet now."

"But you've got to get up," she said.

He half turned. Sunlight prickled black hairs into bronze on his upper lip. "*Why*? Why, in Christ's name, do I *have* to get up?"

"You need a shave!" she almost screamed.

He moaned. "So I have to get up and lather myself at eight in the morning because I need a shave."

"Well, you do need one."

"I'm not shaving again till we reach Texas."

"You can't go around looking like a tramp!"

"I can and will. I've shaved every morning for thirty goddamn mornings and put on a tie and had a crease in my pants. From now on, no pants, no ties, no shaving, no nothing."

He yanked the covers over his ears so violently that he pulled the blankets off one of his naked legs.

The leg hung upon the rim of the bed, warm white in the sunlight, each little black hair—perfect.

Her eyes widened, focussed, stared upon it.

She put her hand over her mouth, tight.

He went in and out of the hotel all day. He did not shave. He walked along the plaza tiles below. He walked so slowly she wanted to throw a lightning bolt out of the window and hit him. He paused and talked to the hotel manager below, under a drum-cut tree, shifting his shoes on the pale blue plaza tiles. He looked at birds on trees and saw how the State theatre statues were dressed in fresh morning gilt, and stood on the corner, watching the traffic carefully. There was no traffic! He was standing there on purpose, taking his time, not looking back at her. Why didn't he run, lope down the alley, down the hill to the garage, pound on the doors, threaten the mechanics, lift them by their pants, shove them into the car motor! He stood instead, watching the ridiculous traffic pass. A hobbled swine, a man on a bike, a 1927 Ford, and three half nude children. Go, go, go, she screamed silently, and almost smashed the window.

He sauntered across the street. He went around the corner. All the way down to the garage he'd stop at windows, read signs, look at pictures, handle pottery. Maybe he'd stop in for a beer. God, yes, a beer.

She walked in the plaza, took the sun, hunted for more magazines. She cleaned her fingernails, burnished them, took a bath, walked again in the plaza, ate very little, and returned to the room to feed upon her magazines.

She did not lie down. She was afraid to. Each time she did she fell into a half-dream, half-drowse in which all her childhood was revealed in a helpless melancholy. Old friends, children she hadn't seen or thought of in twenty years filled her mind. And she thought of things she wanted to do and had never done. She had meant to call Lila Holdridge for the past eight years since college, but somehow she never had. What *friends* they had been! Dear Lila! She thought, when lying down, of all the books, the fine new and old books, she had meant to buy and might never buy now and read. How she loved books and the smell of books. She thought of a thousand old sad things. She'd wanted to own the OZ books all her life, yet had never bought them. Why *not?* while yet there was life! The first thing she'd do would be to buy them when she got back to New York! And she'd call Lila immediately! And she'd see Bert and Jimmy and Helen and Louise, and go back to Illinois and walk around in her childhood place and see the things to be seen there. If she got back to the States. If. Her heart beat painfully in her, paused, held onto itself, and beat again. *If* she ever got back.

She lay listening to her heart, critically.

Thud and a thud and a thud. Pause. Thud and a thud and a thud. Pause.

What if it should stop while she was listening?

There!

Silence inside her.

"Joseph!"

She leaped up. She grabbed at her breasts as if to squeeze, to pump, to start the silent heart again!

It opened in her, closed, rattled and beat nervously, twenty rapid, shot-like times!

She sank onto the bed. What if it should stop again and not start? What would she think? What would there be to do? She'd die of fright, that's what. A joke; it was very humorous. Die of fright if you heard your heart stop. What a paradox. She would have to listen to it, keep it beating. She wanted to go home and see Lila and buy the books and dance again and walk in Central Park and—listen—

Thud and a thud and a thud. Pause.

Joseph knocked on the door. Joseph knocked on the door and the car was not repaired and there would be another night, and Joseph did not shave and each little hair was perfect on his chin, and the magazine shops were closed and there were no more magazines, and they ate supper, a little bit anyway for her, and he went out in the evening to walk in the town.

She sat once more in the chair and slow erections of hair rose as if a magnet were passed over her neck. She was very weak and could not move from the chair, and she had no body, she was only a heart-beat, a huge pulsation of warmth and ache between the four walls of the room. Her eyes were hot and pregnant, swollen with child of terror behind the bellied, tautened lids.

Deeply inside herself, she felt the first little cog slip. Another night, another night, another night, she thought. And this will be longer than the last. The first little cog slipped, the first pendulum missed a stroke. Followed by the second and third interrelated cogs. The cogs interlocked, a small with a little larger one, the little larger one with a bit larger one, the bit larger one with a large one, the large one with a big one, the big one with a bigger one, the bigger one with a huge one, the huge one with an immense one, the immense one with a titanic one . . . .

A red ganglion, no bigger than a scarlet thread, snapped and quivered; a nerve, no greater than a red linen fiber twisted. Deep in her one little mech was gone and the entire machine, imbalanced, was about to steadily shake itself to bits.

She didn't fight it. She let it quake and terrorize her and knock the sweat off her brow and jolt down her spine and flood her mouth with horrible wine. She felt as if a broken gyro tilted now this way, now that and blundered and trembled and whined in her. The color fell from her face like light leaving a clicked off bulb, the crystal cheeks of the bulb vessel showing veins and filaments all colorless . . . .

Joseph was in the room, he had come in, but she didn't even hear him. He was in the room but it made no difference, he changed nothing with his coming. He was getting ready for bed and said nothing as he moved about and she said nothing but fell into the bed while he moved around in a smoke-filled space beyond her and once he spoke but she didn't hear him.

She timed it. Every five minutes she looked at her watch and the watch shook and time shook and the five fingers were fifteen moving, reassembling into five. The shaking never stopped. She called for water. She turned and turned upon the bed. The wind blew outside, cocking the lights and spilling bursts of illumination that hit buildings glancing sidelong blows, causing windows to glitter like opened eyes and shut swiftly as the light tilted in yet another direction. Downstairs, all was quiet after the dinner, no sounds came up into their silent room. He handed her a water glass.

"I'm pale, Joseph," she said, lying deep in folds of cover.

"You're all right," he said.

"No, I'm not. I'm not well. I'm afraid."

"There's nothing to be afraid of."

"I want to get on the train for the United States."

"There's a train in Leon, but none here," he said, lighting a new cigarette.

"Let's drive there."

"In these taxis, with these drivers, and leave our car here?"

"Yes. I want to go."

"You'll be all right in the morning."

"No. No, I won't be all right."

"You'll be all right."

"I know I won't be. I'm not well."

He said, "It would cost hundreds of dollars to have the car shipped home."

"I don't care. I have two hundred dollars in the bank home. I'll pay for it. But, please, let's go home."

"When the sun shines tomorrow you'll feel better, it's just that the sun's gone now."

"Yes, the sun's gone and the wind's blowing," she whispered, closing her eyes, turning her head, listening. "Oh, what a lonely wind. Mexico's a strange land. All the jungles and deserts and lonely stretches, and here and there a little town, like this, with a few lights burning you could put out with a snap of your fingers . . ."

"It's a pretty big country," he said.

"Don't these people ever get lonely?"

"They're used to it this way."

"Don't they get afraid, then?"

"They have a religion for that."

"I wish *I* had a religion."

"The minute you get a religion you stop thinking," he said. "Believe in one thing too much and you have no room for new ideas."

"Tonight," she said, faintly, "I'd like nothing more than to have no more room for new ideas, to stop thinking, to believe in one thing so much it leaves me no time to be afraid."

"You're not afraid," he said.

"If I had a religion," she said, ignoring him, "I'd have a lever with which to lift myself. But I haven't a lever now and I don't know how to lift myself."

"Oh, for God's—" he mumbled to himself, sitting down.

"I *used* to have a religion," she said.

"Baptist."

"No, that was when I was twelve. I got over that. I mean—*later*."

"You never told me."

"You should have known," she said.

"What religion? Plaster saints in the sacristy? Any special saint you liked to tell your beads to?"

"Yes."

"And did he answer your prayers?"

"For a little while. Lately, no, never. Never any more. Not for years now. But I keep praying."

"Which saint is this?"

"Saint Joseph."

"Saint Joseph." He got up and poured himself a glass of water from the glass pitcher, and it was a lonely trickling sound in the room. "*My* name."

"Coincidence," she said.

They looked at one another for a few moments.

He looked away. "Plaster saints," he said, drinking the water down.

After awhile she said, "Joseph?" He said, "Yes?" and she said, "Come hold my hand, will you?" "Women," he sighed. He came and held her hand. After a minute she drew her hand away, hid it under the blanket, leaving his hand empty behind. With her eyes closed she trembled the words, "Never mind. It's not as nice as I can imagine it. It's really nice the way I can make you hold my hand in my mind." "Gods," he said, and went into the bathroom. She turned off the light. Only the small crack of light under the bathroom door showed. She listened to her heart. It beat one hundred and fifty times a minute, steadily, and the little whining tremor was still in her marrow, as if each bone of her body had a blue bottle fly imprisoned in it, hovering, buzzing, shaking, quivering deep deep deep. Her eyes reversed into herself, to watch the secret heart of herself pounding itself to pieces against the side of her chest.

Water ran in the bathroom. She heard him washing his teeth.

"Joseph!"

"Yes," he said, behind the shut door.

"Come here."

"What do you want?"

"I want you to promise me something, please, oh, please."

"What is it?"

"Open the door, first."

"What *is* it?" he demanded, behind the closed door.

"Promise me," she said, and stopped.

"Promise you, what?" he asked, after a long pause.

"Promise me," she said, and couldn't go on. She lay there. He said nothing. She heard the watch and her heart pounding together. A lantern creaked on the hotel exterior. "Promise me, if anything—happens," she heard herself say, muffled and paralyzed, as if she were on one of the surrounding hills talking at him from that distance, "—if anything happens to me, you won't let me be buried here in the graveyard over those terrible catacombs!"

"Don't be foolish," he said, behind the door.

"Promise me?" she said, eyes wide in the dark.

"Of all the foolish things to talk about."

"Promise, *please* promise?"

"You'll be all right in the morning," he said.

"Promise so I can sleep. I can sleep if only you'd say you wouldn't let me be put there. I don't want to be put there."

"Honestly," he said, out of patience.

"Please," she said.

"Why should I promise anything so ridiculous?" he said. "You'll be fine tomorrow. And besides, if you died, you'd look very pretty in the catacomb standing between Mr. Grimace and Mr. Gape, with a sprig of morning-glory in your hair." And he laughed sincerely.

Silence. She lay there in the dark.

"Don't you think you'll look pretty there?" he asked, laughingly, behind the door.

She said nothing in the dark room.

"*Don't* you?" he said.

Somebody walked down below in the plaza, faintly, fading away.

"Eh?" he asked her, brushing his teeth.

She lay there, staring up at the ceiling, her breast rising and falling faster, faster, faster, the air going in and out, in and out her nostrils, a little trickle of blood coming from her clenched lips. Her eyes were very wide, her hands blindly constricted the bedclothes.

"Eh?" he said again behind the door.

She said nothing.

"Sure," he talked to himself. "Pretty as hell," he murmured, under the flow of faucet water. He rinsed his mouth. "Sure," he said.

Nothing from her in the bed.

"Women are funny," he said to himself in the mirror.

She lay in the bed.

"Sure," he said. He gargled with some antiseptic, spat it down the drain. "You'll be all right in the morning," he said.

Not a word from her.

"We'll get the car fixed."

She didn't say anything.

"Be morning before you know it." He was screwing caps on things now, putting freshener on his face. "And the car fixed tomorrow, maybe, at the very latest the next day. You won't mind another night here, will you?"

She didn't answer.

"*Will* you?" he asked.

No reply.

The light blinked out under the bathroom door.

"Marie?"

He opened the door.

"Asleep?"

She lay with eyes wide, breasts moving up and down.

"Asleep," he said. "Well, goodnight, lady."

He climbed into his bed. "Tired," he said.

No reply.

"Tired," he said.

The wind tossed the lights outside; the room was oblong and black and he was in his bed dozing already.

She lay, eyes wide, the watch ticking on her wrist, breasts moving up and down.

It was a fine day coming through the Tropic of Cancer. The automobile pushed along the turning road leaving the jungle country behind, heading for the United States, roaring between the green hills, taking every turn, leaving behind a faint vanishing trail of exhaust smoke.

And inside the shiny automobile sat Joseph with his pink, healthy face and his Panama hat, and a little camera cradled on his lap as he drove; a swathe of black silk pinned around the left upper arm of his tan coat. He watched the country slide by and absent-mindedly made a gesture to the seat beside him, and stopped. He broke into a little sheepish smile and turned once more to the window of his car, humming a little tuneless tune, his right hand reaching over and touching the seat beside him . . . .

Which was empty.